CA...

These are the stories of the Carrier Battle Group Fourteen—a force including a supercarrier, amphibious unit, guided missile cruiser, and destroyer. And these are the novels that capture the blistering reality of international combat. Exciting. Authentic. Explosive.

CARRIER . . . The smash debut thriller about the ultimate military nightmare: the takeover of a U.S. Intelligence ship.

VIPER STRIKE . . . A renegade Chinese fighter group penetrates Thai airspace—and launches a full-scale invasion.

ARMAGEDDON MODE . . . With India and Pakistan on the verge of nuclear destruction, the Carrier Battle Group Fourteen must prevent a final showdown.

FLAME-OUT . . . The Soviet Union is reborn in a military takeover— and their strike force shows no mercy.

MAELSTROM . . . The Soviet occupation of Scandinavia leads the Carrier Battle Group Fourteen into conventional weapons combat— and possible all-out war.

COUNTDOWN . . . Carrier Battle Group Fourteen must prevent the deployment of Russian submarines. The problem is: They have nukes.

AFTERBURN . . . Carrier Battle Group Fourteen receives orders to enter the Black Sea—in the middle of a Russian civil war.

ALPHA STRIKE . . . When American and Chinese interests collide in the South China Sea, the superpowers risk waging a third world war.

SAN DIEGO PUBLIC LIBRARY
CLAIREMONT BRANCH
3920 Burgener Blvd.
San Diego, CA 92110

continued on next page . . .

JUL   2002

ARCTIC FIRE . . . A Russian splinter group has occupied the Aleutian Islands off the coast of Alaska—in the ultimate invasion of U.S. soil.

ARSENAL . . . Magruder and his crew are trapped between Cuban revolutionaries . . . and a U.S. power play that's spun wildly out of control.

NUKE ZONE . . . When a nuclear missile is launched against the U.S. Sixth Fleet, Magruder must face a frightening question: In an age of computer warfare, how do you tell friends from enemies?

CHAIN OF COMMAND . . . Magruder enters the jungles of Vietnam, looking for answers about his missing father. Little does he know that another bloody war is about to be unleashed—with his fleet caught in the crosshairs . . .

BRINK OF WAR . . . Friendly wargames with the Russians take a deadly turn, and Carrier Battle Group Fourteen must prevent war from erupting in the skies. Little do they know—that's just what someone wants . . .

TYPHOON . . . An American yacht is attacked by a Chinese helicopter in international waters, and the Carrier Team is called to the front lines of what may be the start of a war between the superpowers . . .

ENEMY OF MY ENEMY . . . A Greek pilot unwittingly downs a news chopper, and Magruder must keep the peace between Greece and the breakaway republic of Macedonia. But what no one knows is that it wasn't an accident at all . . .

JOINT OPERATIONS . . . China launches a surprise attack on Hawaii—and the Carrier Team can't handle it alone. As Tombstone and his fleet take charge of the air, Lieutenant Murdock and his SEALs are called in to work ashore . . .

THE ART OF WAR . . . When Iranian militants take the first bloody step toward toppling the decadent west, the Carrier Team is the only one who can stop the madmen . . .

ISLAND WARRIORS . . . China launches a full-scale invasion on their tiny capitalist island neighbor—and Carrier Battle Group Fourteen is the only hope to stop them . . .

book nineteen

CARRIER

First
Strike

KEITH DOUGLASS

SAN DIEGO PUBLIC LIBRARY
CLAIREMONT

JOVE BOOKS, NEW YORK

3 1336 05662 5149

If you purchased this book without a cover, you should be aware that this book is stolen property. It was reported as "unsold and destroyed" to the publisher, and neither the author nor the publisher has received any payment for this "stripped book."

This is a work of fiction. Names, characters, places, and incidents are either the product of the author's imagination or are used fictitiously, and any resemblance to actual persons, living or dead, business establishments, events, or locales is entirely coincidental.

FIRST STRIKE

A Jove Book / published by arrangement with
the author

PRINTING HISTORY
Jove edition / January 2002

All rights reserved.
Copyright © 2002 by Penguin Putnam Inc.
This book, or parts thereof, may not be reproduced in
any form without permission.
For information address: The Berkley Publishing Group,
a division of Penguin Putnam Inc.,
375 Hudson Street, New York, New York 10014.

Visit our website at
www.penguinputnam.com

ISBN: 0-515-13230-6

A JOVE BOOK®
Jove Books are published by The Berkley Publishing Group,
a division of Penguin Putnam Inc.,
375 Hudson Street, New York, New York 10014.
JOVE and the "J" design
are trademarks belonging to Penguin Putnam Inc.

PRINTED IN THE UNITED STATES OF AMERICA

10 9 8 7 6 5 4 3 2 1

ONE

There had been a time when Andrei Korsov would have been one of the most powerful men in the world. As commander of the Strategic Rocket Forces, he owned every long-range ballistic missile in the Soviet Union's inventory, as well as thousands of maintenance technicians, operators, and testing and development facilities. His forces comprised more men and more equipment than many small nations.

Korsov's power had not been limited to strictly military matters. The nuclear arsenal was the centerpiece of the USSR's mutual assured destruction policy, or MAD. Korsov consulted daily with the premier—and, later, the president—and advised the Politburo on the readiness posture and responded to political changes in alert status. His circle of influence spilled over into domestic policy, as more and more resources were diverted to support the nuclear forces. He knew the key players in every scientific community as well, as the USSR explored its option in mass destruction. No one in the then-USSR ever failed to return his phone calls.

Privately, Korsov had mixed feelings about MAD. The policy originated in the United States. At the dawn of the nuclear age, as mass destruction and long-range weapons became a reality, a think tank in the United States had explored the possibility of detecting and destroying incoming nuclear missiles. Technologically, it was impossible. Casting about for solutions, the team had finally arrived at the conclusion that the only way to deter a nuclear attack from another nation—specifically, from the Soviet Union—was to make the consequences so deadly and complete that no nation would ever attempt it. Ensuring that America retained the capacity to retaliate under all conditions led to the development of the nuclear triad, with weapons deployed on alert aircraft, in hardened silos, and on submarines. Yes, the analysts concluded, the Evil Empire could devastate the United States, but she would pay with her own life.

While the policy seemed to have worked, at least to the extent of avoiding a nuclear holocaust, Korsov had never completely been able to accept the entire insanity of it. After all, the only nation to use nuclear weapons against another had been the United States herself, at the end of World War II. It seemed to him that that was what led the Americans to live in fear of such an attack. Having made the decision to use them herself, America knew what nations were capable of.

Still, the insanity of MAD had its perks. With America committed to the doctrine, the Soviet Union followed suit, and service in the nuclear weapons forces became the most prestigious of career paths. Rubles poured in to every program, funding submarines and more submarines, mobile land-based launch systems, and scores of bombers. What the nation gave up in domestic prosperity was Korsov's gain.

At the time of the demise of the Soviet Union, Korsov had been deputy commander. When the inevitable search for scapegoats reached his department, he was ready. The commander was urged to retire and Korsov, who had aligned himself with the new powers ruling Russia, stepped in to his billet.

Unfortunately, world reaction to the status of nuclear weapons in former Soviet States brought extreme pressure to bear. Faced with a declining and unstable ruble and a harsh winter pending, Russia and the Commonwealth of Independent States agreed to massive disarmament as a condition of increased aid from America and the rest of the world. Rusting weapons were dismantled, ancient fire-control systems destroyed—or, at least, so it was reported to the rest of the world. In the chaos following the dissolution of the USSR, no one was entirely sure who was keeping records of what. Entire launch systems vanished, some simply destroyed without adequate documentation, others turning up later on the international black market in weapons.

Korsov's connection to the Internet ran at only 9,600 baud, but even that was an impressive accomplishment, given the state of the Russian telephone system. It was sufficient to enable him to log on to AOL and other Internet providers, scan the international news, and keep up an E-mail correspondence with several missile friends.

It wasn't access to the hard news content that really worried the political powers in Russia. It was the lifestyle section, pictures overflowing with riches far beyond the grasp of the average Russian. As long as there was no independent source of information, whoever was currently in power could convince the population that their standard of living was pretty much the same as it was around the rest of the world, particularly in the United States.

But it was the news that interested Korsov most. He had not been expecting to find such a gem in his daily news traffic, not at all. But something inside him told him that he must keep up with it, must, if he was to improve his current situation.

Something about the story in front of him held promise, although he could not say exactly what it was at first glance. He read it again.

It was a short, heartwarming human-interest story about a young boy who needed a bone marrow transplant to combat his leukemia. An international charity had flown him to the United States, but his doctor was not hopeful about finding a donor match. DNA profiling had revealed that the child's frail body held the genes of a small band of indigenous people and there was little hope that a match could be found for the lifesaving transplant. In a short paragraph at the end of the article, the writer explained that the child's doctor had worked on the human genome project and had been part of the team working in the United States that had finally broken the genetic code.

Supercomputers had analyzed every last DNA sequence and now knew exactly which patterns represented which manifestations in the human genome. Research showed that 99.8 percent of the genes found in any human being were identical to those of every other person. It was that .2 percent that accounted for all the individual variations in color, build, stature, and susceptibility to hereditary diseases. While the report did not go into detail, Korsov could easily read between the lines, and fear surged through him.

They know his race. Know it from his genes. Korsov leaned back in his chair, stunned. *Know thy enemy.*

Up until now, a large amount of the data was classified, and Korsov could see why. If the genetic differences were common knowledge, biological weapons could be engineered to attack particular genetic sequences.

Granted, there were problems with designer viri targeted to particular sequences of genes. Most of America and Europe were melting pots of different races. Even Russia had her mongrels, ranging from ancient Tartar blood to the most recent infusion of immigrants from East Germany and Ukraine.

Yet, there were possibilities in this. Astounding possibilities. And Korsov intended to act on them.

His first telephone call was to an old friend, now a genetic researcher at the University of Moscow. Korsov only vaguely understood his friend's research, but knew that he was paralleling the work being done in the United States on the human genome code. His friend's focus was hereditary diseases, with particular emphasis on determining whether or not the ravages of alcoholism in Russians were indeed genetic or environmental. While that might not be exactly on point, if anyone he knew could explain this news to him, it was his friend.

Five minutes later, Korsov had his answer. Russian scientists had taken a different approach to the problem. Instead of analyzing the entire genetic code, they had focused solely on that .2 percent. There were not only answers to the question of identifying race, the weaponeers had solutions as well.

Even in September, Moscow was already in the grip of winter. Old snow coated the streets, masking ancient buildings and covered crumbling concrete of the newer buildings with an all-concealing white blanket. This morning, the city's few snowplows traced their carefully planned routes between the areas where the rich and powerful lived and their probable destinations. The rest of the city was left covered with snow, with the inhabitants left to their own devices in making their way through the roads.

Aside from the elite, few people owned cars. The shops and stores they used were within walking distance, or could be accessed by the public transit system.

Not that there was anything to buy. And leaving their apartments would simply contribute to heat loss, since opening the door would let in ice-cold air. Fuel was expensive, far out of the reach of many. Most apartments relied on a single electric blower or cooking plate, and that only during hours when electricity was supplied. The average Muscovites hoarded their resources, covering the single pane windows with blankets and sheets in an effort to cut down on wind, keeping the door shut, and staying heavily clothed inside.

For Korsov, this was not a problem. He lived a life far different from that of most of his countrymen, but not so dissimilar from his counterparts in the United States. His large, four-bedroom house heated by a seemingly endless supply of propane. There was never a shortage of hot water or fuel for cooking—and, indeed, food was delivered to his house almost daily, coming from the special shops reserved for the elite.

While Korsov understood intellectually the deprivations his countrymen lived under, he had no real concept of the impact on everyday life. It wasn't that he didn't care—he did. But making the translation from intellectual knowledge to truly understanding the gut-wrenching hardships that others experienced was simply beyond him.

What he did understand, and what ruled most of his life, was the dramatic downfall of the USSR. During his early years, Korsov, the son of a member of the Politburo, had been groomed to take his eventual place as part of the reigning royalty in the Soviet Union. He had attended the right schools, made the right friends, and served with the army in Afghanistan. He was politically, ideologically, and physically beyond reproach. Everyone had predicted a brilliant future for him. Korsov basked in the glow of the future that was to come.

With the downfall of the Soviet Union, everything changed. His achievements, his education, even his contacts suddenly meant nothing. For Korsov, it was a crushing blow.

In the years that followed the collapse of the Soviet Union, Korsov's grief over its demise turned to anger, and then determination. He would not have it all taken from him—he would not. The Soviet Union would be restored, albeit under a new name, and he would have his revenge for what had been taken from him. He searched for years for the right way to achieve this, an avenue by which he could strike back at the country most responsible for the Soviet Union's demise.

The culprit was, of course, the United States. He watched with hope as a succession of administrations gutted the military power of his adversary. He could barely contain his glee as the United States became more and more vulnerable to the dictates of the United Nations. And finally, the United States' adventures in the Middle East, not only Desert Storm and Desert Shield, but the attack on the USS *Cole*, had given him his final insights.

From Korsov's study of America's history, he had derived two major understandings. First, she would not tolerate losses in combat. Oh, certainly, the military services understood the risks, at least the senior people did. But in America, oddly enough, public opinion had a great deal to say about how the military conducted its operations. He almost laughed at the idea—an insane concept, expecting a civilian to understand how and why a military must operate. At least Russia had never fallen into the track, although he had to admit that politicians had played far too powerful a role.

But the American aversion went beyond that. They were not willing to tolerate any casualties—*none*. Grand strategy and brilliant tactics were replaced only by efforts to reduce body counts.

Second, after the attacks on U.S. forces in the Middle East, he was finally forced to reach another conclusion—America would not fight back. She would tolerate terrorist attacks, especially ones in the foreign governments, howling and wildly demanding justice in international courts, but they would not strike back.

It was, Korsov knew, a pitiful dream, and one that would inevitably lead to the eventual downfall of America. Powerful nations did not tolerate this, not tolerate it and survive. When challenged, they crushed the opposition. When threatened, they reacted with overwhelming force. When attacked, they destroyed.

But his data points were only from overseas conflicts. He

suspected it would be a far different matter if a conflict took place on the United States' own territory. But, aside from the attack on Pearl Harbor, America had never faced military action on her own soil.

That night, Korsov dreamed of revenge. He saw America as it was shown in the news reports: happy, prosperous, the streets crowded with cars, the chaos on the floor of the New York Stock Exchange, the stores filled with food and consumer goods. Then, beginning along the East Coast, he saw a thin line of red creeping ever westward. The line started somewhere around Washington, D.C., and expanded exponentially, finally covering the entire country, as well as parts of Canada and Mexico.

With the red zone, nothing moved. Crops rotted in the field, cars were abandoned alongside roads. The giant military bases were silent, the industrial complexes deserted. America was dead.

Then, the repopulation began, ships and aircraft converging on the abandoned land from Russia, spilling masses of colonists out onto both coasts. Aircraft filled the center of the country with more people, even more than on the coasts, and the population began spreading out from the center toward the coasts. They filled the empty factories, the abandoned houses, and worked the fields. The faces were happy, smiling, delighted in hard work and with their lives.

And they were speaking Russian.

There would be no war—at least, not one that anyone would recognize. The United States would have to be gutted on the first strike, not allowed time to realize the outrage that had been perpetrated on her, not given an opportunity to retaliate. The strike must be instantly devastating and anonymous. America would not know who had struck her, would not know who to retaliate against. And, not knowing, she would die.

For the first time in ten years, Korsov felt a surge of hope. The effort he'd put into his earlier years would not be wasted. He had friendships, tentacles of power, in virtually every military and industrial complex in the CFS. And among those contacts were people who thought as he did, people now in positions of power. With their resources and the genetic weapons that had been developed, his dream could become a reality.

Still, he shivered at the thought of what he was about to

attempt. Even his most hard-line friends might quail at the prospect of deploying genetic weapons against the United States. He would have to be extremely careful in selecting the members of his team, extremely careful.

Yuri. Yuri Maskiro. He's as ready as I am. He will understand the dream.

For all of his friendship with Maskiro, Korsov always felt a bit intimidated around the former Spetnaz now missile commander. Maskiro retained an air of deadly menace from his days in the Special Forces, and was physically and mentally as tough as they came. Maskiro stood well over six feet tall and every inch of his body rippled with power. Korsov's only consolation was that he had long ago concluded that he was slightly more intelligent than Maskiro.

But this wasn't a matter of intelligence. It was a matter of determination, of visionary ability to see into the future, to a Russia as she should be, and of the will to make that future a reality. Whatever shortcomings that Maskiro might have in the intellectual department, they were more than compensated for by his utter loyalty and belief in Korsov.

It would not do to trust the telephone lines or the mail as he coordinated the plan. No, even though the KGB had changed its name, it still retained its awesome powers within the country. There would be keyword searches, not as sophisticated as those the United States used, but, with fewer telephone lines to monitor, just as effective.

No, this would require personal contact. He picked up the telephone and called Central Command, explaining to the general's chief of staff that he would be away for several days attending to a personal matter. There was no reluctance to grant him leave of absence. Since military officers had not been paid for several months, the general knew that forcing the matter would simply result in a mutiny. He had neither the resources nor the desire to prosecute unauthorized absences.

With that arranged, Korsov booked the first flight he could get into the heartland of Ukraine. He debated calling ahead and telling Maskiro he was coming, but decided against it. Yuri would welcome him with open arms, of that he was certain. Over the years, they had established that they were of like minds, carefully feeling each other out as to political views and determination, both aware that someday the opportunity would come and that they would strike together and form the backbone of a new power structure within the unwieldy CIS.

Yes, Yuri would be glad to see him. And, as commander of all forces along the Black Sea and in the Crimean Peninsula, Yuri would have the resource that Korsov needed—missiles.

TWO

Four hundred miles northeast of Bermuda, the USS *Jefferson* steamed at ten knots inside her assigned exercise box. The guided missile cruiser USS *Lake Champlain* and several frigates kept station on the carrier, each one a prescribed distance and bearing from the centerpiece of the battle group. The battle group was conducting evaluations of some recent tactical proposals.

Several Russian warships, including three troop transports, were 400 due north of the *Jefferson* and her escorts, ostensibly conducting their own tests and evaluations. In reality, they were there to keep an eye on the battle group, to make sure what the United States said was an exercise really *was* an exercise, and to get a look at the new tactics.

The weather was surprisingly calm and clear for that time of year. Later in the season, storms would blow in from the north and be fed by the warm waters of the Gulf Stream current. As winter approached, the full force of the atmospheric fury would descend on the region. During the worst of the storms, even the aircraft carrier would pitch and roll.

But, for now, every ship was taking advantage of the unexpectedly pleasant weather. Weather decks thronged with sailors in shorts and T-shirts, and even if the weather was a bit chilly, they all basked in sunshine.

Admiral "Coyote" Grant was on the bridge, watching the commencement of the latest set of exercises. The object of this short deployment was to practice the latest tactics developed by the Surface Warfare Development Command and test them against real world considerations. Privately, Coyote thought some of the measures were rather farfetched, but he kept his opinion to himself. No point in affecting anyone's performance by letting them suspect he was highly doubtful about some of the maneuvers they had been asked to test.

Even if he wasn't necessarily buying into the revised doctrine, he had found one advantage to having a staff walk through a full consideration of the tactics. While they might not agree with what they were being told to do, it encouraged them to think outside the box, to take a different look, a hard look, at the way they did business. And that, Coyote mused, was not a bad thing. Not a bad thing at all.

On the bridge, there was a stilted formality in the air. That was one of the problems with being an admiral, Coyote reflected. While you might still feel like a fighter pilot—and you were, of course—no one else ever forgot the stars on your collar. He had probably spent more time on the *Jefferson* than everyone on the bridge watch team combined. His first tours had been as a junior officer, just learning the realities of flying the Tomcat. Later, he'd come back as part of both VF-95 squadron and as a member of the Admiral's staff. This would be his final tour on board as commander of the entire battle group.

But, to the bridge officers, he was not just a guy who knew more about the ship than they could ever imagine. Even those who were tempted to ask his opinion and take advantage of his experience were just a little too junior to have the guts to do so. To most of them, he was the one person they didn't want to screw up in front of, the one who might note their mistakes and report them to their commanders, blowing the hell out of their careers.

Not that Coyote would have had to go far to find their bosses—most of them were on the bridge just moments after he arrived, trying very hard to pretend they were there on routine visits. Word traveled fast when the admiral started walking around the ship, and every officer or chief petty officer with any responsibility whatsoever wanted to be where he was in order to make sure his people didn't screw up. But instead of being reassuring, their presence only added to the pucker factor and normally flawless officers and petty officers got nervous and started making mistakes.

But that was part of it too, wasn't it? You had to learn to operate under stress, not to let it get to you. And, besides, it was his battle group, dammit. And he wanted to see what was going on.

The battle group was currently experimenting with a different concept of antiair warfare. Instead of assigning defense areas radiating out from the carrier, the plan was to have the aircraft cover the starboard side of the carrier and the cruiser cover the port side. The theory was that by concentrating the aircraft assets in one sector, there would be less mutual interference with the cruiser. The problems of firing at incoming enemy aircraft when there were friendlies in the way was an age-old problem.

Nobody was particularly happy about this idea, least of all the fighter pilots. Shooting down missiles was problematic at best. Often they ended up in head-on engagements and lacked the sophisticated processing gear found on board the cruiser.

The cruiser was screaming loudly about it as well. The surface ship officers guarded their missions even more rabidly than the aviation commands did. They saw this as simply one more way to cut down on the number of support missions that required two cruisers instead of just one, and they didn't like it one bit.

"Good morning, Admiral," a cheery voice said behind him. Coyote turned to find himself staring into the smiling face of Lieutenant Commander Curt "Bird Dog" Robinson, the new XO of VF-95. "About time to shoot down some drones, isn't it?"

"I hope not," Coyote said calmly. "You remind your folks they're suppose to come close but not actually hit the drones, okay? I don't want any surprises." The drones would make two passes by the carrier. A recovery boat was standing by to pull the carcass out of the water for refueling and reuse.

Bird Dog waved aside his concerns. "Oh, they know that. We take care of our toys, that we do."

"The weather is cooperating," the admiral noted. "I hope the cruiser does."

The admiral studied Bird Dog for a moment, repressing a smile as he did so. Bird Dog had just taken over as executive officer of VF-95, and was clearly pleased as punch about it. Bird Dog was tall, a couple of inches over six feet, with a strong athletic frame. He had dark blond hair and blue eyes, and wore a perpetually cheerful expression. He was an excellent fighter pilot, perhaps the best Coyote had ever seen. Present company excluded, of course. No pilot ever admits that anyone is better than he is. But Bird Dog not only possessed the reflexes and eye-hand coordination to excel, but he also had the most important attribute of a good fighter pilot: luck. Bird Dog had been in more tight spots and deadly conflicts, often as the result of his own hotheadedness, than any other pilot Coyote could think of. He'd punched out of more than one Tomcat and lived to talk about it when most pilots ended their careers with an ejection. All that ought to have earned him a number of black marks on his record and permanently stymied his chances of rising to command, but his punch outs were balanced against an even more startling number of victories. Almost single-handedly, he had resolved the problem in the Aleutians, to name but one. Wherever there was a fight, Bird Dog always seemed to be on the leading edge of it. And, while he had scared more than one RIO shitless, everyone else breathed a sigh of relief when they saw Bird Dog's name on the flight schedule.

"I halfway expected you to be flying the first engagement," the admiral noted. He grinned as he saw Bird Dog frown.

"I tried to," the new executive officer admitted. "But the skipper nixed that. Said I didn't need the practice. Of course, he's right," Bird Dog acknowledged, oblivious to the amusement in the admiral's eyes. "But it seems like there ought to be some good deals in exchange for all the paperwork I wade through every day. You've got no idea, sir. No idea." Bird Dog held up his ring finger for the admiral's inspection. "Look at that. A paper cut."

Coyote clapped him on the shoulder. "It just gets worse, my friend. Trust me on that."

"Vampire inbound," the officer of the deck announced. Coyote checked the time, then nodded with approval. Right on time, the first drone was making a pass at the battle group.

"If it flies, it dies, right?" Bird Dog asked.

Coyote nodded. "Let's see how your boys and girls do."

"Tallyho," a voice said calmly over tactical. "I have a lock."

"Who's that?" Coyote asked.

Bird Dog tried to smile, but it was clear that hearing that particular voice caused an ache in his gut. "Fastball Morrow— you've met him, I think. A good stick, and if he ever gets his temper under control, he's going to be pretty impressive."

This time, Coyote grinned openly. Yes, he knew Fastball, and Coyote was willing to bet that he wasn't the only one who felt a deep sense of vindication that Bird Dog was having to deal with him. *What goes around, comes around, my young friend.*

Washington, D.C.
The Pentagon
1500 local (GMT-5)

Commander Hillman "Lab Rat" Busby had just finished briefing the Pentagon's Joint Intelligence Center on the integration of his intelligence team from the *Jefferson* into the newly commissioned USS *United States* battle group. While the *Jefferson* had been completing repairs from striking a mine, Lab Rat and his crew had been temporarily signed to the Joint Intelligence Center, or JIC, in Norfolk, Virginia. During her sea trials, the *United States* was suddenly broken off from them and deployed to the Far East to intervene in a conflict between China and Taiwan. Since the ship was still in the process of establishing its manning, Lab Rat had offered Coyote the services of his already well-trained and coordinated department. Given the seriousness of the conflict they were facing, Coyote had taken him up on it. Now, however, the *United States* had her own people arriving, and Lab Rat and his people were back on the *Jefferson*.

The Pentagon, concerned with manpower management and maximizing efficiency from detached crews, had been keenly interested in the experience. There were murmurs of approval at Lab Rat's initiative in suggesting the whole scheme to Admiral Grant, and even more approval of the way it had worked out. Lab Rat had been extremely proud of how his people had acquitted themselves and he was gratified to see that some very senior people in the Navy agreed with him.

On the other hand, no good deal ever went unpunished. The *Jefferson* had a five-day port visit scheduled in Bermuda—five days of sun, fun, and relaxation. After the whirlwind conflict between China and Taiwan, Lab Rat felt he deserved a liberty in Bermuda a hell of a lot more than the rest of *Jefferson*'s crew. After all, while he'd been in the thick of it, they'd been bored to death in the shipyards.

But, no, instead of enjoying a mild fall in Bermuda, Lab Rat was trudging through the acres and acres of the massive parking lot with a chill wind biting his ears, looking for the very distant parking spot where he'd left his old Renault. While a commander was a senior officer on board an aircraft carrier, at the Pentagon he was nothing. The place teemed with hot and cold running commanders, captains, and even one stars weren't that uncommon. And while he appreciated the interest from the Secretary of the Navy, he would rather have been in Bermuda with the rest of his crew.

He was pretty sure Chief Armstrong felt the same way. *Senior* Chief Armstrong, he reminded himself. The chief's promotion had come through before the conflict with Taiwan, but Lab Rat still found himself bungling it.

Not that the senior chief deserved that. Senior Chief Armstrong was the smartest intelligence chief petty officer that Lab Rat had ever met in his career. The man possessed an almost uncanny insight into enemy intentions and maneuvers, and had already twice saved Lab Rat's bacon by noticing something askew in satellite photos or in enemy flight patterns.

No, the senior chief had not been crazy about the idea of spending the ship's liberty in D.C., either, but that was life in a blue suit. He hadn't even bothered grumbling. He just fixed Lab Rat with that cold, distant stare, and then shrugged impassively. Lab Rat would find a way to make it up to him.

"I thought that went well, sir," Armstrong said. "They seemed interested."

Where the hell is the car? Hadn't it been in this lot? Maybe it was the next one over—yes, that was it. Lab Rat turned to

his left and started hiking again, Senior Chief Armstrong falling into step beside him.

"Lose the car again, sir?" the senior chief asked, sympathy
in his voice. "If you like, we can head back in, get some
overhead imagery. They got real-time transmissions there. We
could locate it just by the rust signature."

"That is a classic car, senior chief, I will thank you to remember," Lab Rat huffed. "And there's not a speck of rust on
her, as you well know."

"Yes, sir. Though I suspect if you could build up some, she
wouldn't leak oil so bad."

"Entirely normal for her to use a little oil," Lab Rat said.
"It shows she's well lubricated."

"Right." The senior chief smirked, but fell silent.

Senior Chief Armstrong liked the diminutive commander
who was in charge of the carrier intelligence center, or CVIC,
liked him a lot. Commander Busby, he wasn't much to look
at. Maybe a 120 pounds soaking wet, and just a hair over five
feet two inches tall. The senior chief caught himself many
times almost calling the commander by his nickname. It was
too appropriate not to come automatically to your lips.

Commander Busby had short, Marine-clipped, pale blond
hair, and large, translucent blue eyes that seemed to wear a
perpetually trusting expression. If you didn't know him, you
would make the mistake of assuming he was a wimp. But you
only made that particular mistake once.

The senior chief's regard for his commander was, if possible, even higher than the commander's opinion of the senior
chief, although he found himself constantly resisting the urge
to pat his boss on the head. Lab Rat had a sharp, incisive mind,
and tolerated no bullshit within his department. And he took
good care of his people, with the ferocity of a Jack Russell
terrier, and the senior chief had seen the commander rip a new
asshole in more than one person who had failed to treat the
intelligence specialist right, most notably the chief of staff on
board the *United States*.

Yes, it was easy to underestimate Lab Rat. Once.

The senior chief himself was a tall man, well muscled, and
strongly built. His features were craggy, his hair dark and
slightly longer than his boss's. As much as Lab Rat's face was
open and trusting—gullible, some would call it—the senior

chief's was distant and cool. They were an odd-looking pair, but their strengths and weaknesses complemented each other nicely, and the senior chief had to admit the commander was one of the best bosses he'd ever had. The commander's annual evaluation had earned him his last promotion, and he figured if he could keep up with a kid, he would probably make master chief before he left the ship.

"Who knows what they'll do, Senior Chief?" Lab Rat said as he walked briskly down a line of cars. "They're talking about a tiger team, a special unit that they can fly out for a particular area of the world. But we know how that usually works."

"Yep. A tiger team isn't always the answer, although I wouldn't mind some experts around when something goes down."

"Agreed," Lab Rat said slowly, momentarily forgetting his search for the missing Renault. "But, I'm not really sure that's what this entire meeting was about."

"Sir?" The senior chief played dumb, although he had had the suspicion that something was up. But, you had to wait for the officers to get around telling you on their own terms.

"That night you were out with the chiefs . . ." The senior chief winced at the memory, as the evening had dissolved into a night of mourning his lost Bermuda liberty in a series of increasingly interesting bars in the D.C. area. He counted it as one of Lab Rat's strengths that he had not commented on his appearance the next morning. "I spent some time with the two star's staff. There were a lot of questions about our experiences with satellites. And then there were a couple of defense contractors there as well, some guys from Omicron." Lab Rat shook his head, not entirely certain he really understood what was going on. "You know much about lasers, Senior Chief?"

"A little, sir," the senior chief said, his voice suddenly distant.

Lab Rat shot him a sharp glance. "What's that supposed to mean?"

"What's what mean, sir?"

"You said 'a little.' And then you got that look on your face."

The senior chief pointed at the far end of the lot. "Isn't that your car over there, sir?"

Lab Rat stopped dead. "Forget the car for a minute. That look—you had that look."

"What look would that be, Commander?" The senior chief sounded faintly aggrieved.

"You know exactly what I'm talking about." Lab Rat shook his finger at him. "Don't play dumb with me, Senior Chief."

He gets in these moods, you'd think he was six feet tall, the senior chief thought to himself. *I don't care how big he is, he's got the voice down cold.*

The senior chief sighed, stuck his hands in his pocket and stared up at the sky. "I've spent a lot of my time in the Navy staring at computer screens, sir. Some of it has been more interesting than others. Like the tour I spent at Cheyenne Mountain."

"Oh." Lab Rat's mouth snapped shut. Whatever the senior chief had been doing at the Space Command was far too classified to be discussed in any parking lot. "Yes, I think that is my car."

"What do you guess, maybe a quarter mile away?" The senior chief asked.

"About that."

Lab Rat forgot about the cold for a while as they trudged toward his car. The news that the senior chief had spent a fair amount of time at the joint command located deep under Cheyenne Mountain was not surprising, although he had not known it before. That would explain how much he'd known about Cobra Dane and Cobra Judy, the long-range over-the-horizon sensors that had been so critical during the Taiwan-China conflict. It would explain a lot about his ability to glean information from satellite photos as well.

"They asked me about you, too, Senior Chief," Lab Rat said slowly. "About when you were going to retire."

Lab Rat took some satisfaction at seeing shock flash across the older man's face. "Omicron's got its eyes on you."

"No kidding."

Lab Rat nodded. "They seemed to know a lot about you. They want you real bad, Senior Chief. And me, too, for some reason. I take it you know what this is about?"

The senior chief seemed lost in thought. Finally, he nodded slowly. "Yes, I think I do. When we get back on board, I'll tell you what I know."

For the rest of the trip back to the hotel, the senior chief was silent. He seemed to be deep in thought, as though considering his options. Lab Rat couldn't blame him, but wished he knew which way he was leaning on the retirement issue.

Whatever the senior chief made in the Navy, and it wasn't nearly as much as Lab Rat made, he was underpaid. There were people in the civilian world that recognized that, and could offer far more money than the Navy ever dreamed possible. The senior chief had a wife and three kids to support, and Lab Rat knew the prospect of putting all three kids through college was on his mind. Although he would hate to see him go, Lab Rat couldn't blame him if he retired and took a high-paying civilian job.

For his own part, the senior chief was following a similar train of thought. Sure, of course he had thought about working for them after he retired. But that had always been sometime in the far future, not even very real to him. Someday, he would leave the Navy. Maybe at twenty years, maybe at thirty years. He liked the Navy, despite the low pay, long hours, and time away from home. He wasn't sure how he would fit in wearing a suit.

But if Omicron was asking about him, then that meant that they were moving ahead on Brilliant Pebbles. It was a follow-on to the Reagan Star Wars concept, an antiballistic missile defense system intended to guarantee the security of the continental United States. Using a dedicated network of satellites, high-intensity lasers, and long-range antimissile missiles, Brilliant Pebbles looked quite attractive on paper. Sure, there were a number of technical difficulties to work out, mostly those involving the scattering of the laser beams in the atmosphere and command and control circuitry for the antimissile missiles. But if they were talking to JCS and Commander Busby, he was willing to bet that they'd made progress on whipping the technical issues. Made progress, and were ready to go into field-testing. And that, the senior chief thought, was something he very much wanted to be a part of.

And maybe the commander wanted to be part of it, too. "Sir?" the senior chief said slowly, trying to figure out how to tactfully broach the subject. "Would you be interested in seeing what some of the systems can do these days? I could arrange a demonstration."

Lab Rat stared at him. *"You* could?"

The senior chief flushed. "Yes, well—yes, I could. And I think you'd be interested in what Omicron has going on."

Lab Rat smiled at him like a bemused parent surprised by a prodigal child. "Sure, Senior Chief. If you can set it up, I'd like to see it."

New York, New York
United Nations
1400 local (GMT-5)

Ambassador Sarah Wexler had been United States' ambassador to the United Nations for the last three years. During that time, she and the president had come to know each other fairly well, to the point at which they could anticipate each other's reactions and plan accordingly. It had led both of them into some cunning schemes using reverse psychology, and had deepened the respect they had for each other.

Yet, as Wexler tried to analyze the sense of foreboding stirring in her, she knew she would get absolutely nowhere with the president unless she could present facts to back up intuition. He was three years into his first term as president, and he understood diplomacy in a way that many did not. Nevertheless, he tended to discount her gut feelings.

But this time, she had to convince him. She called in Brad, her aide, to rehearse her arguments with him.

"Sit behind my desk," she ordered, vacating her chair and coming around to the visitor side. "Just a second—there," she said, as she adjusted the American flag to his right. "Gives it a little bit more atmosphere, I think. And keep your jacket on. Lean forward, put your elbows on the desk, and stare at me." She surveyed him critically as he complied, then nodded. "Yes, that will do."

"I can have one of the secretaries hunt down a greyhound if you like," he offered. The president's passion for rescued greyhounds and his efforts to ban greyhound racing within the United States were well-known. Two retired racers lived at the White House, and they got more press coverage than any other presidential pet she could remember. When the press could catch up with them, that was. The greyhounds seemed to delight in racing past waiting cameras at their still-respectable speeds of around forty miles an hour.

"Not necessary," she said. "He's usually got one of them in the office with him, and it pisses him off when people ignore them."

"Okay, shoot," Brad said, adopting a Texas drawl. "Ah'm all ears, darlin'."

Wexler marshaled her thoughts and began. "Mr. President, we have discussed the possibility of a reunified Soviet Union several times. And, in the past, we have both agreed that it might indeed be a possibility. I've come today to tell you that I think it may now be happening."

Brad stared at her, unblinking. "Pretty strong accusation, Madam Ambassador. What kind of evidence do you have? Anything like a signed declaration of war? A sunken passenger liner, or such?"

And that's exactly the sort of thing he would say. And would be looking for. But the intentions of nations are more often measured in the small things, not in the atrocities.

"Not yet, Mr. President," she said firmly, and let the silence lengthen.

"What do you mean, not yet? Your saying it's that serious?" Brad said, his Texas twang slipping slightly as he caught her mood.

She nodded. "Perhaps. If it starts, it will start like this."

"I'm all ears," the substitute president said.

"To begin with, the international treaty on the conduct of operations at sea is currently under review by several committees. I briefed you on that last month, and told you that the Russians had promised us a speedy response. I thought we'd hammered out all the essential terms and that it would be signed quickly."

"It hasn't happened?" he asked.

"No. It has not. There's been no response. In fact, the Russian delegation has refused to return phone calls from our people. They've been avoiding them in the hallways, snubbing them in the dining facilities, and generally avoiding us."

"Rudeness doesn't hardly mean World War Three," Pratt observed dryly.

"It's more than that," she said, suddenly feeling terribly inadequate to this task. How to possibly convey the nuances of interpersonal contact, the subtle signals used in the diplomatic corps to express problems or issues. It was almost impossible, but she had to try. The president must understand what was coming—must understand, so he could be prepared, even if he didn't believe her right now.

She tried again. "Last week, the Russian delegation hosted a huge reception for the touring Bolshoi Ballet Company. They've been here touring the country, as you know."

"Saw them myself when they were in D.C.," the president agreed. "So what?"

"The Bolshoi tour has been cut short by three weeks. The Russians say it's due to the illness of the male principal, but nobody believes that. Even if that were true, they always have understudies ready to go on."

Brad let his expression of mild amusement express his disbelief.

"And there's more," she pressed. "As I said, the Russians hosted a huge reception. *We were not invited, Mr. President.* In our own country, we were not invited to a reception honoring dancers touring our country."

"And you find that significant? Couldn't it have just been a screwup of some sort, either in their office or ours?"

She shook her head firmly. "Mr. President, this is a textbook example of the diplomatic corps sending a message. Believe me, the oversight was intentional, and carefully coordinated with the Russian president. Just as with their recalling the Bolshoi Ballet."

"Usually they recall the ambassador, not their dancers."

"That will be next. Within a week or so. That gives us a window of opportunity, Mr. President, to defuse this. We have to find out what's going on over there before we're surprised by it. Things are moving too quickly."

Brad held up a hand to forestall comment. "Now hold on, Sarah. You're moving awfully fast on not much evidence. Can you imagine the Senate Foreign Relations Committee's reaction if I tried to convince them that we ought to base foreign policy on what Russian stars in which ballet? I'd be laughed out of the office."

"I'm not suggesting you consult Congress. I *am* suggesting

that you let the military know, and let them prepare for what might happen."

"Sarah, Sarah. Really—you know that if I pass this on to the military, it'll be all over D.C. in a few hours. They'll be calling me a warmonger again. Listen, if you turn up any hard intelligence or other evidence that we're about to face problems with Russia, I'll act on it immediately. But until then . . ." Brad laid his palms flat on the desk and shoved himself up to a standing position. "Thanks for coming by, Madam Ambassador. I'll see you to the door."

Wexler stared at him. Brad stared back. "That's how it'd go, and you know it."

After a long silence, Wexler said, "Call Captain Hemingway. Ask her if she's got time for a cup of tea."

USS Jefferson
Flight Deck
1920 local (GMT-4)

The C-2 Greyhound banked hard to left, virtually standing on its wingtip as it made its turn onto final. In the back, the passengers were thrown against their restraining harnesses, and more than one let out an involuntary yelp. Among those who silently gritted their teeth and bore it was Lieutenant (junior grade) Clarissa Shaughnessy.

Shaughnessy barely met the height requirements for a pilot. At five feet three inches, she had a slender frame and delicate features. White-blonde hair formed an unruly halo around her face, framing angular cheekbones and deep blue eyes. Her appearance had earned her a nickname in the Tomcat training pipeline—Elf. Whether or not it would stick with her throughout the rest of her naval career would be up to the squadron.

Like most pilots, Shaughnessy hated flying as passenger. After eighteen months in Flight Basic and the Tomcat trading pipeline and two years of enlisted service before that as a plane captain on board the USS *Jefferson*, she knew all too well how many things could do wrong with an aircraft, particularly one that was attempting the always tricky task of landing on the deck of aircraft carrier.

As a young airman, Shaughnessy had been responsible for maintaining her aircraft, coordinating with the more sophisticated technicians as required, and helping pilots preflight and board their aircraft. When it wasn't in the air, it belonged to her. On one occasion, her sharp eyes caught a problem with the control surfaces of a Tomcat that was about to launch. Her quick thinking and disobedience to orders had saved an aircrew's lives. In recognition, Admiral Tombstone Magruder, then the battle group commander, had done everything in his power to see that she was admitted to the Naval Academy.

Now, almost six years later, she was back where she started. But this time as a pilot in VF-95, not as a plane captain. A young nugget, admittedly, but a pilot nonetheless.

And a lousy passenger.

The Greyhound gyrated through the air like a roller coaster as it fought the mass of roiling air in the carrier's wake. At the slower approach speeds used by the COD, the aircraft fought every burble of air. Up, down, sideways, it seemed as though the pilot had absolutely no control over the aircraft.

Shaughnessy tried not to think about the mishaps she'd seen as a plane captain. Instead, she thought of the one she'd prevented, the one good move that had gotten her her appointment to the Naval Academy. The pilot whose life she'd saved had later finagled his way around the rules and taken her up for her first-ever ride in the bird she was responsible for. He'd flown aerobatics, let her fiddle with the radar, and then finally brought her back on deck in what she now realized had been an exceptionally smooth landing.

Lieutenant Robinson, he'd been back then, although she was sure he'd been promoted since then. Bird Dog, the other officers had called him. She'd heard he was still on board the *Jeff*, and she was looking forward to seeing him again. How weird would it be to call him by his call sign? Or, God forbid, would he expect her to use his first name? Could she even do that?

She shook her head, determined to quit being stupid. She wasn't enlisted anymore. She was an officer—hell, she'd even been promoted once—and a pilot in her own right. She'd have to get over this inferiority complex.

With a sickening screech, the aircraft slammed down on the deck, caught the three wire with its tail hook, and jolted to a halt. There was a moment of wild relief among the passengers, a thankfulness that they'd somehow made it through the landing alive. Yet, as Shaughnessy knew, it was no more than a routine landing, one executed dozens of times every day on board this very aircraft carrier.

The crew captain was standing in the aisle of the Greyhound now, and making an announcement over the intercom, ordering them to remain in their seats until they arrived at their spot, the area of the deck that would be the parking spot. Shaughnessy felt the COD lurch backward, felt the thud against the undercarriage as the tail hook withdrew, and a slight surge of power as the COD headed for its spot. Outside, in front of the COD, would be somebody very much like who she had been, a plane captain. It was night, so the plane captain would be using lighted wands to direct them toward their spot on the deck. Once they came to a full halt, the passengers would be allowed to disembark.

Finally, the Greyhound lurched to a halt. After a few moments, the tail ramp dropped down, and cool night air flooded the compartment. Shaughnessy unstrapped herself and reached under her seat for her briefcase. Her large duffel bag was in the baggage compartment, but her briefcase contained her orders, her financial records, and a change of underwear—just in case.

Shaughnessy followed the herd of passengers straggling out across the flight deck and into the ship. "VF-95?" The petty officer standing behind the counter checked her orders, then passed them back to her. "You know how to find it, ma'am?"

"Yes, I do, thanks." *Ma'am. Never thought I'd hear that on board the* Jefferson, *did I?*

"Need any help with that duffel bag, ma'am?" He eyed her doubtfully, comparing the mass and probable weight of the duffel bag with her figure.

"Nope," she said cheerfully, hoisting the duffel bag easily. "I pack it, I can carry it." All her hours in the gym building muscle mass paid off as she saw a new respect in his eyes, but that wasn't the reason she'd sweated away half her free time.

Although the Tomcat flew by guided wire and contained

multiple redundant hydraulic systems, there was no telling
when you might have to manhandle the aircraft all by your
lonesome. Guys, even average guys, usually had no problem
with it. But if you were small, nicknamed Elf, and generally
a physical lightweight, you had to do what she had done: haunt
the gym, pumping larger and larger loads, knowing that you
would never reach the numbers that some of the guys did, but
determined to be able to bench press enough to be safe in your
aircraft.

Shaughnessy moved easily down two ladders, expertly maneuvering the bulk of the duffel bag behind her, to reach the
03 level. The 03 passageway housed most of the squadron
ready rooms, including that of VF-95. The captains, XOs, and
operations officers of the squadrons also had their staterooms
on this level, as did the admiral and his staff.

She made her way forward along the port passageway to
the VF-95 ready room. The passageway smelled of popcorn.
Every squadron had its own popcorn machine, and, as with
everything else an aviator did, the competition to produce the
best possible on-board popcorn was a continual source of contention among the squadrons.

She stared at the door for moment, almost overwhelmed by
her emotions. VF-95—her squadron. And now she was back.
For a moment, it felt entirely too audacious to be entering here
with her duffel bag, as though she were pretending to be something she was not. In one part of her mind, she was still the
young, scared plane captain who worked on the flight deck.

*Nonsense. You're a pilot. And, by God, you're just as good
as any of them.* She shoved the door open and stepped in.

She stood at the back of a large room filled with comfortable
high-back chairs. They were covered in brown leatherette and
numbered about forty. Forward, to the left, there was a small
desk with a telephone where the squadron duty officer stood
his watch.

The compartment was about a third filled, the scent of the
popcorn almost overwhelming. Aviators, most clad in flight
suits, were engaging in horseplay and ragging on each other.
A junior officer at the back of the compartment was fiddling
with a VCR. He looked up as the door opened and was the
first to spot her. A broad smile spread across his face.

"All right!" He stood and made a beeline for her. "Ensign

Shaughnessy—sorry, it's j.g. now I see—not that that makes any difference—you're just in time."

"For what? To see the movie?"

He shook his head, his pleasure unmistakable. "Junior officer in the squadron is responsible for the movies. Until now, that was me." He handed her a VCR tape. "And now it's you. Any questions, call me. I'll be in my stateroom." Shaughnessy stared down, bewildered, at the tape in her hand. What, was she supposed to run the movie *now*? Before she'd even checked in?

"By God, it *is* you!" a voice from the front of the room said cheerfully. "I saw the name on the orders and damned near wet my pants." The owner of the voice, a tall man with a powerful build and a huge grin on his face strode toward her. "Airman Shaughnessy—welcome back." She stared at his hands that clasped hers and pumped repeatedly. "Hell of a coincidence, isn't it? Save any more pilots recently?"

"Not—not recently, sir," she stammered, suddenly overwhelmed by the sheer force of his presence. She didn't remember Bird Dog Robinson as being quite so tall, and quite so . . . well . . . such a hunk. Maybe it was because, as an enlisted technician, she had known that the rules against fraternization prevented him from ever being a possibility. But, now, now that she was an officer . . . well, she shoved that thought out of her mind, and looked up into his broad, smiling face. "It's nice to be back, sir."

Bird Dog dropped her hand, and threw one arm casually around her shoulder. "Oh, hell—don't start on the sir shit. You damn near kicked my ass when I was a lieutenant and you were an airman—and rightfully so. It's Bird Dog now. So, how does it feel to be a pilot?" he asked, leading her toward the front of the room. Before she could answer, he turned her around to face the rest of the ready room. "Ladies and gentlemen, this is my good friend Lieutenant j.g. Clarissa Shaughnessy. Back when she had a real job as a plane captain, she saved my ass. Help her get settled in, folks. This one's a keeper." He turned back to Shaughnessy, and asked, "They tag you with a call sign in the pipeline?"

"Sort of," she admitted with a sinking feeling.

"Sure did," the officer she'd first run in to said immediately. "She's 'Elf'—we all know about Elf." He rocked back on his heels and looked up at the ceiling. "And the word was, the Elf is nobody to fuck with. Don't take your eyes off her for a second, folks—she nailed more of us in Flight Basic than anyone else in the pipeline. Yours truly included."

"Then, Elf it is," Bird Dog said grandly. "Welcome to VF-95, Elf."

"Thank you, sir—I mean, Bird Dog." She glanced at his leather name tag on his flight suit, and her eyes widened. She looked back up into his face, awe in her eyes. "You're the XO!"

"Yep. Just goes to show you, even the Navy makes mistakes sometimes."

"And who's the captain?" she asked.

"Well, you just won't believe this shit," he said, grinning again. "I never thought I'd see the day, and you can believe he rubs it in every chance he gets. You remember Gator, right?"

She nodded. "Of course. He was your RIO. So, he's the skipper?"

"Never lets me forget it. He's been pushing me around since he was just a lieutenant commander, and I listen to him now just a little bit more than I did back then."

"But he was XO before, so it must have been—" She broke off as a sudden silence filled the room.

The normal pipeline for aviators was to serve one tour in a squadron as XO, and then fleet up, as it was called, to command of the same squadron. This resulted in a continuity of command that helped mold the squadron into a tight fighting force. There was far less disruption at change of command in an aviation squadron than there was in a surface command.

But that wasn't the way it had worked out in VF-95. Gator had fleeted up—but a year earlier than he should have, and Bird Dog had unexpectedly been detailed as the XO. The reason was that Commander Joyce "Tomboy" Magruder had been killed in action.

"We don't talk about that much," Bird Dog said finally.

Elf could have kicked herself. Of course it would be considered bad luck to talk about the loss of a commanding officer—she should have known that. And if she'd been paying attention to what was going on in her own prospective squadron, she would have known that Gator was the skipper. But somehow, in a rush to finish the pipeline and the sudden change of orders to report to VF-95, she missed that one little bit of information. She had been in transit when Tomboy was killed.

Not killed. Missing in action. There's a big difference.

"You find your stateroom yet?" Bird Dog asked, breaking the silence.

"No, I just came in on the last flight."

"I'll show you where it is." A woman in a flight suit stepped forward, and held out her hand. She was blonde, but that's where her resemblance to Elf stopped. Her face was hard, her hair slicked back and disciplined. Elf saw shadows in her eyes, a ghost of—of what?

"Hi. I'm Lobo, your sponsor."

Another legend come to life. Shaughnessy had read everything she could find about the only female pilot to have been taken prisoner of war and successfully rescued then returned to flight status. And now, to meet her in person, well . . .

"Don't believe everything you hear," Lobo said wryly. She stepped back, and surveyed Elf's figure and extra small flight suit, noting the twist of muscles in her legs and the hard slope of her shoulder muscles that bulked up the flight suit. Elf saw a flash of recognition and approval in Lobo's dark eyes. Lobo nodded. "You'll do."

Bird Dog laughed. "If I looked you over like that, I'd be facing a court-martial for sexual harassment."

Lobo shot him a dirty look. "With all due respect, XO, you're a poster boy for sexual harassment. Now, if you don't mind, I'm going to get Shaughnessy settled. Come on, Elf— let's find your stateroom." Lobo turned on her heels and left without glancing back.

"Go on, Elf," Bird Dog said, his voice amused. "We'll catch up later."

Elf followed Lobo down the passageway and to the berthing office. She signed for her key while Lobo waited, and then they went down three ladders to the deck her stateroom was on.

"The first thing you do," Lobo said, "is learn your way around the ship. You need to be able to get out of this compartment and to the flight deck with a blindfold on. And you need more than one route in case the first one is closed down."

She waited, expecting a surprised remark. When none came, her brow furrowed briefly, then her face cleared. "That's right—sorry, you *do* know the drill, don't you?"

"Yes, ma'am."

"Lobo. Just call me Lobo."

"Lobo, then."

Lobo turned to leave. "I'll let you get settled in, then. I'll be back in twenty minutes and we'll go grab some late chow. Then we'll catch up with the skipper and the rest of the people you have to meet, as well as the CAG. Plan on being spiffy for the next two days. After you've met everyone, you can grunge around in flight suits all the time like the rest of us. Until then— first impressions, you know. See you in twenty minutes."

Elf surveyed the compartment, astounded by both the size and the disorder. Officer berthing wasn't anything like what she'd experienced as an enlisted sailor. Then, eighty women of all ranks below chief petty officer were berthed in a large compartment packed with bunk beds. There was a storage compartment under each bed and a small locker. The compartment was inspected daily and any loose gear would earn you extra duty chipping paint off whatever undesirable location the master at arms could find.

But evidently the rules were different for officers. If this had been enlisted berthing, there would have been at least six women in it. Instead, there was one bunk bed, two large lockers and two fold-down desks, and every flat space was covered with clothes, papers, or junk. The wastebasket looked like it hadn't been emptied in a few days. And was that—yes, it was! She moved a stack of towels aside to find a sink! Sheer luxury, as far as Elf was concerned. No trekking down the passageway to a communal head just to wash her face or hands or brush her teeth.

Elf stowed her gear in the least-occupied locker, then changed into her khaki uniform, patted her flight suit wistfully and looked forward to the day she could change back into it.

The door burst open and a tall, dark-headed woman rushed in. She skidded to a stop and said, "Oh, hey! You must be Shaughnessy!" She held out her hand. "Ellen Bellson. Sorry about the mess. I thought you were coming in next week."

"Clarissa Shaughnessy. And don't worry about it. I take it this is my locker?"

Bellson looked stricken. "Yes, of course. But, here, let me get it cleared out. I just sort of started using it after Betty left, and—oh, here, I'll take those." Bellson scooped the towels out of Shaughnessy's arms and tossed them on the lower bunk. "Really, I've been on the schedule every day and things just sort of got away from me."

"Don't worry about it," Shaughnessy said, starting to suspect that the condition of the stateroom wasn't at all unusual. A small price to pay for all this privacy, though, and she'd find a way to put up with the mess.

"So. Where are you from? Did you find the Ready Room already?" Bellson pulled out a chair from under her desk, turned it around backward and straddled it. "You a good stick?"

Shaughnessy laughed. "Slow down. I just got here."

Bellson looked chagrined. "Sorry.

Bellson was a good six inches taller than Elf, and for a moment, Elf felt a flash of jealousy. Bellson had long hair pulled back in a twist that her flight helmet had destroyed. A long strand of shiny black hair hung down and clung to her worn flight suit. Her eyes were a dark, deep brown with a hazel tint to them. She was built like a race horse, long and rangy, but strong. She had a presence about her that seemed to suck all the air out of the compartment. Elf felt she herself might as well have been the same color as the paint.

There was no way Bellson would ever be called cute. Striking, beautiful, stunning even—but not cute. No, cute was reserved for people her own size.

"So how's the squadron?" Elf asked. "You like it here?"

Bellson shrugged. "It's about like any other squadron."

Not good. Not good at all. "I met the XO," Elf said. "Good guy."

"If you like the type. A little too pleased with himself, if you ask me. But he's the XO, so you have to get along with him. The skipper's sort of a pain in the ass, too. He's a fuss budget, but he and the XO go way back, so they stick up for each other. Once they get something set in their minds, there's no changing it."

"Like what?"

Bellson looked peeved. "Like if they decide you're not a hot stick, there's nothing in the world that will change their minds. They start telling these stories from *their* first cruises, like they were some sort of super heroes or something."

"Ah." *But they are, in a way. Don't you know who they are or what they've done?*

"Things were better when Tomboy was here," Bellson continued. "At least she knew the whole woman thing. You didn't get all the bullshit you get now."

"She was a pretty tough officer herself," Elf said without thinking.

Bellson's eyes narrowed. "You knew her?"

Damn. I wasn't going to mention all that.

The decision not to mention her enlisted background was something that Elf had arrived at gradually. It wasn't like she was going to try to hide it or anything. It was just that it wouldn't be the first thing she talked about. She was part of this world now, and she was going to have to get used to it. Talking about her enlisted days would be like Bird Dog and Gator talking about their nugget cruises.

"Yeah," Elf said. "I went to the Academy from the Fleet. From *Jefferson*, actually."

"So you knew all these guys before," Bellson said.

"Bird Dog and Gator, yeah. And Tomboy. Back before she married the admiral." A lump started in Elf's throat. How she'd looked up to Tomboy back then!

"Well, excuse me, then," Bellson said, her voice cold. "If I'd known you were so buddy-buddy with them, I wouldn't have talked about them like that. So are you going to trot right back to them and tell them what I said?"

"No! Why would I do that? Listen, we're not old buds or anything like that. I just knew them, that's all. They probably didn't even know my name."

Just then there was a knock on the door. Lobo pushed it open and poked her head in. "You ready for some chow?"

"Sure." Elf felt a faint sense of relief. "You want to come?" she asked Bellson.

"No. Thanks." Bellson's voice was colder than it had been before. "I've got some things to do."

"Oh, join us, Lieutenant," Lobo said, her voice level.

"Thanks, ma'am, but I really do have some things to take care of." Bellson's voice was surly.

"Well, if you're sure." Lobo said.

"Yes. Very sure."

"Come on, then, Elf. If you're late for chow, they run out of ice cream."

Elf followed Lobo down the passageway, worried. Was Bellson going to be a pain in the ass to live with? Did she have some sort of gripe with Lobo? And was Elf going to get caught in the middle?

They went through the speed line, taking hamburgers and fries, and then found spots at a long table half filled with aviators. Lobo introduced her around, and there wasn't a time when Elf could reasonably ask her what was going on between her hero and her roommate.

Finally, when they'd done, Lobo shoved her chair back and said, "Come on, Elf. You've got an appointment with the skipper, and then with CAG. You've got time to get back to your stateroom and get a clean shirt. You've got catsup on that one."

Elf looked down and searched for the catsup. Lobo roared as did the others. "Fish, fish—God, don't tell me you're that gullible about everything," Lobo said, slapping Elf on the back. "Come on, nugget. Let's go."

"So you and Bellson aren't great friends, I take it," Elf said as they started down the passageway.

"Why do you say that?" Lobo asked.

"It just looked that way."

Lobo walked on for another fifty feet before she stopped abruptly and turned down a short passageway to the right. It was far less crowded than the main one. "Let's just say I don't approve of what Bellson does when she's not flying," Lobo said. "In the air, she's fine. It's when she's on the ground that she's a problem. You want to get off to a good start around here, don't become good buddies with her. Keep your distance. Because, sooner or later, she's going down for a fall, and you don't want to get sucked down with her."

"Take a fall? For what?" Elf asked.

Lobo just shook her head. "Just stay out of it, Elf. Keep your eyes open and make your own decisions. There's been enough gossip passed around about me that I know what it feels like. You make up your own mind once you get to know her." Lobo turned and led the way out into the passageway.

Elf followed, wondering if the two-man staterooms might have more disadvantages than she'd first thought.

Sevastopol, Ukraine
Black Sea Command
2022 local (GMT+2)

"I don't know, Andrei." Yuri Maskiro stared down at the plate before him as though its contents were of critical importance. While the rare steak and lightly steamed fresh vegetables were far beyond what most Russians would ever experience, they certainly did not warrant the degree of attention he was giving them. "Yes, what you're proposing is theoretically possible. But, to undertake such a thing—well, you must realize, if caught, we'll be executed."

"We won't be caught." Korsov reached across the table to pick up another crisp bread stick. He broke it open and smeared fresh butter across the exposed bread. "Besides, our planning will include deniability. Should anything be detected, it will simply be blamed on someone else. Trust me, I do know how to set those things up."

"So did Kreschenko."

"What's that supposed to mean?"

Yuri did not answer. Not that he needed to. Both of them knew what had happened to the last naval officer who'd tried to engineer a military coup against the current government. The execution had been public, but the torture preceding it hadn't.

Korsov broke the silence by saying, "Kreschenko was stupid."

"The last commander of the Black Fleet did not think so." Maskiro's predecessor had been part of Kreschenko's inner circle, and had been executed the day after his leader.

For a moment, Korsov felt real fear. Surely Yuri did not regret his involvement to this degree? Not enough to do something about it? And, if so, how much danger was he in right now for having divulged even the general concept of his plan to Yuri, even if he hadn't asked for Yuri's help?

He would not ask, Korsov decided. Yuri would know what he intended, would know and would even now be deciding whether or not to join him.

"The long-range missiles would be impossible," Yuri said finally, and Korsov felt relief surge through him. "The most I could do would be medium-range tactical missiles. And, even then, you would have to be responsible for getting them within range."

"I already considered that," Korsov assured him. "But you're sure you can get them?"

Yuri poked at a stray lima bean. "Oh, that's no problem. No one has any idea exactly how many we have or where they are. Not even me. In fact, I'm sure that about a third of them are on the world market already."

"A third? Are you sure?" Korsov was aghast. While the laxness of weapons accountability within Russia was well known, and was even worse in Ukraine, the prospect of a third of the former Soviet weapons arsenal being sold on the black market was still astounding.

"Of course I'm not sure," said Yuri. "That's exactly the point."

"But, then, this is perfect," Korsov said. "The Americans will find it even more difficult to determine where the missiles came from. And whom to blame."

"The Politburo won't have any problem deciding that blame," Yuri said smoothly. He lifted his gaze from his plate and stared directly across the dinner table at his old friend. "Even if this succeeds, they're going to blame me. Not you, not anyone else—me."

"I have thought of that," Korsov assured him. "Before you release the first weapon, you will be completely satisfied with the deception plan. Completely satisfied, or we will not proceed."

Yuri pushed the plate to the side. "Tell me just how you proposed to do this."

"The key, I think, is China," Korsov said. "China, and the Middle East. A month before we execute our plan, at a time when you have been recalled to the Politburo to testify and your deputy is in charge, there will be a terrorist attack on one of your storage facilities. Your forces will be overwhelmed, and missiles will be stolen. Specific procedures that you have

in place will have been circumvented by your deputy. You
will be outraged. You'll demand action. And you'll mount an
intensive manhunt in an effort to find those responsible."

"What specific procedures?" Yuri asked.

"During routine maintenance, you require an armed guard
when any of the facilities are breached, yes?"

Yuri nodded. "Of course."

Korsov spread his hands apart, palms up. "Your deputy will
have specifically ordered the men to be elsewhere on that date.
A review of his record will show a history of increasing instability. It will appear that he blatantly disobeyed your orders
to satisfy some affiliation he has with a terrorist group.
Chechnya, perhaps."

After long silence, Yuri nodded. "It sounds somewhat promising," he conceded. "However, there is so much detail that
must be filled in."

"Oh, assuredly." Korsov waved aside his objections. "Yet,
in principle, it is a solid plan, yes?"

"In principle."

By unspoken agreement, they moved on to other, more innocuous topics. The discussion ranged over world politics, the
weather, sports, and women. Finally, as evening grew late,
Yuri brought out his finest brandy. He poured each of them a
glass, and lifted his own. "To our success."

"Our success," Korsov echoed. He kept his expression warm
and cordial as his thoughts raced ahead to the day that was
hurtling toward them.

*My success. And, yes, if everything goes as planned, you
will be a part of that. But, if not . . .*

But it if not, Yuri would be his scapegoat just as surely as
his deputy was his.

THREE

Ensign Kevin Forsythe was not having a good day. It wasn't the weather. The forecast predicted a light breeze and blue skies. Soon, the wind would carry the scent of coconut oil, sand, and sea to the submarine from the beach.

Nor was he ill. In fact, he had never felt quite as well as he did that day. Every nerve ending seemed to tingle, the wind was silk drawn across his skin. Every sense was highly attuned, reacting to the smallest changes in his environment.

The source of Ensign Forsythe's discomfort was that he was officer of the day during the *Seawolf*'s first full day in port in Bermuda. Intellectually, he understood it wasn't anything personal. Someone had to stand duty, and it was simply his turn in the rotation. As the junior man in the wardroom, he had few favors to call in to compel a swap and absolutely no seniority. Therefore, when the list came down, he knew immediately he was stuck with it.

However well he might understand that, it still sat hard. The last two months had been especially grueling, particularly since he was a recent graduate of the Navy nuclear training pipeline and not yet fully qualified on board *Seawolf*. When he was not on watch or working, he studied. No movies. No lingering in the wardroom to talk or play cards. No, he did what a good submarine officer was expected to do—indeed, was required to do: He studied. He pounded through massive volumes of engineering text, memorizing diagram after diagram. He toured the ship endlessly, diagramming her peculiarities, the location of her damage control equipment, tracing out her piping systems. Yes, it all had been covered in school, but, as every new officer learns, there is a vast difference between the national submarine on a chalkboard or simulator and an actual living, breathing, honest-to-God boat.

So, given his schedule on board *Seawolf*, he thought that maybe, just maybe, he was a little more ready for liberty than absolutely anyone else on the boat.

Not that anyone else felt that way. He hadn't even bothered to mention it, knowing the sardonic looks and disgust he would garner from the other officers. After all, only he and Ensign Bacon were on their first patrol. The rest of them were veterans, had all done six months submerged on patrol in areas they couldn't even talk about. The fact that Ensign Forsythe had been studying his little butt off for the last two months wasn't even comparable. They had all been there, done that, and had little sympathy.

Oh, sure, he would get his chance tomorrow, and the day after that. The submarine was in three-section duty, so he could expect liberty two out of every three days. Just like everyone else. But, somehow, that didn't seem much of a consolation right now.

To make matters worse, his immediate superior in the watch section, Lieutenant Commander Brian Cowlings, was no happier about having duty than Forsythe was. And, furthermore, Cowlings didn't like him. Didn't like him one little bit. So Forsythe anticipated that to work off his own frustrations, Lieutenant Commander Cowlings would probably spend a good deal of the next twenty-four hours chewing on Forsythe's ass.

Cowlings was an engineer, the chief engineer of the boat. He was one of the men Forsythe would have to convince that he was qualified in order to earn his submarine pin.

Forsythe watched as the off-going duty section streamed down the wooden planked gangway connecting the submarine to the pier. *Like rats deserting a sinking ship.* It was still a few minutes before 0700 but every watch station had been turned over, every watchstander relieved by someone in Forsythe's section.

Since the submarine had gotten in late last night, the offgoing duty section had stood watch from around midnight until 0700. After Forsythe had double-checked everything in his division—he was the auxiliaries officer—gone over his duty roster again, worked out a few small problems connecting to shore services, it was well after 0200. He had contemplated heading ashore for a couple of quick beers and coming back to the submarine and getting up an hour later to assume the watch, but immediately realized that that would be a bad idea. Standing your first in-port duty while still blotto from the night before was no way to impress anyone, and he was quite certain that Lieutenant Commander Cowlings would not only smell the stale beer on his breath but would also be able to peer deep inside his soul and realize just how unworthy a submarine officer Ensign Forsythe was.

"Ready for colors?" a voice behind him asked. "If you don't check, it will go wrong."

A submariner's motto. Check, recheck, and triple-check. Because when you were a couple of thousand feet below the surface of the sea, it was highly probable that anything that went wrong would kill you. Professional paranoia was part of being a submariner.

Forsythe turned and snapped off a smart salute to Lieutenant Commander Cowlings. "Yes, sir. Just went over the roster and verified that everyone is on board. They all know their assignments, we checked with harbor local for the correct time, and there are no special holidays or days of mourning to observe."

"Where's the flag?" Cowlings waited. Forsythe's blood ran cold.

The flag. Dammit, the flag! Where the hell is it? The boatswain's mate would know, but where was the boatswain's mate? Does anyone in the duty section know where it is?

Cowlings smiled slightly. "It's considered highly inappropriate to hold morning colors without an American flag, Ensign. Now, unless you want to get your boys together and start coloring a tablecloth, I suggest you find it. You have—" Cowlings glanced at his watch—"fifteen minutes."

Fifteen minutes. The submarine was crammed with nooks and crannies, and the first place that the Ensign thought to look was the boatswain's mate's locker. But the locker would be secured, accessible only to the boatswain's mate of the watch or someone with a master key. And Lieutenant Commander Cowlings had the master keys.

"Sir, if I might have the master keys, I can—"

Cowlings pulled the keys out of his pocket and dangled them enticingly in front of Forsythe. "You mean these?"

Forsythe reached for them, but Cowlings pulled them back, keeping them just slightly out of his reach. A red flush spread up his face, burning over his cheek bones.

Just what the hell is this? He knows I need them to get in the locker—he's determined to make me look stupid in front of the captain, I just know it. Somebody ashore will be sure to tell the skipper that colors didn't go down right, and the captain will blame me.

But Cowlings is the command duty officer. It will look just as bad for him, because he's responsible for my performance.

"Fourteen minutes, Lieutenant. And counting." Cowlings waited.

A test. This is a test of some sort. The realization dawned in his mind with a blinding flash. *I'm supposed realize something, supposed to understand what I need to do.* The smile on Cowling's face changed slightly as he saw the junior officer consider the problem from a new angle.

He doesn't expect me to be bounding around the deck, trying to grab the keys from him. That's horseplay, not allowed on watch. Besides, it would look undignified, and an officer is supposed to—that's it. An officer.

Forsythe turned to Chief Petty Officer Billdown, the chief of the watch, who was standing slightly behind him. "Chief?"

"Yes, Ensign?" Forsythe could tell by the chief's tone of voice that he's been expecting it, and he detected a note of approval.

"Chief, please locate the American flag and assemble the color guard."

"Right away, Ensign." Forsythe watched him go, resenting the trick that Cowlings had played on him, but knowing he would remember the lesson well.

Cowlings nodded. "Good job. They still teach that story about the new army officer?"

"Yes, sir."

Forsythe knew the story well. A group of army lieutenants was tasked with putting up a standard issue field tent. None of them had ever done so before, and the results, as they issued a series of highly confusing and explicit orders to their troops, were ludicrous. The troops had been told beforehand to obey every order precisely as it was given.

The last second lieutenant watched the others carefully. When his turn came, he turned to his sergeant, and said, "Sergeant, have the men put up the tent." The tent went up in minutes. The moral was that any task could be accomplished much faster and more accurately by doing what an officer was supposed to do: using the chain of command to get the most out of the talents and skills of the men assigned to him.

"Sinks in better with an actual lesson." Cowlings tossed him the master keys. "I'll observe colors with you, then I'll be in my stateroom. Call me if you need me."

They stood side by side as the national anthem rang out and the flag soared quickly to the top of the flag pole. As he listened to the music that never failed to set something aquiver inside of him, Forsythe suppressed a grin. Maybe it wouldn't be such a bad duty day after all.

FOUR

Northern Maine
Omicron Testing Facility
0600 local (GMT-5)

Lab Rat shrugged down deeper in his parka. It was a cold morning, with a biting wind blowing out of the northeast. The sun was still below the horizon.

"This better be good," he grumbled, shooting an aggrieved look at the senior chief. "May I remind you we're supposed to be in Bermuda?"

The senior chief stole a look at his commander and suppressed a snort of laughter. The diminutive man had pulled out a ski mask and pulled it down over his chapped face. He looked like the world's smallest ninja. "You said you wanted to see it, sir. Trust me, it'll be worth freezing your ass off." The senior chief's voice was calm, with just a trace of anticipation in it.

"So, what happens now?"

Just then, the radio that the senior chief held crackled to life. It was connected to the control center of the testing facility, and Lab Rat recognized the voice as the senior controller he'd met the night before. The controller was a former Navy intelligence specialist, and a former shipmate of Senior Chief Armstrong.

"Observation teams, standby for launch. Five, four, three, two—we have a launch."

"Look to the southeast, sir," the senior chief said. "Red lights—it's an old Talos missile, but they have it rigged with reflectors all over it as well as a few embedded red lights. The reflectors are for telemetry as well as visibility."

Just then, Lab Rat saw it, a streak of red on the horizon. He lifted his binoculars to his eyes and tweaked them into focus. There it was, its outline just barely visible and backlit by the now-rising sun.

"What's the range?" Lab Rat asked.

"The ship is eighty miles off the coast."

Lab Rat grunted. It wasn't entirely realistic, not for an antimissile test system. A real ballistic missile would be coming in at a far higher altitude, cruising exo-atmosphere before tipping over, breaking into multiple warheads, and heading for targets. But this wasn't a demonstration of the final system. It was simply proof that the remaining technical issues having to do with the laser and the control system had been resolved.

"Commencing target acquisition," the controller's voice announced, his excitement coming through even over the crackling circuit. "Searching, searching—acquisition now!"

From somewhere to the north of them, a spike of blue-green laser shot up from the coast. It was a narrow beam, too bright for any natural light source, and its intensity washed out the breaking dawn. It speared into the dark sky, burning its image on their retinas, then, in a flash of motion too quick to follow, searched the sky in a quartering pattern. Within seconds, it found the missile and locked on to it. The red lights of the missile were barely visible in the brilliance.

"Target acquisition," the voice announced. "Maintaining lock through transition."

The missile was closer now, its outlines bathed in blue-green light rather than the rising sun. It was running almost parallel to them, its shape clearly visible. The laser stayed with it, seemingly locked on a few atoms at the very tip of the warhead.

"Sometimes this is enough," the senior chief murmured, quiet awe in his voice. "The high-powered beam burns out electronics pretty fast. A soft kill, but that may not be good enough. Depending on the warhead, it can still do a lot of damage if it makes land."

Lab Rat stared at the laser beam. He had heard rumors of testing in the desert, of lasers flickering among the remote mountains in Arizona and New Mexico, but he had had no idea that the system itself was so close to implementation. The technical problems alone in maintaining the focus over distance of the laser light, in generating sufficient power and in target discrimination, had been reported as overwhelming.

"Fire one," the controller's voice said. Immediately, from somewhere in the vicinity of the laser, he saw fire arc up from the ground. For a moment, it looked like some god was throwing thunderbolts, but Lab Rat quickly realized it was simply the fire and exhaust from the tail of a small antimissile missile. It shone pure gold and white, stark against the primary colors of the laser and the red-lighted target. It spewed white exhaust in its wake in a faintly spiral pattern that gradually tightened and settled into a straight line.

Unerringly, the missile followed the laser beam, running just to one side of it and correcting its course as it arced up. The symmetry of the entire evolution was completely stunning, and the combination of colors, the time of day, and biting cold gave the entire scene a surreal feeling.

The antimissile missile winked out of existence. For a few microseconds, Lab Rat wondered if it had missed its target. Then a fiery explosion lit up the northern sky, a fireball of white and gold and black smoke, now illuminated by the sun coming over the horizon as well as the laser. The blue-green light played over the billowing clouds of black smoke and fire, as though it were hunting for any last remnants of the missile.

"Hard kill," the controller's voice announced with satisfaction. "All observation teams, return to base. Muster in conference room eleven for debrief."

An expression of sheer joy lit the senior chief's face. He stared up at the sky, his eyes transfixed and his face transformed. Finally, when he noticed Lab Rat staring, he turned back to his commander. "That's what I was working on, sir. A lot of the targeting module is mine."

"Is it deployable now?" he asked, unable to believe what he'd just seen. "If this works, it changes everything, doesn't it?"

The senior chief nodded his agreement. "Oh, it will work. And, yes, sir, it does change everything. Now the question is: Do you want to be a part of this or not?"

Lab Rat's mind reeled. If Brilliant Pebbles was deployed, there would be far less need for the nuclear arsenal the United States now maintained. He could see the submarine fleet standing down, ballistic missiles disarmed, and a flood of officers entering the job market. Maybe the senior chief was right— he should get in now, on the ground floor, before there was too much competition.

"It seems to me that they've got a ways to go, though," Lab Rat said slowly, as he strode over the frost-encrusted ground, following the senior chief back to the humvee that would take them back to the compound. "The trajectory problems alone— we've discussed those. Head on it's a tougher shot than on the beam. And tying this all in to the early warning systems, even into Cobra Dane and Cobra Judy—well, that will take some time."

"It will. But can you imagine it, sir?" The senior chief's voice was low, but filled with more intensity and passion than Lab Rat had ever heard before. "I grew up in the sixties, sir. I remember nuclear attack drills in elementary school, where we were supposed to get under our desks and put our hands over our heads. I remember the warning sirens. No, it never really came to that, but can you imagine never having to worry about that again? To be able to guarantee our continental safety and sovereignty? Sir, that's worth fighting for."

"Yes, I suppose it is."

They walked in silence until they reached the humvee, and Senior Chief Armstrong slipped automatically into the driver's seat. Lab Rat watched him for a moment, and a feeling of profound sadness swept over him. "You've made up your mind, have you?"

The senior chief looked uneasy. Finally, he nodded. "I think I have. It's not that I don't love the Navy, sir—I do, and working with you has been a real honor. But to be part of this"—he gestured, taking in the entire expanse of the horizon—"that would be something. I've got twenty-one years in— I can retire anytime."

"Give it a few days' thought," Lab Rat urged.

The senior chief nodded. "I will. And, sir, you might give it some thought yourself."

Tomcat 103
300 miles northeast of Bermuda
1100 local (GMT-4)

Elf put her Tomcat into a hard climb, then kicked in the afterburners. At the top of her climb, she rolled the Tomcat over, inverted, as she pulled out into level flight. Then she dropped the nose back down, kicked the afterburner off, and let gravity do its thing. She descended 5,000 feet in a hard dive, then gently pulled the Tomcat out at 7,000 feet. She followed up, just for the hell of it, with a couple of barrel rolls, then a hard break to the right.

Silence in the back seat. Elf sighed, glanced at her checklist and continued on to the next maneuver. The new skipper, Commander Gator Cummings, had welcomed her warmly when she'd reported to his stateroom with Lobo. He talked to her about his philosophy of combat, discussed her background with her, most of which he already knew, and then congratulated her again on making the transition from enlisted sailor to officer. "It won't always be easy," he warned. "There are people on the ship right now that will remember you from your plane captain days. And the whole fraternization thing— well, you're the one ensign that I won't have to explain that to, right?"

"Right, sir."

"Well, then, check in with Safety and get your NATOPS quals taken care of. Unless Safety objects, ask Lobo to get you on the schedule for tomorrow. It'll be a fam flight, your first hop. I'll be your RIO and Bird Dog will be your wingman. He'll put you through your paces, see what they're teaching in the pipeline these days, and get you up to speed on all the local procedures."

Elf groaned. Sure, she knew that she'd have to have a few check rides, but she had expected somebody from the safety department to do it. That it would be her new executive officer had not occurred to her.

"Something wrong, Ensign?" Gator asked.

"No, sir. Not at all." She stood, and started to leave.

Gator held out his hand. "Welcome aboard again, Ensign. It's good to see you again, and I'm extremely impressed with what you've accomplished. I've looked at your transcripts from the Naval Academy—outstanding, simply outstanding. If you've got half the smarts in the air that you've got on the ground, you're going to be a real asset."

"Count on it, sir," she shot back. A grin broke out on her face. "And it's a real treat to be back here, especially with you and the XO."

After that introduction and her first meeting with Bird Dog in the ready room, she expected a casual approach to check flight. But from the moment they commenced a preflight brief in the ready room, quizzing her on the rules for avoiding incidents with the Russian task force to the north, through the preflight checklist and the start-up checklist, then right on through the cat shot, both men have been . . . well, cold wouldn't be exactly the right word, but there was certainly none of the easiness she'd expected. She was acutely aware of both Bird Dog and Gator watching every move. Even Bird Dog's RIO seemed to be taking notes, and he was only four months ahead of her.

But that was four months of experience that she didn't have. Yet.

The preflight had gone well, as had her taxi to the catapult. Once on the catapult, she felt the butterflies start. After all, it wasn't like she had all that many launches under her belt.

The flight deck technician gave her the final hand signal to check her control surfaces. When he saw everything cycle as required, he snapped off a sharp salute. Already full power, she returned the salute. The catapult officer dropped to the deck and pointed forward.

A hammer slammed her in the back. The Tomcat raced down the catapult and seconds later she was airborne.

Behind her, she heard Gator give a sigh of relief. She didn't take it personally—RIOs were like that. The most common fatal error on a cat shot wasn't anything she had control over—it was a soft cat, insufficient steam power at the shuttle that would result in the aircraft failing to attain takeoff speed and dribbling off the end of the deck. If they were to launch under insufficient steam pressure, she would have only microseconds to punch them out, and even that was fraught with dangers. In a low altitude ejection, there was a serious risk that their chutes would fail to open, that they would be ejected onto the flight deck, or that the chute would open, drag her under the ship, and become entangled in one of the ship's four propellers.

Elf put the Tomcat into a hard turn, banking away from the *Jefferson*. As she came around the ship, sun glinted off her superstructure and off the gentle swells. The cruiser and frigates were standing well off, more than 10,000 yards away.

As she ascended, Elf's radar picked up a close formation of ships to the north. At this range, the radar blips were so close together that it was almost impossible to make out individual contacts. It was the Russian task force, still staying well clear of the *Jefferson* but now only one hundred miles to the north. She noted they were steaming southwest.

For the next twenty minutes after launch, it was as though Gator was conducting an accelerated review of everything she had learned in the last eighteen months. They went from basic flight maneuvers to formation flying, then aerobatics. Finally, when he was satisfied that she knew the performance characteristics of the aircraft, he said, "Bird Dog, you're now a MiG. Get lost." With that, he flipped off the input to her heads-up display, or HUD.

Bird Dog peeled off. She tried to watch where he went, but he wheeled around behind her, and Gator ordered her to maintain straight and level flight. Twenty seconds later, her HUD snapped back on and Gator said, "Okay, kid. Let's see what you've got."

She quickly surveyed the contacts on her screen, and immediately pinpointed the one that was likely to be Bird Dog. It was outside commercial air patterns and routes, and it was behind and above her.

"Talk to me, Elf," Gator ordered. "I want to hear what you're thinking as well as see what you're doing."

"That's probably him," she said, designating the radar lozenge she believed was Bird Dog's aircraft as a possible hostile contact. The symbol changed, indicating her assignment. "He's breaking for a mode four, although that could be a Brit in the area as well." Mode four was the classified, encrypted portion of IFF, or international friend or foe. If aircraft or a surface ship radiated mode four, it was proof positive that it had the correct friendly gear loaded with the correct daily crypto codes.

"And mode three?" Gator prompted.

"Can't use it, sir. In a real situation, they'd have it turned off anyway." Mode three indicated the type and nationality of a contact, but mode three could be changed inside the cockpit.

"Okay. So what are your plans, assuming you're right?" Gator asked.

The answer rolled out of her mouth easily, although both knew that translating knowledge into the actual practice was a horse of a different color. "The MiG's performance characteristics make it tighter on turns, so I'll want to avoid overshooting him. The Tomcat has a superior power-to-wing ratio, making me better in climbs. Right now, he's above me, so I'm going to want to break out and climb, and then try to come into position behind him?"

"But he can turn tighter than you can," Gator said. "What makes you think you can get in behind him?"

"I probably can't in two dimensions—or, at least, it's difficult to do in a one-on-one. If I had a wingman, that would be a different story. So, I can't work in two dimensions, I have to work in three. That means I either have to break behind him, going head-on while I climb, or try to gain altitude quickly before he can turn in behind me."

"Let's see you do it."

Elf slammed the throttles forward into afterburner, clicking past the detente. The Tomcat responded immediately, slamming her back against her ejection seat. She heard a grunt of protest from Gator in the back.

"Damn pilots. You're all alike," Gator said, forcing the words out against the G forces.

Both she and Bird Dog had been heading in a general southerly direction. As the afterburner kicked in, she started climbing, banking around in an eastern direction as she did so. She rolled the Tomcat slightly to keep him in visual range. "Watch him, RIO," she said calmly. "Tell me the second he starts turning."

"Turning now," Gator answered.

The acceleration was building now, and Elf eased off
slightly on her rate of ascent. The powerful Tomcat would put
more vertical distance between the two of them, and she
needed the time to move to position. In an out-and-out run for
the money, the MiG could keep up.

At the same time, she had to trade some horizontal distance
to increase her vertical distance. She watched her heads-up
display, noting that Bird Dog was descending slightly, intending to slip in behind her at exactly the right moment.

"He's got a lock on you," Gator said. He then favored her
with his own imitation of the ESM warning buzzer.

"Chaff, flares" she said. She rolled the Tomcat hard to the
right, clearing the area as chaff and flares spit out from the
belly of the fuselage.

She heard Gator swearing behind her again. "Damn, it's bad
enough I have to put up with it from Bird Dog. Could you
give me a little warning at least, the next time you try to pull
a maneuver like that?"

"Warning," she said calmly, and snapped the Tomcat back
into a hard turn. She'd seen on her heads-up display that Bird
Dog was now boring straight in on her, intending to take a
second shot. She hit the afterburners again, accelerating their
rate of closure to well over 1,000 miles an hour. And increasing.

"AMRAAM," she said crisply. "Your dot, Gator."

"My dot," Gator acknowledged, "Fox three," simulating the
firing of the all-purpose, long-range, antiair missile. "I would
remind you that there are briefed rules of engagement for this
exercise that are—"

"Warning," Elf said again, interrupting him. She dropped
the Tomcat nose-down sharply, increasing the clearance between the two aircraft, then pulled back hard to start ascending
again, flashing in behind Bird Dog. "Golf, golf," she said,
announcing that she had just taken shot with her nose cannon.
"I see flames."

"You do not," Gator snapped. "What you see is a missile
incoming—"

"Warning," she said, interrupting him again. "Your dot,
RIO—Sidewinder."

"Fox one," he acknowledged as she snapped the Tomcat
into another series of hard turns and radical changes in altitude,

simulating shaking off an enemy missile lock. "It's still got you, Elf," Gator warned. "Still coming, still coming—"

Elf jammed the afterburners on, pitching the aircraft's nose straight up and heading for the sun. She rolled the Tomcat over just as she reached the apex of the climb, and stared down through the canopy at Bird Dog, now below her. She made another hard right turn, coming in behind and slightly above Bird Dog. "Golf, golf," she announced again.

"What is it with you guys and guns!" Gator shouted. "I can't tell you how it pisses me off that you and Bird Dog keep trying to get me killed."

"You're still alive," she snapped. "And if you don't like the way I fly, you got options."

The comforting roar of the Tomcat was the only sound in the cockpit. Reality came crashing in on Elf. She had just told her new commanding officer that if he didn't like the way she flew, he was welcome to take his chances by ejecting. This was not the way to pass a check ride.

The silence dragged on, and Elf tried desperately to think of something to say. Should she apologize? Under normal circumstances, she and RIO would be fighting the aircraft together. But in the end, even with a more senior RIO, she was the pilot.

"Stop the clock, stop the exercise," Gator said finally, his voice showing no trace of his earlier emotion. "Bird Dog, we'll join on you for a return to the carrier."

Elf turned and vectored in on Bird Dog, dropping neatly into position off his right wing, and following him back to the boat. She waited as he made his approach, snagging the three wire neatly. Then she turned in on final, shutting all of her concerns about the previous engagement out of her consciousness. Landing on a carrier was a good deal more dangerous than getting shot at with pretend missiles, and this was no time to be wondering about what Gator thought. There would be plenty of time to hash that out later.

"Two zero three, call the ball," she heard Pri-Fly say.

"Roger," she acknowledged. Just as she said it, she saw the green flash of the Fresnel lens to the left of the stern. "Two zero three, ball."

"Two zero three, LSO," a new voice chimed in. "Say needles."

"Needles show high and right," she said, referring to the crosshair indicators that showed whether or not she was on flight path. Her needles showed she was off the glide path slightly.

"Two zero three, I understand high and right. Roger, concur, fly needles." LSO's voice changed from a bored rote recitation to a more friendly tone. "Okay, Elf, let's get you back on board."

The landing was almost anticlimactic. Elf made small corrections to her course and attitude, slamming down on the deck to catch the three wire. Not a perfect landing, not like Bird Dog's had been. But, still, a pretty damned good effort for a first approach on a new boat, she thought.

There was not a word from the back seat.

After she'd followed the plane captain's directions to her spot, she said "Commencing preshutdown checklist." She announced it crisply, her voice betraying no hint of her nerves. "Are you ready, sir?"

"Yes, go ahead." As she ran through the checklist, Gator made the necessary responses, his voice distant and detached. Finally, she shut down the engines and popped the canopy and came down the boarding ladder. She dropped lightly to the deck, flexing her knees as she landed. Bird Dog and his RIO were waiting for her. Gator followed slowly, his knees cracking as he landed.

"Little eager with those guns," Bird Dog said. She saw a scowl on his face.

"It seemed like the best option at the time, sir," she said formally.

"Well, there are a few points we might go over," Bird Dog said. Then, as though suddenly remembering his place, he took a step back and glanced over at Gator.

"Well, thank you," Gator snapped. "Awful thoughtful of you, XO, to allow me to express my opinion."

"Ah, sir, come on, I didn't—"

Gator waved him into silence. He turned and fixed Elf with a glare. All her worries and fears she'd put aside during the trap came crashing back down in on her. Was it possible she could be stripped of her wings after only one landing—even if she hadn't crashed? "Sir, I just want to say . . ." she began, suddenly frantically trying to find a way to salvage her career as a naval aviator. How could she tell her parents that she'd been shitcanned after only one trap?

"Shut the fuck up," Gator snarled. He turned to Bird Dog. "She's just as bad as you were at her age. If not worse." With that, he turned sharply and stalked off.

A broad grin broke out on Bird Dog's face. He held out his hand, smacked it hard palm-to-palm against hers. "High five, Elf!"

"But—" she began.

Bird Dog cut her off. "What, you were worried? Hell, coming from a RIO—my old RIO, that old fusspot Gator in particular—that's about the highest compliment you can get. Come on, I'll buy you some popcorn. We'll talk about MiGs and guns. I got a little experience with both of 'em."

FIVE

Yuri Maskiro pitched forward slightly in his seat as the Boeing 747 made its first screeching contact with the runway. The tires emitted a high-pitched yell, bounced off, then immediately settled back down. After a few seconds of rollout, the nose dropped gently and the front tire hit the runway.

There was a loud roar as the pilot immediately reversed the thrust of the engines and deployed all speed breaks. The aircraft settled in to a gentle roll.

The pilot and the flight attendants made the usual announcements about remaining seated until the aircraft came to a complete stop. Maskiro waited, excitement surging through every millimeter of his body. Close, so close—and no one even suspected he was here.

Between his contacts and those Korsov had, it has not been difficult to make his way from the Black Sea to Greece. There, he changed identities and boarded a scheduled transatlantic flight to Bermuda. He paid for a first-class ticket, on the theory that no one would suspect that as much. Besides, Andrei told him that the first-class passengers were often moved through Customs more quickly.

Customs had not proved to be a problem. Maskiro's passport was indistinguishable from the real thing, primarily because it had been made by someone who worked in the passport department of the Greek government. No matter that he spoke no Greek. Instead, they had agreed that Maskiro would simply ignore anyone who spoke to him in Greek, insisting that he wished to practice his English. And if the accent sounded a little off to some, well, he could count on the wide range of British and American accents to help disguise him.

He passed quickly through Customs, speaking a few words of English to the functionaries, then moving with his luggage to the flight terminal itself. There, he scanned the crowd and finally located a small, dark-skinned man who matched the description he had been given.

"Sir, I'm supposed to meet you." The man's tone was respectful.

Maskiro nodded. "My luggage is all here." He gestured to a suitcase.

"That's it?"

Maskiro nodded. "Let us go."

The man handed him a long gym bag made up in bright colors, advertising itself as belonging to a guest of the Hamilton House. "Everything you required," he said finally, patting the matching bag on his own shoulder. "Come, follow me. You have reviewed the diagrams?"

"Yes, of course," Maskiro said. Even in a place like Bermuda, the locals knew where to obtain weapons. This should be quite simple, really.

Quite simple in part because security at the airport was remarkably lax. He noted uniformed men and women in short pants and some sort of official-looking shirt clustered randomly about the terminal. None of them was armed with anything more than a billy club. Judging from the way they were talking and laughing, few of them had any military training and even fewer had experience for what they were about to face.

Or, maybe not. One man standing at the fringe of a group looked toward Maskiro and an uncertain look crossed his face. He studied Maskiro for a few moments, as if considering whether or not he should do anything. But then a poke in the ribs from one of his compatriots and a new round of jokes drew his attention back away from the Russian.

"Down here," the man said, leading Maskiro down the hall.

There was a door that required a pass to open. The man produced a thin, credit-card-sized security pass and swiped it through the scanner. Something clicked and he pushed the heavy door open.

"Up four flights," he said. "There is an elevator, but we won't use it."

"And at the top of the stairs?" Maskiro asked.

"Just a hallway, and then a well-marked door. No security, no more locks."

Unbelievable. Even though Maskiro had heard about the legendary slackness at this airport, he still found it difficult to understand. Control the airport and you control access to the country. The first priority of any landing force was to obtain access for aircraft.

Maskiro trotted up the stairs, not deigning to use the handrails and holding his weapon well away from his body. He paused at the very top, not even the slightest disturbance in his breathing, and glanced across at his associate. "You understand, there are to be no shots fired. For this to be successful, no one must know we're here."

"They will, soon enough," the man said.

Maskiro nodded. "Soon enough gives us enough time. Remember, no shots."

At the top of the stairs was a small foyer with one door leading off of it. On the door was a large red sign that warned, AUTHORIZED PERSONNEL ONLY—STRICTLY ENFORCED. But there was no card reader, and no other security measures.

Maskiro could have laughed out loud. Easy, far too easy. As would be the rest.

It wasn't necessary to kick the door in or even to use any force at all. Maskiro simply turned the knob, opened the door, and walked in.

The room was dark, circular, and lined with radar screens. A low murmur of voices filled the compartment as the air traffic controllers worked their various parts of the skies. British accents of the native voices mingled with American voices and the overall impression was one of controlled chaos.

There was one loud yell from a woman, and then all the heads not covered with earphones turned toward him. A man in the middle standing on a podium, turned, scowled, and shook his head. He opened his mouth as though he were about to give an order, and stopped abruptly when he saw the weapons.

"Don't move. Not an inch," Maskiro ordered. He saw the supervisor's hand inch toward a button—a security alarm of some sort, no doubt—and Maskiro lifted the barrel of his weapon ever so slightly to point directly at him. "No alarms. Do as we say and no one will be harmed."

Without taking his eyes off Maskiro, the man said, "Everybody, just keep doing your job. Do exactly what they tell you." He raised his hands slightly, palms facing toward Maskiro, as though to demonstrate he had no weapon. "What do you want?"

"I want you to keep doing exactly what you're doing," Maskiro said. His companion moved off to the side to keep an eye on the other air traffic control operators. "The only difference is there will be several unscheduled flights arriving. I expect you to give them the highest priority, and to bring them in safely. They will taxi immediately to the far end of the runway. At that point, you will hold all incoming traffic for a period of thirty minutes. After that, you may resume normal operations and we will be gone."

"Is that all?" Now that he was over the initial shock, the supervisor seemed to be regaining his courage. Maskiro hoped he would not be foolhardy.

"That is all."

"And when will we see these flights you're talking about? And how many of them?" He moved two steps toward Maskiro, who shook his head warningly.

"I believe your people will be able to inform you. And I would prefer that you stay right there. Hands where I can see them, please. And, all of you," he continued, raising his voice slightly, "just remain calm, do your jobs. If an alarm sounds or your security forces are otherwise notified, this man will die first. And she," he said, gesturing to woman who screamed first, "will be next. It doesn't matter what happens to us, you understand. This is a holy war."

And that little piece of this information should keep your security forces busy for quite a while, figuring out what this means. I hope that they will assume we are Islamic. Foreign accents—they all sound alike to these people.

"Notify me immediately if you have any unidentified contacts," the man said, raising his voice slightly to be heard by everyone in the room. A series of quiet "Rogers" acknowledged the order.

Air superiority—the most critical part of any military operation, and yet so often overlooked in civilian contexts. Security checks concentrate on passengers arriving but not those people who come in from the outside to greet them. And there are weapons available everywhere in the world—yes, even here. Especially here.

Then, Maskiro heard what he'd been waiting for.

"Unidentified air contact at . . ."—the air traffic controller reeled off the latitude and longitude—"at thirty-one thousand feet, speed four hundred and fifty, descending; please advise of your intentions."

There was no answer. Maskiro motioned to the supervisor with his weapon, and he crossed over to stand behind the air traffic controller watching the area to the northeast of the island.

"Unidentified contacts, I repeat, state your intentions. I do not hold you on any flight plan or regular commercial schedule."

The technician kept his gaze locked on the scope, but toggled a button so that his voice spoke in Maskiro's ears. "I think this may be what you're looking for."

"Any IFF?" the supervisor asked.

"No," the air traffic controller said. "Nothing."

"That is it," Maskiro said. "You'll bring him in immediately, as well as the next two aircraft following."

"What kind of aircraft is it?" the supervisor asked, and then an impatient look crossed his face as Maskiro started to raise his weapon. "Don't give me that—I don't care who you are or what you want. All I want is to get you out of my control room. I need to know what sort of aircraft we're talking about to get them on the correct runway. Otherwise, he rolls off the end, smashes into a couple thousand pieces and we're both real unhappy. So, just tell me—how big is it?"

"It is the equivalent of a very large transport aircraft, perhaps a 747. Do you understand?"

"Yeah, I got it." He clicked over to the next circuit, and said, "Allen, bring it in on thirty-one." Without looking at Maskiro he said, "That's our longest runway—I don't know how loaded down he is or how much fuel he's carrying so I'll give him every foot of runway I've got."

"That will be acceptable," Maskiro said. Even though he deplored their security measures, he marveled at the way they went about their business, as if a major disruption in the flight schedule occurred every day. And perhaps it did—perhaps they trained for this very possibility. If they had been Russian troops under his command, they certainly would.

Voices coming from the inbound aircraft were protesting the go-arounds they were given, pointing out that they would be behind schedule, that their passengers would not make their connections. As if that would matter—making their connections was the least of their worries at this point.

The minutes ticked by and aircraft inched closer on the scope. He and the supervisor moved from console to console, tracking the aircraft as they came in. His companion watched the rest of the room.

Finally, a monitor pointed at the runway showing the first massive transport touching down. It touched down the very farthest point of the runway, still going too fast, and seemed like it would roll out forever. For just a moment, Maskiro was afraid it would not stop in time.

Then, ever so slowly, its speed decreased, and it finally rolled to a stop with only 200 feet of runway left. It turned, cleared the end of the strip, and rolled in to the terminal area. As it did, the second transport touched down. Just as the third was touching down, the back ramp on the first transport lowered. Troops with automatic weapons poured out and vanished into the terminal building. Maskiro watched as the second, then the third, repeated the maneuver.

Moments later, they heard feet pounding up the stairs to the tower. The door slammed open and four heavily armed and fully combat-ready Spetznatz stormed in. Without speaking, they took positions around the room. One sat down at the approach controller's console and held out his hands for the earphones. The Bermudian controller yielded them up immediately.

The three troop-transport aircraft backed away from the terminal and began taxiing toward the service area just off the ramp. Maskiro said, "Refuel them," then turned to the lead man. "Report."

The man saluted crisply. "All positions secured, sir. Estimate complete control of all critical facilities within one hour." A slight expression of disdain crossed the man's face. "They are not well prepared, sir."

"I noticed that." Maskiro said. "But overconfidence will kill you quickly. Do not expect it to go quite so easily at the American naval base."

The leader stiffened at the reproach. "Of course not, sir. But we are prepared to deal with them."

"Very well." Maskiro felt the familiar thrill of adrenaline course through him and felt a brief flash of regret that his responsibilities required him to remain at the airport. How he would have enjoyed watching them take the base! "Keep me posted," he said, regret in his voice. "I want to know the second that the military base is secured."

Naval Station Norfolk
Flight Operations Terminal
1700 local (GMT-5)

Lab Rat was at the terminal building, waiting for his flight to be called. The senior chief would be flying back out to *Jefferson* tomorrow, after he completed an inventory on some additional material they were picking up for CVIC. Lab Rat felt faintly guilty about leaving the senior chief to finish that onerous task, but he had to admit that a few days away from the senior chief would be welcome.

It was evident that the senior chief had made up his mind to accept Omicron's offer, and his enthusiasm for his new life was evident. There was a new fire in his eyes comprised of equal parts hope and expectancy. No, he had not slacked off on a standard military bearing or courtesy, but Lab Rat could sense it was chafing at him. The senior chief seemed to be yearning for his new civilian world. He would no longer be kept out of certain decision-making loops because he was only a senior chief, not an officer, even though he was far more qualified to command than many officers Lab Rat had met. Now, the senior chief would take his much-delayed and well-deserved place in the highest levels of management.

For his own part, Lab Rat felt confused. He still had two years to go before he could retire from the Navy, and the idea of wasting those eighteen years of service without staying for retirement was deeply troubling. No, not wasted—but he worked hard for it, hadn't he?

I was never working for the retirement. And it still seems so far away—I'm here because I like what I do, because I like the people, the ships, and the deployments. And because what I do makes a difference.

But wouldn't his work at Omicron make a difference as well? Maybe even more than staying in the Navy, if the system were truly deployable. Lab Rat leaned back, felt the hard plastic edge of the seat cutting into the back of his neck. Choices, too many choices.

Am I uncomfortable with that? To put it bluntly, do I prefer the Navy because there are fewer choices? Someone tells me when to go to work, what to wear, what time to get up—is that what it is?

It was all too much. He would get back to the ship, think it over, see if his world seemed different now that he knew he had options.

"Mr. Busby?" a voice asked. Lab Rat opened his eyes, immediately on edge but determined not to show it. It wasn't someone in the Navy—no one in the Navy would call a full commander "mister." Not unless he was in serious trouble.

"Yes?" Lab Rat answered.

There was a man in the seat next to him. His hair was too long for military, and he was dressed in jeans and a casual sweater. An expensive watch gleaned at his wrist. He held out his hand. "Bill Carter, from Omicron. I wanted to catch up with you and make my pitch before you headed back out to the ship."

Lab Rat pulled himself upright in the chair, and rolled his neck. "Your people already made a pretty strong case, Bill. I'm not sure what you could add."

"Pretty impressive stuff, wasn't it?" Carter asked, as though Lab Rat had not spoken. "And Armstrong speaks highly of you. He asked me to take another shot at getting you on board."

"Senior Chief Armstrong knows I'm not even eligible to retire."

Carter nodded. "I know, he was very clear about that. But he's really hot and heavy on getting you on the team, too. I know you're the only person he's considering for his number-two slot."

That got Lab Rat's attention. "His number two?"

Carter looked puzzled. "Yes, of course. You'd be working directly for Armstrong as his chief of staff. And I must say, we have a number of people who are very eager to take the slot—and who are very well-qualified."

Somehow, this particular configuration of responsibilities had not occurred to Lab Rat. He just assumed that if they were both at Omicron—well, but that didn't make sense, did it? The senior chief had extensive experience with the system, had even been involved in the development.

"I see," Lab Rat said slowly. *Does that make a difference? Am I too good to work for Armstrong because he's just a senior chief?* The possibility that that was indeed how he felt sounded ugly.

"I wanted to introduce you to what we might call a signing bonus. You can think of it as a buyout offer." Carter extracted a sheaf of papers and handed them to him. "If you agree to come on board with Omicron, we will give you an annuity that will pay you an amount each month equivalent to what your current retirement pay would be. The payments start two years after you sign up with us, and are guaranteed whether or not you stay. In other words, you live on your Omicron salary for two years, and then start getting your Navy retirement just when you would have originally."

Lab Rat's jaw dropped. "You can't be serious."

"I'm quite serious. Here, look over the details and talk to the lawyer on the ship. Armstrong can fill you in on anything you need to know. And as for living on your Omicron salary, well—how does triple your current pay sound?"

Lab Rat felt stunned. This was all moving too fast.

Just then, Lab Rat's flight was called. He stood and slipped the papers Carter had given him into the side pocket of his suitcase. "I'll think about it."

"Nice to meet you, Lab Rat," Carter said easily.

Lab Rat groaned. It was clear that the senior chief had made the nickname known to Omicron. *Will I never live that down?*

"Just let Armstrong know when you reach a decision," Carter continued. "I hope to be working with you next year. I think you'll find that it's very gratifying to make a difference for world peace."

"I've got to get going," Lab Rat said. "Yes, I'll let the senior chief know."

"Officers first," a flight technician called. Lab Rat walked numbly to the front of line, aware of just how much his way of life would disappear if he accepted Omicron's offer. And, yet, it was still very generous—and very very tempting.

I'd be working for the senior chief.

Just as he reached the gate, a petty officer wearing headphones stopped him. "There a problem?" Lab Rat asked, suddenly anxious to be back on *Jefferson*, where the issues were much clearer.

"Don't know, sir. I'm getting reports that—hold on—" And then the petty officer's jaw dropped and his face turned pale. "Holy shit." He turned to Lab Rat, disbelief in his eyes. "Sir, we've been put on hold. Three unscheduled troop transports just landed in Bermuda."

"So?" Lab Rat said.

"They're Russian, sir. Russian. They're not on any flight plan and now the tower in Bermuda is not answering up. *Jefferson* is northeast of Bermuda, and, until they figure out what's going on, they don't want the COD launching."

"Russians troop transports?"

The petty officer nodded, his eyes unfocused as he concentrated on the voice coming over his headphones. "Might as well go back into the terminal, sir. We're cleared to launch in twenty minutes—as soon as a fighter escort arrives!"

USS Seawolf
The Navy Pier
Bermuda
1931 local (GMT-4)

If anything, the sunset was even more glorious than sunrise had been. Ensign Forsythe made his rounds below decks, checking each watch station, observing the general condition of the ship. He stopped by Cowlings's stateroom and gave him a brief rundown on the status of the ship, including engineering plant configuration, depth of water in the bilges, and the status of shore power. When he was done, Cowlings nodded. "It's been a quiet watch so far, but don't let that fool you. Expect it to get busy after midnight. You know the procedure for picking up somebody that shore patrol has taken into custody, right?"

"Yes, sir."

Cowlings leaned back in his chair. "How you coming on your quals?"

"A lot to study, sir. There are so many details—prototype school didn't cover the half of it."

"It will be that way on your next boat, too. Not quite as bad, though."

"Sir?" Forsythe asked. "About this morning . . . well, I understood the point you were making. But I'm wondering, the stuff I'm learning for my qualifications is an awful lot of detail. Things like the engineering equivalent of where the flag is kept. How do you decide what you have to know and what you can look up if you need to? There's no way I can remember everything. And I'm supposed to use my chiefs' and my troop's expertise, right? But I'm supposed to know every detail of their jobs as well, right?"

"Good question. I'll see if I can explain it." Cowlings closed his eyes for a moment, and then continued, "There's two reasons for making you study the details, the where-is-the-flag stuff. First, anybody can have a dumb-shit attack. Even a chief can overlook something that's just so painfully obvious that you question his sanity. You're a safety valve for those dumb-shit moments. No, you can't second-guess him on every detail, but you can do a sanity check. Sometimes, the chief has a solution in mind that he needs to run by you. He can't use you as a sounding board if you don't have a clue what he's talking about.

"And that brings us to the second point: context. Your chief is an expert in every area of his own spaces, and knows a lot about the rest the ship as well. But his time and attention are spent in his own division. You, as an officer, have broader responsibilities, up to and including, when you get more senior, actually taking the ship into combat. Sure, you're not ever going to know as much about engineering as a chief in engineering does—but what about when you're talking to an operations-type chief? Then you'll be the one who knows more about engineering, and you'll be the one who can think across departments to come up with an answer. The sonar man might know that certain equipment can cause an artificial signal, or artifact, on his gear. But he probably won't know that we changed bearings on the number-two reactor coolant pump two days ago. You probably will. You can think across departments because the chief knows more about the details. That makes sense?"

Forsythe nodded. "It's an awful lot to learn."

"No shit. But that's why they pay you the big bucks. Have the men put up the tent, right?"

Forsythe stood and said, "Thank you, sir. I guess I understand. I'll go check on evening colors now."

"Oh, Ensign?" Cowling said as Forsythe started to leave. "Do you know where the flag is kept now?"

Forsythe smiled. "For evening colors, it can be found at the top of the flag pole. Sir."

Sunset that day would be at 2018, according to the ephemeris. The chief had not only worked the calculation manually, but had also double-checked with the harbor master to make sure they were coordinated. At 2008, the evening colors detail was assembled and took their positions around the flag pole. Forsythe stood to one side, observing as the chief gave the orders.

Five minutes before sunset, the chief called the detail to attention. Forsythe waited, the evening breeze warmed against his skin, the prospect of liberty in his mind. Sure, it might be a long duty night as intoxicated sailors staggered back on board, but tomorrow it would be history. Finally, his first long-awaited liberty. And in Bermuda, paradise.

The chief lifted his portable radio to his lips, and spoke softly in it, confirming the time with his counterpart on the senior ship present in port. Forsythe marveled again at the sheer amount of planning, coordination, and precision with which both the morning and evening evolutions were conducted. You wouldn't think it was such a big deal to everyone, getting it precisely on time.

But it was. The sharpness during colors was a reflection of the discipline and training of the crew. Every flag on every ship hauled up at precisely the same moment, precisely at the moment that the sun first broke the horizon. And around the world, as the hours passed, every other military unit executing precisely the same drill in turn.

Just then, off in the distance, Forsythe heard a chatter of gunfire. *Automatic weapons?* He was no expert, although he had qualified on the handguns and shotguns used in the Navy.

The local police? The Navy? Forsythe stared across at the chief, growing concern on his face. The chief stepped away from the color guard, started for the quarterdeck then hesitated. He turned to Forsythe. "Sir?"

We can't screw up evening colors—we can't. Just for a moment, Forsythe attempted to ignore the noise, to proceed on schedule. Nobody could fault him for doing that, could they? After all, he was supposed to observe evening colors. It was on the schedule. And if Lieutenant Commander Cowlings found out that he screwed this up, too, then . . .

But Lieutenant Commander Cowlings was below decks. He wouldn't have heard the gunfire. He wasn't present to make the decision.

More gunfire. Forsythe could hear it coming from different directions now. Then a loud siren broke out, one that took him a moment to identify. The chief, who was fifteen years older, recognized immediately.

"That's an air-raid siren!"

"Chief, get the flag down! *Now!* Have the color guard standby to cast off all lines on my order."

The deck of the submarine exploded into motion. The chief yelled, "Grab the axes," and started hauling down colors himself as the rest broke from formation and headed for the mooring lines. The chief stood in the middle, directing them, roughly folding the flag but not taking time to do it precisely.

Forsythe ran to the forward hatch, slid down the ladder, and grabbed the microphone. "All hands, this is the Officer of the Deck. Make all preparations repel boarders. Engineers, disconnect us from shore power immediately and make all preparations for getting underway. Command Duty Officer, Control Room."

Forsythe grabbed the getting-underway checklist and began

going down it, monitoring reports from the chief over the radio. Five seconds later, Cowlings burst into the control room.

"Gunfire, sirens, and air-raid sirens. The chief has the flag and I have the color guard standing by to cast us off."

Cowlings blinked twice, and some of the color drained out of his face. Then he nodded. "I'll take that." Forsythe handed him the checklist and the mike. "Get top side and sever the shore power lines and the mooring lines. Use the axes if you have to."

"Already issued. On my way." On his way out, Forsythe grabbed another of the portable radios, tuned it to the same channel, and ran out on the deck.

In theory at least, each duty section contained every necessary rating and necessary officer to get the ship underway in an emergency. Like every other requirement in the Navy, submariners took this one seriously. As Forsythe headed back up the ladder to the forward deck, he ran over the names on the watch section, mentally putting them in their underway duty stations. Yes, they could do it—but just barely. On paper, they had all the right qualifications. What they lacked was experience. Half of the enlisted sailors were just as junior and inexperienced as he was.

The chief had sailors staged next to each mooring line. Each one held a firefighting ax at the ready. The chief seemed to be everywhere at once, checking on the engineers, giving last minute instructions.

Amidships, engineers scrambled to disconnect the cables that provided hotel services, the potable water, sewer services, and compressed air to the ship while her own power plant was on standby. The connections had quick release fixtures, and one by one, the sailors snapped them off and tossed them back on the pier. The sewer return line, known as the CHT, dumped a couple of gallons of foul-smelling liquid into the ocean. Under normal circumstances, there would be serious civilian and military penalties for polluting the water.

Deal with that later. In fact, if we're doing the right thing, no one will ever say a word about it.

The primary responsibility of the in-port duty section was to keep the ship safe. In this case, when it sounded like all hell was breaking loose ashore, that meant getting underway.

There was nowhere in the world they were as safe as below the surface of the sea.

"Cast us off, Chief," Forsythe shouted as he trotted up to them. "Can you turn things over to the boatswain's mate here? We could use a hand below decks on the navigation plot."

"Aye-aye, sir. Can do." The chief passed the boatswains mate his radio and double-timed back to the forward access hatch.

Forsythe turned to the boatswain's mate. "What am I forgetting?"

"Nothing, sir. Be nice if we had somebody on the pier to haul the rest of those lines so we make sure they don't get tangled in the shafts. I'm pulling aboard the lines on this end, just for that reason."

"Can you get someone down on the pier to do it all?"

The boatswains mate nodded. "But it'll be tricky, sir. With a mooring lines detached, if you start the ship moving too fast, we'll pull away from the gangway and leave him on the pier. And I don't think any one of us wants that. All lines have been cut except for the two lines abeam, so we're ready to go on short notice. I send one guy down to the pier and we're disconnected from everything else." The boatswains mate shrugged. "It's as safe as we can make it here."

"Do it," Forsythe ordered. "Cast off the moment everyone is back on board."

Things moved rather quickly from that point, and Forsythe stepped back out of the way, letting the boatswain's mate run things. His radio crackled with a steady stream of orders as, below decks, Cowlings ran through the getting-underway checklist. For just a moment, he thought he felt the turbine come up to speed, and then sensation faded. Everything on board the submarine was shock mounted for maximum acoustic silence, and that included the main turbines.

The man on the pier hauled all the lines in out of the water, and then ran back on board. The final line was severed on board the ship, and, because of the tension it was under, it slashed back across the pier, narrowly missing the sailor. He jumped nimbly out of the way, then hauled the bitter end out of the water. The process was repeated at the forward spring line.

"Come on, Billy!" The boatswain's mate shouted. "Move your ass!"

There was a low groan as the bolts holding the gangway to the ship took the whole stress. The submarine was not underway yet, but now it was subject to the currents and wind, and both were pushing it away from the pier.

The young sailor, a yeoman, darted up the gangway, leaping over the last six feet to land solidly on the deck.

"Now!" the boatswain's mate said. Engineers snapped off the cotter pins and the gangway pulled away from the ship, screeching its way down the side and leaving marks on the antiechoic coating.

The boatswains mate pulled a whistle out of his pocket. He issued one sharp blast on it, then shouted, "Underway." He repeated the announcement on his radio.

"Everybody below decks, Boats," Forsythe heard Cowling say. "Ensign Forsythe, you take conning tower, but be ready to clear the decks on short notice. I don't plan on staying surfaced any longer than I have to."

"Aye-aye, sir," Forsythe said. He watched as the sailors scuttled down the forward hatch, pulled it shut behind them and secured it. Forsythe then climbed into the conning tower and took his station. The distance between the submarine and the pier increased and water roiled around the bow as the propeller and the bow thrusters began to operate.

More gunfire, closer this time. At the land end of the pier, a cluster of men with automatic weapons were assembling.

"OOD, Conning Officer. I'm under fire."

"Secure the watch and get your ass down here," Cowling snapped. "Now."

Forsythe ducked down into the lockout chamber in the sail, pulled the hatch down behind him and continued down the ladder a short distance. He spun the wheel behind him, securing the hatch, then made his way into the control room to stand behind the chief of the boat, his normal underway station as conning officer.

"Green board, sir," the chief of the boat said, indicating that the telltale indicators showed all hatches secure.

"Pressurize the submarine," Cowlings ordered. Seconds later, Forsythe's ears popped as blasts of compressed air increased air pressure inside the subway slightly, testing every seal.

"Pressurization set," the chief said. "The ship is ready for sea, sir."

"Very well. Conning officer, periscope depth. Or, just a little less than that—I want the decks awash, but not the entire sail. Be ready to dive as soon as we're clear of the channel and commercial shipping."

"I recommend seventy feet, at the keel, sir," the chief said immediately.

"Very well. Make your depth seventy feet." Cowlings turned to Forsythe. "Get the antenna deployed and get an OPREP message out to Second Fleet and COMSUBLANT. Tell them what you heard, that we're underway, and that, unless otherwise directed, my intentions are to head for deep water. Once I'm satisfied that we're in no immediate danger, we'll come to communications depth for further guidance. If they've got a major problem with that, they can reach us on ELF." Cowlings's mouth quirked slightly. "Put it in a little more tactful terms, but make sure you tell them that we're out of contact for about eight hours, other than ELF."

SIX

Washington, D.C.
The Beltway
Advanced Solutions
2200 local (GMT-5)

To an outsider, Advanced Solutions looked like any one of a number of small defense contractors known as the Beltway Bandits that lived and died off defense industry contracts. They sprang up overnight like mushrooms, flourished briefly on one or two contracts, and disappeared just as suddenly, either through insolvency if unsuccessful, or being absorbed into larger corporation if they were so lucky as to actually make a profit. Indeed, the exterior office had the requisite mauve and blue furnishings, metallic veneered name plates, and other accoutrements of prosperity that tried to give the impression of solvency without actually achieving it. The receptionist could spout knowledgeably about Advanced Solutions's prospects, the current and anticipated contracts, and their hiring requirements. Unemployed aerospace professionals provided a steady flow of remarkably similar résumés, but Advanced Solutions never seemed to have any openings. And this, too, was typical of most Beltway Bandits.

But behind the facade, a highly professional and skilled team was at work. The two recruiters, nephew and uncle, were

funded as a black operations project, so far off the books that
their budget never even raised an eyebrow in defense oversight
circles. Indeed, their expenditures were so small compared to
most of their ilk that no one would have noticed anyway. They
drew primarily on military personnel on detached assignment,
and, with Uncle Thomas doing the brainstorming and Tombstone the mission planning, they were able to do far more with
far less than any other covert organization. Their skills were
specialized, not used in every conflict, but called in to play
whenever the United States needed small, sensitive aviation
missions executed with the utmost secrecy.

At present, the staff of Advanced Solutions consisted of only
four people—the two Magruders, Greta, the receptionist, and
Tombstone's backseater, Navy Lieutenant Jeremy Greene, also
a Tomcat pilot. On this particular morning, all except Greta
were gathered in the conference room, a secure, carefully
shielded space that was cleared for the most sensitive information in defense circles. They were reading the message traffic coming in from the fleet and getting their updates from
CNN, just like the rest of the world, and most especially the
military establishment.

Tombstone swore quietly as he saw yet another Russian
transport land heavily on the airfield. One part of his mind,
the part that didn't give a damn about national security or
anything else except flying, noted that the landing was a
clumsy one. The transport bounced three times before it finally
decided to settle down, and the Bear's initial taxi had almost
run her off the strip.

Beside him, his backseater seethed. An excellent pilot in his
own right, he was increasingly proficient as a RIO, although
the assignment often annoyed him. Still, all of their aircraft
were configured for two pilots, and having him aboard assured
him that someone could get them home even if Tombstone
were incapacitated.

Of the three, his uncle was the quietest. His gaze was fixed
on the screen, his fingers drumming monotonously on the fake-
wood table. A deepening scowl framed his eyebrows and
strong features.

"Damn, I should have stayed with my squadron," the
younger aviator said. He shot up out of his chair as though on

afterburner and started pacing the room. "Something's going down, and I'm not going to be part of it."

"Settle down," Tombstone said mildly. He stared at the younger man, seeing himself fifteen—okay, twenty—years ago. "You really think we're going to bomb the Russians out of Bermuda? A few quick strikes and it's over? Because I have to tell you, that's not going to happen. There's too many civilians there, natives, tourists, everything else. No, this isn't going to be over quickly, not at all."

"You mean we'll just sit here and let them land Russian forces on American soil?" The younger man demanded incredulously. "How can you sit there and watch this?"

An embarrassed silence hung in the room for a moment. Tombstone and his uncle exchanged a telling glance, one that was simultaneously confident and slightly amused. "What?" Greene demanded. "I hate it when you two start the telepathy stuff."

Finally, Tombstone spoke. "It isn't our soil," he said quietly. "We forget that sometimes. We can't just go storming in there without an invitation of some sort. A United Nations' resolution, a request from the Bermuda government, something of that sort."

For a moment, the youngster looked befuddled, but he recovered quickly. "I know it's not a state. But it's right off our coast! You mean to tell me that we're going to put up with that? What about Cuba, or something like that? We didn't put up with nuclear weapons there. Why should we put up with it in Bermuda?"

"Oh, we won't," Tombstone assured him. "You can be sure of that. But it's not a simple matter when a foreign government is involved. And the question of civilian casualties—well, every nation in the world knows how sensitive we are to that, especially since the Middle East. All they have to do is invite CNN to broadcast pictures of a dozen sunburned tourists being held at the airfield and we'll back off immediately. We're not going to risk their lives. And, even if we are invited to take action, there will be some pretty strong restrictions to avoid collateral damage, not only to the tourists and people, but to the tourist industry infrastructure as well."

The young pilot flung himself into a chair, a look of disgust on his face. "Special forces. Get the hostages out, then bomb the bastards."

"And that can't take place overnight," Tombstone said, striving to keep a tone of reason. "Look, everybody feels the same way you do. But going in without the proper preparation just means people get killed."

"It's not like we'll have anything to do with this anyway," the pilot said, his voice dejected. "This will be strictly an active-duty operation."

For the first time, the senior Magruder spoke. "Don't be so sure." They all turned to look at him.

"Talk," Tombstone said. "What do you have in mind?"

"It's not what I have in mind," his uncle answered. "But I did talk to Don Stroh early this morning. He has some interesting insights into this, to say the least."

"Seal Team Six?" Tombstone asked.

His uncle nodded. "As you said, the only way to do this is with special forces. And since its on foreign soil, the CIA is right in the thick of it."

"Did they know it was going down?" Tombstone asked, a hint of disbelief in his voice. "Because, if they did, and they didn't do anything to stop it, then—" He stopped, as the full import of his words hit him. *If the CIA knew this was happening and didn't put out a warning, then there's going to be hell to pay.*

But his uncle was shaking his head. "I don't think so—at least, not in advance. There may have been some signs of it, in retrospect, but hindsight is always twenty-twenty. No, they didn't know and decide not to tell the rest of us. It's not a Coventry situation."

During World War II, after the Allies had broken the Enigma Code, they had intercepted a message indicating that the Germans planned a bombing raid on the village of Coventry. They were faced with the agonizing choice of warning the village and stopping the attack with air power, or allowing the attack to proceed in order to avoid compromising their intelligence sources. In the end, it had been decided that revealing to the Germans that Enigma had been broken would cost more lives than allowing the attack on Coventry.

"So, now Don Stroh is calling you?" Tombstone asked.

"Who is he, anyway?" the younger pilot asked. Tombstone glanced over at his uncle, who shook his head.

"What?" the younger pilot demanded.

"You don't have a need to know," the senior Magruder said bluntly. "For now, let's just say that Don Stroh is sometimes involved in some military operations. And this time, we may be tasked to support him."

"How?" Tombstone asked.

"As you said, one of the problems is that a foreign nation is involved. It would seem to be in our interest to avoid having the United States look like it's the solution to this problem. Rather, we would like for Russia, Bermuda, and the United Kingdom to solve this one on their own. So, any involvement by the United States is going to be in the form of covert operations."

"Are you saying we've been asked to get involved?" Tombstone asked.

"Certain people have certain information about what's going on behind the scenes. In particular, apparently there is a renegade Russian general in charge of this. He's holed up in Chechnya, and you can guess how much the Russians want to start a new offensive there. It's like digging a rat out of a hole—you need a good terrier to do it."

"I still don't see what we have to do with this," Tombstone said.

"You have to remember, the Russian military is in a state of disarray. Many of their officers and enlisted men have not been paid in months. Their loyalty, quite frankly, is questionable. And this man, this Korsov fellow, is a popular officer. But the last thing we want is further instability in Russia. Therefore, this mission has to be accomplished by the Russians—or, at least, it has to appear that the Russians have done it. The objective is to behead the snake. Without Korsov, the entire operation will fall into disarray."

"I still don't get it," the younger pilot said. "What does this have to do with us?"

For the first time since he'd turned on the television, a trace of a smile crossed the senior Magruder's face. He looked squarely at his nephew and asked, "How you feel about flying a MiG?"

USS Seawolf
Off the coast of Bermuda
Saturday, November 10
0300 local (GMT-4)

It was only after they were well clear of the channel and in deeper water, running at a depth of 500 feet, that the impact of what they'd done really struck Forsythe. Before that, they'd been running on adrenaline, reacting to the gunshots, frantically struggling to get underway, and then sweating out exiting the harbor channels and avoiding other traffic. Cowlings had proved to be unflappable. It was as though he had done this every day of his Navy life, although Forsythe knew nothing could be farther from the truth. Cowlings had never gotten the ship underway without the captain and the XO on board, and he had certainly not done it without tugs, except perhaps the simulator. And never, ever, with only a third of the crew on board. Yet, to look at Cowlings, you would have thought this was a completely normal and unremarkable operation.

And Forsythe saw how that attitude transmitted itself to the crew. Without even leaving the Control Room, Cowlings seemed to be everywhere at once, keeping track of the engineering configuration, dictating messages to Second and Sixth Fleet, and, in one quick moment, even ordering the senior mess management specialist to conduct an inventory of their supplies, reminding him that they would need to eat at their battle stations if the ship went to general quarters.

Already the ELF, or extremely low frequency, receiver was slowly printing its digitally coded messages. The data rate over ELF was extremely low, and the messages consisted of preformatted codes to cram the maximum amount of information into the minimum amount of bandwidth. But after they outchopped the harbor, once they settled in at normal cruising depth and speed, it wasn't even the fact that they had no operational orders in hand to tell them what to do next that brought home to Forsythe the seriousness of their situation. No, it was that no one came to relieve him. Normally, at this point, they would have secured the sea and anchor detail, and commenced the normal watch standing rotation. However, with only a third of the crew on board, the reduced manning just blew the hell out of any watch bill ever conceived for the ship.

Cowlings looked over at the chief, and they seemed to reach an understanding about something without a word being spoken. The chief nodded.

"Chief, you have the conn," Cowlings finally ordered. He motioned to Forsythe. "Captain's cabin."

Forsythe knew a moment of shock. Underway, the officer of the deck belonged in Maneuvering, right there, supervising the conning officer and other watch stations. Cowlings was only five steps away, since the captain's cabin was located immediately behind maneuvering, but even that small distance amounted to heresy.

As though reading his mind, Cowlings grimaced. "It's the least of the compromises we're going to be making at this point. We need to talk. I'm keeping the deck because I don't want him solely responsible if something goes wrong."

Once they stepped in the captain's cabin, all the energy seemed to drain out of Cowlings. He slumped down in the captain's chair, boneless, and seemed to have barely enough energy to point at the captain's couch. Forsythe took a seat, remembering not so long ago when they had been in the same positions in the engineer's stateroom.

"So. Here we are." Cowlings took a deep breath, and shook his head, as though unable to believe what they'd done. He closed his eyes for a moment, rolled his neck to loosen the shoulder muscles, and then rubbed his temples with his fingertips. With his eyes still closed, he said, "Good call, getting them moving immediately on the mooring lines. I'm not sure we would have made it otherwise."

"Are we in a lot of trouble?" Forsythe asked hesitantly. "I mean, I've never heard of this being done before."

"Neither have I. Not since Pearl Harbor. But there's no point in second-guessing that now. Under the circumstances, I did what I thought was necessary to protect the ship."

"We did," Forsythe said firmly.

Cowlings shook his head. "It doesn't work that way." He finally opened his eyes and stared directly at Forsythe. "I was the command duty officer and I'm the one qualified as officer of the deck underway. Whatever else happens, you are in no way responsible for that decision." He held up one hand to forestall comment. "Don't get me wrong. We have to stand together on this, at least in front of the crew, and I appreciate the fact that you understand that. But let's get it straight between the two of us. It was my decision, and I will take sole responsibility for it."

"But you—"

"Enough, Ensign." The note of command in Cowlings's voice was unmistakable. "We will not discuss this again."

"Yes, sir." Forsythe fell silent.

"So, the question is, what do we do now?" Cowlings continued, reverting to his earlier tone of voice.

"Come to communications depth and find out what's going on?" Forsythe suggested.

"Soon enough. When I'm sure we're safe."

Fifteen minutes later, the reply from Second Fleet was short and to the point. Under no circumstances was the *Seawolf* to return to Bermuda. Instead, she was to remain on station until relieved by the USS *Tulsa*. Second Fleet ordered Lieutenant Commander Cowlings to assume temporary command of the submarine until relieved by his commanding officer, and to advise Second Fleet in the event that he was unable to comply, either through lack of training or material deficiencies, with any detail of the order. Arrangements were being made to provide a qualified senior officer as commanding officer within a few days, but there was currently no ship with helicopter capabilities within range. Cowlings was advised that Second Fleet had every confidence in his ability to carry out its orders as stated, and wished him good luck. And, finally, almost as an afterthought, Second Fleet noted with approval Cowlings's decision to get the ship underway and the ability of the crew on board in carrying out that order.

"Well, it looks like we dodged that bullet," Cowlings said, passing the message to Forsythe. "They put that all at the end of the message to make a point—that what we did was just what we'd been trained to do. If they'd made a big deal about it, it would be like saying we surprised them by doing the right thing. Second Fleet's got a way with subtle compliments, wouldn't you say?" He glanced over at Forsythe. "Guess that makes you the temporary executive officer. Can you handle it?"

"Sir, I'm not even a qualified officer of the deck underway yet," Forsythe said. "How can I be the XO?"

Cowlings stared at him for a long moment, and said softly, "Under the circumstances how can you not?"

"Conn, Sonar. Sir, *contact*. Subsurface, classify possible Russian Kilo class diesel! And there's two—correction, *three* of them, sir!"

Forsythe stood behind the sonarmen at the display. Not an unknown subsurface contact, not even one Russian—then suddenly there were three. And there wasn't any assurance that there weren't more.

"I think we know who was responsible for the gunfire," Cowlings said quietly. "Battle stations, Chief. And set quiet ship."

"Aye-aye, sir," the chief answered. He turned to the navigator and said, "Pass the word—now."

The petty officer left, and moved back down the long passageway running down the centerline of the submarine, whispering "Battle stations. Quiet ship." A red light began flashing in the control room, indicating battle stations.

"Chief, come left to course two seven zero. Drop us down to nine knots—and get us down to below the layer depth, if there is one. I want to clear the area, and do it quietly."

"Recommend seven hundred feet, sir," the sonar man said. "There's a radical drop-off just above that—if we stay below the layer, chances are they'll never hear us. And besides, I'm not sure, but that may be below their normal operating depths."

"Make it so." Then, for the first time since they'd heard the gunfire, Cowlings appeared to hesitate. Indecision flashed across his face, and Forsythe noticed that his breathing increased slightly. "Chief, have weapons ready in tubes one and two. Keep the outer door shut, but I want them flooded as soon as we are below the layer."

"Roger, sir. I understand." The chief's face settled into an expression that Forsythe had never seen before, but one that looked entirely too well-practiced. "Like the old days, sir."

"Yes, I imagine it is. I'll keep that in mind."

"Sir, the contact report is ready to transmit and we're still above communications depth," Forsythe began. "Nobody else knows there are subs in the area. Shouldn't we—?"

Cowlings cut him off. "Get your priorities in order, mister.

Protect the ship first. That means getting clear of these fellows. Until we're clear of them, I don't give a shit who knows that they're there."

Forsythe felt his face flush. "Of course, sir."

Cowlings studied him for a moment, his expression stern. "If anything happens to me," Cowlings said slowly, "here are my orders. I want you to first take every measure possible to preserve the safety of the ship. Second, you are to clear the area, avoiding all contact with any unknown surface or sub-surface vessel. As soon as you are in a position of safety, you are to come to communications depth and immediately advise Second Fleet of your situation. Under no circumstances are you to delay reporting my . . . incapacity . . . to Second Fleet. And you are not to attempt to prosecute any contacts or in any other way do what you think I would do under the same circumstances. Get clear and report in. Got it?"

Forsythe stared in confusion at Cowling. "But what do you mean, sir? Nothing is going to happen to you on the *Seawolf*— or, at least, if something happens to you, it's not likely I'll survive, either. So I don't see the point—"

Cowlings cut him off. "This isn't a discussion, Ensign. It is a one-way conversation. And yes, I'm fully aware of the capabilities of this boat." He leaned forward, jabbing his finger at a Forsythe to emphasize the point. "Anticipate the unanticipated. Whatever you plan for will not happen. So the more things you plan for, the less chance there is for things to go wrong. And, remember, there is not a finite number of mistakes in the world. Even when you've thought of everything, something else will happen."

"Yes, sir. I understand."

But Forsythe didn't, not really. And, furthermore, his pride was hurt by Cowlings's lack of confidence. After all, hadn't they gotten underway shorthanded? And hadn't he, Forsythe, correctly identified the potential danger and preparations for getting underway even before he spoke to Cowlings? Okay, so he was on his first cruise. But there was a first time for everything, wasn't there? Like Cowlings getting underway without the captain and without tugs.

If he's dead, I'll be in command. I won't have to obey his orders. The Navy will expect me to use my best judgment, and, given the fact that there are three diesel submarines out here and no relief in sight, I know what my best judgment tells me.

"So where do we start, sir?" Forsythe asked. "We can't attack three submarines at once, can we?"

"Of course we can't." Cowlings voice was firm. "And, besides, maintaining continuous contact on them probably isn't a way to go about it."

"But that's what our orders are, aren't they?"

Cowlings shook his head. "Just to locate them. Look, the Russians know these waters. They spent decades on ballistic missile patrols around Bermuda, before they developed long-range missiles. They know how to operate in this area with two or three boats at a time, and I'm willing to bet that they're just as cautious about mutual interference as we are. And with these diesels, it could be a real problem when they're on battery. So, what they've probably done is divide up the area around Bermuda into different operating areas. Three operating areas at least—although we can't be certain that there aren't more boats out there, can we?"

"I guess not."

"So, what we have to do," Cowling said, sketching out his plan on a piece of paper, "is pull the data on their historical operating areas during the Cold War and figure out if they're still using the same boundaries to avoid mutual interference. At the same time, we need to find out exactly what they've got deployed here. It might not be just diesels. A few old Yankee or Delta ballistic missile boats could be in the area, too. We need to know the exact composition of their forces as well as where they probably are so we'll have a general idea of where to start looking for them if the balloon goes up or if we have to do something about them."

There might be more—yeah, that makes sense. And, why just diesels out here? Why not a couple of old Yankee class ballistic missile boats?

"So," Cowlings continued, "We stay around the edges for now. Get more detections, try to figure out what their boundaries are. At the same time, we want to maintain a weapons posture that will allow for immediate weapons free. Not that I think it'll come to that, but let's be prepared."

"It won't happen if we prepare for it?" Forsythe said, echoing Cowlings's earlier statement.

Cowlings nodded. "Right. So, we'll start with the southern-

most contact and work our way north. Now start putting together a plan while I see the chief about the galley." A weary
smile passed over Cowlings's face. "A well-fed crew is a
happy crew."

"Yes, sir."

"Okay, then. Let's get on with it. As I recall, you're pretty
sharp on sonar. Go take a look at things, decide what we have
to do to get locating data on each of those three contacts. Talk
to the sonarman—he understands how to do this. And the
chief's no stranger to this, either. Get back to me as soon as
you have a plan, but no later than one hour from now."

"Yes, sir. And where will you be?" Forsythe asked.

"Well, I figured you and I aren't going to be getting much
sleep for the next couple of days. I want one of us awake at
all times. Therefore, since you're going to be in Manuevering
for a while, I'm going to take a nap." Cowlings stretched out
on the captain's couch and kicked off his shoes. "First lesson
of combat operations—eat, drink, sleep, or piss anytime you
can. Because the odds are, you won't have time later." With
that, Cowlings shut his eyes. "Turn off the lights on your way
out."

SEVEN

Bermuda Airport
Control Tower
Saturday, November 10
0300 local (GMT-4)

Maskiro leaned against the back wall of the control tower, fighting off exhaustion. They had released most of the control tower crew, keeping only five people as a hostage contingent, four women and one man. They were now stretched out in the middle of the room trying to get some sleep. His guards had already started their sleep/watch rotation, and there was really no reason for Maskiro himself to be awake right now. Better that he sleep while he could. It was far too soon for any of the American forces to mount an attack on the tower. Hostage rescue required planning, planning, and more planning. Probably at least two days, he decided, stifling a yawn. Maybe three.

So why am I still awake? My element commanders know how and when to contact me. There's no need for me to be awake.

He knew what it was—the escape of the American submarine. A frigate and a destroyer in port had been easily subdued, their security forces clearly poorly trained and not prepared to react. They had not even attempted to leave port,

instead mistakenly depending on a few sailors with shotguns
to take care of any problems.

But the submarine—ah, that was a different matter. Were
the American nuclear forces simply more cautious? Perhaps
their commanding officer had been aboard and had ordered the
ship underway. Yes, that had to be it.

The sergeant in charge of this detachment was eyeing him
warily. Maskiro ignored him, but knew that it would be just a
few moments before the sergeant, in the special way that senior enlisted men had of dealing with officers, would suggest
that perhaps Comrade Captain might wish to stand down. He
could even hear the tone the sergeant would use, slightly aggrieved and offended that the captain did not adequately trust
his sergeant to maintain the watch, yet with the full measure
of respect due to a senior officer.

Only two aircraft had been permitted to land after the troop
transports were on the ground, and that was only because they
reported that they were critically low on fuel and unable to
divert. The transports had remained on the ground until the
area was secure. Then, the troops had returned to unload the
ZUK-88 trucks with their attached missile launchers. Once
they had verified that all the trucks and launchers were operational, the missiles had been loaded on by specialist teams
and the trucks departed the airport with armed escorts. From
the main road, they would spread out into the countryside,
moving to higher elevations and dispersing themselves about
the island. By dawn, the last one would be in position. Along
with the one squadron of MiGs on the ground, they would
maintain air superiority around the island. Additionally, they
were loaded with the most potent deterrent to American intervention—medium-range launchers equipped with special warheads. While the range was insufficient to cover the entire
expanse of America, it was more than sufficient to reach
Washington, D.C., Norfolk, New York, and other center-of-
gravity targets. One squadron of MiGs was on the ground,
under heavy guard, and another squadron was en route and
would arrive in two days.

One squadron would be sufficient to maintain air superiority, even with the carrier lurking to the north. The Americans
would not dare engage the MiGs over the island, not and risk
civilian casualties, even assuming that the Bermuda govern-

ment gave their permission for American intervention. Not everyone welcomed American forces and their sometimes heavy-handed way of dealing with things.

The sergeant was starting toward him. Maskiro debated ignoring him, but decided against it. The problem was, the sergeant was right. He held up his hand to stop the man. "I know. Toss me a blanket, would you?"

"Yes, Comrade Captain." The sergeant changed directions and swung by the table to pick up a blanket. He handed it to his commander with a glint of amusement in his eyes. "I will call you an hour before dawn, yes? Or as otherwise required."

"Fine, fine." Maskiro slid down to the tile and pulled the blanket around him. In seconds, he was asleep.

USS **Jefferson**
TFCC
0300 local (GMT-4)

The reaction on board the carrier had at first been one of complete disbelief. Surely this was a prank of some sort, somebody's idea of a bad joke. Russians invading Bermuda? It couldn't be real.

A quick voice confirmation was immediately forthcoming. No one was entirely sure what was happening, but all the local Bermuda government sources were either not answering telephones or had gone off the air. The only immediate source of information was an ACN reporter on vacation with a cell phone, and ACN was jealously guarding that contact, relaying information to the Pentagon only after it had been broadcast.

When it finally became apparent that there was indeed a squadron of MiGs and a division of troops on the island, the *Jefferson* immediately turned southwest and kicked her four massive propellers up to flank speed. The cruisers paced her, while the frigates dropped slightly behind, unable to sustain the thirty-five knots plus that the *Jefferson* was capable of maintaining.

In TFCC, Coyote stared at the large screen tactical display, his emotions alternating between pure adrenaline highs and

utter incredulity. Clustered around the airport were hostile air—
hostile air—symbols! And reports were just coming in from
overhead imagery that the transports had unloaded the ZIL-85
antiair defense systems vehicles and that they were already
being dispersed about the island, hidden under the canopy of
trees in the interior.

Coyote turned to the senior Marine, his CLF, or Commander, Landing Forces, and noted, "Bitch trying to dig them
out. You'll get thermal signatures from the satellites that will
pinpoint their locations, but the terrain's going to be rough
going for your men."

Colonel Avery Forrester smiled dryly. "Not a problem. I've
already got my people working on it."

"Boy Scouts, aren't you? Always prepared."

"We try to be." Forrester frowned. "Although I'm not so
sure we're going to get the chance to take a shot at this. If I
know the SEALs, they'll be chomping at the bit to get in
there."

"Yep," Coyote acknowledged. "It is the sort of thing that's
right up their alley. Their bread and butter, if you will."

"Yes, Admiral, but—"

"And frankly," Coyote continued as though the Marine had
not spoken, "a covert landing followed by some shooting and
looting sounds like a SEAL mission rather than one for your
people. They're going to have to swim in, you know."

"We can take the Osprey in," the colonel said.

Coyote flicked his laser pointer at the chart. "With the ZILs?
I don't think so—not until we know how effective they are.
You start decimating the only operation Osprey squadron in
the fleet and nobody's going to be very pleased."

"To the contrary, sir, with all due respect. The Osprey is
ready for an operational test just like this. She's got enough
spoofing and jamming gear on board to deal with the ZILs,
even assuming your aircraft misses her with HARMs. Using
the Osprey now would answer a lot of questions, Admiral. We
need this."

"It might raise more questions than it answers, Colonel. You
realize that?" Coyote studied the man for a moment, wondering how to proceed. Sure, it should be a straight tactical decision. In theory, at least. But it never really was, was it? The
political forces back in the Pentagon always had their own

agendas, most of which including winning wars in such a way as to ensure their next reelections.

"We *are* ready. The *Osprey* is ready."

No use sugarcoating it. The colonel is a big boy. "I understand that. I'll wait and see what my staff recommends, but my inclination is to use your troops as the first wave ashore after the SEALs neutralize the ZILs. Assuming, of course, that we're ordered in."

The colonel's face clouded over. "With all due respect, Admiral, is there a little favoritism going on here?"

Coyote regarded him levelly, his face hard and cold. "I'm going to forget you said that, mister."

The colonel flinched, then his own expression matched the admiral's. "As the admiral wishes. If I may be excused?"

"Yes." Coyote watched the colonel go, his back ramrod stiff and his posture every inch Marine. There hadn't been any easy way around that one. The colonel was way out of line to even suggest favoritism.

That's why they gave you the stars, amigo. So you could make these calls. But, damn, that's a man I want on my side, not against me. Well, we'll see. If he sucks it up and acts like an officer, he'll be fine. And, if he doesn't, he'll learn real fast what it's like to dance with elephants.

Chechen Military Camp
0400 local (GMT+4)

Korsov surveyed the ragged collection of prefab buildings, ramshackle stores and tents that made up the rebel troops' command center. Politics makes strange bedfellows, and allying his interests with those of the Chechen forces had at first seemed an impossible coalition. But the Chechens were desperate. They could not hold out forever against the Russians, and they eagerly jumped at Korsov's promise of complete autonomy. They had their sympathizers inside the Russian command structure as well, and, in exchange for the use of their insurgent network in certain matters, they had proved to be if not entirely hospitable at least more receptive to his needs than his own government.

The commander of the Chechen forces was an old, battered Russian colonel, now elevated by the fact of his mutiny to the rank of general. Ilya Petrovich had seen action in Afghanistan and knew what the Russians were capable of, both in a military sense and in the likely treatment of the Chechen forces once they were overrun.

Petrovich's face was deeply lined, his skin rough and burned. His eyes were a faded blue, his short hair silver around his face but glossy black at his crown. He seemed to have problems concentrating on what Korsov told him, as though he were continually listening to another voice just out of earshot.

And perhaps he was, Korsov thought, as he started to review operational security procedures for the third time. It was the sound of his ancestors talking to him, preparing to welcome him to the other side.

Like many Russians, both Korsov and Petrovich had deep streaks of superstition running through their souls. It underlay the patina of the Eastern Orthodox church, so long banned but never really suppressed in Russia, and tainted all of their planning with a dark fatalism that was not often understood by their opponents.

Korsov started again from the beginning. "I can't give you the flight plans. With all due respect, comrade, it would be too dangerous. Both for you and for me. Should your opponents find out that I am here, they could accelerate their timetable, putting you in jeopardy before I can ensure your future."

Petrovich seemed amused. "Jeopardy." He pointed at a deadfall of rubble at the far end of the camp. It was the remains of a barracks that had been bombed the week before. "What would you call that?"

"An atrocity," Korsov responded promptly.

"Yes. Yes, of course. But comrade"—and suddenly Petrovich seemed fully alive, more alert than Korsov had seen him before—"if you do not give me your flight plans, I cannot alert our antiair batteries. It would be a shame to shoot you down in the name of operational security, would it not?"

"I will give you the exact details. At the appropriate time." *And not far enough in advance that you can betray me in exchange for Russian mercy, if there ever is such a thing.*

Petrovich shrugged. "I have explained to you our equipment

limitations. Communications with all of our outposts are not the most reliable." He peered down at Korsov from his slightly greater height. "These are not conventional forces, you understand. Our patriots work differently."

Korsov nodded, feigning respect. "Of course. I understand and am willing to take that chance." *What you mean is that you hide some defenses in the civilian population. As though that would stop anyone from attacking them.*

"Very well. Six hours' notice, then," Petrovich said, apparently assuming that the final determination was his to make.

Korsov nodded his understanding, if not his agreement. *Six hours—no. Perhaps thirty minutes. And if your forces are so foolish as to target me, I will destroy them on my way out.*

Wexler's townhouse
0500 local (GMT-5)

Even though her townhouse was air-conditioned, dehumidified, comfortable, and completely covered by security forces, sleep eluded Wexler. She shoved the blankets off for the third time in the last ten minutes, then immediately pulled them back up. Finally, concluding that her restlessness was not attributable to anything outside her own mind, she gave up. She pulled on an old bathrobe and plush slippers and headed for her office.

"Good morning, ma'am," a voice said from her living room.

"Morning. Can't sleep," she answered shortly. She could have ignored him completely, she supposed. Brad had promised her that the increased security would be completely transparent to her, and part of the deal was that she could pretend that they were not around. But there was a deep streak of innate courtesy in her bones that prevented her from carrying out what she'd insisted on. "I'll be in my office," she concluded.

"Can I get you anything?"

"No. Thanks."

She shut the door behind her with a firm click, then leaned back against it and sighed. First the intrusions into her private life, and now the president's blind ambition. Didn't he see what could happen? Didn't he understand that short-term political expediency would do more to lose the election for him than any number of civilians killed in Bermuda?

Oh, sure, she understood his reasoning, and, on one level, she was tempted to agree with him. Among the current crop of politicians, he was indeed the best person to occupy the Oval Office. A shudder ran through her as she considered what sort of president the other party's nominee would be.

Are you being completely honest about this? Aren't you just covering up the fact that if he loses, you lose?

Her appointment was a political one. If the other party swept the White House, she would be asked to resign. Not in so many words, but it was an accepted fact of this life that she'd chosen that she'd be expected to tender her resignation immediately.

So what? I was a good lawyer before I took this job—I'll be a good one after I leave the U.N. Nobody stays here forever, you know.

A pang swept through her. There was so much still left to do in the U.N., so many possibilities for peace and prosperity.

Ah. So it is about the power, isn't it?

No, it wasn't.

Was it?

The telephone broke into her increasingly uncomfortable musings and she trotted over to her desk to answer it, grateful for the distraction. The LCD read out indicated it was a secure call originating at the White House. She picked up the handset and simultaneously began spinning the dials on her safe, retrieving the crypto key that would enable the telephone to synchronize with the one on the other end. "Wexler," she said, still fumbling with the dials. "Give me a moment to go secure."

"Take your time, Sarah," the president's voice said. "And get comfortable. This is going to take a while."

After the president had concluded the call, Sarah Wexler slumped back into her chair, her security key in her hand. Unbelievable, absolutely unbelievable. And it couldn't have come at a worse time, either. It had not been so long ago that she'd discovered that the Russians had planted a listening device in her office. While she'd been able to turn the tables on them then, and had since stepped up her electronic security measures, the incident had left a residue of distrust and uneasiness between the American and the Russian delegations. Reactions from the other members of the CIS had been all over the board, with some of them quite privately gleeful over the comeuppance Russia had received while publicly protesting American policies.

Russia herself had recalled her ambassador and replaced him with a man she had yet to get to know. The few times they had met, he had been cold and distant, formally correct, but showing absolutely no inclination to develop the sort of working relationship that normally characterized the U.N.

Nevertheless, there was no getting around it. She needed to talk to him, and talk to him immediately.

She pulled out her Palm Pilot and dialed his number.

EIGHT

USS **Seawolf**
Saturday, September 10
0530 local (GMT-4)

Cowlings came out of the captain's cabin, bleary and pale. His eyes looked unfocused and distracted. Forsythe, who was fighting off his own fatigue, passed him a cup of coffee. Cowlings fumbled for it, then took it gratefully.

"I was just going to call you," Forsythe said. "One of the Kilos has turned back toward us. There's no indication she sees us yet, but she's within twenty thousand yards."

Cowlings yawned. "Okay. Go rack out for a while."

Suddenly, a sharp *ping* cut through the control room like a knife. Forsythe felt his stomach lurch. "How can they—how did they know—we didn't—"

"It doesn't matter. We'll—"

"Conn, Sonar! I'm holding air bubbles from the Kilo—classify as depth change and outer torpedo doors opening! Recommend snap shot procedures followed by—*torpedo in the water! Torpedo in the water!*"

Cowling swore quietly, then stepped over to the sonar shack, tripping over the rubber gasket as he did. "Ensign, you have the deck."

"Aye-aye, sir," Forsythe said. "I have the deck—belay your reports."

"Hard right rudder, make your depth fifteen hundred feet," Cowlings said sharply. "All ahead flank."

Forsythe relayed the orders, knowing what Cowlings intended. The sudden increase in their speed, as well as the hard turn and change in depth would create massive air bubbles in the water. With any luck, the torpedo would be deceived into thinking that was the target and would detonate while the *Seawolf* made her escape.

But what if it is an acoustic homer? Then it will ignore the air bubbles.

"Layer depth is one thousand and fifty feet, sir," the sonarman announced. "Estimate we'll be there in ninety seconds."

Suddenly, the deck pitched down hard as the *Seawolf's* helmsman selected a large down bubble and steep angle of descent. It was followed by a slight shove as the propellers ramped up to flank speed and the deck tilted down to the right. It was an unusual sensation on board a submarine, normally a stable, motionless platform. Forsythe felt exposed, vulnerable, suddenly conscious of just how far below the sea they were. Fifteen hundred feet—at that depth, even the slightest leak had the force of a sledgehammer. A thin stream of water would cut through flesh and bone like superheated steam. They would never have to worry about drowning, no—they would be smashed to unrecognizable jelly by the pressures before that could ever occur.

"Cavitating, sir," the sonarman announced.

"Maintain course and speed," Cowlings said. "We're heading down." As the pressure increased, the cavitation would decrease. Cavitation was dependent on pressure, as determined by depth and propeller speed. Cavitation was normally something every submarine tried to avoid, since the bursting air bubbles dumped massive amounts of sound into the water and made them an all too attractive target.

Forsythe turned around and stared at the sonar screen to see exactly where the torpedo was in relation to the ship, as though there was something he could do about it. But there wasn't, and his duty now was to oversee the control room team, along with the chief, and let Cowlings watch the sonar. He could almost feel the torpedo creeping across the screen behind him, felt it as a sickening itch between his shoulder blades.

Suddenly, he heard a deep, painful sigh, as though a soul were being ripped from flesh. Cowlings had one hand on the bulkhead—nothing unusual about that, he could have been steadying himself during the turn—but his face was pale.

"My head," Cowlings said, almost conversationally, a trace of puzzlement in his voice. "It hurts." His eyes closed and he leaned toward the bulkhead, holding out one hand to support himself. His elbow bent and his arm went limp. He slid down to the deck.

The chief sonarman caught Cowlings as he crumpled, and then looked across at Forsythe, panic on his face. "Sir?"

"Maintain course and speed," Forsythe said, staring at Cowlings. "Chief, get the doc to sonar."

"Passing eight hundred feet," the planesman announced.

"Very well." Forsythe answered automatically, still staring aghast at Cowlings.

What did you mean to do once we got below the layer? Were you going to lay another knuckle in the water? Cut speed just before we went through the layer, change course below the layer—yes, that's it. That's what he would have done. I know that's what he was going to do, it just seemed to make a lot more sense when it was him doing it, not me.

The doctor came running into Maneuvering, a black medical kit in his hands. He dropped down on his knees beside Cowlings and began making his assessment as he said, "What happened?"

"Passing one thousand feet," the planesman said.

I know what you were going to do. Don't I?

"I said, *what happened?*" the doctor snapped. "Come on, somebody. Anybody."

"Passing one thousand one hundred feet."

"Conn, Sonar. Layer is at one thousand five hundred feet." Petty Officer Pencehaven's voice was pointed. "Sir, what are your intentions?"

"Sir," the chief said quietly, "priorities. You can't help him if we're all dead."

The torpedo noise was now clearly audible inside the submarine. Forsythe saw the doctor turn his face up to stare at the overhead.

"*Sir,*" the chief said, his voice urgent.

"Continue to one thousand two hundred feet," Forsythe said,

his voice not nearly as confident as Cowlings's had been. "Then, hard port rudder and steady up one hundred and eighty degrees off our former course." He glanced over at the chief and saw him nod almost imperceptibly. "Navigator, deal with the doctor. Sonar, notify me if there's any change in the layer depth and stand by for snap-shot firing-point procedures." A snap shot would be blindly firing a torpedo down the bearing of the attacker without refined targeting to throw the other submarine on the defensive and buy time for a deliberate attack.

A chorus of acknowledgements, and Forsythe could feel the crew's confidence return.

"Get him to sick bay," the doctor ordered. "He's not—"

"No," Forsythe said. "Not until we're clear of the torpedo. No unnecessary movements. And put that down," he continued, indicating the sailor that was already unstrapping a transport frame from the bulkhead. "We're at quiet ship."

"I need him in sick bay," the doctor said, his voice louder. He took a step toward Forsythe, who had turned his attention back to the sonar screen. The chief stepped forward and caught the doctor by his arm, a look of foreboding on his face. The doctor started to protest, then thought better of it.

Overhead, the noise of the torpedo gradually faded. There was one last hard *ping* from the Kilo's sonar, then silence.

Pencehaven breathed a sigh of relief. "We've lost them, sir. Recommend we clear the area and then return for a deliberate attack. Better than playing tag around the layer. I don't know if she can make this depth—I'm pretty sure we can go deeper—but there's nothing to stop her from getting close and letting her tail drift below the layer. We'd never see her before another attack."

"Concur." Forsythe shut his eyes for a moment, considering course and speed.

"Sir, the navigator has a recommendation for evasive maneuvers." The chief's voice was quiet and polite. He dropped his voice to a whisper. "You're doing okay. We'll walk you through this, Ensign. Just pay attention."

Forsythe nodded. *Chief, put the tent up.* "Navigator, recommendations?"

Thirty minutes later, when they'd cleared the area with no further contact on the Kilo, Forsythe drew the chief aside into the passageway just outside of maneuvering. "Listen, Chief, I don't know what else is going to come up, but—well—you know—I just want to say—"

The chief cut him off. "You're welcome, sir."

Wexler's townhouse
0630 local (GMT-5)

The duty staff at the Russian Embassy did not appear overly eager to connect Wexler with her counterpart. Whether it was from simple slovenliness or on direct order from the ambassador, she wasn't certain. Whatever the reason, the Russian ambassador was not answering his cell phone nor was he returning her phone calls. Just when she was close to calling the president and reporting that the situation was far more serious than they'd thought, the Russian ambassador finally returned her call.

"Sir, I need to ask you about—"

"I know what this is about," he said gruffly. "Bermuda, yes?"

"Of course. Is there an explanation for what appears to be a highly irregular deployment"—*read invasion, my friend; you know what I'm saying*—"of your troops? Of course, this is not U.S. soil, but an island nation so close off our eastern seaboard naturally has a rather special status in our view."

There was a long silence broken only by electronic hum on the line. Wexler's pulse was pounding, her breathing starting to quicken. Was this the start of another Cuban crisis?

Finally, the ambassador said, "As soon as we have an explanation, I will contact you."

"What do you mean? What is your government's position on all this? I must tell you, sir, that the president is prepared to increase the alert level of our military forces worldwide within the next hour. It was only with the greatest difficulty that I was able to persuade him to hold off long enough for me to contact you." *A small lie, but an expected one.* "I'm afraid I can't be responsible for what has been happening, given the delay in reaching you."

"We have no position," the ambassador said bluntly. "This is not a government operation."

"*What?*"

"I thought my command of the English language was sufficient. This is not a government operation."

"Then who—? Oh, dear God," she said, her heart sinking. The ambassador and his country might be duplicitous idiots, but at least she could deal with them.

"It appears that Russian military assets are involved. They were, as you know, on peaceful operations"—*spying on the carrier,* she translated mentally—"in international waters. They have received no orders to approach Bermuda and no orders to disembark troops. The squadron of MiGs, as well as the three heavy transports, are similarly acting contrary to orders."

"I see," she said, her mind racing. "Are you in contact with any of the forces in Bermuda?"

"No. But we intend to be." There was the slightest trace of embarrassment in the ambassador's voice. "I will not tender an apology, since neither your government nor mine is directly involved. However, be assured that Russia solves her own internal problems. It will take some time to arrange, given the distance and logistics involved, but be absolutely assured that Russia will deal with this. We will notify you when direct action is contemplated in order to avoid any confusion or interference."

The line went dead. She stared at the receiver for a moment, then dialed the number she knew by heart. When the president answered, she said, "We've got a problem."

USS **Seawolf**
0800 local (GMT-4)

Half of sick bay was occupied by an examination table, but the compartment beyond that was for isolating contagious cases. The hatch between sick bay and the isolation chamber had a small thick window in it.

The doctor stood beside the examination table. The sheets on it were slightly rumpled and there were a few spots of blood on it. "There was nothing we could do. It will take a full autopsy to determine the cause, but I suspect an aneurysm. Based on his comment about his head, followed by his sudden collapse—yes, an aneurysm."

"He can't be dead," Forsythe said, still stunned by the turn of events. "He can't be."

"There's also the question of his medical history," the doctor said, continuing as though Forsythe had not spoken. "Lieutenant Commander Cowlings had orders to see a specialist while we were in port. He was having headaches—severe headaches, migraine type. They became so severe that he was temporarily blinded. At times. Not constantly, of course."

"That's impossible—I never heard anything about that," Forsythe snapped. "If he was that sick, the captain wouldn't have let him deploy with us."

The doctor shook his head sadly. "He didn't tell anyone. He found ways to cover it up. The spells didn't last long and, so far, he had not been on watch when they happened. I think he believed that if he could figure out what caused them, he could stop them without ever having to tell anyone. Because, as you well know, it would have ended his career immediately."

"He took a terrible chance—a completely unacceptable one. That's not like Lieutenant Commander Cowlings," Forsythe said. "I can't believe it."

"I know. But just before we pulled in, he must have realized how serious it was. He came to me and admitted what was happening. I took him off the watch bill, of course, and talked to the captain. He would have been transferred out immediately. Any routine medical workup would have caught the aneurysm. It's possible it was operable, and if so, they could have saved him."

"He knew that?" Forsythe asked.

The doctor nodded. "He knew everything I'm telling you now. And still he came back on board. I think the captain figured there was no harm in letting him stand watch in port."

He knew it could kill him. Knew it, and got underway anyway. Because he knew I couldn't handle it on my own, not the way I was acting.

A deep sense of shame rolled through him, followed shortly by an icy cold determination. In that moment, Forsythe knew that he would not obey Cowlings's last order. The *Seawolf* would not turn tail and run, he would not surface the ship and radio for help. Although the torpedo had missed the submarine, it had scored one casualty. And Forsythe would make her pay for it.

"What's the procedure?" Forsythe asked. He pointed at the isolation chamber. "With—?" He caught himself as he almost said, "with the captain."

"Body bag and stored in the reefer," the doctor said. "If you think it's a health hazard, you can order him buried at sea."

Using the garbage chute. No, I don't think so—he deserved better than that. And, even though it gives me the willies to think of his body in the refrigerator, I owe him that much.

"I want to see him," Forsythe said abruptly. *I don't, but I feel like I have to. It's what the captain would have done—what Cowlings would have done, too.*

The doctor nodded, as though expecting that. "There's a hole in his throat—I was putting in a trach tube, trying to find a way to keep him breathing. It's all stitched up, of course."

The doctor led the way, opened the hatch to the isolation chamber, and stepped aside. "We will have to inventory the contents of his pockets and his stateroom," the doctor said. "That requires both of us."

"Eventually—probably when we get back to port," Forsythe said.

He stared down at Cowlings's body, trying to see exactly what it was that made the difference between being alive and being dead. He had never seen a dead body before, not outside of medical programs on television. It was an eerie sensation, looking down at someone he knew well, seeing Cowlings's familiar features, the short clipped brown hair. He tried not to look at the jagged hole in Cowlings's neck, but his eyes were drawn to it. It was a clean incision about an inch long. Blood had run down the side of it, creating a circle around Cowlings's neck. Some of it had been cleaned up, but there were a few traces of smeared blood still there.

Had Cowlings felt the doctor cutting into his neck? Or, had he been dead by then? Forsythe touched his own neck, imagining how it would feel to have a knife slice through his skin just above his Adam's apple, and hoped Cowlings had already been gone. There was a sense of stillness about the body, a sense of, well, lifelessness. You're a rocket scientist, he thought, then realized he had really never understood what lifeless meant. Not until he saw Cowlings's body, flesh deprived of spirit.

And what am I supposed to? I'm not particularly religious— was Cowlings? Maybe. I should find out.

Forsythe reached out and laid one hand on Cowlings's forehead. The flesh under his fingers was still warm, but starting to cool, a few degrees below what you'd expect to feel. The skin was still resilient.

Father, into your hands, I commend his spirit.

Forsythe tried to think of what else he should say, some prayer—there was probably a Navy-issue prayer book somewhere around, but right now he didn't have time to look for it. Cowlings would understand, and by now would have been chiding him for being away from Maneuvering.

Where do they keep the flag? Where do they keep the prayer book? There's so much I don't know.

Out loud, Forsythe stumbled through the Lord's Prayer, then took his hand off Cowlings's head. *It's the best I can do, sir. And I'll do the best for the ship, too.*

Forsythe straightened, then turned to the doctor. "Go ahead with what you need to do. I'll be in the control room if you need me."

Forsythe started out of sick bay, but the doctor, a full commander, caught his elbow as he walked by. "What are you planning on doing?"

"What he would have done," Forsythe said, jerking his thumb back toward the isolation compartment.

"You're not ready for this, Ensign. What we need to do is get out of here and call for help. Look at the ship. It's practically empty. You don't have enough people to maintain safe watches, you don't even have any other officers on board now, except for me. I'm afraid I must insist—"

"Refer to your copy of *Navy Regulations*," Forsythe said, his voice hard and cold. "You are not a line officer—you're not in line for succession to command. I am."

"You don't know what the hell you're doing," the doctor shouted. "You'll get everyone on this ship killed."

Forsythe stared him, letting his anger build. "I intend to carry out our mission, Doctor."

"You're just an ensign. I'm a commander. You have to listen to me!"

Forsythe shook his head. "No. You are the doctor. I am the senior line officer present on board. And the *Seawolf* has a job to do."

Washington, D.C.
Advanced Solutions
0645 local (GMT-5)

Finally, just after dawn, the last detail was nailed down. It was essential that it appear that Russia herself was solving the problem, but the current president of Russia was adamantly opposed to anyone finding out that Tombstone would be flying a MiG. It was an awkward position for him, since he supported the American plan. He simply wanted complete deniability, and that meant he was neither willing to provide Tombstone with a MiG nor participate in any training.

Fortunately, not every member of the CIS felt the same way. In the end, Armenia agreed to provide both training and hardware. Covering Russia's butt appeared to serve some political purpose for her, and she had been quite eager to cooperate. In exchange, the United States agreed to attempt to behead the snake immediately before Maskiro's command element could reach the island. That would make the mop-up operation all the easier. There was even some speculation that the forces on the island would simply surrender once they knew Maskiro had been eliminated. Current intelligence reported that the rebel leader had sought sanctuary in Chechnya, to the irritation of the Russians and the amusement of the Armenian government. This was the quid pro quo—Korsov would be eliminated in Chechnya. After countless international phone calls, the plan was ready.

Since the plan was not being channeled through normal Defense Department command, getting accurate intelligence proved to be the most difficult part. Sure, there was overhead imagery of Bermuda, of Chechnya, and probably of Korsov himself. But getting it meant telling someone that they wanted it, and, more importantly, telling them exactly *why* they wanted it. That was not acceptable. But U.N. Ambassador Sarah Wexler, one of the few people who knew the details, provided an unexpected answer. Captain Hemingway from JCS, Wexler said, understood the challenge of working under unusual circumstances.

Tombstone and his uncle, retired Admiral Thomas Magruder, formerly Chief of Naval Operations, both stared at Captain Hemingway. For the past fifteen minutes, she'd been filling them in on various concerns having to do with the Commonwealth of Independent States. As she detailed Ambassador Wexler's concerns and correlated them with available military intelligence, Tombstone's expression and his uncle's expression grew somber.

Finally, she finished. "Well, that's that. What do you think?"

Neither Tombstone nor his uncle spoke for a moment. Each was occupied with his own thoughts. His uncle, a Cold War veteran, knew all too well what the Russians were capable of. And Tombstone had seen first the Soviet Union and then Russia and the CIS intervening in international conflicts whenever the opportunity presented itself. Russia had always been a player, always, if not on the front lines, then certainly behind the scenes.

"It would solve a lot of their problems," his uncle said finally. "Particularly if they retake Ukraine—food and oil are in critical shortage in Russia, and Ukraine has more of both. With modern technology, some of those oil sites around the Black Sea could be productive again."

"It makes sense," Tombstone added. "Ukraine has always believed that she is the birthplace of modern-day Russia. Culturally and politically, Russia and Ukraine are quite compatible. And if those two merge, Armenia, Georgia, and most of the states with predominately Muslim populations will go along with it."

"Aren't we going to have to worry about the Pan-Arabic coalition?" the senior Magruder asked. "Seems like we've had trouble out of them from time to time."

Both Tombstone and Hemingway shook their heads. There was something about his uncle's mindset that had been formed during the Cold War that tended to see strong alliances in every situation.

"No," Hemingway said, after Tombstone deferred to her. "From what we've seen in the past, the Middle East nations have been able to form short-term working alliances, when it was in their economic interest to do so. But as far as long-term allies, no. The deep divisions within Muslim society supports that conclusion. Additionally, Russia and Ukraine are used to working in tandem. Especially in military matters. We know that they can work in concert long-term."

"So." The senior Magruder stood. "We have contingency plans, of course, and we remain at JCS's disposal. But, until we know the exact nature of any planned Russian aggression, we can't realistically assess our chances of operational success. But thank you for the heads-up." He made a move as though to show her to the door.

Hemingway didn't move, and something in her expression made his uncle pause. "There's more," she said finally, and looked away from them both as she reached into her briefcase. She pulled out a red file folder, and without looking at Tombstone, held it out to him.

Tombstone opened the folder. It contained one grainy, slightly blurred picture. Two men, one woman, the woman in the center.

Tombstone felt as though he'd been sucker punched. His breathing stopped and the blood drained from his face. The edges of his vision grayed, and for a moment he was confused, because he wasn't in a Tomcat pulling max G forces and losing oxygen to his brain, but that's what it felt like.

"Stoney? You okay?" His uncle moved around to stare over his shoulder at the picture and sucked in a hard, sharp breath. "Sweet Jesus, it can't be."

Tombstone still could not speak. The fragile world he'd built around him shattered, the dams he'd constructed against the overwhelming pain collapsed.

The figure in the photo, the woman staring directly up at the sky, had petite delicate features over a strong, forceful jaw, and topped by a halo of ragged red hair, was undoubtedly his wife.

"When? Where?" Tombstone managed to say finally. Hemingway handed him the analysis that went with the photograph.

"Siberia," Tombstone moaned. "That explains the snow." Neither his uncle nor Hemingway reacted to his attempted humor. Tombstone felt cold horror grip his heart. "We can—you can—we have to do something." He looked wildly from his uncle to Captain Hemingway, searching for their acknowledgement of what must be so obvious. "Now that we know where she is, we can get her out!"

Hemingway stared at a corner of the room, apparently completely engrossed by a dusty plastic plant on top of a file cabinet. When she spoke, it was with a distant tone of voice, as though trying to distance herself from his pain. "There was a great deal of debate over whether to show you this," she said finally. "Most people said it would be cruel, since the photo isn't that clear. Better to go ahead and let you believe that she died when her Tomcat was shot down."

"It's her. I'm certain of it," Tombstone said.

"That's not what they were worried about, Stony," his uncle said, a note of infinite sadness in his voice. "Was it?" he asked Hemingway.

She shook her head. His uncle nodded. "I've been on the other side of these discussions. Once or twice. Not often."

"*What* discussion?" Tombstone said, not able to believe what he was hearing. He couldn't sit there any longer, he couldn't. They should be on the airstrip, preflighting, loading up bombs, moving ships into position, and getting ready to bomb the hell out of anyone or anything that got in their way. Tomboy was *alive*—what was there to discuss?

One part of his mind knew. Knew, and refused to shut up.

They won't go in after her. The intelligence sources they'll compromise, the political ramifications—they won't. Because Russia has no excuse for having kept this a secret, none at all. And whatever's going down over there, we're not going to push them over the edge with this. They're not going to.

"They can't get her out, Stony. They won't even try," his uncle said gently. Then he looked over at Hemingway, a new respect in his eyes. "And you lost. You were ordered not to tell him about her, weren't you?"

Hemingway didn't answer. She didn't have to.

Tombstone felt as though he was being flayed alive. He stared up at her, tears starting in his eyes, agony coursing through his soul. "Thank you," he said, his voice thick. "I know you're risking your career telling me this. 'Thank you' isn't enough." He took a deep breath, then continued. "But you understand, don't you? You *know* that I can't leave her there. You knew I couldn't when you decided to tell me."

Hemingway nodded, infinite sadness in her eyes. "And if things ran the way they were supposed to in this country, no one else could, either."

His uncle spoke quietly. "If you solve the Bermuda problem for the Russians and we can find a way to convince them that no international recriminations will follow, we may be able to convince them to let her go." He held up a cautioning hand. "I'm not saying it's even a probability. Just a possibility. Say what you will about them, the Russians do have a streak of fairness. Their loyalty is to people, not nations. It may make a difference."

"Have they put it in those terms? Bail them out and they'll give me my wife back?" Anger started in the pit of his stomach and flashed through his entire being, so strong and hard that it threatened to consume him.

Hemingway shook her head. "No. But your uncle is right. All politics is personal. And if they're holding the wife of someone that's bailed them out of trouble instead of holding just another American aviator . . . No promise, you understand."

"Why are they holding her, anyway?" Tombstone asked. "We're not at war with them. This isn't Vietnam. There's no reason for them to keep her."

"We don't know," Hemingway admitted. "It may be that they're hoping to use her as a bargaining chip some time in the future. Maybe turning her loose would reveal something about their intelligence sources. Or maybe some junior officer just screwed up holding her in the first place and there's no way to back out of it now without international consequences."

"That's not right!" Tombstone said, his voice breaking. "It's not right."

"Of course not," Hemingway said briskly. "Neither is our failure to get her out. But it is what it is. Do you want to bitch about it, or do you want to fly this mission and see if it makes a difference?" She paused and shot him a considering look. "And if you think you can just go public and cause enough outrage to force them to release her, think again. I can tell you this for certain: The only thing you would accomplish would be to ensure that they start covering their tracks as fast as they can. Starting with getting rid of her. Are you really prepared to take that risk?"

"I'll leave today," Tombstone said, avoiding her question. "Tell the Armenians to expect me."

NINE

As the airliner touched down on the Armenian tarmac, Tombstone breathed a sigh of relief. No pilot likes to fly as a passenger, and Tombstone was no exception. He glanced over at Lieutenant Jeremy Greene and saw relief in his eyes as well.

"Nice landing, Tombstone said coolly, letting the understatement express his relief to be on the ground again.

"Yeah. Not bad." Greene was just as determined to be cool.

A mixture of languages flooded the compartment, primarily Russian but with other dialects as well. The passengers behaved as airline passengers do everywhere, getting up quickly, trying to organize their belongings and jockeying for position in the aisles. Like their American counterparts, the Russian flight attendants pleaded with the passengers to remain seated until the airline had come to a complete stop, and, like their counterparts they were mostly ignored.

Finally, the aircraft taxied to a halt outside the small, low terminal building. A metal rollaway ladder was pushed up and the plane began to empty. Tombstone and his copilot had carry-on bags containing a few essentials in case their luggage was lost. Neither of them had much faith in the Armenian baggage handling system, and doubted that the Russians would be any more efficient.

Inside, long lines had already formed at the Customs stations. Tombstone and Greene gathered up their luggage and looked at the lines with dismay.

"I thought we didn't have to do this?" Greene asked.

Tombstone shook his head. "We're not supposed to, but maybe something got screwed up. It wouldn't be the first time and it won't be the last time. Let's get in line and try to look inconspicuous. Remember, we're attending a religious conference."

The fact that an international Russian Orthodox church conference was scheduled in the city at the same time was fortuitous. His uncle in particular had appeared to enjoy the idea of his two pilots traveling as visiting priests. Tombstone's somewhat vehement objection to the appropriateness of pretending to be priests, and in particular to wearing the white collar, was overruled. To his surprise, Greene appeared not to mind at all. He ran a finger around the clerical collar, scratched, then said, "Chicks love these things." Tombstone and Greene got into line, trying to appear inconspicuous, and waited to see if the system would work as it was supposed to. They had advanced just ten feet toward the inspection station when a man in clerical garb approached them. "Father Stone?"

Tombstone nodded. "Yes. And you are . . . ?"

"Gregorio Russo," the priest said, holding out his hand. "Welcome to Armenia." He glanced at the line and said, "Come, there's no need for this. After all, if one can't trust a priest, who can one trust?"

Tombstone and Greene followed the priest away from the line to an unmarked door at one end of the room. Father Russo led the way, talking idly about the weather, the city, and the scheduled events at the conference. Tombstone tried to keep up his side of the conversation and finally said, "Jet lag, you know. I'm sure you understand."

Father Russo was instantly solicitous. "Of course. Please forgive me. Your hotel is not far—we'll get you settled in and you'll have time to rest up and prepare for vespers. There is a reception planned for this evening. A driver and escort will be by to pick you up at six this evening."

The Armenian priest's demeanor was so convincing at that moment that Tombstone wondered if there'd been a serious FUBAR in the plans. But as he looked closely at Russo's dark, inscrutable eyes and stern face, the priest winked slightly. Tombstone relaxed.

At the hotel, the two pilots were shown to adjoining suites, each modest by American luxury hotel standards, but more than adequate for their purposes. After all, they didn't intend to spend much time there.

"Six o'clock," Russo reminded them.

"Right. Vespers," Tombstone answered.

Once alone, they opened the door that connected the two rooms. Both had been extensively briefed on the probability of surveillance and certainly weren't going to take the risk of discussing the mission. Yet, what did priests talk about amongst themselves? Tombstone wondered. Somehow he doubted that Jeremy Greene's analysis of the potential for meeting Armenian women would be suitable.

"Suppose they have room service?" Greene asked, and Tombstone breathed a sigh of relief. His copilot's other abiding passion, in addition to chasing women, was eating.

"Let's find out," Tombstone suggested.

In short order, they learned that not only did the hotel have room service, but that they had a concierge who spoke English exceptionally well. They placed an order for breakfast for Tombstone and lunch for Greene, as their biological clocks were in different time zones.

The food came quickly, and Tombstone found it more than acceptable. Greene stripped off his collar and dug in with his usual gusto. Even as he was polishing off the last of his steak, he was eyeing Tombstone's hash browns.

After refueling, Tombstone settled in for a nap, vetoing Greene's suggestion that they go for a walk and insisting that the other pilot/priest remain in his room until their escort came at six.

At precisely six o'clock, Father Russo rapped on Tombstone's door. He stepped in and grinned at the two pilots, who had reassembled the bits and pieces of their clerical garb. He straightened Tombstone's collar, checked the tuck on Greene's shirt, then announced, "If you're ready, we'll go to vespers now."

He drove them in an old Zil to an ancient stone church and they followed him in. Tombstone was just starting to wonder just how far Russo would take the charade when Russo turned in to a small chapel. He led them to the altar and past it to a door in the back. They followed him through a dimly lit corridor that seemed to run the length of the back of the church. It opened out onto a small garage. Another Zil was waiting for them.

"Let's go," Russo said, his voice more animated than before. "There are enough Zils heading in and out of here that we'll be able to slip away. Somewhere around eight hundred priests will be attending vespers, so I don't think anyone will miss us." Again Russo took the wheel. "Stay low until we're away from the church, though."

Fifteen minutes later, he signaled that they could sit up. Tombstone was starting to feel a bit uneasy at the total lack of control he had over their comings and goings, and it showed in his voice when he said, "Mind telling me exactly what's up?"

"Not at all," Russo said, his voice jovial. "We're heading for a small private airfield to get you some time in a MiG. That's what you're here for, right?"

"You seem to know a lot about us," Tombstone said.

"Not as much as I will in a little while," Russo said, and turned to look back at him, grinning.

"What's that supposed to mean?" Tombstone snapped. *What the hell is this? I don't know what he's been told, what I can say, who the hell I'm supposed to meet.*

"I'm about to kick your ass," Russo replied. His grin broadened.

"So I take it you're not a priest," Greene said, his voice surly. "What the hell is going on around here?"

Russo pulled the car into a parking area. Not far away, two MiGs waited at the end of a runway. "Cool your jets, young man. And, yes, I am a priest, but don't let that bother you." He turned to face them, a hard look of joy on his face. "For the next two days, I'm your instructor pilot. I'll either teach you to fly a MiG or I'll pray for your souls when you fuck up and auger in. Your choice."

USS **Jefferson**
CVIC
0800 local (GMT-4)

Conversation stopped when Lab Rat walked back into CVIC from a briefing in TFCC. Petty Officer Lee, a linguist in the department, asked, "Are we going in, sir? We gonna go kick some Russian butt?"

"Not yet," Lab Rat answered. "Politics, ladies and gentlemen. Stay loose, stay ready—we'll get our chance."

The briefing had been less that encouraging. The *Jefferson* was ordered to stand by, and, from the reports they were seeing over ACN, it didn't look like that was going to change anytime soon. Public furor over the possibilities of casualties was already starting to pick up, and the White House had been oddly silent about the whole affair.

Lab Rat had taken advantage of a lull in Coyote's schedule to ask to talk to him about the Omicron offer, and that had also been less than satisfying. Wasn't there anything to career counseling other than being told to stay in the Navy? That was a lot of help—he could've told himself that.

Senior Chief Armstrong was unloading the additional database documentation he had brought back from Norfolk. He was smiling, and humming a cheerful song as he worked. He glanced up as Lab Rat walked in, and smiled. "How's it going, sir?"

"I've been better," Lab Rat said. The senior chief was the last person he wanted to talk to right now.

"Sorry to hear that, sir. Armstrong was still smiling, looked anything but sorry. "Have you thought anymore about what you're going to do?"

"I've been thinking of little else, to tell the truth," Lab Rat said. "It's a tough choice to make."

"It is, and it isn't," the senior chief said.

"Believe me, sir, we'd love to have you. But, I can understand if you want to stay in the Navy, too."

"Yeah, well. I'm still thinking, okay?"

Something changed the senior chief's face. He put down the volume he was working on and turned to face the commander. "Sir—could I ask a question?"

"That's a question itself, isn't it?"

"Yes, sir, it is. But it's not the one I've got in mind."

"Sure; shoot."

"Sir, this offer from Omicron that you're thinking about—is there any problem with the fact that you'd be working for me?" Armstrong looked straight in Lab Rat's eyes with a trace of dismay on his face.

"No, of course not," Lab Rat said. "How could that possibly make any difference?"

The senior chief sighed. "With all due respect, sir—of course it makes a difference. And to pretend it doesn't—well, I thought we were a little beyond that."

"What do you mean by that?" Lab Rat asked, now irritated.

The senior chief shrugged. "I'm not certain, sir. It just seems to me that it does make a difference—after all, we've both spent almost twenty years in a system where who you are is determined by what's on your collar. And if we're both at Omicron, well . . . that would reverse everything, wouldn't it? All I'm asking is if that makes a difference in your thinking."

"It doesn't." *It does. God help me, but it does.*

The senior chief stared at him steadily now, disappointment in his face. "If you say so, sir.

"And what is that supposed to mean?"

Armstrong shrugged. Whatever you want it to, sir."

Lab Rat slammed his hand down the desk. "Enough! If you have something on your mind, go ahead and say it."

"Why should I?" The senior chief shot back. "You're not."

Lab Rat's jaw dropped. Sure, the senior chief had always been willing to stand up for what he believed in, but it had never been on a personal level like this. For the senior chief to question his decisions, well, that was just too much.

But he's right. It does make a difference, I'm just not willing to tell him that it does.

The full implications of what had just happened sunk in. And Lab Rat felt a surge of relief. This, then, was the critical issue to deal with, whether or not he could cope with working for the senior chief. Once he decided that, everything else would fall into place.

Am I that rigid? Do I value people more for their rank than for who they are? If you asked me, I wouldn't have said so,

*but this is certainly putting a different light on it, isn't it? And
one that's not very attractive.*

Just then, the vault door swung open and a small woman
peered in. "Commander Busby?"

"Yes," Lab Rat said, not taking his eyes off of the senior
chief. "What is it?"

She stepped into the vault and extended her hand. "Lieutenant Johnnie Davis, sir, with VF-95. I have a few questions
about what might be on the island and the skipper told me you
were the person to talk to."

"I'll be right with you," Lab Rat said, finally looking away
from the senior chief. "And Senior Chief," he said, "We'll
continue this discussion later. At my convenience." He hated
himself even as he added the last phrase.

The senior chief's face was an impassive mask. "Of course,
sir. At your convenience."

Lieutenant Davis spread out the proposed flight schedule on a
table in front of her. "It's the first time I've done this for an
entire air wing. I've only been in strike planning for two
weeks. Anyway, before I make a fool of myself in public, I
wonder if you might take a look and tell me if I've missed
anything from an intelligence perspective."

"Sure." Lab Rat pulled the flight schedule over in front of
him and ran his finger down the assignments. "Looks good—
you're on a one-point-five cycle, which is fine. The air wing
is broken up into just two flights—why is that?"

"That was my guidance from the strike officer," she said.
"Of course, it's always subject to change, but he wanted to be
able to take on two separate missions if necessary. So I figured
that, absent any other guidance, I'd just be making them both
about the same composition."

Lab Rat leaned back in his chair, slightly relieved to be on
familiar ground. He studied the lieutenant in front of him. She
was small, barely his own height, and small-boned at that. He
could tell she worked hard to make up for the problems her
size could pose in her aircraft. Sleek muscle rippled over her
bones and she looked exceptionally fit. A healthy glow suf-
fused her face.

"There are some advantages, of course, to proceeding that
way," he said, continuing to study her. Attractive, exception-

ally so. He wondered if she was seeing anyone.

"What did you say you name was again?

"Johnnie Davis. But everybody calls me Rat."

"Rat?" Busby's voice was incredulous. "You've got to be kidding me!"

She shook her head, a woeful look on her face. "Nope. They tagged me with that in Basic, because I was small. The instructor said I could weasel into small places. I could hear that one coming on and couldn't stand the thought of spending my Navy career days known as Weasel. So I popped up fast and said, 'You mean, like a rat, sir?' It was the best I could do on short notice, I'm afraid. But Rat is still better than Weasel."

"Oh, no doubt." He hesitated for moment, unsure of whether to proceed. "But that gives us something in common, doesn't it?"

She looked confused. "Sir?"

"I got my nickname the day I checked in at AOCS. I have no idea why, but my drill instructor decided to name me Lab Rat. I'm afraid it stuck."

At that, she laughed out loud. "A few more Rats on board, and we'll have us a whole species, won't we?"

"We will," he agreed. "*Rattus carrierus*, you think?"

She nodded. "Well, sir, I have to admit, that makes me feel a bit better."

"So, who do you usually fly with?" Lab Rat asked, more to make conversation that anything else.

A mournful look crossed her face. "Brad Morrow.

"Fastball? My condolences. Especially if the Padres are losing." Lab Rat doubted that there was anyone on board who didn't know about Morrow's obsession with the San Diego Padres. "He still wearing that Tony Gwinn shirt under his flight suit?"

"Sure is. Although with the season they had last year, I don't know if that's such a good idea."

"I understand he's quite a handful." Word had it that Davis had been paired with Morrow to cool his heels, and that their last cruise together had been a rugged one.

She shrugged. "He's young. He'll outgrow it. If he lives that long."

Lab Rat leaned toward her. "Now, about this flight plan—remember, you need to worry about the terrain as well as what

sort of threat you'll encounter. We're not certain how much
they have on the island, but it's probably old, and it'll have to
be something mobile, something they brought with them. I'd
bet on at least one antiair installation, maybe two. You've got
to figure that you want to take those out at some point, which
means you should have a different weapon load on standby.
It's a different situation when we're operating with the Air
Force. They send their own Wild Weasel—there's that word
again—antiradiation aircraft in ahead of us. But out here,
we're going to be on our own. So, if there's an antiair radar
problem, we'll have to take care of it right up front."

"That makes sense." She leaned forward, and Lab Rat got
a whiff of something that might have been perfume, or could
just have been soap or shampoo. Whatever it was, it was in-
toxicating. He founded himself distracted as he concentrated
on the plan in front of them.

For the next fifteen minutes, they discussed the possible missions to Bermuda, how the problems might shape up, and what
impact the initial reconnaissance missions would have on the
air wing flight plan. When he finally ran out of things to go
over, Lab Rat quit talking.

Rat stood, and held out her hand. "I can't tell you how much
I appreciate this, Commander. You just kept me from making
a fool of myself in front of my boss."

Lab Rat waved away her thanks. "My pleasure. And, since
we're members of the same species, call me Lab Rat."

TEN

As early as the end of the second day, Forsythe could already see the strain starting on the faces of the crew. It wasn't that they complained—far from it. In fact, since the death of Lieutenant Commander Cowlings, a new, grim determination had seemed to settle over them. A fire for vengeance burned in their eyes, and no one wanted to be the first to admit the strain was getting to him.

Forsythe and the doctor continued to take their meals in the small wardroom, although with only two of them it almost seemed pointless. In fact, the doctor had suggested that they begin messing with the crew, simplifying life for the three mess cooks on board. But Forsythe had decided not to, and not simply because the doctor suggested it—though the fact that that thought had crossed his mind made him somewhat ashamed. Later, he realized his instinct had been correct. He needed a bit of distance from the crew, and while the doctor might not be particularly his favorite company, he would have to do.

"They're wearing out," the doctor said, pointing his fork at his interim commanding officer as he spoke. "You can't keep this up for long."

"When there are complaints, let me know," Forsythe said. There was a reason for the rank structure on a submarine, perhaps even more reasons for it than on a larger ship. The chiefs ate in their one small corner of the crew's mess, behind a divider, and pretended to ignore the rest of the crew. That allowed sailors time to blow off steam. But, had their very junior captain been in the same compartment, they would have been silent.

"I'm already seeing the signs of stress in them."

"Has someone complained?" Forsythe asked, keeping his eyes down on his plate.

"No. They won't, you know. But, it's only a matter of time. You have to listen to me in matters like this, you have to." The doctor's voice was smug and demanding.

"Listen to doesn't mean obey." Suddenly, Forsythe's appetite was gone. He shoved the plate back slightly. The one concession to the reduced manpower had been that he and the doctor would obtain their food from the crew's mess, eat it in the wardroom, then take their own dishes back to the galley. "Until then, keep me posted."

"The enlisted people aren't the only people who are my responsibility," the doctor said softly, his voice carrying a note of menace. "Last night you suggested I read Navy regulations—I suggest you review them yourself. If and when I believe that you are becoming a danger to this crew, I will relieve you. Will relieve you for medical reasons, and order you confined to your stateroom. Between the Chief and the troops, we can get the boat back to the surface and the message out."

Forsythe turned, icy menace clear on his face. "Then I think we both adequately understand our duties, doctor. And, yes, I am familiar with the passage to which you're referring." He could smell the rank stench of fear on the doctor now, and it disgusted him. "That said, I will tolerate no more insubordination from you. Just who do you think the crew will obey? Watch their eyes, doctor. You claim to know the mood of the crew—watch their eyes. Because I can guarantee you, what you're seeing isn't stress. It's pure, one hundred percent pissed off American sailor. Right now, they'd follow me to hell and back if it meant avenging Commander Cowlings. And I suggest you try to stay out of their way."

"Captain to the Control Room!" The chief's voice blared

out of the speaker on the bulkhead. "Sir, it's urgent."

Forsythe picked up his plate and tossed it on top of the doctor's "Take that to the galley with yours. And, in case it isn't perfectly clear to you, that's an order." He turned and raced out of the compartment.

As he raced down the single central passageway of the submarine, Forsythe's heart was hammering. For a split second, he wondered if he was experiencing some sort of medical problem like the one that had killed Cowlings. In the next instant, he dismissed the thought. He was perfectly healthy, not carrying a ticking time bomb in his head as Cowlings had been.

"What is it?" he asked as he skidded in to Control.

"The Kilo, sir," the chief said. He pointed at the sonar display. "She just turned and is heading directly for us."

Forsythe studied the waterfall display, and at the same time said, "Set quiet ship." He heard the word being passed softly down the passageways. "And battle stations." The second word went out as well, but with a touch of electricity in it.

"She must have heard a transient," the sonarman said, his gaze glued to the screen. "And, if she did, then her hearing's better than we thought it was." He shook his head, not denying the fact, but musing over the possibilities. "We need to re-evaluate this whole plan, then, sir." He looked up at the lieutenant, his face thoughtful. "Our plan is based on certain assumptions. No, not cancel the plan," he added hastily, seeing the lieutenant start to shake his head. "Just re-evaluate how far we want to stay from her. Out of her weapons' range, maybe, a little bit farther away. I can still do it," he concluded.

Back off from her? I don't think so. But if her sonar is better than Cowlings thought, we have to take that into account. The unexpected—what you can't plan for. I can't be afraid to change our plans. Cowlings wouldn't have been. For some reason, the thought of what the late operations officer would have done weighed more heavily on him than what he thought his captain would have done.

"She's not going to leave her box," Forsythe said, with more certainty that he felt. "But let's move out to seven thousand yards. Can you still hold contact at that range?"

"Yes, sir." Pencehaven said, although Forsythe could see

doubt on Jacob's face. "We can always move in closer if we lose her."

"Right. But—" Forsythe stopped as he watched the display shift ominously. "Down doppler—she's turned away from us," he said.

Why is she doing that? She was heading straight for us like she knew where we were. And then she turned away—why?

Seconds before it was confirmed, he knew the answer. The hard squeal of tiny propellers followed by a hard pinging against the hull of the submarine gave him his answer.

"Torpedo in the water!" Jacob said, his voice carrying even though it was at a whisper. "Recommend evasive maneuvers."

"Down doppler on the torpedo." Pencehaven corrected, his more sensitive ears telling him what the display had not yet picked up. "Sir, the torpedo's not heading for us. It's headed for the bird farm."

USS Jefferson
2333 local (GMT-4)

"Evasive maneuvering" Coyote howled, knowing it was useless, but not willing to give up without a fight. The officer of the deck had not waited for his command. Even as he spoke, he felt the ponderous ship start to turn, the deck shifting ever so slightly. The collision alarm beat out its staccato warning over the 1MC overhead, and he heard the pounding of feet as people raced toward their battle stations. Even though general quarters had not been set, everyone knew that it would be, in a few seconds.

The symbol for torpedo popped into being on the tactical screen, small, red, and deadly. It inched toward the aircraft carrier, bearing in unerringly. The speed leader for the *Jefferson* was already showing her turn, but there was little an aircraft carrier could do to avoid a torpedo. It was like an office building maneuvering to avoid a tornado.

Still, they had to try. They had to.

USS **Lake Champlain**
2335 local (GMT-4)

Captain Coleman stood beside his battle chair, his headphones tethered him to the elevated brown leatherette chair. Theoretically, he should be sitting there, strapped in, but he found it almost impossible to hold still when the ship was in physical danger. It was as though he could control her by pacing the deck, toughen her skin, and keep her sensors turned in the direction of the threat.

"TAO, Sonar! Sir, it should miss us by two thousand yards—it's headed for the carrier, sir!"

"Time to CPA?" Coleman demanded.

"About ten seconds or a hair less," the sonarman replied.

Coleman swore quietly. Ten seconds—not enough to get within range and eject noisemakers and decoys, although the carrier would certainly be doing that on her own. Still, it was worth a try. He gave the order, knowing that the entire crew had already anticipated it and was simply waiting for the command.

God, he hated being helpless. To sit here watching as the torpedo arrowed in on the one ship that wasn't supposed to take a hit, the centerpiece of the battle group. Without the carrier, they had no chance of regaining control of Bermuda.

"Five seconds to CPA, sir," the sonarman said. Coleman could see the geometries playing out on the screen in front of him, the torpedo squeaking past his ship, the hard turn the carrier was attempting—and the inevitable result.

"ASROC, sir?" the TAO asked. The antisubmarine torpedo could be launched from a vertical launch cell on the ship, and had the range to reach any possible submarine.

"Can't," Coleman said shortly. "Our locating data on the *Seawolf* is twelve hours old—and, at last report, she had been stalking a contact in this very area." If the ship were to launch a torpedo into the box, there was every chance that it would find the *Seawolf* instead of the enemy sub. No, this was the *Seawolf*'s battle—and there was nothing anybody on the surface could do about it.

USS **Seawolf**
2336 local (GMT-4)

"Got her solid," Pencehaven said, his voice as calm as if it were a drill. "Your orders?"

"Are we within weapons range?" Forsythe asked.

"Yes, sir. Two tubes loaded and flooded, waiting for weapons release."

"Weapons free," Forsythe said softly. "Two shots—now."

Even as Forsythe gave the order, Pencehaven mashed down the red button. The submarine shook slightly as compressed air forced a torpedo out of the tube. Its tiny propeller immediately began whipping the water into a froth as it came to life, checked its orders to intercept the target, and pick up speed and headed off on its mission. A second later, another torpedo followed.

Forsythe watched the screen, desperately praying that he had done the right thing. Yes, he could ask the chief if he'd done the right thing—even the doctor, if he had wanted to. But, in the end, it was his decision to make, his responsibility to fight the submarine.

And, until that very second, he had not realized how lonely that could be.

Kilo One
2338 local (GMT-4)

Captain First Rank Sergei Andropov turned on his psychological services officer. "You said they would not fire!"

The man beside him was pale and shaken. He had not understood initially what the hard, buzzing noise was from the speaker, but the crew had quickly filled him in. He would be lucky if he lived long enough for the torpedo to kill him.

"Every projection said that they would not," he said, aware of how very lame his explanation sounded. "They would not risk it—they are too conscious of their body count, too afraid to take any casualties. They would not—"

"They did!" Andropov grabbed him by shoulders, shook

him violently, then transferred his grip to the man's neck.

"You imbecile, you have killed us!"

The Russians could not presume to know the American mind any more that the Americans could know the Russian psyche. For just one second, he wondered if the Americans had advisers such as this.

USS Lake Champlain
2339 local (GMT-4)

Coleman saw the two new bursts of noise on the display, and watched as they resolved into the characteristic shapes of torpedoes. Cold fear clutched at his gut, followed immediately by relief as they turned away from him.

"They're ours, Captain. Ours!"

Good old Seawolf. *She's pulling us out of this. Now, if I can do so well on the air battle, we may have a chance.*

Kilo One
2339 local (GMT-4)

"Two thousand yards, Captain!" Stark terror filled the sonarman's voice. "Bearing constant, range decreasing. Captain, your orders? Captain?"

"Hard left rudder, flank speed, and . . ." For just a moment he paused, uncertain of himself for the first time in nearly twenty years. Classic evasion tactics called for him to go deep, forcing the torpedo to follow him down, leaving hard knuckles in the water as he went and ejecting decoys and noisemakers. The theory was that the torpedo could be tricked into attacking one of the phantom targets as the submarine slipped safely below the thermocline.

But the hard, cold knot in his gut told him it wouldn't work this time. Couldn't work—no, they had no chance of evading this torpedo using classical tactics. Therefore, his only option was to attempt something radical.

"Surface the ship," he ordered after what seemed like

minutes, but in reality had been a few seconds. "Surface the ship."

"Captain?"

The Captain reeled around to glare at the conning officer, murder in his eyes. The body of the psychologist stretched out across the deck was ample proof that he was prepared to follow through on his threats. "I said, surface the ship." He waited.

The junior officer glanced down at the dead psychologist and made his decision. "Surface the ship, aye, sir."

"One thousand yards—bearing constant, range decreasing."

I may be too late, he thought, watching the torpedoes move across the time-versus-bearing display. *I hesitated—I should not have done that. The other captain—he did not hesitate.*

USS **Seawolf**
2341 local (GMT-4)

"Oh, no you don't," Otter said. The other submarine's acoustic signature was changing. Otter made a tiny correction with the joystick, turning the wire-guided torpedo. "You're a bad, bad little bastard, aren't you?"

"What are you doing?" Forsythe asked. "You're bringing the torpedo shallow! That sub's not coming shallow. That would be insanity. She's got no chance on the surface."

"She's got no chance either way, Captain," the sonarman said quietly. "And she *is* surfacing—she *is.*" He pointed at an interference pattern on the screen, tracing out the details as he spoke. "She's shallow right now, and she's going to surface. And," he said with conviction, "she's going to die."

She's going to die. He called me Captain. Again, the full weight of what he'd done bore down on Forsythe.

But when had there been time to do anything differently? There had not been time to surface and ask for instructions, not the way that things had unfolded. There had not been time to make a stealthy approach on the enemy sub and carefully set up a killing shot.

No, this was undersea warfare the way it really was. Not some tidy game of angles and maneuvers in a classroom, the relative positions outlined in different colors of chalk on a two-dimensional board. Not a trainer, where you knew that the result would be the instructor calling, "Stop the problem, stop the clock," followed by a detailed and unforgiving debrief in front of your classmates. How he had dreaded those moments, when his errors would be exposed to everyone else, the teasing that would follow. Not that he had been anymore gentle when it was someone else under the gun, no. That's not the way it was done.

And this was why, he saw, watching as his torpedoes reached the end of their wires and were set free on their own. *This* is why it was done that way. Because real warfare was nasty, bloody stumbling around the dark, acting and reacting on insufficient information, praying to God that you hadn't screwed up. Because, if you have, it's not just worrying about a hard time your roommates are going to give you or the bad marks on a fitrep. It's knowing that thirty other people will die along with you.

"There they go," Pencehaven said as the wires snapped. He could no longer control the torpedoes with his joystick. "Damn, they're just like little bloodhounds—look at them go! You hear that, Captain? You hear that?" The sonarman pointed at the speaker. The series of shimmering pings from the torpedoes' seeker heads were growing higher pitched, coming faster now. It sounded eager, certain about what it was doing—

Stop it. Don't anthropomorphize it. It's a weapon, not a bloodhound.

"Fifteen seconds until contact," Otter said, his mood more closely matching Forsythe's own than Pencehaven's did. The sonarman raised his hands to his earphones, ready to peel them away from his head. He glanced over at his friend and nudged him. "Don't forget this time. Last time, you couldn't hear for two days."

"Yes, yes," the other said, still smiling broadly.

Hours of boredom punctuated by seconds of sheer terror. But at least for them, not for us.

"Five seconds," Pencehaven said, pulling his own earphones off. "Stand by for it, folks. It's going to be a doozy."

Kilo One
2341 local (GMT-4)

"Passing five hundred feet," the Russian sonarman said.

Not good enough. We're not going to make it in time. "Emergency blow," the Captain ordered, feeling his skin crawl. The sonar pings sounded like ball peen hammers on his hull, an incessant hammering that would drive you insane if you listened to it long enough. But he wouldn't have to, would he? That was the whole point—he wouldn't listen to it that long at all.

"Emergency blow, aye," the officer of the deck said. A loud *whoosh*ing filled the submarine and his ears popped, as every bit of available compressed air was dumped into the ballast tanks, forcing out seawater, and jerking the submarine toward the surface. The captain felt heavier as the submarine surged up under him. Then, the submarine tilted hard to the right, and loose gear went flying, cascading down from the elevated front parts of the submarine. It could not fall all the way to the stern, of course. Watertight hatches stopped the debris's progress, and piled up at the rear of every compartment.

"Five seconds!" someone shouted. There was no need for silence now, no advantage at all. A blind man could follow their progress through the ocean.

USS Seawolf
2342 local (GMT-4)

"Will you look at that?" Otter said, pointing at the screen. "Man, she's one noisy bitch on emergency blow, isn't she?"

"Is that what that is?" Forsythe said, a terrible certainty starting in his heart. "Emergency blow?"

Both sonarman nodded. "No doubt about it, sir. She's scared and running for daylight."

"Can she make it to the surface?

Neither sonarman answered.

Kilo One
2343 local (GMT-4)

"One hundred feet," the Russian sonarman said, the relief plain in his voice. Depth was measured from the keel of the submarine, and if the keel was at one hundred feet, the conning tower was just twenty-five feet below the surface. They were near enough to get out if they had to. If they could.

"Captain, are we going to—?" The officer of the day never had a chance to finish his question.

The torpedo struck the ship in the aft one-third of the hull, about twenty feet forward of the propeller shaft. As its nose dented the steel hull, the force shoved the igniter back into the warhead. The torpedo detonated, instantly vaporizing the seawater around it and producing a massive pressure gradient along the hull of the submarine.

The force of the explosion, coupled by the sudden change in pressure, popped rivets along the junction between two plates. The sea took advantage of the submarine's weakness immediately, pouring in, as though trying to demonstrate the principle that nature abhors a vacuum.

The sea acted like a giant wedge, forcing the two steel plates farther apart. Incredible forces brought to bear on buckled steel, mangled with nature's force everything man had so carefully machined.

Inside the submarine, the effect was devastating. The original split in the hull filled the space with water, and the force twisted the inner hull out of shape. Given the submarine's steep angle of climb, and the forces already in play on her, it didn't take much to breach her hull completely.

The original leak—if such torrential force can be called by such an innocuous name—was located in a machinery space. The stream of water hit with the force of a fire hose, immediately enlarging the hole. The watertight bulkhead to the passageway held for five seconds, then, under the stress of the hull deformity, the rubber seal pulled away from the coming. Again, the water followed.

The submarine was divided, like a surface ship would be, into a series of watertight compartments designed to withstand considerable pressure. But every engineering design works on the assumption that the hull would remain intact.

The passageway running the length of the sub was empty. The submariners were in watertight compartments on either side, at the battle stations, torn between the duty and the compulsion to race forward or aft to one of the escape hatches. Everyone knew what the steep angle on the deck meant—they were surfacing, surfacing hard, and there was only one reason to do that with a torpedo in pursuit. Each one vowed silently that when he heard the submarine break the surface he would abandon his post and head to the escape hatch, protocol and duty be damned.

The ocean, however, had other plans.

The next to the last segment of the passageway flooded first and the watertight hatches on either side of it collapsed almost immediately. As the ancillary equipment room filled with water, it became heavier, deepening the submarine's already steep angle of ascent, and severely slowing her forward progress. The submarine had enough inertia built up, however, that even the fatal breech of the hull could not stop her from reaching the surface. Still, she broke the surface at a sharper angle than her designers ever intended.

As she breached the surface of the ocean, the sea broke through the aft watertight door. Now, with the full force of the sea behind it, it smashed into engineering, cold seawater surging over the hot main propulsion engines. The engines flashed the first cascade of water into steam, then shattered, metal torn apart by the sudden change in temperature as more water followed.

There were three sailors in that compartment, each with his own general quarters station. The first was assigned to monitor the oil pressure and temperature over the main engines. The second was the damage control petty officer, standing by to coordinate any repairs or actions in an emergency. The third was a very junior member of the crew, whose only job in life was to watch the bilges and make sure that the seepage never rose above two inches.

They had approximately four seconds warning before the ship began to break apart, long enough for a prayer or a curse, depending on each one's temperament. Long enough for the senior rating to scrabble up the ladder to the escape hatch and begin desperately twisting the heavy wheel, hoping against hope that he could somehow manage to get it opened, get inside, and get out before he was trapped. The other tried to follow what he was doing, but got in the way. While the senior rating might have had time to get the inner hatch open, it was almost certain he would not have had time to climb inside the escape chamber, shut the hatch behind him, and reseal it. Even if he had time, the pressure and forces acting on the hull would probably have warped the chamber itself, either preventing the hatch from securing or keeping the outer hatch from opening.

In any event, the others had forgotten to grab emergency egress breathing devices and would have drowned as the chamber filled.

As it was, the sea broke through suddenly, slamming into the compartment and flooding it instantly. The youngest seaman was slammed into a bulkhead and his neck snapped. He had a few seconds of fading consciousness, but not enough time to feel the cold, clear panic and fear flooding the other two.

The senior petty officer, the one who had climbed the ladder, was knocked off his perch. He took a deep breath, held it, and moved through the compartment, hoping to find an air bubble trapped there. The man in the middle panicked. He became completely disoriented. In trying to emulate the other in the complete pitch darkness and cold water, he swam for the stern of the ship. By the time oxygen starvation forced his mouth open in an instinctive insistence that he could indeed breathe seawater if he just tried hard enough, he had realized his mistake.

The third man lived—at least for a few more minutes. He had time to realize what was happening, to watch the water rising around him, to hear the sudden crack as the hull gave way. He was completely conscious as the water quickly rose, the cold leeching the heat almost immediately, the water filled with oily debris. He could not see the water rise, but followed its progress as it crept up his body, the heavy pressure on his chest, the icy oil against his skin, seeping into his tightly closed mouth and invading his nostrils.

He knew the submarine better than his own house and he tried to make his way forward. He pounded against the first door he encountered, but the man on the other side rightfully refused to doom the rest of the ship by opening the hatch. Finally, as he verged on unconsciousness from oxygen starvation, his mouth opened and he breathed in seawater.

Those in the forward compartments who were strong and acted quickly survived. As they heard the torpedo hit, they ignored their standing orders, opened their hatches and streamed forward. They secured the hatches behind them as the went, moving forward against the flood, struggling against the ever deepening inclination on the deck. Eventually, they reached the control room.

Inside the control room, utter chaos prevailed. The captain had roared out a hasty abandon-ship order that was not necessary. Every one of them instinctively knew that to stay in the submarine would be to die. No damage control effort could begin to staunch the flood.

At the bottom of every watertight hatch is a port, known as the telltale. Because there are no windows between the watertight compartments, the telltale provides a way of determining whether the other side is flooded or not.

The control room crew heard the frantic pounding of the others on the hatch, and, in an act of superhuman courage, one of them stayed behind and popped open the telltale. When he saw no water, he opened the hatch and helped drag the rest of the crew through it. After the last one was in, as he saw water seeping into the compartment they'd just vacated, he slammed the hatch shut and twisted the wheel. Except for the captain, he was the last man to leave the dying submarine.

USS **Jefferson**
CVIC
0308 local (GMT-4)

"Come on, *Jeff*," Coyote said softly. He wasn't sure if it was an order or a prayer.

Beneath his feet, the deck was now tilted as hard over as he'd ever felt it. He had to give her credit, the old girl was strong, but she just couldn't maneuver like the smaller boys could.

On the screen in front of him, the torpedo symbols inched

closer and closer, their positions reported by the *Lake Champlain* from the cruiser's sonar detections.

No time, no time. We're not even all buttoned up—if it hits directly under the keel, we're in serious trouble.

Outside the compartment, Coyote could hear feet pounding down passageways as sailors scrambled for their general quarter stations. The damage control crews were the most critical part of the entire evolution, since they would be the ones who determined whether or not *Jeff* stayed afloat.

If it hits. Just turning now—we may be able to confuse it.

Evasive maneuvers worked—at least in theory. How well depended on what type of torpedoes had been fired. The acoustic homers would have no difficulty tracking her, although a straight wake homer might be confused by a sudden change of course.

Suddenly, *Lake Champlain* skipper's voice came over the circuit, ferocious joy in his voice. "*Jeff, Champlain*—they're gone! My sonarmen said they simply slowed down then stopped. Massive explosions under the water, too, sir, immediately before. They were probably still on wire guidance, the *Seawolf* took out the submarine, and the torpedoes went stupid."

Cheers broke out in TFCC, and Coyote drew in a deep, shuddering breath. So, the *Seawolf* was on the job—and just how had she accomplished this? Everything Coyote had read said that the *Seawolf* was tasked only as an intelligent asset pending relief on station.

The details spelled out in the P4 had been far more alarming. Coyote had whistled softly as he read it, unable to believe that the submarine's watch section had gotten her underway without the captain or the XO on board. In fact, the senior line officer present on board was a lieutenant commander.

Coyote folded up the message and tucked it into his shirt pocket. "Good on you, *Seawolf*," he said. He shuddered at the thought of being shorthanded so far below the surface of the ocean, while marveling at the man who had managed to pull it off. No, they weren't aviators—but, for the first time in his career, he was awed by someone whose max speed was just over thirty knots.

USS Seawolf
0500 local (GMT-4)

Forsythe stood stunned, watching the silent death unfold on
the sonar screen in front of him. All around him, the sonarman
and the sailors mouthed quiet cheers, arms pumping vigorously
in the air, pounding each other lightly on the back. Even in
the midst of their exhilaration over a successful war shot, they
remembered the first rule of life below the surface: Silence is
safety.

The sonar chief jabbed Forsythe in the ribs. "Get with it,
sir." The chief stared at him with a silent intensity, as though
willing Forsythe to read his mind. He let Forsythe see him
glance around room, taking in the sailors and their silent cel-
ebrations, and then returned his gaze to Forsythe's face, eyes
narrowed, shoulders back.

Suddenly, Forsythe understood. The chief was doing the job
that all chief petty officers do in the Navy, although under
somewhat different circumstances. He was training a junior
officer—the officer commanding the *Seawolf*, true, though
only by a quirk fate, but a junior officer nonetheless.

The crew needed him, Forsythe realized. He had to show
he approved of what they'd done to make the killing of the
other submarine something that they could live with. Because,
at some level, each of them knew what happened was not just
pixels on a sonar screen. It was the death of the ship and her
men, men very much like themselves. Russian, yes. Diesel-
propelled instead of nuclear. But within the double-hull con-
struction there were men with families who would miss them,
sons and husbands who would never go home. And that, Forsythe realized, his own men must not be allowed to think
about. Not now. Not yet.

Maybe someday, when they left the depths and were back
on the surface, when they could look at what happened again
in the sunlight, consider it without thinking immediately that
it could have been them.

But, how to do that? Forsythe's mind raced furiously, and
he saw the chief's face relaxed as he realized he'd made his
point. How would Lieutenant Commander Cowlings have handled it?

Forsythe stood a little straighter, feeling the weight of command on his shoulders. He lifted his chin, braced slightly, and said, "Good job. Now let's nail those other bastards."

Otter and Pencehaven nodded in unison. "We'll get them, sir," Otter promised. "We'll get them or I'll volunteer to hot rack with him the rest of the cruise."

Laughter broke out among the crew, although quiet, still so quiet. There would be no hot racking on this mission, Forsythe realized. That there would be little rack time at all didn't seem to occur to them.

"All right—let's make it three for three, shall we?" Forsythe asked. He turned to the sonar chief. "Chief, I need a recommended course and depth to intercept the next contact."

"Due north, Captain," the chief said, nodding in approval. "I recommend we make our approach below the layer—that seems to be working for us pretty well, I'd say."

"Very well. Make it so." *What else? What am I forgetting?* An after-action report, certainly, but there wasn't time to stop and transmit it just yet. Maybe on ELF—were there appropriate codes for it?

A sudden, gut-wrenching thought occurred to him. He drew the chief off slightly to the side, and said, "Good job. You know what I mean." The chief nodded. "But there's something else. There could have been survivors, Chief." He held up one hand to forestall comment. "I know, I'm not about to surface and take a look for them. But we need to alert somebody, just in case . . ." He couldn't finish to sentence.

"They were shallow when it hit, *Captain*," the chief said, emphasizing the last word ever so slightly as if to remind Forsythe who he was right now. "Real shallow. Plenty of time for most of them to make it out." The chief considered the matter for moment, and said, "A message buoy, delayed transmission. I'll set it for six hours. That will give us time to clear the area before it starts transmitting." He shot a glance at his very junior captain. "I'm assuming you don't want it screaming bloody murder directly overhead."

"To whom?" Forsythe asked.

"Second Fleet. They'll get the message to the appropriate civilian and military vessels in the area. I'm not sure whether Bermuda's Coast Guard is going to be in any shape to respond, but there's plenty of surface traffic in the area. And the water's warm—they can wait it out if they're smart."

No hypothermia—just sharks. Forsythe remembered the briefings on the waters around Bermuda. The profusion of fishing and passenger vessels resulted in lots of garbage, which attracted sharks. That, and the warm-water fishing.

"Good thinking. Now, let's go after that other one." Forsythe turned and started to walk back into the control room. The chief cleared his throat. Forsythe turned. "Something else?"

"Yes, sir." The chief came closer. "It's about the crew, sir. They're flying high now, and they will for a while. But, sooner or later, they're going to start wearing out." The chief passed him a piece of paper. On it were listed the most critical watch stations on the ship, with two names next each position. "Some of them are completely qualified, at least on paper. But, under the circumstances, everybody's capable of handling most everything on each watch station. I recommend you give them about forty-five minutes, then stand half of them down for rack time. We'll be transiting for awhile to get to the next operating area, and if there's ever a chance to go skimpy on the watch, it would be now. Give the first group three hours off, then put the second crew down for three hours. Then restart the regular watches. We can keep that up a lot longer than if we keep everybody awake at once."

"I'm not on here," Forsythe said, as he scanned the list. That earned him a small wintry smile from the chief.

"No, sir. You're not. The captain never is.

As Forsythe watched, acoustic signatures of the enemy torpedoes wavered across the screen. They moved from the right to the left, indicating that they were slowing down. Finally, they trailed off the left edge of the screen and disappeared.

"Dead in the water," Pencehaven said softly. "We snapped the wire before they could acquire the targets on their own."

The chief grinned and slapped him on the back. "Unbroken record, right?"

Pencehaven nodded and tried not to look too pleased with himself.

"Record of what?" Forsythe asked.

"Of not buying drinks. After every deployment, every man and woman on the carrier wants to buy him a beer. I doubt he's spent a penny on booze or food in the last two years. Right, Pencehaven?"

"I bought my mother dinner once."

"Yeah. But then that frigate guy came up and bought you both a drink, didn't he?" the other sonarman chimed in. "Besides, doesn't count when it's your mother."

Forsythe put his hand on Pencehaven's shoulder. "We get home, I'm buying you one myself. Hell, I'll buy you an entire bar!"

ELEVEN

MiG 101
Armenia
1800 local (GMT +4)

Tombstone stared down the long, gleaming white expanse of concrete stretching out before him. The runway was comparable to any that he'd seen in the United States. Sure, there were a few differences in the placement of lights, the numbering system, but in general airfields all over the world had certain similarities. Function drove form. There had to be places to keep aircraft out of the weather. There had to be a way to fuel aircraft, a control tower, and at least some facilities for maintenance. Associated ground equipment and ground crew were another constant, and he had been impressed with how well the Armenians were trained. Had it not been for the accent of the tower controller, he would have believed that he was on an airfield somewhere in the United States.

The MiG itself was impeccably maintained. Its engines thrummed with a comforting rhythm, and even if pitched differently from a Tomcat, reassuring all the same. His aircraft wanted to fly, surged against the brakes as he held her back, coming up to military power in preparation for takeoff.

After his first lesson in the MiG, he'd come to a new appreciation of the MiG's capabilities. Before, he'd seen MiGs primarily as adversaries with weaknesses that he memorized and exploited. Now, her weaknesses were something he had very much in mind. Primary among them was the appetite of this MiG and the relatively small size of the fuel tanks. She also carried a lighter loadout of ordinance, more on par with what a Hornet would handle than his own massive Tomcat.

On the upside, she was more nimble, quicker to turn in the air and to gain altitude. And, during ascent, she could manage a full negative angle that a Tomcat couldn't match. Aerodynamically, she was an exceptionally stable, nimble fighter. In air-to-air combat situations, he would not have minded flying her.

But this was an air-to-ground mission, and the lighter loadout of ordinance worried him. Still, a dirt mission might be preferable to ACM. In air-to-air combat, decades of flying the Tomcat would influence his every decision, and he thought that he might miss exploiting some advantage that the lighter aircraft had. With air-to-ground, the adversary stayed the same.

"We're very certain of this," Russo had said. "Our intelligence sources are, well, let's just say they are highly placed. He will be leaving Chechnya tomorrow afternoon, and this will be our last opportunity for a strike."

"Our last chance for a ground strike," Tombstone had corrected.

"Yes, of course. But, that's far preferable to having to track him down after he launches. The difficulties inherent in shooting him down over a populated area are considerable. The whole point is to avoid civilian casualties, and we could help his cause more by shooting him down over a hospital or an orphanage.

Tombstone nodded. Yes, this was a way to do it, although both of them had pointedly avoided mentioning how many people on the ground at his base might be killed as well.

But those were the military people, weren't they? And that made a difference, didn't it? They had to know when they'd signed on with a renegade that they were putting their lives at risk for something like this.

"Hunter, you're cleared for takeoff. Launch at your discretion."

Tombstone disengaged brakes. The MiG surged underneath him, hungry to be airborne. As he had every time for the last

wo days, Tombstone marveled at her sheer speed, her will-
ingness to slip the surly bonds of Earth. Such a long runway,
and so little of it needed.

The MiG sliced through the cold air like a scalpel through
skin. The cold air was dense, and provided more lift, virtually
vaulting her into the air.

His orders had been explicit. Once they were clear of the
Armenian airfield, there would be no further contact from any
of the air controllers. The forces on the ground were simply
told that he was a military aircraft on independent operations.

"So far, so good," Greene said over ICS. "Now, as long as
the Armenian's intelligence is good, we're okay."

The photographs Russo had showed them were obviously
taken from a satellite. The resolution was grainy and the details
less distinct than Tombstone expected from American satellite
shots. At first, he was inclined to chalk that off to inferior
technology, and then he caught himself. Would Americans
show the very best satellite shots to a foreign national? No.
Tombstone knew better than that from countless Allied and
NATO briefings. Even the closest allies were shown products
that did not reveal the full capabilities of the system. Why
would foreign nations do anything else?

So, Tombstone had fished delicately for details, asking questions about the better photographs. Russo had answered each
question with more detail. Perhaps it was ground intelligence,
but Tombstone doubted it. The Russian fighter-jock priest
knew more than he was telling. And, had their situations been
reversed, Tombstone would have done exactly the same thing.

"A little late to be worrying about the intell, isn't it?" Tombstone asked.

"Better late than never," Greene grumbled.

And what was it with his young pilot? For the last twenty-
four hours he'd been in a surly mood. Not openly disrespectful
or contentious, but Tombstone could tell he had something on
his mind. A less than successful encounter with one of the
Armenia women he'd been introduced to? Or maybe a touch
of the flu—maybe even doubts about his mission. Well, whatever it was, he better not let it affect his performance in the
backseat.

Chechen Camp
1810 local (GMT +4)

Warrant Officer Joseph Starskii had never intended to be a rebel. Most certainly, he had not intended to be part of a losing rebel force trapped in a makeshift camp, working on radar that had been modern during Stalin's days, and under the command of officers and senior warrant officers far more brutal than those he'd known in the Russian Naval Air Service. He most certainly had never planned on military field rations as his primary subsistence.

Starskii had been comfortably retired from the service for three years and living in his native Chechnya. Sure, there were food and fuel shortages, but he had a hard time imagining any part of the world where that wasn't so. He had a small garden, a few chickens, and, while it was hardly a luxurious or even dependable life, there were no inspections, no officers, and nobody shooting at him.

All that had changed during the first Chechen rebellion. Momentarily caught up in the furor of patriotism sweeping across the area, he had reported as ordered to the rebel commander. Once they'd found out that he could not only operate a radar but repair one as well, his fate had been sealed.

The rebel forces had spent the last five days on full alert, and the strain was starting to show. Tempers flared, careless accidents happened, and conditions were made no easier by cold military rations as their only food, and by rudimentary sanitary facilities. They smelled of too many men too long unshowered and the stench filled their operations center, although you didn't notice after the first thirty minutes. But the initial shock of it during the moments you first walked inside was enough to stun you. It made concentrating on briefings difficult.

Even knowing they might be attacked at any moment did little to increase the state of alertness. There was only so long you could run on adrenaline, only so long, and they'd passed that point weeks ago. Now, it was a matter of conserving resources, waiting for the moment you had to act or die.

Starskii checked the contact on the screen, noting that it was radiating the appropriate IFF signal for a civilian airliner, Aeroflot, and their location matched flight plans already on file. They were the same flights he'd seen on the last two watches, and there was nothing out of the ordinary.

Suddenly, from the front of the room, he heard raised voices. Both were readily recognizable. One was his immediate supervisor, the watch officer, and the other was their operational commander. Comrade General Korsov.

The watch officer wasn't a bad guy. They'd shared a few drinks off duty and had cautiously felt each other out on their respective views on the Chechen forces and prospects. Under different circumstances, they would have been close friends.

Korsov, however, was another matter altogether. The few times Starskii had encountered him, it had had the unexpected result of refiring his passion for the Chechen cause. Korsov represented everything bad Starskii had ever seen in the Russian Naval Air Force.

"I don't care who told you, it was still a violation of operational security," Korsov shouted. "If we are so sloppy with planning, how will we be during the execution?"

Starskii's supervisor's voice was at first placating, then defensive. "How can you expect us to do our jobs if we don't have adequate information? If we're not notified when you expect to launch, we would assume that you were hostile air."

"You would have provided confirmation of my flight's identity," the Russian shouted. "And now, you fool, you have compromised the entire evolution."

"I have compromised? Sir, I was simply told that your aircraft would be departing this evening."

"And who did *you* tell?" The Russian's voice grew louder as he turned to face the operations center.

Starskii ducked down behind his consul, hoping to avoid notice. Yes, he had been one of the ones told, since his sector of airspace would be involved. A sensible precaution, and he'd thought no more of it.

Within moments, Korsov loomed over him. "And you—what do you know about the flight plans for this evening?"

Reflexive self-preservation immediately took over. "Nothing, sir. The only thing scheduled is an Aeroflot flight or two, but they are all well north of us." Starskii stared into the Russian's eyes, frightened to his very soul. Korsov had dark, penetrating eyes that seemed to peer into his brain. Korsov knew he was lying—Starskii was certain of it.

To his surprise and relief, the general grunted and turned away. He turned back to the Starskii's supervisor. "Who, then?"

To Starskii's relief, the supervisor immediately took his cue. "No one, sir. They would have been told at the appropriate time."

A long silence followed.

Had Starskii not been so involved in trying to watch the argument without being detected, he might have noticed a small air contact wink into being at the very eastern edge of his area. He might have seen it grow two or three pixels stronger for just a moment then fade away. He might have wondered what caused it.

But he never, ever, would have interrupted the argument taking place to report it.

MiG 101
1814 local (GMT +4)

The gentle warble of the MiG's ECM detection gear was markedly different from that of a Tomcat. Tombstone heard Greene swear softly as he fumbled with unfamiliar dials. The frequency of the detection was displayed on the edge of Tombstone's HUD.

"Standard ground search radar," Greene said finally. Tombstone had already figured that out from the parameters.

"They got us yet?"

"I don't think so. It looks like it's just in general search mode. The thing is, Tombstone, they didn't brief us on any ground station search radar. And if they didn't tell us about that, what else didn't they tell us about?"

"Like what?"

"Like ground-to-air missiles, maybe."

Tombstone held his temper. There was no point in bitching about it, and it wasn't unreasonable to be detected by radar. It was probably just a small airfield, maybe just a tower, that handled cross-continent flights. "We'll deal with what's there, Jeremy. Is it in targeting mode?"

"No."

"Is it one of the radars normally associated with a mobile antiair platform?"

"I don't know that that matters," Greene said, his voice growing cold. "It may not be directly slave to one, but it could be used by any of them. Even a Stinger could get some initial indications off of one. And the Stinger has a two-mile range and we're going to be well within that on our final approach."

Tombstone felt his irritation growing, more at Greene than at the prospect of antiair defenses. The latter he'd expected—the former he didn't. All aviators were capable of compartmentalizing their minds, putting aside any other concerns and focusing on the task at hand. There was no threat near—and Greene knew that Tombstone knew that. So, why all this flack in the cockpit?

"Jeremy—just shut the hell up," Tombstone said with a cold note of authority in his voice. "We've got a mission to fly. Whatever other problems there are, we'll settle them when we get back on the ground. Got it?"

"Got it. Sir."

"Time on top?"

"Ten minutes. Sir. All the landmarks may look a little different." Greene's voice was coldly professional now.

"Roger," Tombstone acknowledged. Turning to the east to slip out of the radar envelope would add a degree of difficulty to their run, but not an insurmountable one. By losing altitude now and using the hills to block the radar signals, Tombstone hoped to be able to approach undetected for a longer period of time.

At least by the Chechens. But the Russians, ah—that is a different story, isn't it? The land bases will see us coming, and getting through is going to depend on whether or not our Armenian friends can convince them that we're a routine flight. And, on whether they're loyal to a bad guy.

Well, there was no help for it now. He wasn't going to cancel the mission just because there was an air search radar they didn't know about.

Chechen Base
1815 local (GMT+4)

"You are relieved," Korsov said coldly. Starskii peeked up over his consul, trying not to be caught snooping. Since they had moved away from his consul, their voices had been quieter for a time. From what he could gather, Korsov did not completely believe his supervisor's explanation.

"I did nothing wrong, sir," the superior said, an almost desperate note in his voice. They were committed now to the story that he told, and it was clear that he intended to justify himself when the wiser course might have been to simply roll on his back and whine.

A sudden sharp spike of noise echoed through the compartment. Starskii's jaw dropped. Korsov had slapped the supervisor across the face, moving with such lightning speed as to be scarcely detectable.

"You are relieved," Korsov said. Starskii saw Korsov examining the room, carefully evaluating each man there. Finally, Korsov pointed at Starskii. "You. Come here."

Starskii moaned, his stomach whirling and churning. He walked on unsteady feet over to the two. His superior refused to look at him. "Yes, sir?"

"As of this moment, you are to assume his duties." Korsov peered closely at him. "What is your name?"

"Joseph Starskii, General." Cold swept over him, radiating up from his gut, and threatening to make him lose the heavy, indigestible rations he'd consumed just hours before. "Sir, I think there are others more qualified."

Korsov stepped closer, and Starskii felt the heat radiating off him. It was as though Korsov were superhuman, possessing a metabolism different from that of a normal person.

"Yes," he said, studying Starskii carefully. "But loyalties still means a great deal to me, do you understand? And if you are to be loyal, I would prefer it to be to me."

He knew! He knew I lied, and yet he let me live. Relief rushed over him.

"Come," Korsov said, drawing him out of earshot of the others. Two military police hustled his former supervisor out of the room. "We must talk."

Starskii could feel everyone else trying very carefully not

to see him. Eyes were averted, heads turned away. Whatever mistake he had committed, they wished to be careful to avoid it.

"You understand my concern over the compromise of this mission, yes?" Korsov asked softly. His eyes bore into the uneasy air traffic controller.

"Yes, sir."

"Regardless of who you have or have not told, the fact is that the knowledge should have never been in this room. And now, since the remote movements are compromised, there must be a change of plans. I will be departing immediately. As supervisor, you'll tell no one of this. You will make sure that your actions are appropriate. When we appear on your radar scope, you'll order our contact not reported. Is that clear?"

"Very, sir."

"Ninety minutes later, you'll evacuate the center personnel and proceed immediately to the airfield. There, you'll board a transport and you will follow us to Bermuda. Is that clear?"

"Yes, commander."

"You have no questions, do you?" Korsov's voice made clear what the appropriate response was.

"No, comrade. In ninety minutes, then."

Starskii's answer appeared to satisfy Korsov. He rocked back slightly on his heels, his hands jammed deep in his pockets, and fixed the controller with a dark stare. "Succeed and you will be well rewarded. Disobey me and the consequences will be immediate and severe." Without further word he turned and stalked out of the room.

Starskii let out a long, shaky breath. Behind him, the normal sounds and voices of the mid watch resumed.

I will tell no one. But, in ninety minutes—well, I'll decide then what to do. Because with comrade general out of the room, and airborne himself, things are entirely different.

MiG 101
1820 local (GMT +4)

"Three minutes," Greene said. "Recommend you come left on course zero nine four for twenty seconds to retain original flight profile."

"Acknowledged." Yeah, that might be the better idea. Pop in between these hills, pick up his original route rather than deal with approaching from another angle. The more that was familiar, the better off they were.

Tombstone cut the nimble aircraft hard to the left, counted out loud, and turned just as Greene updated his advice. "Come right now to course zero one five, descend to two thousand feet."

"Time on top?"

"Ninety-two seconds," Greene answered. "Recommend descent to eight hundred feet in thirty seconds."

"Roger." *Just like the original profile said. Man, if I can't lay these bombs down his chimney, I'd better hang up my spurs.*

Tombstone rolled inverted to take a closer look at the terrain as he descended and located the landmarks they'd picked out from the satellite photos. They were flying a perfect approach, exactly on schedule. And, any second now, all hell was going to break loose.

Chechen Airstrip
1820 local (GMT+4)

Korsov climbed into the cockpit of his aircraft, feeling the cold seep through his flight suit and into his undergarments. Though winter was still a month off, already he could feel it coming on. All too soon, the wind would blow steadily, cold and harsh down from the north, and the snow would complicate even the simplest of maneuvers. The Russians had known for generations what the Germans learned the hard way—do not attack during the winter.

Ah, but winter in one place was not the same as winter every place, was it? He could almost feel the Bermuda sun on his hands, feel sunburned skin tight across his chest, marvel at sweat rolling down his back in the middle of November. Yes, Bermuda in winter was entirely different from Chechnya in winter.

His aircraft was already preflighted, and his assigned regular copilot waiting for him. Years ago, he been able to comfortably relinquish tasks such as preflight, checking fuel status, and such. Those who worked for him knew well the consequences of making a mistake.

He clambered up the boarding latter, feeling the cold reach deep into him through his fingertips. The plastic ejection seat was hard and unyielding. Before he even buckled his ejection harness, he reached down to flick the heater on. Hot air gouted out under his feet, and he felt the Bermuda sun on his skin again.

The flight line technician fastened his ejection harness, double-checked that the safety retaining pins were removed, showing them to Korsov for his inspection. Behind him, his copilot did the same. Then, as the technicians climbed down and, even before they were on the ground, bad guys slid the canopy forward and locked it into place.

In front of him, another ground traffic controller stood in front of the aircraft, lighted wands held steady in front of him. When all the other technicians cleared the area, Korsov was signaled to proceed, and then handed off along the line to a second technician, who guided them toward the runway. As he reached the apron, the second ground tech snapped off a sharp salute with his lighted wand and pointed toward the runway. Korsov turned and continued his taxi.

He paused for a moment at the end of the runway, stepped hard on the brakes, and ran the engines up to full military power. They sounded sweet, operating perfectly. There was no tower to control takeoffs or landing—they had all been killed during the first rebel attack on the airfield. Not that there was much need for them now—the only aircraft coming in or out were his, and he knew when each was scheduled.

It has not been a fatal mistake to warn base operations of his departure that afternoon, he admitted. He would have done so himself, but certainly not that far in advance. No, half an hour before his intended departure would be fine to prevent any confusion in the antiair batteries.

"Ready?" he asked his copilot.

"Yes, comrade," the man replied.

"Well, then . . ." He let off the brakes, and the MiG surged forward evenly. She bolted down the runway, gathering speed every second, and leaped in the air as though she were going home.

Their next stop would be in Bulgaria, both as a brief maintenance stop and to rendezvous with a squadron of MiGs that would be joining them there. Korsov wasn't entirely sure what Maskiro had told the squadron commander, a subordinate of his in the Black Sea Fleet, but Maskiro appeared confident that the MiGs would be there. He relayed that information to his copilot, who had not known until the time where they were headed, although he certainly had been able to guess the final destination.

"Comrade! Air contact, bearing one one zero, range six miles!"

An air contact? Nothing scheduled to be in this area. Perhaps a private aircraft?

"Speed, four hundred and twenty knots, altitude eighty seven hundred meters," the copilot continued, thus eliminating that possibility. "Comrade, it must be a military transport—there are no civilian flights scheduled."

It was just as he had feared—someone knew that he was leaving the airfield, someone knew.

His copilot's voice trembled. "Radar in search mode only, sir. No targeting. Should we radio a warning back to our operations center?"

They'd know in a few minutes. Know, and pay for their mistakes.

There had been no air transport scheduled to evacuate them in ninety minutes. In fact, there had been no provisions made for them at all. As he watched the unidentified aircraft descend, turning toward the air base, and then descend again, he knew exactly what it was. There was only one particular mission that fit that flight profile. Soon enough, the operations center would know as well.

"No," he said. "They have detected the contact on their own radar by now."

"But, sir, if they haven't, we must warn them." The copilot said disbelievingly.

A babble of voices, some shouting, some crying, came over the tactical frequency now. Korsov smiled grimly. There was no need to warn them now—they knew exactly what was coming.

Chechen Base
1821 local (GMT +4)

Starskii stared at the screen. There was no doubt in his mind what the blip represented, not with that flight profile. Even now it was decreasing speed, descending again, and any second it would—

"Everyone out!" he shouted, his gaze still glued to the radar screen. Korsov's aircraft was just rolling off the runway, and they surely must see the incoming contact. And would have seen it before the controller, since his greater altitude was giving him a longer range. "There's only one target—I know what that is, on that flight profile. Everybody out! Get as far away as you can!"

The fifteen remaining watchstanders needed no further urging. They abandoned their consoles, some of them running away with headsets still on, and headed for the single door leading into the reinforced structure. From there, they raced down the short passageway separating the operations center from the unclassified portions of the building. A few shouted warnings to the others as they ran, but did not slow to assist them.

Once outside, they headed in various directions. Starskii himself ran straight ahead, heading for the gate, shouting at the guards to unlock it. They had no way of knowing he was the senior person in charge of the operations section and were slow to obey him. A few men ahead of him started climbing the fence, frantic to be clear of ground zero.

Even an Olympic medallist would not have been able to run fast enough to make any difference. The controller and his own compatriots might be battle-hardened soldiers, but they were hardly world-class runners. They ran nonetheless, praying, some of them for the first time in years, hoping against hope somehow to make it far enough away to survive.

MiG 101
1822 local (GMT +4)

Tombstone rolled back over into level flight and continued his descent. By now the targets were clearly visible just in front of them. It was a ramshackle cinder block building, the exterior in severe disrepair, and surrounded by a rusty chain link fence.

"Man, look at that," Greene said, leading forward and watching over Tombstone's shoulder. "They're running like ants."

"You would be, too." Tombstone was intent on making minor corrections to his lineup.

"For all the good it will do them," Greene said.

"Time to release?" Tombstone said.

"Ten, nine, eight . . ."

Tombstone stared forward, now close enough to see their faces. Without exception, stark terror distorted their features into something almost less than human. He felt a flash of pity for them, and then remembered the pictures of the dead civilians in Bermuda.

"Seven, six, five, four . . ."

Despite the best intentions of military men and women everywhere, it came down to this, didn't it? There was no way, despite the long-standing American dream, of limiting casualties to just the military. No way at all. And, no, the men running away from him below might not actually have been on the ground in Bermuda, but they were just as responsible for what had been done there as if they had been.

"Three, two . . ."

"Hunter, abort! Target is gone—repeat, your target is gone!" Russo's voice broke through the cockpit like a wave of cold water, shocking each man.

Without even acknowledging, Tombstone broke hard to the right.

"What are you doing?" Greene howled. "Tombstone, we're only two seconds—"

"You heard the man," Tombstone snapped. "There was only one real target on this mission, and he's gone."

"How do you know that? How do they know? What is this, waiting until the last minute? Hell, it would have been safer to release than to abort, you know that!"

"We have our orders. And we're going to follow them."

But—" Greene broke off as a movement on his screen caught his attention. "That must be him, Stony! That air contact—it's another MiG. We can catch him. We can put an end to this right now."

Tombstone knew Greene was right. That was their target flying the other MiG. It was close, so close—only one minute separated them. They were within range even now.

"Forget our load out?" Tombstone snapped.

Greene swore violently, directing his oaths equally at the Russians and the Armenians, and the ordnance techs who'd loaded the MiG only with ground attack weapons. Short of dropping an iron bomb on top of the other aircraft or ramming it, they had no way to attack. Even the nose gun had not been loaded.

Just then, a hard tone cut through the cockpit. It was louder and more insistent than the earlier ESM alarm. Tombstone glanced at the frequency and pulse rates on the alarm display, and knew immediately what it was.

"SAM! Get us out of here!" Greene shouted. "Tombstone, it's got a seeker head and—"

Tombstone broke hard to the right, and kicked the MiG into afterburner. He glanced down at his fuel gauge, keeping up his scan, absorbing all the information from all the sources immediately, integrating them into a coherent threat picture, and calculating his options without even being conscious of it.

He knew instinctively he could not outrun the missile. They were too close, and had too little time. And, if he used the afterburner now, there was a good chance they would not be able to return to base.

"Do you see it?" Tombstone demanded, keeping his attention on the terrain ahead. They were now at 500 feet and still descending.

"No, I—yes! I got it, ten o'clock low. It's got a lock!"

"That's what they're supposed to do. Options?"

"Faster!"

Tombstone didn't answer. Ahead of them were the low hills that had shielded them from the air search radar as they were approaching. Now, they would serve a similar function, only in reverse. But the descent angles would have to be calculated perfectly. Since the missile was rapidly gaining altitude, it would have a look-down capability that would negate the masking effect of the hills. If he could just entice it down, then cut back behind the terrain, it might work.

"What are you doing?" Greene screamed. "You're heading back toward it!"

"Tell me when it turns!" Tombstone demanded. He pulled the MiG into a tighter turn, decreasing the range to the missile, dividing his attention between the HUD, the terrain, and the missile. This close to the ground, a hill could kill him just as fast as a missile.

"It's got us, it's got us." The tone sounding in the cockpit increased in frequency and pulse rate, indicating the missile had a lock on them.

"Hold on!" Now the trick would be to see if he could shake it.

Tombstone put the MiG nose down, still in afterburner, and headed for the deck. Eighty feet, seventy feet—Tombstone yanked up hard at forty feet. He maintained level flight for a few moments, and watching for the missile to react.

"It's coming after us," Greene said, his voice disbelieving. "Damn you, you—"

Tombstone dropped the MiG's nose down hard again, grunting to maintain the blood flow to his brain, then jerked the MiG back up. Already he could feel the G forces eating away at his vision, threatening to rob him of the only sense that would keep them alive. Greene was unprepared for the new maneuver, and let out a moan of protest.

"Stay with me!" Tombstone snapped. The missile was closing, only 200 feet behind him now, and just for a moment he felt despair. It wouldn't work—there wasn't enough time—they would have to punch out, take their chances on the ground, which was no chance at all, not at this altitude, not in Chechnya.

"Oh," Greene moaned. "It's—it's still coming, Tombstone." His voice, while slightly fuzzy, contained none of his earlier panic.

"Hold on. This is our only chance." Tombstone dropped the nose of the MiG down and headed for the hill in front of him.

The area around base was composed of a mixture of ridges and valleys, with hardwood trees and pines dominating the hills. The hardwood trees had already started to lose their leaves, but the evergreens formed a solid line thirty to forty feet above the cold ground. Tombstone aimed directly at a group of pines. At max speed, the deciduous trees were little more than sticks against the gray sky, and the evergreens were easier to see.

"No!" Greene howled. "No, you can't—"

"I can't," Tombstone screamed, shouting not only at his backseater but against the Fates as well. "I can!"

The trees were so close, too close. At the last second, he yanked the MiG over on her side and pulled her up hard. Almost too late—the aircraft jolted violently as the top branches smacked against her wingtip. She started to cartwheel, but for the first time Tombstone was part of her, melded to metal as he'd never been before. Her wings part of his body, her hydraulics lines and cables his blood vessels and ligaments. He reacted without having to think, countering the aircraft's insistence that she must rotate, *had to,* pulling her out of it by demanding more of her control surfaces and engines than anyone had ever done before.

In a Tomcat, he would have been dead. He knew that with cold certainty. And even in the MiG, so light, so responsive, so willing, it was a close thing. Time stopped and the trees seemed to creep past him. He had time to examine each branch, each needle, it seemed.

Greene was screaming, no words just inchoate sounds of terror and protest, scrabbling forward with his hands as though to reach for the controls but too panicked to remember that he was strapped in. As the MiG careened past—*through*—the trees, Tombstone felt nothing but cold, utter, focused peace. If it was to end here, it would end. If not, it wouldn't. Nothing else mattered, not Tomboy, not the screams coming from the back seat, and least of all his own body. All that mattered was that he fly, right now, right this second, better than he'd ever flown before.

Suddenly, they were clear of the trees, climbing hard, the dense cold air caressing the fuselage and urging the aircraft to fly, fly. Time resumed its normal progression, and the feeling of detachment started to disappear. He noticed dispassionately that his hands were trembling ever so slightly at the fingertips, the only sign of the adrenaline that was flooding through him.

A hard blast of air rocked the aircraft, threatening to destroy her precarious aerodynamic stability. He calmed her as he would an unsettled horse, letting his hands and feet form the words on her controls.

"It detonated! It hit the trees! Or the ground! I don't know which—oh, dear God." Greene was almost sobbing. "There was nothing I could do. I was—I was—" Greene's voice dissolved into sobs.

It struck Tombstone at that moment precisely what Greene's problem was. It had nothing to do with courage or with his confidence in Tombstone. No. That wasn't it at all.

The problem was simply that Greene was a pilot. And no pilot, no matter how good or how bad, no matter how brave or how timid, ever tolerated being a passenger.

A pang struck Tombstone. He had done this. He had asked another pilot to fly back seat, to go against every instinct and reflex in his body.

Would he have done it, if asked?

I wouldn't have. I wouldn't have lasted as long as he has. No way.

"As soon as we get back on the ground, I'm getting you an aircraft," Tombstone said, pretending that Greene had not been crying. "I should never had done this, asked you to fly back seat this long. And we're heading for the *Jefferson*. You want a fight, I'll get you a fight."

No answer. Tombstone didn't expect one. Words were cheap, but he'd prove he meant what he said as soon as they were back on the ground.

TWELVE

Sarah Wexler stormed down the passageway to the Oval Office, past Secret Service agents and the chief of staff and the press secretary and past a group of Boy Scouts waiting in the hallway. The head of the president's protection details stepped in front of her. "Just what the hell are you doing, Madame Ambassador?" he asked.

She stood with a steely glare. "Going to see the president. As is my right."

"He's not free right now," Leahy replied, trying to gently ease her away from the door, and applied more force. "Come on—you know the drill," he cried, exasperated, as she resisted.

"The drill doesn't count today," she snapped.

Leahy motioned to the other agents now standing behind the Ambassador, wrapped his arms around her, and lifted her off the ground with a groan.

Enraged, Wexler twisted her body and snapped her leg back, flexing it at the knee. She connected. Leahy let out the strangled yelp, stumbled, but didn't put her down.

"What the hell is the meaning of this?" the president said, stepping out of the Oval Office and shoving his way through a crowd of Secret Service agents who were increasingly convinced that the Ambassador to the United Nations had lost her mind. "Sarah, would you mind explaining yourself?"

"Tell your goons to put me down," she snapped.

"Put her down, Jim. The Ambassador isn't going to assassinate me."

"Maybe." But, with a grateful sigh, Leahy deposited her on the floor, "You might want to talk to her about protocol, Mr. President."

"Among other things." The president motioned her into the office and stepped aside to allow her to proceed him. Two Secret Service agents followed them and positioned themselves rather more closely to Wexler than was usual.

"Mr. President, you've got to turn *Jefferson* loose on Bermuda, and you've got to do it now. They've already got one squadron on the ground. Once they build up air superiority, we're going to have a bitch of a time taking the island back."

The president shook his head. "That would put all those tourists at risk."

"All those American tourists, you mean."

"If it comes to that."

She studied him for a moment, disgusted by what she saw. She had known that the president had a strong political side, but never had it been so obvious. Over the last year, as the time for his re-election grew closer, she sensed a shift in his values, a cold distancing from what was actually right and wrong in the world. She had ignored it—had made her staff ignore it, too, because it would have been impossible to acknowledge what he was becoming—or whom he had been all the time—and continue to be his representative in the United Nations.

But now, it comes down to this. "It would be very difficult for you to be re-elected if that many tourists were killed during your term of office, wouldn't it?" She said it carefully, with no rancor, her words precise and clear.

Anger flashed on his face, to be replaced immediately by a blank expression. "Now, Sarah. That's a bit unfair, don't you think?"

She shook her head. "Not from where I stand. But suppose I grant you that this is purely a military decision. And suppose I assume that this is a decision you made after consultation with your secretary of defense and secretary of state—not after talking to your campaign manager." She held up one hand to forestall comment. "This is how I read it. There's a squadron of MiGs on the ground in Bermuda. I learned this morning that another is on its way. If you allow them to establish a couple of squadrons on the island, along with their antiair defenses, there will be no way we can gain air superiority immediately. And without air superiority, there's little hope of dislodging them. Bermuda will become a frontier for Russia, a base like the Philippines was for us. Now, if that happens before the election, how do you think the American people will react?"

"There will be no strike on Bermuda," he said at last, looking away as he did so. "Don't you think I have discussed these options with my staff?"

"Yes, I think you have. And I think you have made the wrong decision."

He stood suddenly, turned his back to her to the window overlooking the Rose Garden. A few blooms still flourished among the bushes, but most had shed their flowers as well as their leaves in preparation for the winter. Were there specific orders to pick up all the rose petals as they fell, she wondered. And where did all the flowers go—were they used for special presentations, to honor those visiting this seat of power? Or, were they merely for show, never used, simply allowed to bloom and die?

"Mr. President," she said, a new note of formality in her voice. "You and I have seen what our military forces are capable of. Sir, we spent a lot of time and money developing the most potent systems in the world. Use it now, Mr. President. Whatever they launch from Bermuda, the Aegis cruiser can take it out. I'm sure your advisers have told you that the resulting explosion will neutralize antibiological or chemical threat. The nuclear material would be dispersed harmlessly over the sea. Send in the SEALs, disarm what you can, and let the Navy take care of the rest. That's the way it's got to be, Mr. President."

"And if I disagree?" he asked, his back still to her.

"Then you will be remembered as the antithesis of John F. Kennedy," she said grimly. "You have been an excellent president in peace—yes, even when regional conflicts have broken out I know you have the mettle to withstand this, to react appropriately, Mr. President. I've seen you in action before. And I don't understand why you have taken the wrong path now—no, that's not true. I understand what is on your mind, I think. But I'm asking you to reconsider your decision. I have no leverage, no way to force you to. But you know I'm right."

He turned then, and she was struck by the anguish on his face. "If I lose the election, there is no hope. You know who the other party has nominated—can you see him in this White House? Making the decisions that you and I have had to make over the past three and a half years?" He shook his head. "No, for the good of the nation, I must consider my re-election.

"Then, you will be remembered as a president who failed to act. Who allowed a hostile government to establish an outpost virtually off our coast. And what will be next—Cuba? Once you have established this precedent, it will be impossible to back down from it. That will be your legacy, Mr. President. But if you do what is right, the people will understand."

The president turned to Leahy. "I suppose you agree with her?"

Leahy looked as though he wished desperately to be anywhere else except where he was. But he cleared his throat, fixed his gaze on the president, and said firmly, "Yes, Mr. President. I do."

A long, contemplative silence settled over the four. Wexler felt no pressure to speak. She had said her piece, done what she felt was best for the nation, and she recognized that Leahy had taken a similar risk. Now it was up to the one man the people had trusted to preserve their nation.

"Get me the secretary of defense and the secretary of state," the president said finally. "Now."

USS Jefferson
500 miles west of Bermuda
1000 local (GMT-4)
Sunday, September 12

The message arrived simultaneously at all the ships in the battle group. The USS *Jefferson* and her battle group commander were the only action addees. The rest of the ships were addressed for information purposes only, but it was information they greatly appreciated getting. Knowing now what the admiral would be planning would help them prepare for their own part.

The message flashed first over the computer system, ahead of informal traffic, warning of formal traffic to follow. The message was brief and to the point.

> DO NOT ALLOW ANY MORE RUSSIAN AIRCRAFT TO LAND IN BERMUDA. COMMENCE PLANNING TO DEFEND AGAINST MISSILE LAUNCH FROM BERMUDA, FOLLOWED BY ESTABLISHING AIR SUPERIORITY AND RETAKING THE ISLAND WITH THE ASSISTANCE OF BRITISH FORCES. SPECIAL OPERATIONS PLANS FOLLOW BY SEPARATE MESSAGE.

Coyote was in his cabin, having a late lunch, when the message arrived in TFCC. He frowned as he heard howls coming from his watchstanders, and was just about to go see what the hell was happening when his chief of staff burst in, a grim expression on his face. He handed Coyote the message. "We're going in, Admiral. Finally."

"About time," Coyote grumbled, as he scanned the brief message. "Let me know when the detailed order comes in. In the meantime, I want all department heads and COs on board in my conference room, thrashing out final details. We knew this was coming. Now, it's just a matter of making sure we've covered all the bases."

"He's putting a lot of faith in the Aegis, isn't he?" his chief of staff asked.

Coyote nodded. "With good reason. It flies, it dies, according to the Aegis community. I don't think the stakes have ever been quite so high, but if I know those cowboys over on the ship, they're just itching to take a shot at this."

Coyote went back to his lunch, figuring that the oldest adage of warfare still applied: Eat and sleep when you have a chance, because you won't later on. He just polished off the last of his hamburger and contemplated a second order of french fries—his cooks, he knew, would make them, but it would take a few minutes. What if he didn't want them by the time they were done? Was he really prepared to deal with the slightly reproachful look on the chief's face if he wasn't?

No, he decided, he was not. He patted his stomach, still flat and ridged. He was determined not to gain weight on this cruise. Maybe, some night when they were all tired and on edge, he would ask the chief to bring french fries for everyone. Yes, that would do it.

Outside his cabin, in the admiral's conference room, he could hear a low murmur of voices. There was an occasional victory cry. He smiled at that. They were ready to go, had been since the news was announced. They would be polishing their plans to cope with any last-minute requirements from the president, but in his heart he felt unleashed.

USS Seawolf
1100 local (GMT-4)

Forsythe studied the crew. Red-rimmed eyes, willing but exhausted, stared back at him. After three days, the men were starting to look unkempt. Not that their appearances were a reflection of what was in their hearts. Forsythe knew that they would willingly follow him anywhere.

But should he ask it of them? For perhaps the millionth time since Cowlings had died, Forsythe wished for someone around to ask what to do.

But there was no one. Even the chief, as much insight as he had into the crew and operations, could not help him on this one.

They're following me. Not the chief, not Cowlings, not the real captain. I'm the reason they're awake, at their stations, and ready to fight. A sense of awe, of crushing responsibility filled his heart. To hold their lives in his hands, knowing that his decisions would either get them killed or keep them alive, was a sacred trust past all understanding. They were his crew, *his.*

And, I am the only one who can stand them down. They won't take it from anyone else.

The USS *Nashville* was due in their area in six hours. The reasonable thing to do would be to withdraw, retreat to a safe distance away from this last submarine's operating area, and wait for *Nashville* to show up. A fresh submarine, one with a fully manned and rested crew, was the weapon of choice in this instance.

They had come so far, done so much with so little—but there was a time to call it quits. That time was now.

Forsythe took a deep breath, ready to give the order. It would be a disappointment to many, coupled with a relief they dared not expressed. He would let them grumble about the order, insisting that they were ready to go on, as he knew they were.

But before his lips formed the words, a hard, shimmering *ping* reverberated through every scrap of metal on the ship. Once, faintly, then again, harder and louder. The tone shifted up, the beats coming closer together.

"Captain, Sonar. I classify this contact as a Soviet Yankee-class submarine. Unable at this time to determine whether she is a ballistic missile boat or one of the modified guided missile ones."

"Make your depth twelve hundred feet," Forsythe ordered, now moving almost automatically through the process of breaking contract, evading and setting up for the kill. "Chief, how are we doing on decoys and noisemakers?"

"Two decoys and seven noisemakers left."

"Fine. Have a man standing by with them." Forsythe summoned up a determined tone from some deep inner resource he didn't know he had. "Okay, men. We've done this before. Let's do it again." For a moment, he wished he could think of some more ringing words that would echo in their minds, but what he said was evidently enough. It fired them up, their attention now focused on the task and away from the fear, and commands and reports flowed smoothly around him as though he were a boulder in the middle of a stream, observing it all, taking it in, letting it flow over and around him.

By now, the chief was accustomed to the way he worked. He took the submarine down smartly, executed two sharp turns to generate masses of bubbles, then slowed and dove quickly below the layer. The sonar pings followed them, wavered, and faded out as the warmer water above them deflected the acoustic energy toward the surface.

"Sir, recommend we kick her up to fifteen knots then circle around behind."

"Very well. Make it so." And why wasn't there anyone to give *him* a pat on the back, to remind *him* of how much they accomplish, to inspire *him* to go on? Forsythe rubbed his hand across his eyes, which were dry and scratchy.

"Here." The doctor appeared at his side and pressed something into his hand. "This will perk you up."

The mug contained fresh, hot coffee, the steam still rising off its surface, the color dark and oily as only submariners can make it. Forsythe glanced up at the man in surprise, then shook his head. Maybe he had misjudged him. They had had their differences of opinion, but when it came right down to it, the doctor was a submariner, too. He understood what they were up against.

"No drinking during general quarters," Forsythe said, reluctantly. He could almost taste the dark bite of caffeine, feel the warmth trace its way down his throat and spread through his body. But he couldn't, not now. Not when the other men were not allowed any. He started to shove the cup away, but the doctor touched his wrist lightly. "I think you can break the rules just this one time, Captain. Consider it medicinal. Besides, I brought enough for everyone." He held up a carafe, and stack of foam cups.

"Very well." Forsythe could resist no longer. He lifted the cup, took a second to savor the aroma, his gaze still fixed on the sonar screen as he watched the ship maneuver. He took the first sip, held it in his mouth for a moment, and reveled in the heat. He swallowed, took another gulp, and then another. Finally, when he finished, he passed the cup back to the doctor.

"Steady on zero nine zero, speed fifteen," the chief said. "There's no indication that they see us, Captain. Recommend another three miles before we come above the layer."

"Very well. Make it so."

This doesn't sound like me. My tone—and where did I learn those words? But, it sounds right. At least, they act like I'm saying the right words. Good thing they don't know. . . .

He knew a moment of panic as he remembered how quickly Cowlings had died. One second alive, studying a problem just as he was at this moment. A second later, falling against the bulkhead and passing out.

What? He reached out to steady himself against the same bulkhead, then felt a flash of surreal fear. What the hell was happening?

"Sir, are you all right?" The chief was at his side, anchoring him to navigation plot. "Captain, what's wrong?"

"I—I don't know. All at once my balance is off." Cold horror ran through Forsythe as an ugly possibility came to mind. He shook the chief's arm off, and turned to stare in disbelief at the doctor. The man was watching him, his face expressionless.

"He did this," Forsythe said, aware now how seriously his words were slurred. "What did you put in the coffee?"

"Nothing, Captain." The doctor studied him for a moment, then nodded. "It's just coffee. Perhaps you're more tired than you realize."

Rage swept through Forsythe, sweeping away the drowsiness creeping upon him. "You fool! Don't you realize what's happening? Get me something to counteract this—and get it now."

"Counteract what?" the doctor asked quietly. "All I see is an overstressed junior officer finally succumbing to the pressure."

"Oh, yeah?" the chief asked. He picked up the coffee cup, examined it, and turned to the quartermaster serving as navigator. "Bubble wrap. Completely. I don't want anything to evaporate." He turned to glare at the doctor. "I think the Navy lawyers might want to take a look at this.

"You're just as bad as he is," the doctor said, a note of triumph in his voice. "We've got no business being out here, not like this." He gestured toward the rest of the group. "How could you do this to them? They can't fight, not with him in charge."

From his belt, the chief produced a set of handcuffs. He moved swiftly, like a cat, and before the doctor could voice a protest, he snapped one cuff around the doctor's wrist, lifted it to a chill water pipe, and snapped the other cuff on. He stepped back and looked at his work with satisfaction. "That will hold you. He took the coffee pot that the doctor had brought in and set it safely aside. "Nobody touches that," he ordered, then he turned back to Forsythe. "Sir—how are you?"

Forsythe smiled wanly. "I've been better."

Black waves swarmed over him, threatening to swallow his consciousness. He fought them off, tried to stay focused on his anger, but the darkness crept ever closer, settling down on him in layers, blanking off the edges of his mind. He couldn't succumb, not now. Not with the Yankees on their tail.

"Do you realize what you've done?" the chief said softly, glaring at the doctor. "You may have killed us all."

Think, think. He had to pay attention—he couldn't afford to lose focus. Not now. Something warm pressed itself against his hand and he opened his eyes, surprised to find that they'd been closed. Another cup of coffee. He pulled back immediately.

"I made this one myself, sir," the chief said. "Go on—this one's okay."

The same dark, earthy smell, the same sense of anticipation, but this time tinged with wariness. He glanced over the chief, then realized he had to trust someone. The chief had done nothing so far to warrant suspicion, nothing at all.

Forsythe took a large gulp, and another. It seared the delicate lining of his mouth, his throat, and the caffeine immediately seemed to insinuate itself into his body. He almost choked on the bitterness—it was at least twice as strong as any coffee he'd ever had on board the submarine, and that was saying a lot.

Nevertheless, the effects were almost immediate. He felt the sudden rush of energy, felt the pressure in his head and chest increase as the caffeine constricted his blood vessels and raised his blood pressure. No, the effects of the drug weren't gone, but he felt capable of fighting them off now. He pushed himself away from the navigator's table, figuring that having to stand up would help keep him alert. "Situation?"

"You were only out a couple of minutes, sir. We're continuing north, still below the layer. We should turn again in about five minutes, according to the original plan."

Forsythe paced back and forth, aware that the jitters were sweeping over him. It wasn't comfortable, but he welcomed it. Better nerves than sleeping. "Run me through the contacts again," he ordered.

Jacob's screen showed five contacts of interest. "Here's the battle group," he said, pointing to the west. "I imagine they're going to stay a safe distance out from shore, especially after that last torpedo attack. In here," he continued, tapping an area just off the coast of Bermuda, "I think is a couple of large Russian ships. They're at anchorage, not moving, so I'm not holding a lot off them, but they're still there."

"How far off the coast?"

"About a mile. Well within their landing capabilities for small craft, or for an easy dash in to the beach if they want to offload heavy equipment. And, finally, our playmate," he said, indicating the last position that they held on the Yankee. "Of course, all of this is ten minutes out of date," he said in an apologetic way. "As long as we're below the layer, I'm not holding them."

"Okay, I got it." Forsythe turned to the chief. "Continue on our original plan. Then surface at the indicated time—real quietly, if you catch her napping. Keep in mind that this is a whole new game. The Yankee may be old, but she's probably been backfitted with a lot of acoustics gear. And some of those crews have spent a lot of time in this part of the ocean. But, if we can get to her before she knows we're here, we can take her."

The chief nodded. "Time now, sir."

"Very well. Take us up, Chief."

Forsythe kept his gaze locked on the sonar screen as the ship crept slowly up. Every sonarman was in the compartment, listening, waiting, trying to catch the first sniff of the Yankee. They came up slowly, bare steerageway, so that the noise of their propeller did not give them away.

"Eleven hundred," Jacobs murmured. "Any second now, sir."

A hard blast of noise echoed through the submarine.

"Shit!" Jacob said. He ripped off the headphones, an expression of pain on his face. "She's got us!"

"Snapshot," Forsythe ordered. "Two torpedoes, bearing-only launch."

Jacob's fingers were flying over the fire control panel, dialing in the bearings and launching the torpedoes even while another hard blast of acoustic energy buffeted them.

The Yankee's sonar drowned out the noise of the torpedoes' launching, but the acoustic gear quickly picked it up. They saw their torpedo start up, head down the bearing, and turn toward the Yankee.

"How did they get us?" Forsythe demanded.

"Probably dragging her tail, sir," Jacobs said. "Stayed above the layer herself so we couldn't hear her, but going slow enough to drop her towed array down below the layer. It takes some fancy footwork, but we could do it. I guess they can, too, because there's no way she was below the layer. No way at all, sir."

"Torpedo inbound!" Renny shouted. "Recommend evasive maneuvers, Captain!"

"Chief, take us down to two thousand feet," Forsythe ordered. Then a hard turn, wait one minute, then an emergency blow to get us back up above the layer. With any luck, she'll try to follow us down."

"Two—no, four torpedoes inbound, sir. Same bearing." Renny said.

"Captain, the water here is only three thousand feet deep," the chief said.

"Plenty of room," Forsythe assured him.

But it wasn't, not really. Not for what he wanted to accomplish.

Forsythe grabbed onto the chill water line as the submarine tipped nose down and headed for the depths. They could hear the noise of the torpedo on the speaker faintly now, growing louder. The beat of its propeller mixed with the two the *Seawolf* launched, until they could no longer tell which one was from them and which one was after them.

Just as the submarine passed 2,000 feet, the chief jerked the sub into a hard left turn. Just as she steadied up, Forsythe ordered, "Emergency blow!" The chief turned to stare at him, incredulous. Forsythe just nodded.

"Emergency blow, aye, sir." The chief turned a valve.

Compressed air flooded the ballast tanks, first reversing the submarine's speed and momentum, then thrusting her toward the surface. The effect was almost immediate.

There was a distant sound of an explosion, and Forsythe shot a questioning look at Jacob.

"Theirs," the sonarman assured him. "One down, three to go." Forsythe wasn't so sure he would ever be able to tell the difference between torpedoes by audio alone, but he took Jacob's word for it.

"And ours?"

"Still heading for her," Jacobs assured him. "Another ninety seconds."

"Passing five hundred feet and ascending," the planesman sang out. "Passing four hundred.

"Hold on, everybody. This is going to be rough," the chief warned.

All at once, the water around the submarine seemed to disappear, her momentum changed, and Forsythe knew what was happening. She was hanging bow up in the air, trying to fly, but not built for it. The odd sensation lasted just a moment, and then she slammed back down in the water, entering the water with a force that she hadn't experienced since her original sea trials.

The shock from the impact ran through Forsythe like an electrical charge. "No," Forsythe moaned, as a new wave of blackness threatened to overwhelm him. "Not now."

"We can't keep this up forever, Ensign" the chief warned.

From captain, to sir, to ensign again. "I know, I know," Forsythe said, his mind working frantically. *Expect the unexpected, expect the unexpected*—"Chief! Give me a course to the nearest Russian landing ship."

"Zero eight four, ten thousand yards," the chief said without even having to look at the plot. "But, sir . . ."

"Come left, steer course zero eight four—flank speed, Chief." Forsythe could feel the certainty coursing through him.

To his credit, although his face was doubtful, the chief did not even hesitate. Seconds later, the submarine was headed into the heart of the Russian task force at flank speed.

There was no need for conversation now, no need for orders or advice or reports. This was simply a flat-out race for their lives—8,000 tons of submarine shoving her way through the sea at her absolute top speed, the fires of her nuclear reactor burning at 120 percent of capacity, the propeller biting hard into the water, getting a grip, the speed of the propeller at the propeller tips so great that the temporary vacuum sucked dissolved gases out of the water, creating cavitation.

Although the crew was silent, moving about the ship like ghosts, *Seawolf* was as noisy as he'd ever heard her. The reverberating rattles, creaks, and assorted complaints from joints and seams were frightening at the most visceral of levels. *Seawolf* was running for her life, her speed almost two knots above what she done during sea trials, every system redlined at max capacity and beyond.

There was no second chance. The three remaining torpedoes were gaining on them, following them with hard, icy pings, the scent of their prey hot in their electronic nostrils.

The graphic display spelled it all out. Ahead, shallow water, the massive bulk of the Russian transports. Behind, the Yankee submarine and three remaining small torpedoes that had barreled out from her.

"Two thousand," the chief said, his voice cold and professional. "Planesman, take us up ten feet."

"Ten feet, aye." The change in depth was not even perceptible.

Depth was crucial this close to the island. The continental slope crept up toward the coast, the shallow water a more dangerous environment. There were wrecks here, some of them still uncharted, and Forsythe and chief were doing their best to avoid them by maintaining some distance from the bottom while still trying to stay as deep as possible. The shallower they went, the less dense the water, and the more turns per knots of speed required.

Something slammed into the side of the submarine and traced its way down the hull, fingernails on a chalkboard. One sailor yelped, then fell quiet, his lips tightly compressed as though to hold in his fear. The rest of them were shaking.

"One thousand yards," the chief said.

Are we going to make it? Is it even going to work? The charts—how accurate are the water depths? I must be insane to try this—I must be insane. But if there's any other way, then I don't know about it. This is all we've got left.

The pings from the sonar were harder now, faster, excited. The torpedoes were actively homing, as well as following the wake and the acoustic signature of the submarine. There was no way they could miss the *Seawolf* now, no way at all. And their speed, while not as fast as the latest generation torpedoes, was more than sufficient to enable them to catch up.

"Five hundred yards."

"Make your depth one hundred and ten feet," Forsythe ordered. Assuming the Russian ships had a draft of thirty-two feet and the submarine eighty-five, that would give them just enough clearance to sneak by under the ships. Maybe. There was still too much he didn't know: exactly how much water the transport drew depended on how heavily laden she was, how much fuel she had on board, and whether or not there have been any design changes since the reference books were written.

"One hundred feet." For the first time, the chief's voice showed the tiniest shiver of emotion. Forsythe wasn't sure anyone else would have noticed.

Their own sonar showed the bulk of the transport ahead, a massive steel cliff in the water.

It was not the first prayer that Forsythe had murmured since they left port, but it was certainly the most heartfelt. Most of the crew was staring at the overhead, as thought they could see the giant ship overhead and somehow duck if they came too close.

And then they were under her, the pressure wave surrounding the submarine hitting the ship's beam and keel and the pressure forcing her down slightly. The water depth at this point was 140 feet, and there was no guarantee that the debris on the bottom wouldn't decrease that.

It was as though they could feel the ship overhead. The water around them was saturated with the sounds of machinery, stamping feet, almost with the sound of voices. They were so close that someone standing on the conning tower could have reached up to touch the barnacle-encrusted hull above them.

"Emergency back full," Forsythe ordered, and saw that hands were already poised over controls. "Emergency blow." The sharp hiss of compressed air being pumped into ballast tanks filled the submarine.

Even as small as she was compared to the ship, *Seawolf* could still not stop on a dime. It took time to slow her down, more time than it took to come shallow. But how long—had he miscalculated? Could she surface and turn in time to—?

The *Seawolf* slammed sideways, throwing everyone not strapped in against the port bulkhead. Loose gear went flying. A massive groan that seem to encompass their whole world filled the submarine, far more overwhelming and powerful than any sonar they had heard so far. It went on and on, angry, screaming, the sound of metal tearing and fuel exploding. It crescendoed, increasing to the point where there was nothing left in the world except the sound of the massive transport dying.

The force was sufficient to rotate the *Seawolf* around her long axis, and to shove her through the water with her conning tower parallel to the bottom of the sea. Her speed decreased quickly, and by small increments, she righted herself. In the forward part of the compartment, the planesman and helmsman struggled for control of the ship, powerless against the massive forces acting on her.

Just when it seemed neither steel nor flesh could endure it any longer, *Seawolf* slammed to a stop. A cacophony of sound filled her, less agonized than the tearing of steel.

"Chief, surface the ship," Forsythe ordered, still on his side along the port bulkhead but struggling to his feet. For some reason, his right leg wasn't working the way it should. He felt numbness extend from his waist down to his feet, worried for a second, then dismissed it. It was preferable to the pain that would certainly follow.

"Surface the ship, aye." A thin trickle of blood ran out of the corner of the chief's mouth. "Planeman, surface the ship."

A groan arose from the planesman's position. The sailor was leaning sideways in his straps, struggling to sit up straight and reach for the planes controls, but clearly disoriented and confused. Forsythe crawled across the deck to him, used the man's chair to pull himself into a standing position, and leaned over him, bearing all his weight on his left leg. He grabbed the controls and yanked back, putting *Seawolf* into a climb.

"Depth?" Forsythe asked, studying the indicators.

"Ninety feet, sir," the chief answered. "But I'm not certain that—"

Suddenly, they both felt it, the change in the weight and inertia of a submarine that is no longer completely submerged. Forsythe restored the controls to neutral position and made his way to the center of the compartment to the periscope. It still operated, although with a noisy squeal as it extruded from its housing. He spun it around and looked back the way that they had come.

At first, he could see nothing. He thought the periscope was broken, a cracked lens or something. Then he realized that what he was seeing was fire. Fire, water, and steam obscuring the picture, making it difficult to make out any details.

"We did it," he said, then all at once felt every bit of adrenaline vanish from his system. He hung on to the periscope to keep himself upright. "We did it." The torpedoes that had been following them had hit the three Russian transports. Even if they'd been trying to follow the *Seawolf*'s maneuvers, the torpedoes couldn't have maneuvered to avoid them.

Forsythe leaned against the bulkhead. The blackness was back, eating at the edges of his consciousness, inviting him, enticing him, and he fought against it. There was still too much to do, too much to . . .

Forsythe crumpled and slipped to the deck. The chief watched, and turned to the planesman who was now completely conscious.

"Benson, take us down. Real slow. We are a feather drifting down through the water. I want to sit us on the bottom and stay at quiet ship. Then, we'll wait here until the captain comes around and tells us what to do." The chief glanced around the control room and saw heads nodding in agreement. The ship settled gently to the bottom of the sea. They waited.

THIRTEEN

MiG 101
Sunday, September 12
1132 local (GMT-4)

The threat warning receiver in the cockpit screamed, indicating that he'd been targeted by fire control radar. Tombstone's pulse pounded, and he could hear Greene swearing quietly in the back seat.

Had his uncle gotten the message to the *Jefferson*? Did it get lost somehow aboard ship before the right parties got it? And did somebody remember to tell the cruiser? Hell of a thing to get shot down by friendly fire.

"Home Plate, this is unidentified air contact bearing one eight zero, range twenty miles from you. Be advised that this is a friendly contact—no IFF, but you should have verification on board of our identity."

"Roger, unidentified contact, we hold you at that position. Say again your identity and interrogative your intentions?" The operation specialist's voice was suspicious, but was replaced almost immediately by a different voice.

"Unidentified contact, this is Home Plate CO," indicating that the commanding officer was speaking. "Be advised that we are in receipt of the traffic you mentioned. What assistance do you require?"

"A green deck," Tombstone said promptly. "And a tanker.

Get Rabies up if you can—I need a good one."

There was a long silence, and Tombstone could only imagine the incredulous conversations taking place on board the carrier. Finally, the captain's voice returned. "Unidentified contact, are you aware that this is an American aircraft carrier?"

"Do you think I could put this down on a cruiser?" Tombstone snapped. "Of course I know it's a carrier. Now get me some gas in the air or you're going to need a helo to get me on board. And believe me, if I have to punch out of this bitch due to lack of fuel, I'm going to be one royally pissed off aviator."

Another long silence, then, "Roger, we have Texaco aircraft in your area at this time. And, as luck would have it, Commander "Rabies" Grill is the pilot in command. And, unidentified contact . . . ? Is there something we ought to call you, something besides unidentified contact?"

"Sure. Call me Stoney One," Tombstone said promptly. "Composition one, two souls on board, state one point six, and I'm really getting thirsty up here."

"Roger, sir," the operation specialist said, evidently having decided that, unidentified or not, this was something he did know how to do. "Suggest you come left, sir. Texaco is fifteen miles from your location, and he'll be waiting for you. Oh, and sir, no disrespect, but Commander Grills . . . well . . . he asked me to ask you . . ." the controller's voice trailed off.

"What?" Tombstone demanded.

"If you know how to do this, sir. Tank, he means. And if you know him personally."

"Yeah, I can manage it. And tell Rabies that since he's so concerned about it, I'll let him sing his latest song during the approach."

The controller kept the mike open to allow Tombstone to hear him chuckle. "I guess you do know him, sir."

"All too well."

"Button three for coordination."

"I don't have a button three. How about a frequency?"

"Roger, wait one . . ." The controller then reeled off the frequency associated with that preset channel on an American aircraft. Then he continued with, "Sir, just out of curiosity—

just exactly what is it you're flying? The deck wants to know for the tension line settings."

"A MiG-37," Tombstone replied. "And if you've never seen one close-up, I'll be glad to give you a personal tour once we're on deck."

"Roger, copy a MiG-37," the controller said, his voice as calm as though this were an everyday occurrence. "I will advise Texaco."

"Hell, don't mind me," a familiar voice broke in on the circuit. "Just get your ass on up here before I change my mind about committing unnatural acts. Tanking is bad enough, but doing it for a MiG really sucks."

Outside of landing at night on the deck of a carrier, few evolutions are as dangerous as tanking. Tombstone had done it so many times in so many American aircraft he thought he could probably do it in his sleep, but he knew the dangers of complacency. And, even though the evolution was familiar, the MiG was still a new aircraft to him. He had less than thirty hours in her, and while he'd grown to appreciate the aircraft's nimble handling and performance characteristics, tanking with an unfamiliar cockpit configuration would test his skills to the limits.

He already had radar contact on the KS-3 tanker, and a vector from the controller took him right in behind the aircraft. The tanker was trailing the familiar basket and Tombstone settled in low and slightly behind the KS-3.

"Is this who I think it is?" Rabies asked over their private control circuit.

"Probably," Tombstone answered. "No names, okay?"

"Yeah, right, I got it. What the hell are you doing flying that bitch?"

"Long story, and now is not the time." Tombstone glanced down at his fuel indicator. "Let's get this done and we'll catch up when we're back on board."

"Roger. Take it slow. I'll keep her steady for you."

One of the advantages of the S-3 airframe as a tanker was it was an exceptionally aerodynamic platform. All the S-3's series liked to fly and did it easily. They had exceptionally long endurance, and their stable, aerodynamic characteristics made them an excellent choice for tankers.

Tombstone finessed the control surfaces, allowing the MiG to gain altitude almost inch by inch. She was more than glad to accommodate him, and seemed to understand exactly what he was trying to do. When he attained the correct altitude, with his refueling probe lined up on the basket, he tapped the throttles forward ever so slightly.

The MiG bolted forward. Tombstone swore, and pulled back, dropping well behind S-3.

"Easy, big boy," Rabies warned, and Tombstone could hear the tension in the pilot's voice. "You got all the time you need to do this right—but no time to do it wrong."

"Roger, she's a little too loose on the throttle," Tombstone acknowledged.

"Try doing it with control surfaces instead," Rabies suggested. "I saw them doing it at an air show once."

Still at the correct altitude, Tombstone adjusted the control surfaces and then compensated with the throttle. The MiG slowed noticeably and he tapped the throttles so that he was keeping the correct distance from the tanker. Then he eased off the speed brakes ever so slightly, allowing her to drift forward. The distance between the two aircraft closed slowly.

"That refueling probe—you sure it'll fit?" Rabies asked.

"I think so. It's supposed to."

"All right, let's do this."

Attitude, attitude. Watch your line up. Keep your eyes on the basket. That's right, slow and easy. You can do this.

But it didn't feel right. The probe was closer to the cockpit than it was on the Tomcat, and was set slightly farther back. He would be perilously close underneath the KS-3.

"They must use a longer tanker probe, and trail the basket back farther," Tombstone said.

Tombstone slid the MiG forward, almost holding his breath. It looked like he was going in smoothly, but then he heard a *thump* and a shiver ran through the MiG.

"Off center," Rabies said. "Slide back a bit and try it again. And, remember, that refueling probe is off to the right a bit, not midline.

Tombstone pulled back slightly, readjusted his speed, and tried again.

Come on, baby. You can do it. Now!

The refueling probe slid into the basket smoothly and locked into place. A green light appeared on Tombstone's control panel. "We got a lock."

"Roger, concur lock. How much you want?"

"Four thousand pounds."

"That much?" Rabies said, doubt in his voice. "I thought you were heading in for landing."

"Yeah. But if you think refueling for the first time was tricky, imagine the trap. I want to be a little heavier, have plenty of time for a couple of go rounds."

"Roger, you got it." Another green light on the panel lit up, indicating fuel was flowing. "You sure you know how much she holds?"

"That is one of the things I do know," Tombstone answered.

The MiG proved to be an exceptional refueling platform once he figured out how to plug into the basket, and the aircraft gulped down the fuel quickly. Within a few minutes, Tombstone was able to reduce speed and drift away from the tanker.

"Thanks," Tombstone said. "I'll see you on the boat."

"Roger. If you have any problems with a trap, I can give you some pointers." Rabies voice was smug. He was known as a hotshot who rarely missed a perfect three wire trap.

"I think I can manage." Tombstone chuckled.

"Some kind of fun," Greene said from the back. Except for a few quiet comments during Tombstone's lineup, he had been silent during the entire evolution.

"Yeah. You can try it next time."

"Wonderful." Again Tombstone detected a note of surliness in the younger pilot's voice.

"Now, let's see if we can get back on board." Tombstone switched away from the coordination frequency back to the tower frequency. "Home Plate, this is Stoney One. Request permission to come on board."

"Roger, green deck, and you have priority in the stack. We've recalculated your weight to account for the fuel you took on and we're ready for you."

"Roger, I'd like to make two passes over the deck before I actually try it. And put the Hornet LSO back there, would you?"

"Roger, you got it."

Tombstone descended and slowly turned, getting a feel for the handling of the aircraft now that she was fully fueled again.

He came in behind the carrier at five miles, lined up on her and proceeded to the two-mile point, intersecting what his glide path would be for a Tomcat, then commenced his descent.

"Stoney One, call the ball," the controller said.

"Roger, call the ball," Tombstone acknowledged. Moments later, he saw the Fresnel lens. "Stoney One, ball."

"Stoney One, LSO. First for both of us, sir. Looking good at this time, on path, on altitude. Say needles?" the calm, professional voice of the LSO requested.

"No needles," Tombstone said. "We'll do this by visual."

"Roger, copy no needles. Disregard needles, well, fly visual, Stoney One." The LSO reflexively fell into the standard patter he used with an approaching aircraft.

"Disregard needles, aye," Tombstone answered.

For a few moments, he simply let the aircraft fly, his hands light on the controls as he made his approach. The MiG was so much lighter than the Tomcat he was used to and he was sure that would shortly play a major factor.

Astern of the aircraft carrier is a mass of roiling, disturbed air, and every aircraft approaching for a landing runs smack into it. This area, known as the bubble, makes it difficult to hold on glide path, particularly in an unfamiliar aircraft. For his first approach, Tombstone would approach intentionally high, avoiding ramp strike.

"Stoney One, you're above glide path, on course," the LSO said. "I understand you're doing a fly by?"

"Touch and go," Tombstone said, feeling confident with the way the MiG was handling. He would touch wheels to the deck well forward of the arresting wires, continue maintaining full power, and take off again immediately over the bow. "Two touch and goes, and then we'll do it for real."

"What are your tires rated for?" the LSO asked.

Tires. Another spec we didn't cover. But there's only so much you can absorb in two days. I think they'll take it, but I don't remember. Maybe I should just try it. Tombstone groaned. "I don't know," he finally admitted. "But, to be on the safe side, cancel the touch and goes—we'll do a fly by instead."

So, no actual contact with the deck prior to the trap, he thought. "You ready for this?" he asked Greene.

"Yep. We're in command eject, and I got my hand on the bar. We run into trouble, I'll have us out of here."

That worried Tombstone a bit. Would Greene panic and punch them out unnecessarily?

"It's going to feel different," he said. "A lot harder landing than it would be in a Tomcat."

"Don't worry—I know what to do."

And now the boat was coming up at them quickly, a massive steel tower, its deck cluttered with aircraft and people. He saw sailors lining up outside the green line, staring up in wonder at the sight of a MiG flying over their deck. Vulture's Row, the observation area on the weather decks at the 0–10 level, was also crowded. A few people waved as he went by.

He flew down the length of the deck, then pulled up sharply and peeled off to the left. "Nice pass, Stoney One," the air boss said.

"One more, and we do this for real."

Tombstone circled around and this time intercepted the flight path at just over two miles from the boat. He lined up again, eased her in, and followed the LSO's directions, getting used to the sound and rhythm of the LSO's coaching. This time he took her down even closer to the deck, so close that in a Tomcat his wheels would have been touching. Again, he continued his pass on down the deck, then peeled off to the left. Behind him, Greene muttered a word of encouragement.

"All right, this time is for real," Tombstone announced as he veered away from the carrier once again. "I'm taking bets on the three wire."

"You're on," the LSO said promptly. "I bet two sliders that you nail the three wire."

"I hope you're hungry," Tombstone warned.

The aircraft felt right, so very right. He knew with a sudden surge of confidence that there would be absolutely no problem with the trap, that he would nail the three wire cleanly, easily, righteously.

"A little high, sir. Down just a bit," the LSO coached. "That's right, that's right, looking good," he continued, as Tombstone bled off the speed slightly. "Watch your speed, sir—not as much needed in the smaller bird."

Tombstone increased his speed slightly and corrected his course as the MiG veered in the bubble. The LSO was right.

The lighter aircraft could land a bit faster than a Tomcat could, and had less of a margin for error in minimum airspeed.

"You're right a bit, sir. That's it, that's it—right on path right on altitude. Bring her on in, looking good," the reassuring patter from the LSO provided Tombstone with instantaneous updates on how he was doing. He glanced one last time at the Fresnel lens, at the bright green glow, a friendly welcoming sight, and then fixed his gaze on the deck. He was committed now.

All at once, the carrier loomed up at them, massive and inhospitable. It was always at this moment in any landing that he was convinced, just for a microsecond, that he wasn't going to make it. And it passed just as quickly as it always did.

"Power back, power back," the LSO said, as he came over the flight deck. "Now!"

Tombstone pulled throttles back, and let the MiG slam down on the tarmac. "Full power," the LSO ordered, and Tombstone slammed the throttles forward again.

For one terrifying moment, he thought he had missed all four wires. Or perhaps the tail hook had been down—no, the LSO would have seen that and warned him. Then, he felt the neck-snapping jolt that threw him forward against his ejection seat straps, and the MiG slammed to a halt. For the next several seconds, it strained against the arresting wires, engines burning at full power, ready for take off again should the wire snap.

Then a plane captain stepped up front him and signaled for him to reduce power. Tombstone eased back on the throttles until the engines were barely idling. He backed up slightly, then retracted the tail hook. "Good job, Stoney One," the LSO said. "I'll see you in the dirty shirt mess. We got a lot of folks who owe us a slider or two."

Tombstone followed the directions of the plane captain and taxied to his spot. The handler elected to place him with the Hornets. Tombstone powered down the engines. The crowd around him stood back, wary. Finally, as a wide-eyed plane captain scrambled up the boarding ladder, Tombstone popped the canopy back. Fresh air rushed over him, cool and welcoming. He smiled, as the plane captain said, "Welcome aboard the USS *Jefferson*, sir."

● ● ●

Before Tombstone was even out of sight of the MiG, Lab Rat had his people swarming over her. They took pictures, made measurements, and Tombstone could tell they were itching to completely disassemble the entire aircraft.

"Don't do anything that will disable it," he warned, as a safety observer led him toward the island. "It's not ours—not yet."

"Don't worry, sir," Lab Rat reassured him. "They're not allowed to touch anything that moves."

"I mean the avionics as well," Tombstones said, scrutinizing Lab Rat carefully. "You know what I mean, Commander. Don't down my bird."

"Promise, sir," Lab Rat said.

Not completely satisfied, but unwilling to stand watch on the aircraft himself every second of the day, Tombstone let the white shirt lead him away.

As he walked down the so-familiar passageways, Tombstone felt wave after wave of nostalgia wash over him. It was here that he started his career so many decades ago as a nugget aviator, served as CAG, and later as commander of the battle group, the billet Coyote now held.

His escort took him straight into flag spaces, and people he passed in the passageways stopped, then turned to stare, their jaws dropping. Many of them recognized him, and seemed to understand that he did not want to be acknowledged. But they still cleared space for him just as though he were still an admiral, and he heard a few quiet comments of "Good trap, Admiral," as he passed by.

He walked into the conference room, then back through it into TFCC. Coyote was watching the screen, asking questions and shouting orders as he watched the battles progress. He paused just long enough to slap Tombstone on the back, then turned his attention back to the screen.

"I'm not even sure you have a security clearance, old buddy," Coyote said. "But if you've got any suggestions or comments, speak up. The president wants us to deal with this and deal with it now." Coyote shook his head wonderingly. "I've never seen such a strong directive. So I sent in the SEALs to deal with as many of the missile launchers and antiair weapons as I could. We're taking on the MiGs at the same time and trying to prevent a second squadron from reinforcing them."

Tombstone shook his head, watching the scenario unfold. To the north of Bermuda, half the air wings fighters were decimating the remaining Russian MiGs. The Aegis was standing by in case the missiles were launched. Coyote was providing voice updates to the National Command Center every thirty seconds.

Coyote swore quietly. He turned to Tombstone, anger in his eyes. "It's the damned mobile antiair platforms," he said. "The Russians are sticking close to shore, and backing off to lead us in closer."

"You got anything airborne with HARMs?" Tombstone asked, referring to the antiradiation missiles. HARMs were intended to destroy enemy radars. They homed in on radar signals and the later versions of the missile could even remember where the radar was, even if it was shut down immediately.

"No. Strictly antiair load outs. I'm having two loaded out right now, but it will be another fifteen minutes before they launch. But they've got long-range antiair launchers on the island. I don't think we can get close enough to target them before they can target us." He shook his head, glaring at the screen. "But the real priority is the missiles. If they make it past the Aegis, the East Coast is in deep shit. The cruisers along the coast are deployed to take them out on final, but there're no guarantees they can take them, either."

Suddenly, an idea occurred to Tombstone. It was outrageous, completely outrageous—but it just might work. He waited for break in the action, and grabbed Coyote by the arm. "Have you got any really, really smart weapons and intelligence people?"

"Of course." Coyote didn't take his gaze off the screen. "What do you want them for?"

"See if they can jury rig those HARMs on the MiG. I might be able to get in closer and faster than they can—I'll have the transponder on and I'll show up on their radar as a friendly. I can be on top of them before they know what hits them."

Coyote looked at him, doubt on his face. "Never work. The avionics are—"

"Are stolen from us," Tombstone finished, remembering the lecture his instructor pilot had given him on the avionics. Even hard points, the fixtures on the wing to which the Russian missiles attached, were strictly American specs. "It'll work— I know it will. It's worth a shot."

Coyote thought for a moment, which seemed like an eternity in the fast-paced environment in TFCC. "If nothing else, you could launch as an antiair platform," he agreed cautiously. "Come up behind them, even up the odds."

"Yes. Give me two HARMs, the rest antiair."

Coyote shook his head, still not certain he believed what they were discussing. "Can you even launch that bird off the cat?"

Tombstone nodded. "More borrowed technology. Rather than building their own catapult systems from scratch, the Russians studied ours. They're completely interchangeable."

Coyote turned to a chief. "Pass the word for Lieutenant Commander Gurring and Chief Harding. I want them up here on the double." He turned back to Tombstone. "Those are your men. If anybody can do it, they can."

USS Jefferson
VF 95 Ready Room
1410 local (GMT-4)

Bird Dog had called in every favor he could in order to have himself included in the air combat mission. Sure, the land attack group would see plenty of action, but it wasn't the kind that he preferred. Give him a fight against a MiG any day, to dumping iron on stationary targets. When the flight schedule was posted, though, he was in for a disappointment. He turned to the CO and pointed at the offending line item. "What's this?"

Commander Gator Cummings, the commanding officer and a RIO, peered at the offending item over the top of his reading glasses. "It's you and Shaughnessy. What's the problem?"

"I don't fly with her," Bird Dog said, feeling his temper start to rise. "I thought I made that pretty clear."

Gator shut his eyes for a moment as though replaying the

conversation in his mind, and finally said, "Yes. Yes, I believe you did."

"Then what's this assignment? I don't want her on my wing. She's too—too hotheaded."

At that, Gator roared with laughter. He turned to the rest of the pilots, who were milling about, checking their gear and talking excitedly among themselves. "Hey, listen to this. Bird Dog thinks Shaughnessy is hotheaded." A wave of guffaws and rude comments swept across the ready room, as every pilot chimed in.

Bird Dog thought someone was too hotheaded? Well, it was about time he knew what it was like to be on the other side of things for change.

"Hey, I'll swap," one of the pilots said. "He could have Boomer—I'll take Shaughnessy any day."

"What's that supposed to mean?" Boomer snapped. Boomer was a lieutenant on his second cruise and had already earned a reputation for being an extremely cautious pilot. "You got a problem with the way I fly?"

The first pilot slapped him on the back. "Naw, not a bit. It's just that Bird Dog wants a conscientious wingman, and well, you fit the bill, don't you think?"

"Prudent," Boomer insisted. "Prudent, that's all. I like to make sure of my shots." From around the room, other offers to swap wingmen with Bird Dog were called out.

Finally, Gator held his hand up. "Pipe down, everybody. They'll be no swapping—the flight schedule stands as written."

"Why?" Bird Dog asked, aware that he was starting to whine. "I don't see why I should have to—"

"Follow orders like anyone else?" Gator snapped. A sudden silence descended on the ready room. "What makes you think you're entitled to your choice of wingman? You think that maybe, just maybe, I might know better than you what's best for this squadron?"

"But I—" Bird Dog started, and Gator waved him off.

"Try looking in the mirror sometime, asshole. Half the time, you'd see Shaughnessy's face staring back. The only difference is you got more time under your belt. She stays your wingman. Got it?"

"I don't suppose I have any say in this?" Shaughnessy said,

walking to the front of the room. Cold fury infused her delicate features. Electricity seemed to crackle off her. "Because if I do, then I—"

"No," Gator said simply. "You don't, either. Now, unless both of you want to be assigned permanent squadron duty officer while everyone else flies, I suggest you get your asses up to the flight deck and start preflight. You fly together, or you don't fly at all."

Shaughnessy beat him to the ladder heading up the flight deck, and he had to admit that hurt slightly. She was smaller and weighed less, he told himself. She squirmed through holes in the crowd that you couldn't expect a guy his size to go. And, climbing the ladder, well, she had a lot less weight to carry around, didn't she?

By the time Bird Dog arrived on the flight deck, Shaughnessy was already well into her preflight checklist. The plane captain stood by her side, nodding and smiling, and that bothered Bird Dog, too. It was his favorite plane captain, and he resented the defection. Just because Shaughnessy herself used to be a plane captain, they were all over her like she was still one of their own. Well, she better learn about the responsibilities and burdens of being an officer. She couldn't keep sucking up to a stupid airman.

"Sir?" his own plane captain asked. "Are you ready?"

"Of course I'm ready," Bird Dog snapped. "I'm always ready."

All around them, the flight deck buzzed with frantic activity. An outsider watching might have concluded it was uncontrolled chaos, but everyone on the carrier knew better. It was a delicate, complex ballet, each sailor with his own starring role, all under the watchful eye of the Air Boss located in the tower seven decks above.

Forward, the alert five aircraft that had been sitting manned on the catapults were already launching. Steam boiled up from the catapult line as the piston came up to full power. The catapult officer ordered one final check of control surfaces, and the Tomcat wiggled every moving part. Then, satisfied that no last-minute gremlins had crept in, the plane captain popped off a sharp salute. The pilot returned it, the catapult officer dropped the deck and pointed and released his finger from the pickle.

The aircraft shot forward as the shuttle began its run down to the end of the deck. It picked up speed at an astounding rate, taking less than five seconds to reach minimum takeoff speed. First one, then the other alert five aircraft launched.

As the jet blast deflectors lowered, a long line of steam curled lazily away from the shuttle. A familiar vibration rang throughout the deck, a gentler echo of the one produced by the launch, as the shuttles ran back to their starting position. Already Tomcat and Hornets were vying for position. From the middle of the deck, a helo lifted gracefully from its spot, then moved off to the side and took station astern of the carrier.

Bird Dog performed his preflight quickly, almost automatically. How many times had he done this? Why, hell, he had more time preflighting than Shaughnessy had in the cockpit, he'd bet. Finally satisfied, he pulled down the boarding ladder from the side of the aircraft and started to climb up. As his eyes cleared the fuselage, he could see that Shaughnessy and her RIO were already buttoned up, canopy down, and waiting to taxi to their shot.

Dammit, she shouldn't be getting ahead of him. She was his wingman, not the other way around. He added this offense to the list of infractions she had committed just to piss him off.

A plane captain followed him up, helped him with the ejection harness fastenings, and pulled the safety pins from the ejection seat. He held up the ejection pins for Bird Dog's inspection, then put them in his pocket. "Good hunting, sir. Kill one of those bastards for me, would you?"

"You got it, buddy. Bird Dog started to slide the canopy forward.

"And, sir?" The airman pointed over at Shaughnessy's bird. "Bring her back. She's still kinda new—she doesn't know what she's doing like you do. But, I know she always watches to see what you do. She says you're the best pilot she's ever known in a Tomcat. So, keep her out of trouble. We'd all really appreciated it."

"No sweat. That's what I'm here for, isn't it?" Bird Dog locked the canopy down and turned to taxi.

So, he wasn't the only one who realized what Shaughnessy was facing, was he? Even her own former peers realized it. Hell, knowing where she came from, maybe that made her a little desperate to succeed. Maybe she tried too hard, felt like she had something to prove.

But she was a hot stick. Did she know that? Did she know how really good she was? Good enough not to have anything to prove to anybody. *Not even to me.*

Maybe she didn't know that. He considered the possibility as he kept up his scan of the deck and followed the plane captain's motions to taxi forward. Shaughnessy fell in behind him and her own plane captain held her back and waited for Bird Dog.

Good thinking. Maybe between the plane captains and her RIO, they could keep her from screwing up.

The shuttle locked on and the Tomcat jolted slightly. He watched the plane captain and the catapult officer, cycled his stick on signal, saluted, and braced for launch. Seconds later, he was airborne.

Once clear of the ship, Bird Dog circled around to the marshal point and waited for Shaughnessy. One way or another, along with killing his share of MiGs, he was going to bring her back alive.

FOURTEEN

Under any other circumstances, Lieutenant Bruno Parto would have considered this a tropical paradise. Towering palms swayed gently in the light breeze, and the foliage was dense with a wide range of exotic flowers. Everywhere he looked it was green, the colors running the gamut from the pale yellow shades to dark, almost black greens. Hibiscus blossomed seemingly at random, deep red and yellow splashes against the green canopy.

This far up the mountain, there were few sounds of civilization. No trucks, no internal combustion engines. No aircraft. Instead, the air teemed with shrieks and raucous cries of birds as they went about their daily tasks.

Yes, paradise. Except for the area immediately in front of him.

Someone had been brutal about clearing the area, as well as quite thorough. A cleared path slashed through the forest, leading down to the main road he'd observed from the air. Up here, the road widened into a clearing forty feet in diameter. Within the cleared area, everything was trampled to the ground. Ugly stumps seeping sap poked up, raw and wounded. The debris was tossed around the edges of the circle, already turning brown and melting down to join the compost on the tropical floor. Parked in the center was the rocket launcher, its rails extending up from the bed, a missile already in place.

Parto ran his hand over the ground, letting the rich loam sift through his fingers. Even the most brutal treatment by men could not permanently stop nature. Already, only a week after the area had been cleared, the jungle was trying to reclaim its own. Small sprouts of green poked up through the debris, and twigs were visible in the center of the tree trunks. Within another week, the ground would not be visible as foliage started to sprout, and in perhaps as little as three months he would never have been able to tell it had been cleared.

But, for now, it was an ugly scar on the land, easily visible from the air, although a bit more difficult to find on the ground. The dense foliage screened it until you were almost on top of it.

It was the smells that first gave away the location even before he had visual contact on it. The scent of people, cooked meat and tobacco, sweat, and the oily, noxious odor of machinery. He motioned to the members of the squad, and they dispersed silently around him. They advanced slowly, each with his own assignment, knowing that time was running short.

The previous three sites had been easily taken down. The SEALs had approached like Ninjas, undetected, and during the night had silently and finally eliminated the soldiers asleep in their trucks. After everyone was dead, Parto himself had run through the simple sequence of input commands on the attached fire control panel, canceling all preprogrammed launch instructions. As a final precautionary measure, they carefully detached the warhead sitting on the bed of the truck and rolled it off onto the ground. It would be impossible to remount on the launcher, and other teams would be along later to dispose of it.

But they had run out of darkness before they had run out of trucks, and the result was that they were making their approach on this one in the afternoon, already worn out after a night of operations.

Parto could smell something cooking, as well as coffee, and he swore silently. He would have preferred to catch them just as they stumbled out of their beds, when they were still caught in the no man's land between sleep and alertness.

But you played the cards you were dealt, and Parto was not one to demand a recount.

Just as he was about to give the command over his whisper-mike, the technicians scrambled over the missile. They began raising the launch arms, putting it at the angle necessary to launch through a narrow hole in the canopy overhead.

As the launch arms rotated upward, the mounting platform under them complained. A good coat of grease would have prevented the metal-on-metal grinding, but Parto knew how hard it was to maintain equipment in the warm salty air. As the missile launch rails reached the angle of approximately twenty degrees above vertical, something snapped. The entire assembly jolted hard to the left.

"Not yet," Parto whispered. He waited. There was a sharp crack, and then a seam near the tip of the missile opened. From it gouted a burst of white vapor, a fog that wafted in the gentle breeze toward the depths of the jungle.

The men around the truck panicked. Some grabbed gas masks, others fled wildly into the jungle. With cold dread in his stomach, Parto knew what the warhead was.

"Fall back," he ordered, moving himself away from the site. "Get as far away from here as fast you can—it's a chemical warhead, and it's leaking. Head down slope, into the wind— we'll form up at Charlie point."

His men needed no urging. He heard them moving out, sacrificing stealth for speed. If they didn't escape the deadly cloud heading for them, there would be no second chance of this mission.

Which nerve agent? It didn't matter. Not if he didn't get out of range fast enough. He had the standard antidotes in self-injecting vials in his pocket, atropine and a few others, but they weren't effective against everything. Some nerve agents didn't even need to be inhaled. The slightest touch of their vapor on skin would be immediately deadly.

Was he clear of it? Did he feel muscle tremors starting now? No—he was imagining things. It was the normal, comfortable feel of adrenaline pumping through his body as he put out maximum physical effort.

He was the second man to arrive at the muster point, but the others weren't far behind him. There was something peculiarly terrifying about chemical and biological weapons. For all the SEALs' strength, for all their physical prowess and weapons, they had no sure counter to this enemy. What they could not see, what they could not touch, they could not fight. And that was a very odd sensation for each one of them.

"What now?" one asked. Despite the hard run, Parto was breathing normally.

"The last thing I heard before all hell broke loose was a launch order. They're planning on letting them rip sometime in the next hour. Every site still around is raising launchers, setting in coordinates, and preparing to fire. If we are going to stop them, we have to do it now."

"Metal fatigue, probably," one commented. "You don't maintain something, you use it too hard, that's what happens. They should have known that."

"I wonder if all of them are in the same shape," another said.

"Probably—or close to it. Makes our job easier, huh?"

"No. That was a one-in-a-thousand mishap," Parto said firmly. "We've got an hour—if we move fast enough, we can take out two more."

Not one of them would have expressed doubt openly, but he could see it in each face. Hell, he felt it himself, the gut feeling of revulsion and fear that made him want to beat feet as far and as fast as he could from this place.

But that's what they were here for, wasn't it? To take the risks that they didn't want to subject their families and friends to back in the States? They were the hard spear tip of the American military, protecting the soft underbelly of the civilian population, and sometimes it came down to this—put up or shut up.

He didn't have to tell any of them that. They would make the connection in their own way, come to the same conclusion. There was no help—they had to take out the ones that they could.

Suddenly, he heard a crashing in the bushes. Chief Petty Officer Jesus Lacar held up a hand, nodded, and silently slipped out of the group. He would find whoever was approaching and dispose of the problem.

The noise stopped. A few moments later, he reappeared. His face was pale and tight.

"Whatever it was, it got him," he said, his voice steady,

maybe too steady. "Definitely a nerve agent. He had blood coming out of his mouth and was in convulsions when I got there. Big red boils all over his skin, some of them breaking open. And his eyes . . ."—the man could not repress a shudder—"his eyes were solid bloodred. They must've been hurting bad because he was trying to claw them out."

"Better here than at home," Parto said finally. "Come on, let's move out."

The next crew they approached was much sloppier. The guard had his back to him as Parto approached, and he died quickly and quietly. They were in the clearing in a heartbeat, moving silently, but not as carefully as they had before. The clock was ticking.

On signal, six handguns rang out with a double tap, dropping six men, and then again until everyone was dead.

If we hit the missile . . . He shuddered to think how close to disaster they may have come before.

"One more," Parto said, as they hastily regrouped. "We have twenty minutes—we'll use them."

Bermuda Airport
Control Tower
1430 local (GMT-4)

Maskiro's people disliked giving him bad news. Over the previous three days, he'd gone from an aggressive, canny tactician into an easily irritated manic. So, when the Russian air traffic controller saw the spate of aircraft symbols appear around the American aircraft carrier, he groaned.

Maskiro was behind him in an instant, stinking of sweat. "What is that?"

"It appears to be aircraft launching from the carrier, comrade," the controller said, trying to keep his voice level.

"Impossible. They will not take the chance of incurring civilian casualties. I have that on the best authority and we are not." Maskiro's voice trailed off as he saw the aircraft symbols merge into a single mass, and then break apart into two separate flights. One group headed for the island. The second turned north, staying out of range of the antiair weapons, but clearly intending to intercept the reinforcement MiG squadron now approaching the island.

"No." Maskiro picked up the portable radio that connected him with the medium-range land attack launchers. He paused for a moment, and the controller thought he saw a flash of sanity and sorrow. Before he could speak, the radio came to life.

"Command, sector one commander. Comrade, three stations have failed to conduct their hourly status reports. I have been unable to raise them by radio. I think we must consider the possibility that American special forces are now on the island." The sector commander had no hesitation in voicing his opinion, since he was out of Maskiro's immediate reach. "I have ordered additional security measures, but I cannot guarantee our security here. Comrade, your orders?"

Maskiro howled in rage. He slammed the radio down on the desk and turned insane eyes around the room as though seeking someone to take the brunt of his anger. The radio blared again. "Comrade, your orders?"

Maskiro grabbed the radio. "Launch. I repeat, all land attack site launch! Now!" He then turned to the air controller. "Notify the inbound flight and Comrade Korsov that we are under attack." Maskiro drew his personal side arm and chambered around. "And that we will fight here to the death."

FIFTEEN

USS Jefferson
Flight Deck
1432 local (GMT-11)

With a slider in one hand and a cup of coffee in the other, Tombstone was on the flight deck with Coyote's two weapons experts. They'd spotted the MiG just aft of the island to stay clear of the long line of fighters waiting to launch. Greene was ignoring the MiG, staring hungrily at the catapult and the Tomcats.

Coyote's experts made a cursory examination of the exterior of the MiG, then the chief broke out a multimeter and started taking readings. "You're sure they told you it was the same?" the chief asked, shouting to be heard over the launching aircraft.

Tombstone had no idea whether the chief recognized him and didn't care. "Yep. That's what he told me."

The chief put away his gear. There were four carts loaded with missiles and aviation ordnance men standing by, just waiting to download the antiair missiles Tombstone had flown in with. "You understand, I can't get into the guts of it, not with a lot more gear and a lot more time."

Tombstone nodded. "But the fact that the hard points match up says a lot, doesn't it?"

Gurring spoke up. "Yes, of course. But we don't even know

how the system is grounded. If it doesn't work the way ours does and you catch a stray shot of voltage you could light off a missile and not be able to get it off your wing. If that happens, you're out of there."

"I know. It's a risk I'm willing to take."

The chief looked at the younger pilot. "And how about him?"

Tombstone turned to Greene. *Yes, how about you, my moody little sidekick? Just what the hell is going on with you?* "You don't have to go," Tombstone said. "This is strictly volunteer."

An offended expression crossed Greene's face. "You think I don't have the guts?"

"I never said that. But you have to admit, you've been off lately."

Greene waved away his concerns. "Maybe. But no way you're going to try this without me. No way. Of course I'm in."

Tombstone nodded, pleased. "Okay, let's do it. We shoot the HARMs then buster back here. The admiral's got a Tomcat with your name on it as soon as you land."

Tombstone had never seen any weapons crew work more quickly or more efficiently. There was not a single wasted motion. The techs waltzed around each other as they went through the precise business of downloading one missile from hard points, lowering it to a carry cart, and sliding the HARM cart underneath. Uploading the two missiles took less than eight minutes, with the team on the right side edging out the team on the left by a few seconds.

The chief grunted "Not bad." Tombstone turned to him, astounded.

"Chief. *Not bad?* Your crews upload HARMS onto an aircraft they've never seen before and do it faster than I've ever seen anyone load up any missile—and you say *not bad*? Where did you get these guys? Are they robots?"

"Naw, sir. We've just done some training."

An understatement if I've ever had heard it. But he's determined to be cool about it. Tombstone stepped forward and said, "Gentlemen, thank you. That has to be the finest job I've ever seen."

Every last one of them tried to look cool, tried to pretend it was no big deal, but Tombstone could tell they were pleased with themselves. More than pleased—damned proud, and with every right to be so.

Greene had already started preflight and Tombstone decided not to double-check him as he normally would have. Instead, he climbed up the boarding ladder and strapped in, then began his preflight checklist. A few moments later, Greene climbed up and started his as well. They ran through the remainder of the checklist at record speed, glossing over a few steps with no more than a cursory glance. Three minutes later, the engines were turning over, the cockpit buttoned up, and they were taxiing toward the catapults.

The catapult crew had watched the ordnance men, and were determined not to be outdone. Watching them, you'd think they launched a MiG every day of the week. All routine, so routine—and yet every evolution was handled with the utmost professionalism. The MiG was directed to the catapults, the shuttle attached with a retaining pin, and a jet blast deflectors raised. Tombstone made a complete cycle of his control surfaces at the catapult officer's direction. He returned the sharp salute and braced himself.

A split second later, the MiG started rolling down the catapult. Tombstone knew a moment of terror—it felt so different from the much larger Tomcat that had so much inertia. By contrast the MiG was so light it seemed like they were already airborne.

Finally, with a sharp thump, they were airborne. The MiG dipped slightly toward the waves as her wings caught the air, but less than a Tomcat would've done. He was able to pull her up and begin to climb almost immediately. He pulled off to the left, gained altitude, and headed for Bermuda.

"The missiles look okay?" Tombstone asked over ICS.

"I'm getting all green lights," Greene said. "Everything checks out fine so far. But we won't know for sure until we try to fire them."

"If we've got solid green lights, then there shouldn't be a problem." A green light indicated that the avionics were talking to the weapons and getting the right answers to their electronic inquiries.

"Theoretically, yes."

"Okay, let's go over how we're going to do this. I'm going in at low altitude, trying to stay out of the radar's envelope.

If we go in on the right approach path, the MiGs will think we're one of them."

"And what about the Hornets?" Greene asked. The HUD showed a mass of Hornets engaging the original squadron of MiGs between the carrier and the island. Tombstone and Greene would have to maneuver around them in order to reach their targets.

Tombstone shrugged mentally. "The Hawkeye will be keeping an eye out for us—they know who we are. And if anybody starts to look like they're interested in taking a shot, they'll break them off."

"If there's time."

"Right. There will be."

Hornet 102
1435 local (GMT-4)

Thor picked his first target almost before he was off the catapult and certainly before his wingman, Captain Bennie Randy, formed up on him. To no one's surprise, Thor targeted the lead MiG on the western edge of Bermuda even before he'd fully pulled up from his launch and settled in to level flight.

"Roger, one oh two," the Hawkeye said, as Thor identified his contact. "You going to let anyone else take a shot this time?"

"If there's a need for them to," Thor said, his hands moving as he pulled the Hornet around to head east, his finger already toggling off his first weapon, his eyes searching for the next target. "You got one Marine, I don't know that you need much more."

"Hey." Randy's voice sounded aggrieved. "Thanks a lot."

"Don't mean you, buddy," Thor assured him. "Go ahead, get rid of some of that shit on your wings and let's get down to business.

"Roger." Thor saw a flash of fire and smoke as Randy shot an AMRAAM. "Okay, you call it."

"Take high," Thor said promptly. And watch your distance to the island—you move in too close, you're in range of those antiair launchers. For now, we pick off what we can from a distance and wait until we can move in closer to do some real damage."

"Roger," Randy acknowledged.

Tomcat 302
1440 local (GMT-4)

"Come on, oh two," Bird Dog's impatient voice said over tactical. "You take any longer launching, I'm going to have to refuel."

"On your wing now," Shaughnessy said, seething. He knew where she was, he had to. Not only was her transponder lighting her up on his HUD, but she was within visual range as well.

"About time. Take low station and stay where I can keep an eye on you," Bird Dog grumbled.

"I don't need a baby-sitter," she snapped.

"Matter of opinion."

"Oh, yeah? Well, opinions are like assholes."

Silence for a moment, then Bird Dog said, "Look, let's just get over there, okay? Head north, then turn east once you've cleared the island. We should be able to engage the reinforcement squadron before we get within range of the antiair batteries. Stay tight with me."

Shaughnessy complied, seething. *Right, stay tight. That's because you think I'm a hothead. That I take chances I shouldn't take. Like you should talk. Fat chance, mister. I waited too long for this, put up with too much shit from you when you were an ensign. I see a chance, I'm taking it. Because I'm every bit as good a pilot are you are—maybe better. And, sooner or later, you're going to have to admit it.*

MiG 101
1450 local (GMT-4)

Five minutes after the MiG was airborne again, she was in the midst of the light fog along the coast at 5,000 feet. Tombstone was counting on the confusion factor, with each pilot focused on only his individual engagement, to allow him to sneak into the pack. While he was behind the fur ball, he gained altitude and circled around like he was a MiG spoiling for a fight.

"Give me the frequency," Tombstone said. Greene reset the radios and they heard an inquisitive Russian voice coming over it. Tombstone could pick out a few words, but his language skills fell far short of being able to answer.

The coast was only a short distance away. It would be no more than two minutes until they were dry. The voice over the radio grew increasingly insistent, then finally quit speaking altogether.

"Any reaction behind us?" Tombstone asked.

"Nope. I think maybe the controller wanted them to break off and take a look at us, but they're all a little busy right now. With any luck, he'll just decide that we're having radio problems."

"Great. Okay, first target. My dot," he said. "Cross your fingers." He toggled the weapons selector switch to select the radar homing missile, he paused, his finger over the firing button. "Be ready to punch us out if we have to."

"That's my job."

"Tombstone punched the button.

The MiG pulled hard to the left as a missile sprang off the right wing. The sudden loss of weight coupled with the hard backdraft from the missile proved too challenging for the lighter aircraft. Tombstone regained control immediately and brought her back into level flight. "Second target now—your dot, Jeremy."

"My dot," Greene acknowledged, then toggled the second missile off.

The white exhaust from each of the two missiles was visible for a few minutes as they arrowed toward the island. The two remaining missile radars were located at the opposite ends of Bermuda.

"We're targeted," Greene said, as the ECM system howled. "Missiles."

"Let's get the hell out of here," Tombstone said. "And if the missiles work, no more problem in a few minutes."

Tombstone put the MiG into a hard climb, kicked in the afterburner, and headed south. "Keep an eye on them."

"Roger." Greene turned around in his seat to watch the island behind them. A few moments later, he saw two explosions, followed by fire. "Hard kill, I think." The radar warning
signal fell silent. "And missiles have gone dumb. We did it!"

Tombstone switched to the tactical frequency. "Home Plate,
this is Stoney One. Two HARMs fired, two kills. Request you
have the Hawkeye confirm."

"Roger, Stoney One," the Hawkeye said. "Confirm two radars off line."

Howls of anticipation echoed over tactical as the Tomcat
pilots turned back into the battle within the renewed deadly
intent on the remaining MiGs. With shore-based missiles no
longer complicating the picture, the matter of sweeping the
sky clean became increasingly less complex.

SIXTEEN

Mig 102
1455 local (GMT-4)

Korsov and his flight were cruising at an altitude of 29,000 feet. He kept a close eye on his fuel indicator. In theory, at this altitude, the incoming aircraft should have more than sufficient fuel to reach Bermuda, with even some to spare should they have to delay their landing.

But he'd never planned to engage in a full-on dog fight and have to fight his way into the landing strip and refueling area. No, between Maskiro and his truck-launched weapons and the Americans' reluctance to risk casualties, it was supposed to be an unopposed landing. Looking at the radar now and the gaggle of American fighters sweeping north along the west side of the island, he knew that would not be the case.

No matter. The mood among his group of aircraft had been growing all day, all of them hyped on adrenaline and itching for a fight. They were fighter pilots, and the drive to see combat was never far from the surface in each of them. Deeper down was the fear, the knowledge that you might not make it, the memory of having seen so many comrades lost in training, stupid accidents, or in combat. But it always happened to someone else, never to you. You would have been smarter at the last second, have made the right choice, have known immediately what to do instead of wasting precious seconds and altitude realizing you were in deep, deep shit.

The tension in the group had eased during the long transit, but now, with the island a fuzzy blur on their radar and the American fighters heading for them, everyone was on edge, itching for a fight. When the warning bowl of the ESM gear sounded, Korsov almost jumped out of his seat. "Where?" he demanded.

"To the west—Tomcats. It's the AWG-9 system, no doubt," his backseater said, his voice rushing over the words, talking too fast. "They're out of range of the trucks—they're headed for us."

"Well, what of it? They want a fight, they'll get one." The adrenaline was surging through his system now, blanking out any possibilities that there was anything but one logical conclusion to the pending encounter. "How many?"

"Ten—no, sixteen. Maybe more."

Did they launch the entire fighter complement off the aircraft carrier? No, they wouldn't have—not and leave the carrier unprotected. There were still the MiGs already on the island to contend with, although they had remained on the ground since they'd landed. Still, just knowing that they were there would keep the aircraft carrier off balance.

"Roger," he said. "Lenin flight, remained on course, engage at will. Bolshoi flight, follow me." With that, leader pulled off half of the squadron and ascended, increasing his radar range as well as gaining valuable altitude. Altitude meant safety.

"Lenin flight—do nothing until you have launch indications," he ordered. "Same thing, Bolshoi flight—if we can get on deck and under the antiair cover, that's what we'll do. And if not, well, we'll wipe the sky clean, won't we?" Listening to the cheers rattling over the circuit, he could feel the combat lust that filled each cockpit.

He put Bolshoi flight into a long, slow turn to the south, lining up now on the island. He could see it easily from his canopy, a lush, green expanse, its edges trimmed with white. The beaches, he'd heard, were outstanding. Not that he would have a chance to see them. None at first.

But perhaps later. Yes, definitely later. A walk along the beach, barefoot, the sun bleaching my hair, with a piña colada

*in my hand and a woman—no, two women—with me. They
will be—exotic.*

*And the only thing standing between me and my beach is a
few Tomcats.*

Tomcat 301
500 local (GMT-4)

"Half of them are heading for the deck," the Hawkeye announced. "They probably intended to do a quick refuel while
the other half covers them."

"Be nice if we could keep that from happening," Bird
Dog said. "And I got just the thing that might persuade them."

Bird Dog listened to the warnings over international air distress and military air distress, ordering the MiGs to turn away
from the island. There was no response to the repeated warnings, each one promising dire consequences and harsher terms.
Finally, after the last one, Bird Dog heard Coyote's voice.
"Weapons free. All Russian targets declared hostile. I repeat,
weapons free."

"Tally ho on the lead MiG," Bird Dog said promptly. "Your
dot, RIO," he said, giving his backseater permission to fire. It
was a privilege he normally would have reserved for himself,
but he was trying to make amends. "Shaughnessy, take your
shot—AMRAAM now. Maybe we'll scare the little bastards
off."

"Roger. But I get the feeling they came to play, not to run."
As she spoke, an AMRAAM shot out from under her wings,
nosed over a bit, then headed straight for the second MiG in
the pack.

At the first missile launch, the MiG flight broke formation,
scattering into fighting pairs in the same style that the American used. Bird Dog listened as voices called out targets over
the circuit. Sixteen Tomcats against twenty MiGs—well, that
was close enough to being fair. The AMRAAM would even
up their numbers quickly, and they'd polished off the rest of
them at their leisure.

He bore in on it, keeping the MiG targeted, hand poised
over the weapons selector switch, watching the AMRAAM

close in. The MiG knew it was in trouble, and began jinking around the sky, frantic to evade the missile. Finally, two seconds before the missile intersected the fuselage, the canopy blew off and the Russians' ejection seats shot out at right angles to the plane. Bird Dog watched them floating down to the ocean, glad in some way that they made it out.

"Good kill," the E-2 said. "You too, Shaughnessy." Bird Dog moved his pip to the next target.

"MiGs! They've got a lock!" his RIO shouted. Bird Dog saw it immediately. He punched out chaff and flares, initiated jamming, and watched as the missile arced down cleanly from above, seeking out the Tomcat 5,000 feet below it. Bird Dog toggled off an AAMRAM at the aggressor.

MiG 102
1502 local (GMT-4)

Korsov snarled as he saw the missile symbols emerging from the Tomcat symbols. "You think that long-range weapons worry me?" he sneered. "I have a little something for you as well." He pickeled off his own long-range antiair missile, then turned his attention to the countermeasures and maneuvers he would need to evade the American missiles.

The Russian missile was not new technology. The seeker head was reverse-engineered from the American AMRAAM, the missile slightly longer, while the payload remained about the same. This particular warhead contained a net of expanding steel rods that would snag a Tomcat out of the air like a cat dipping into a fish tank. The missile was a bit slower than the AMRAAM but made up for it in endurance. It possesses a retargeting capability as well.

Because of the extended range and retargeting capability, it also possessed the small IFF receiver in the nose. In theory, it could tell friendly aircraft from enemy ones—in theory, at least. He knew that in every operational test so far, the system has proved less reliable than the rest of the missile. He would bet his life on it, but it did provide an additional measure of safety.

The disadvantage to the long-range Russian missiles was

that, since it was slightly heavier, the MiG could carry fewer of them. And, like the Hornet counterpart, the MiG packed less overall firepower than one Tomcat. Still, the MiGs were adept at working as small wolf packs and several smaller aircraft could easily bring down any number of larger ones as long as they worked together.

But working together without a GCI, or ground control interceptor, was a relatively new skill for them. Sure, they'd practiced, drilled, and trained for it, but in actual fact, maintaining coordination was only slightly more difficult than getting the IFF to work.

Still, as Korsov tracked the incoming AMRAAM, he saw his own missile was having the desired effect. The American forces below him were already scattering, breaking apart into pairs, some dodging and twisting now trying to evade the missiles homing in on them, others remaining rock steady and launching their own missiles before executing evasive maneuvers.

"Bolshoi flight, engage at will," Korsov ordered. "Lenin flight will refuel and rejoin on you shortly."

Bermuda
1502 local (GMT-4)

The SEALs moved west and south, seeking out the next missile launcher location on their chart. The final installation was downwind slightly from the mishap area, a fact that worried Parto somewhat. But, it seemed to be far enough away that the nerve agent might be disbursed before it reach them—or maybe not. They would watch the birds overhead carefully as they approached, assessing the possibility of danger. At this slightly lower altitude, the vegetation was even thicker, and it was almost impossible to move quickly and silently. But there was no time for caution, no time for a careful, invisible survey of the scene, a deliberate approach to maximize their advantage.

Whoever commanded this detachment ran a tight ship. Or perhaps someone had put out a warning, noting that four other truck installations had failed to answer routine security checks.

Whatever the reason, there were four men with weapons at the ready, each one intently scanning the jungle around them, alert and ready to act. The SEALs would have to do this one the hard way.

"On my command," Parto said, his voice barely audible as he spoke into the whisper-mike. "Guard's first, then the rest of them. Watch the missile." A series of clicks acknowledged his command.

Right, like I had to tell them that. Not after what Lacar saw.

The guard nearest to Parto was making the classic error of any watchstander. He was clearly assigned to cover a sector of ninety degrees of the jungle, and he had taken to pacing back and forth along his perimeter, falling into a rhythm as he scanned the jungle for intruders.

Suddenly, the radio slung on one man's hip blared to life. Parto could make out words, but he couldn't tell what they were saying. It sounded like Russian—he crept closer, hoping to be able to make out the orders.

"—launch now—" was the only phrase he was able to decipher. That alone was enough to make his blood run cold.

They would have to move in, and move in now. If there was a launch order, then there was no time to waste.

Parto waited until the man was as close to him as possible, and whispered, "Now!"

Before he could finish the word, gunfire crackled in the jungle. Parto fired himself, bringing down his man with a short burst of three rounds. The SEALs charged forward, weapons at the ready, to the very edge of the camp.

The Russian team was panicking, but panicking with a purpose. Everyone had a weapon drawn, and they were formed up in three small clusters, their backs to each other as they covered all angles of approach. One brave soldier scrambled to the control panel and was frantically typing, glancing over his shoulder as he did. The missile launcher started to move. It was already completely extended. A second round of gunfire rang out and the three clusters of men dropped. They were firing as they died, the shots going randomly to the jungle. But a random shot could kill you just as easily as a well-aimed one. Leahy hit the ground, sighted in on the man standing at the console, then put one round through his lower back, hoping that it didn't ricochet up into the missile.

It didn't. But before he died, the man had evidently completed his task. As Parto's last shot rang out, the missiles belched fire from its ass. A second later, it rattled off the rails, vaulted through the gap in the canopy overhead, and arrowed out into the blue sky.

Lacar fired at it as it came off the rails, hoping against hope to hit it, knowing that if he did he may have killed them all. But it launched untouched, and for a moment he wondered whether some subconscious instinct of self-preservation had skewed his aim. But sometimes lousy shooting was just lousy shooting.

"They got it off!" Lacar said, as he pointed up at the sky. He followed with a string of curses, as any of them were prone to do when they failed to do the impossible.

"But six others didn't," Parto pointed out.

All across the island, missiles were boiling up out of the green hills, gleaming white and shining against the deep blue sky. They were visible for only a few moments before they were out of range. "Could be more," one said, and Parto wasn't sure whether he meant that they could have eliminated more, or that there could be more launched. Either way, it didn't matter. Their window of opportunity was over.

"Come on, let's get out of here," Parto said. "We've got things to do."

SEVENTEEN

USS **Lake Champlain**
1540 local (GMT-4)

For just a moment, the Aegis computer stuttered. The flood of new contacts did not come close to overwhelming its capabilities, but they still had to be organized, assorted, assigned track numbers, and then processed for display. This took an eternity in computer time, almost two seconds in human time.

"Chief, get those little bastards designated," Coleman shouted. "I want a ripple shot, missiles on top of each one of them, now!"

"Roger, sir, switching to full auto," he said. He would let the computer do the assigning, weighing the priorities—he could do it himself, of course, but the computer was far faster, and with the number of targets arcing out from the island, speed mattered. "Sir, friendly forces are in the way! They need to descend to below ten thousand feet and clear a bearing sector out from our ship."

The TAO picked up the mike to make the call over tactical. "Hold fire, Chief. Wait until I give the word."

It wasn't like the aircraft could break off from everything they were doing simply to clear the area. Blue and red symbols were intertwined so closely it was almost impossible to tell what the boundaries of the air battle were. To turn tail and run would simply be to expose the most favorable target aspects to the enemy. Yes, they could move the battle to the south, but it would take a few minutes—and a few minutes was what they didn't have.

"All but three clear," he said. "Sir, the missiles will be out of range in approximately ten seconds. We have to fire now."

And risk those three aircraft that stood between the ship and the missiles? He had to. If the intelligence reports were correct, the nuclear, chemical, and biological warheads on those missiles were an order of magnitude greater threat than the loss of a few aircraft.

A few aircraft. He blinked, surprised that he was able to put it in those terms. Each one had two officers on board, officers that, if they weren't quick enough, would never see their families again.

"Weapons free, Chief," he said, his voice hard and cold. It was the right decision, but one that he already knew he would have to live with for the rest of his life.

MiG 102
1502 local (GMT-4)

Korsov checked his chronometer again. Ten seconds. Should he watch? Yes, he decided. He had to. He deserved it. He veered off course slightly, heading southeast, not giving up all of his forward progress but allowing him to watch the island. As the seconds ticked by, he felt his gut tighten.

And then there it was. Small puffs of smoke from the hill-tops, flying telephone poles emerging, heading straight up and then disappearing from sight. They would proceed to an altitude of 31,000 feet, then level out and begin the flight cruise toward the United States. Once within range of the coast, they would nose down, gain speed as they descended, and hit their preprogrammed targets.

The missiles were not terribly accurate. But, then, they didn't have to be. The chemical warheads would begin spewing their aerosols of sarin into the air during their descents. The fast-acting nerve agent would cause convulsions, choking, hemorrhaging, and speedy death.

The biological agents would follow up by disbursing their

particular brand of death. They were programmed to pull up out of their descent to conduct a spiraling descent to their targets, with aerosol disbursement initiated at one hundred feet. Some of the warheads contained anthrax spores, others a deadly African hemmoragic virus.

And, finally, the jewel of the entire arsenal, the three nuclear-tipped tactical weapons. Their accuracy was far greater than that of the biological or chemical weapons. By modern standards, their warheads were small. One was aimed at the White House, the other at the United Nations, and a third at Naval Station Norfolk. Their effects would be devastating.

Too bad he couldn't stick around to watch it. But, then, duty called.

He pulled back on to course and expanded the range of his radar screen. He could see most of the weapons now, in flight, continuing on exactly as planned. The Aegis cruiser was a problem, of course. He did not make the mistake of discounting her ability to knock down his missiles. She was, in fact, a frighteningly capable ship. But he was counting on the involvement of the air wing with the MiGs to muddy the picture, to clobber the area with contacts so that the Aegis would have to fire between them to reach the missiles. By the time the battle group could get the air wing out of the way, the Aegis missiles would be in a tail chase and it would be far more difficult to shoot them down.

Hornet 101
1502 local (GMT-4)

Thor heard the call to clear the area. Unfortunately, he was a little bit preoccupied at that moment. Two MiGs had decided that his little Hornet was just the target that they wanted that afternoon, and he was busy keeping track of them, dancing around the sky to avoid a missile lock, all while trying to line up for his own shot.

And where the hell was his wingman? Was he that black spot just at the edge of Thor's peripheral vision? He wasn't answering call ups—radio trouble? Or, was he already in the drink, inflating his life raft and watching the battle progressing overhead? Looking up from the sea, the life-and-death struggle taking place overhead would be barely visible, probably no more than sun glinting off metal.

"Thor, I'm coming in on you," a voice said over international military distress. "Lost frequency control."

Okay, it was radio problem. If Thor had had time, he would have felt relieved. But one of the MiGs was just then sliding into position behind him, its missiles hungry for the hot exhaust spewing out of his tailpipes. Thor tipped the nose down and flashed past the other aircraft as a streak of silver. He then pulled up hard, heard the Hornet howl its complaints as he exceeded recommended G forces, fought off the gray threatening his vision, and rolled back into position. His thumb toggled the weapons selector and he fired a Sparrow, performing exactly the shot that the MiG had intended just moments earlier.

"One zero one, clear the area—now! You're fouling our line of fire, mister."

"Listen, buddy, I would if I could," Thor said between clenched teeth, fighting to stay conscious, "but I'm a little busy right now. Maybe you noticed."

"Roger, sir, but we have launch indications from Bermuda. It's now or never."

"Do what you have to, buddy," Thor snapped. "If I can stay out of a MiG's line of fire, I sure as hell can avoid yours."

"Roger, sir, I'll do what I can to get you clear."

"Quit bothering me," Thor said. The MiG under his wing burst into a fireball, and Thor broke his Hornet hard away to avoid the flames.

"Randy, where are you?" he said over tactical. "What's with your damned radio?"

"—intermittent—too much data—" He heard Randy's garbled voice come back.

"Listen, if your receiver's okay, take low station. Where's that other MiG?"

And then he saw it. While he'd been preoccupied with the other one it had circled around and was now arrowing down out of the sun, intent on the kill. Thor's ECM warning system shrieked, and Thor pulled up his nose in order to face the incoming aircraft. In front of him, he saw a flash of silver, as

Randy's Hornet cut across at a right angle, guns blazing, trying for the knife fight kill.

"Inside minimums! I need to open on him," Thor shouted. "Randy, keep him occupied for a minute, then go buster when I tell you."

Had his wingman heard him? It looked like it—Randy broke off, pulled a tight, gut-wrenching turn, and was now diving back in on the MiG. Now that it was two on one, it was a far, far better situation to be in.

Thor raced away from the fight, keeping an eye out for telltale flames or hydraulic links. If Randy's guns had connected, then a missile shot might not be necessary at all. But from what he could see, the MiG was undamaged.

Fine. We'll do this the hard way.

With Randy playing cat and mouse with the MiG, Thor opened up the range to one mile, turned, and started back in. He got a solid lock on the MiG, then shouted, "Break now, Randy!" his finger poised over the weapons release button. "Come on, man, you're fouling my shot!"

But the Hornet and the MiG, almost equally matched in performance characteristics, had drawn themselves in to a close, tight circle, chasing each other, each trying for the tail shot, neither one willing to break out of the circle for fear of being the target. Thor circled above them, watched in frustration, hoping for a clear shot. Maybe if he went in with guns, and tried to pull them apart—yes, that might work. He was just starting in, closing to within one quarter mile when fire flashed in the MiG's wake. Thor immediately pulled out of his approach, popping chaff and flares as he did so, but he knew instinctively that was too late. Just before the MiG's missile reached him, his hand closed over the ejection handle and he yanked down.

How long was I out? Not long—shit, I'm still way up here. Did Randy get the MiG? As Thor regained consciousness, he had no loss of memory. It seemed as if a brief black flash had swept over him, to be replaced immediately by the realization that he was hanging suspended in the air beneath his parachute.

He saw an explosion in the air off to his right. A pressure wave of air swept over him. The noise of the explosions was muted by the rush of air as he fell.

Randy? Or the MiG? Then he saw the Hornet emerge from behind the fireball and turn toward him. Randy pulled up sharply as he approached Thor.

Damned fool is going to foul my chute if he's not careful.

He was cold, so cold. And it would get colder yet when he hit the water below him. But, if everything worked according to plan, he'd be picked up soon enough. He debated for a moment pulling out his rescue radio, but immediately decided against it. Too much danger of dropping it. Randy had seen him, seen the chute, and the helos would be on him after he splashed down. It wasn't like he could do a special forces midair recovery.

He saw it just then, a flash of silver off to his left, and swung himself around to face it. It was a missile—one of the cruisers? No, it was headed away from Bermuda. Damn, they'd gotten a shot off! And from the looks of it, the Aegis had missed it.

Thor was spinning around in a circle now, the result of the jet wash from Randy's Hornet. Thor drew his legs up to his belly and reached down into a side pocket that ran along his calf. His cold fingers fumbled with its zipper, trying to find purchase, and eventually he managed to snag the metal tab. He jerked it open, then reached in and closed cold fingers around the even colder grip of his nine millimeter pistol.

Careful, now. Don't blow it. But hurry.

He got two hands around the pistol butt, lifted it free of his pocket, and, operating on instinct, took aim on the missile that was broadside to him. He fired off three rounds, paused, then added another three.

At first, there seemed to be no effect. But, then he saw vapor streaming out of a hole in its side, enveloping the aft section in a white cloud. The missile veered sharply away then began tumbling ass over elbows out of the air, departing controlled fight in a truly impressive manner.

Thor watched with satisfaction for a moment. The motion of the parachute increased violently, an indication that he really needed to pay some serious attention to the risers if he expected to make it down to the surface of the ocean. He started to drop the gun, then tucked it down the front of his flight suit. He still had two rounds left, and no Marine ever wastes ammo.

I'm claiming that one, and I don't care who believes me. The ocean surged up to meet him.

EIGHTEEN

With his binoculars, Maskiro could see tiny streaks of black smoke in the air to the north, indiscernible to the naked eye and just barely visible under magnification. His missiles, launching, heading for the United States with their deadly payloads.

For perhaps the thousandth time since Korsov had approached him, Maskiro wondered just how reliable the genetically targeted warheads would be. Korsov had wanted to refit all the long-range weapons with them.

Maskiro had not been convinced. Yes, it was a wonderful idea if they worked as advertised. Yes, he too would be pleased to see the American continent resettled with Russian citizens. But, try as he might, he could not convince himself that the plan was as infallible as Korsov claimed. So the new warheads were mounted on only one-third of the missiles. The remainder contained tried-and-true chemical, biological, and nuclear warheads. One way or the other, America would suffer.

And how was Korsov's part of the plan proceeding? He tried to correlate what he saw with the chatter over the tactical circuit, but there was no way to be certain whose aircraft had been hit. He knew his resupply squadron would be low on fuel, and this battle had to be finished quickly and decisively.

Reports on the radio were complicated by the fact that there were far more kills reported than there were aircraft in the sky. If the pilots were to be believed, every Russian aircraft that launched a missile scored a kill—and that he found hard to believe. He felt an increasingly uneasy conviction that if Korsov were left to his own devices, the entire reinforcement squadron would be lost. And that was not acceptable.

"All flights, disengage. I repeat, disengage," Maskiro said. "Break off as soon as consistent with safety of flights, and proceed due east. Then turn hard south, increase speed to maximum, and descend to three thousand feet."

"Three thousand feet? Sir, our fuel reserves—" a voice said.

"I know about your fuel consumption rates," Maskiro cut in, scowling. "If you descend to three thousand feet, I can fire over you at the Americans and they will break off long enough for you to land. You'll be refueled immediately, and relaunch. Do it now. You can stay airborne long enough to win this fight."

"This is not your decision," Korsov's voice cut in. "We agreed that the air elements were under my sole command."

Rage rushed through Maskiro. Everything depended on having enough MiGs to maintain air superiority, and Korsov was risking everything. "Stay airborne if you will," Maskiro said coldly. "But in one minute I am launching a massive antiair attack. You know that the missiles are supposed to distinguish between friend and foe. Are you willing to bet your life on it?"

There was silence on the circuit for a moment, then a reluctant, "Roger, acknowledged. Breaking contact, turning east."

Tomcat 302
1504 local (GMT-4)

Shaughnessy studied the MiG's maneuvers. First they broke into two segments, and now they were reforming into a single flight. A change of plans? But, why?

"Bird Dog, what do you think they're doing?" she asked.

"Don't know, don't care. Kill 'em all and let God sort them out," her lead replied immediately, firing another AMRAAM.

"But don't you think that we—?"

"You don't think. You do what I tell you. I'm not going to be responsible for you buying it on this mission, you got it? Now get back up to altitude."

They're trying to get to the base to refuel, Shaughnessy suddenly realized. *Refuel and rearm. But why do they feel like they can risk turning their backs on us right now? Why now?* She wasn't certain, but she was determined to find out.

NINETEEN

Infuriated, Korsov watched the rest of his flight head toward the island. So, they would obey Maskiro rather than him, would they? Well, that would be their undoing.

Korsov had no illusions about being able to permanently hold out against the Americans. Indeed, he was willing to sacrifice a certain percentage of his forces—a large percentage—for the eventual victory. As long as they could hold off the Americans for a while, the Americans would soon have other worries besides Bermuda. With the missiles in flight now, it was simply a matter of time until they could consolidate their position on Bermuda unopposed.

Korsov had prepared for the possibility of a temporary defeat. Maskiro had not.

Somewhere, approximately 400 miles to the south, there was an AGI, a Russian fishing boat. For decades the AGIs had patrolled off the coast of the United States, yes, indeed fishing, while they performed other missions as well. Their superstructures bristled with antennas, far more than one would expect on a simple fishing boat. And, inside, half of the upper deck contained electronics and interception devices. Yes, the AGIs knew these waters well, and would respond immediately to his emergency distress beacon.

Korsov did not consider himself a coward, although to many running away from the fight would appear to be exactly that. He thought of his invasion plans in terms of the larger picture. He was the one with the vision, the determination to restore Russia to her rightful place in the world. It was essential that he survive. And, to that end, this was the entirely necessary and logical course of action to conclude the Bermuda operation.

He estimated that it might take as long as a week for the Americans to completely abandon their attack on Bermuda and turn their attention back to their own mainland. Korsov was prepared to wait them out, counting on Maskiro to keep any other aircraft from landing for just a few days. After that, the Americans would have already embargoed Bermuda.

He switched the radio transponder over to the preassigned frequency, and contacted the AGI. The master answered immediately, his voice uneasy. He hadn't been told of all the details—it had not been necessary. But by now he would have some clue as to what was happening, both over the military channels he had access to and local radio reports.

Fine, it made no difference at all. The master would still do his duty and retrieve Korsov from the sea.

And then it would begin again.

Tomcat 301
1524 local (GMT-4)

"They're running," Bird Dog yelled, glee in his voice. "Couldn't take the heat, could you?"

"And just where are they running to?" Shaughnessy's tart voice asked. "You think they're planning on heading out to open ocean and ejecting? Because I have to tell you, Bird Dog, I find that pretty improbable. They're heading for the island to refuel, and I for one would very much not like that to happen."

"Where the hell are you?" Bird Dog demanded, a cold feeling starting in his gut. Surely she wouldn't try to take on half a squadron of MiGs on her own? "I don't have you in the LINK."

"Neither do I," the Hawkeye confirmed. "She's not breaking mode four."

"Shaughnessy, you are RTB—I repeat, RTB. Your mode four is down, sweetheart, and I don't want to take the chance that you—"

"I'm not breaking because I secured my IFF," Shaughnessy's calm voice replied. "I'm due south of you, eight miles off the coast—pretending to be a Cessna."

Bird Dog's jaw dropped. "You're my wingman," he shouted. "What the hell—?"

"Oh, but you don't need a wingman, do you? Or, at least that was the impression I got in the ready room."

"I don't. But that doesn't mean you can take off on your own and secure your IFF," Bird Dog shot back. "Dammit, Shaughnessy, you turn that gear back on and get back up here. You know that what you're doing is—"

"Intercepting them before they can turn back to the island?" she finished for him, her voice sharp. "Maybe if you'd been less worried about the chase and more focused on the eventual objective, you might have noticed what they were doing. I tried to tell you, but you didn't want listen. So I came out here to handle it myself."

By then, Bird Dog had turned south, kicked in the afterburner, and was heading buster for his errant wingman. One look at his HUD showed that every member of the flight was doing the same.

Her tail number flashed on his HUD, indicating she had turned her IFF back on. "Catch me if you can," Shaughnessy said.

Air Traffic Control Tower
1526 local (GMT-4)

War was a hard business. There were always casualties. The trick was to pile up more on the other side than on your own.

Somewhere along the way, Korsov's original dream of a Russian resettlement of America had gradually transformed itself into a victory of a more personal nature for Maskiro.

Certainly, the glory of Russia remained the most important consideration. Of course it did.

Didn't it?

Yes, of course. Maskiro ran a finger around his collar, wondering if the launch of the special weapons had somehow tainted his own air. He felt odd, disoriented. So much had gone wrong.

Of the twenty MiGs comprising the second flight, only eleven remained. And, of that eleven, ten were flat out running for the island, all at 3,000 feet. Their fuel consumption at that altitude was brutal due to the drag of the denser, thicker air. Only the tail-end aircraft was still above 3,000 feet, and he was descending rapidly. But he'd started too late, and the geometry wasn't going to cut him any breaks.

If I don't act now, the American aircraft will be within weapons release range. If they're carrying ground attack missiles, everything is lost. If the missile discriminator IFF is ever going to work, it has to work now.

Knowing he had the Aegis to deal with and that he might be signing the last MiG's death warrant, Maskiro ordered all the remaining antiair batteries to open fire on the Americans.

TWENTY

Tomcat 301
1531 local (GMT-4)

The area around the coast fuzzed out. For a moment, Bird Dog thought they were experiencing equipment problems, but behind him his RIO was swearing quietly. As he watched, what had looked like interference resolved into individual contacts spaced so closely that at extended range they appeared to be a single band of green on the radar screen.

"We got a launch, ZUS-9!" his RIO shouted. The warble of the ESM cut him off, confirming his conclusion.

The missiles fired from the trucks were far less accurate at long range. Their primary use was against ground attack aircraft, and they were deadly at short ranges due to their exceptionally short reaction time. But they weren't as fast as the missiles carried on the MiGs, and thus were easier to evade.

But they don't need to kill us, do they? Just keep us away. They're accurate enough for that.

Or are they? I'm faster, better reflexes, all that, right? And they are limited on turns. I remember that from the briefing. So, if I get close and don't give them any time to react, they won't be that difficult to avoid, will they?

"Listen up," Bird Dog ordered. He described his plan over tactical, talking over the expressions of disbelief he heard coming from the other aircraft as he explained the dynamics of what he proposed. He concluded with, "Not everybody can hack it, I know that. So, I'm leaving it up to the RIOs. You know who you're with—if you trust your pilot enough to try it, join me."

"Piece of cake, Bird Dog," Shaughnessy said, her voice lazy and almost amused. "The defenses are so slow and clumsy it's like trying to beat you up the ladder to the flight deck. Just stay loose, watch what they're doing, and you can turn inside every time." As Bird Dog watched, Shaughnessy's tail number entered the green blur around the island, dancing through a storm of enemy missiles.

"If she can do it, so can I," one voice said.

"Me, too." Without exception, they were all in.

Bird Dog could see Shaughnessy below him, maybe 10,000 feet below him, a silver spec trailing con trails as it streaked across the whitecapped ocean. She was alone, violating the first commandment of fighter combat—never leave your wingman. Nevertheless, she had, and Bird Dog was seriously pissed.

But not pissed enough to abandon her.

Time seemed to slow down, even as his mind raced. The missiles rising up from the ridge running down the center of the island were creeping up to the sky, moving so slowly that he could see every detail of their shape. It seems like he had forever to evade them, but he knew that overconfidence killed at least as many pilots as enemy fire.

With the Tomcat moving at almost Mach 1 and a missile closing at slightly less than that, reaction time was measured in seconds. And there was no telling how many warheads they had on each missile. No, it was like a picket fence that stood between him and Shaughnessy, even assuming that the seeker head on the missiles had a lock on her.

Behind him, the rest of the flight was thinking exactly the same thing. But picket fence or no, they would have to wind their way through it. Because, just in front of Shaughnessy, and already curving back around to catch her, was a pack of MiGs. One had curved off from the course the others were on as though curious, taking a look back along their six to see the lone Tomcat trapped below a layer of missiles. Bird Dog could imagine the pilots evaluating her predicament like a pack of wolves stalking a young elk separated from the pack. However good a pilot she might be, Shaughnessy couldn't stand up to an entire flight of MiGs.

The other possibility was that she could run the missile picket fence herself and rejoin the rest in the Tomcat flight. But in the long run, that would leave them in no better position than they were in right now. There would still be a flight of MiGs to be destroyed and there'd still be the missile trucks next time they tried.

No, better to finish this once and for all. If Shaughnessy could find her way through a cloud of launching missiles, Bird Dog could, too.

"Home Plate, Bird Dog. We're going in." A flurry of clicks on tactical from the other aircraft acknowledged his order.

"Alpha flight, this is alpha leader. You heard what the lady said—they're slow and dumb. Keep your airspeed down to have time to react, but not so slow that they have time to catch you. Just be slightly faster, and a hell of a lot smarter. It should take you about ten seconds to transit the danger zone, and I want every last one of you pumping countermeasures as we go through it. All right, follow me."

Bird Dog nosed the Tomcat down and decreased his airspeed slightly. Four hundred knots—yes, that should do it. "Keep your eyes glued to your radar screen," Bird Dog ordered. "Call out the closest threat so I can get a visual on it."

"They've got some sort of coating on, Bird Dog," his RIO answered. "Not the greatest radar contacts in the world. Some of them are fading in and out."

"Jamming of some sort?"

"I don't think so," the RIO answered, but his voice was doubtful. "Maybe. It's more likely that they've got some sort of stealth coation on them. I'm getting a scatter effect, sort of—keeps them from having a solid return."

"First one coming up in about five seconds," Bird Dog said. "Like I said, stick to the radar—I'll handle visuals, unless you tell me the radar is totally useless."

"Roger. Recommend you descend four hundred feet, come right hard. That should put us underneath it. Even if it locks, is going to have a tough time making a hundred eighty degree turn."

"Concur." Although his HUD display provided him enough information to make the same call himself, Bird Dog didn't even bother with it. His eyes were his combat information system; they told him the angle of approach and the relative speeds more accurately than any set of sterile numbers ever could.

Bird Dog snapped the Tomcat down and hard to the right. "Take it easy," his RIO said. "Or, at least warn me."

"Next target," Bird Dog said.

"Come left, ease back a bit, then back hard right and continue descending," the RIO said promptly.

So far, the plan seemed to be working out really well. He could hear over tactical that some of the pilots were cutting it a bit too close, mainly by the anguish howling from their RIOs. Still, there were no explosions.

It was almost like playing a video game. After he evaded the first few, it took on a feeling of unreality. Were those really live missiles or just pixels on a screen? One part of his mind knew better than that, and he tried to pay attention to that, tried not to relax.

"Bird Dog, they're on her!" his RIO shouted. Shaughnessy and a flight of MiGs were below him and slightly aft, and Bird Dog had lost a visual on them. He jerked his gaze back to his HUD. His RIO was right.

"We're taking too long," Bird Dog snapped. "We've got to get down there."

"If you go any faster, you're going to screw it up," his RIO said, his voice now seriously concerned. "I'm doing the best that I can."

"I'm not," Bird Dog said grimly. He jammed the throttle forward. "Coming right for two hundred feet, another right turn, then down five hundred feet. Double check me."

So this is how it would work best. He would do what his gut told him was right, counting on the RIO to catch it if he made a mistake.

The feeling of being in a video game disappeared abruptly. Everything was moving much faster, so fast that there wasn't even time to think. It was all reflexes and nerves. He doubted that most of the squadron could keep up, but he was counting on their own good sense and their RIOs to know what their limitations were. But it was his wingman down there and he was going to get there in time, or die trying.

"She's got three MiGs on her, Bird Dog. One's got a lock.

She's trying to shake him—there, it took the chaff. But the other two are trying to box her in."

Dammit, Shaughnessy, hold on. I'll be there in a second—just hold on.

Bird Dog stared straight ahead, not even daring to blink. At this speed, the few microseconds it took to shut his eyes and open them might get them killed.

"No!" the RIO shouted. "Hard right—now!"

Bird Dog hesitated for a split second, and almost made a fatal mistake. He was near the bottom of the missile field now, and the MiGs were rising to greet him. If he continued the maneuver he'd planned, he'd fall right into a perfect firing position on them. The RIO's plan was risky, but it might just work.

Time stopped again. The Tomcat seemed to respond so slowly that he wondered if he'd lost control surfaces. But the instrument panel was solid green lights, and he could feel the thrum of the aircraft biting into the air at a different angle.

As he came around, his wings swept back at maximum angle, he saw the missile. It was inching toward them, gleaming white, wobbling ever so slightly in the air as it rammed through his jet wash. It seemed to be staring at him, watching, determined to take him out. He knew where it would hit, too, felt it as a crawling sensation on his skin as though he were melded with the fuselage. Just after the cockpit, on the left side. It would destroy the wing first, plunging the Tomcat into a terminal barrel role, then continue on into the fuselage itself, detonating just after penetration. The fireball and the destruction would be instantaneous.

"No!" Bird Dog howled. He jammed the Tomcat down into a vertical dive, not sure if there were more missiles in front of him, but not caring. If he didn't get out of this one's way within the next few seconds, it was all over.

"Pull up!" the RIO shouted. "You're past it! Pull up, Bird Dog."

"Bird Dog, I can't shake this one," Shaughnessy said, her voice shaky for the first time since he'd known her. "I tried everything, but it's like it's reading my mind. Every turn I try—"

"Break hard to the right," Bird Dog ordered, now diving straight for her. "Now, Shaughnessy—now! Break!"

Shaughnessy obeyed instantly. Her Tomcat rolled over, dived toward the ocean in a hard right turn and the MiG followed. As the MiG turned, it exposed its tailpipe to Bird Dog. He snapped off a white Sidewinder, which shot out and immediately acquired the blazing hot exhaust from the MiG. It accelerated, slamming into it before the MiG even realized he was no longer alone.

"Get back up here," Bird Dog ordered. He brought the Tomcat around the hard turn, and saw the rest of the MiGs heading back toward him.

But the rest of his flight was now descending through the thicket of missiles, and the lead aircraft fired an AMRAAM into the pack, forcing them into evasive maneuvers and dispersing them. From their superior altitude, the Tomcats wreaked havoc.

"We're in the line of fire" Bird Dog shouted to Shaughnessy. "Buster, to the north!"

"Roger," Shaughnessy said, her voice still shaky, and Bird Dog saw that she was turning even before she responded.

They headed north to clear the AMRAAMs and resulting fireballs, then arced around to rejoin the rest of the flight. A few of the remaining MiGs had the same idea and also headed north, but the Tomcat flight quickly dealt with those. Finally, when they'd established complete control of the air, Bird Dog said, "Come on, people. Let's get those trucks."

Southeastern tip of Bermuda
Truck Station Four
1439 local (GMT-4)

Sergeant Oleg Kaminiski shouted frantically at the conscripts swarming over the missile launchers. The ripple launching had gone well, so very well that there should've been no way for the Americans to survive it.

But survive it they had, and he didn't need a control tower to tell him that. His own rudimentary targeting radar showed the clouds of interference generated by the chaff, then the harder discrete contacts emerging from it. There would be a second round of missiles, and then a third if necessary. They could not keep this up forever.

He was sweating heavily, the salt water trickling down his spine and soaking into the waistband of his pants. He could feel more sweat rolling down his face and his scalp itched where it collected.

Damn this hot weather. It wasn't right, expecting a man to live in this.

"Hurry, or you'll kill us all!" Oleg crawled up onto the bed of the truck. He shoved aside the conscript who was holding one end of the firing cable in his hand, staring at it as though it were a snake. "Have you forgotten everything? Connect it then get clear. Move, I'll do it myself."

How far away where they? Were they even now firing antiradiation missiles, seeking out the warm scent of his radar?

"There!" He jammed the housing home, and a green light on the panel went on, indicating a solid fire control circuit. "Stand by to—"

But the conscript he'd shoved out of the way had forgotten more than how to connect the cable to the housing. He'd also forgotten every basic safety precaution. Before Oleg could finish his sentence, before he could even get clear of the tail of the missile, the conscript punched the firing button.

Oleg had just a second to stare in horror as a high-pitched sizzle started behind him. He turned just as the rocket engine ignited, toxic fumes spewing out from its tail seconds before fire burst out.

Every inch of his skin was incinerated immediately. It clung to the remainder of his body, masking the slow cooking taking place underneath charred flesh. His hair flashed into fire and then ash, as did his eyes.

By the time Oleg's body fell from the truck bed to the dark, rich ground, he was already dead.

MiG 101
1523 local (GMT-4)

"Who's that?" Tombstone said, indicating a lone radar contract to the south. "He's pretty far away from the fight—is he waiting on us?"

"I don't think so." Greene's voice was puzzled. "He's heading due south—but he's off axis of our course."

"Hawkeye, got any idea?"

"It's a MiG out of area. There's nothing to the south of us in the air."

Tombstone recalled the large-scale briefing plot he'd seen in TFCC. A possibility occurred to him as he remembered the AGI to the south.

"I think I know where he's headed," Tombstone said. He put the MiG into a hard turn to the south. "And I think I'll stop him from getting there."

TWENTY-ONE

MiG 102
1550 local (GMT-4)

With seventy-five miles of airspace between his aircraft and the island, Korsov was beginning to relax. The rest of the flight had hardly noticed when he departed, and, although there had been one question from the flight leader, no one has followed up. They had their hands full dealing with the waves of American aircraft coming at them. The shore-based missiles were giving them some cover, but he gathered from the radio traffic that most of the ZUS-9 trucks had been eliminated somehow. Something about a MiG firing on them—no, that was impossible. While it wasn't inconceivable that there could have been a defector, there could have been no motivation to destroy their own antiair missile sites, none whatsoever. Not with the Americans breathing down their necks.

He was holding the AGI on his radar now. It was only a matter of minutes before he was in area for a quick pick up. He had used afterburner the entire way—no use worrying about fuel consumption now, not when he expected to abandon this airframe shortly.

The sudden *deedle deedle* of his ESM warning system snapped him out of his pleasant anticipation of the future. Who was . . . ? He glanced at the scanner, and noted it was another MiG. But why would another MiG set off his warning system?

It wouldn't. Not unless he'd been swept by fire control radar specifically in launch mode.

Another contact snapped into being on his screen and he stared at it in disbelief. The sheer shock stunned him for a second, and then he began working rapidly.

An incoming missile—and from another MiG! Had they somehow detected his treachery and broke off one covertly to follow him? A MiG, of all things—he could understand a Tomcat chasing him down, although most of their attention was still fixed on the air battle off the coast.

Why another MiG?

Well, no matter. He had been a senior instructor at their advanced fighter tactics school not so long ago, and anything the pilot facing him knew Korsov had taught him. He should've known it would come to this. Everything had gone far too smoothly. There would have to be one final test, one final confrontation.

Korsov turned back to face the other MiG, now regretting the long sprint in afterburner. He would have to watch his fuel, and watch it carefully. He began climbing rapidly, pumping chaff and flares as he did so, creating a curtain of metal and heat behind him, hoping it would hide him for even just a few moments. He also activated his IFF transponder on the off chance that a missile IFF seeker head wasn't malfunctioning. Finally, he gained altitude, knowing that he might be able to outmaneuver the other pilot.

The other MiG was heading straight for him, ascending to meet him, searching for another lock on him. But the avionics resisted targeting a friendly, now with his IFF on, and that would work in his favor as well.

The first missile selected a particularly attractive flair hanging in the air and detonated inside its plume, satisfied that it had found its target. Korsov considered abandoning his dash to the south. He could turn north and try to circle in behind the other MiG.

But whoever was chasing him had already thought of that. The MiG cut around in a curve, trying to position itself behind him for a tail shot. The simple heat seeker wouldn't care that his IFF was screaming out a warning. It would see only heat— nice, tasty heat—and it would home in on it.

The other pilot was also smart enough to keep the sun behind him, producing not only a glare in Korsov's eyes but an enticing target for the no-brainer heat seeker that Korsov wanted to fire.

Who is it? Korsov ran through the faces and names of the men assigned to the first squadron and rejected each one as lacking sufficient balls even to attempt to come after him. Could it have been someone from the second flight? No, they were still too far to the east and dealing with the mass of Tomcats intercepting them.

No matter. He would make short work of him, and then continued his intercept to the AGI.

MiG 101
1551 local (GMT-4)

"This is no novice," Tombstone said, grunting against the G forces. The light, quickly accelerating MiG was constantly challenging his ability to remain conscious during maneuvers that would have been prosaic in a Tomcat. "Whoever he is, he's good—real good."

"Tombstone—you know I have some time in Hornets," Greene said. "You're good, real good in this MiG. You already proved that. I'm just reminding you, pilot to pilot. You're fighting an equal now, not a Tomcat. Remember, as maneuverable as he is, you are too."

"I know that," Tombstone said. "But, you're right—this is going to take both of us. Eyes and ears, Jeremy. If you got any thoughts, I want to hear them."

"I'm trying get a lock on him, but damn!" Greene said. "The avionics do *not* want to target another MiG—they do not. Whatever IFF is built into it is recognizing him as a friendly."

"Does it work the same way for us?" Tombstone asked.

"It should. The bottom line is, I wouldn't guarantee that either one of you can fire smart weapons on the other."

"Then he knows that, too."

"I imagine so. There's a reason he has the gain turned up on his IFF."

"Okay. We do this the hard way." Tombstone put the MiG into a hard turn. The other pilot was already climbing, exposing his tailpipes to Tombstone, but, before he could toggle off a heat seeker, the MiG abruptly turned, and came back down toward him head-to-head, and closing fast.

"Shit!" Tombstone felt the MiG shudder and swore quietly. "Any damage?" He tried all the controls, assessing her response. "I don't think so."

"Looks all right back here—wait, no. I lost radar. We must have taken a round in the radome. And I wouldn't vouch for the communications, either."

"Two can play this game," Tombstone said. "Where is he? You're going to have to keep him in visual for me."

"Low, three o'clock."

Tombstone rolled his MiG inverted and located his target. The other aircraft was rising to meet him. Tombstone flipped nose on to him and pivoted, so nimble that the turn was almost midair, and then launched a heat seeker. The other MiG immediately filled the air with chaff and flares, but the missile had achieved its main purpose, that of shaking up the other pilot and breaking his concentration. Every time he had to stop to evade a missile, there was a chance he would make a mistake.

"I don't see any damage," Greene said, his voice strained as he twisted in his seat to keep the MiG in view. "He's climbing again, Tombstone—seven o'clock and going high. And I think east—*missile launch!*"

"I hope you're right about the IFF," Tombstone said quietly. "Because I'm about to try something."

Tombstone ignored the missile completely. The other pilot was counting on it to shake him up to make them break off from the offensive, into the defensive, for just a moment, just as Tombstone had done a moment ago when their positions were reversed. But if Greene was right, the missile couldn't target them, and he could play on the false assumption. Play on it and win. Tombstone put the MiG into a short arc, intending to make it look like the beginning of an expected evasion maneuver. But, instead of completing the turn, he turned back toward the other contact while simultaneously ejecting his own mass of chaff and flares. With any luck, there might be one, maybe two seconds when the other pilot didn't know what was going on.

He was at a perfect angle for a gun shot, the other aircraft beam on to him. He let rip an extended blast from the nose cannon and had the satisfaction of seeing a short line stitched down the metal fuselage. But had he hit anything vital? Judging from how well his own MiG had absorbed several rounds, he suspected that key components had additional shielding he hadn't been told about.

"Any damage?" Tombstone shouted, turning away from the contact and climbing for altitude. "Hydraulics, anything?"

"I don't see anything, but I can't see it all," Greene shouted, frustrated beyond measure. "I know you got him, but I can't see what it did."

MiG 102
1553 local (GMT-4)

Korsov swore quietly as he saw the other aircraft ignore the smart missile and continue toward him. His aircraft shuddered as the rounds from the nose cannon connected and warning lights popped on. The main hydraulics line had been punctured, and he was losing hydraulic fluid. He toggled the primary valves shut electronically and switched to the secondary loop. The MiG had triple redundancies built in to all control systems, so, while leaking hydraulic fluid certainly posed a fire hazard, it wouldn't cause him to lose control.

He circled back around to meet the other contact, still trying to figure out what happened. There was something inconsistent in the other pilot's reactions. After the first missile, he behaved as though he thought it would actually target him. But any MiG pilot would have known that such could not be the case, that the only thing he had to worry about was the heat seeker and the guns. Could he have forgotten? Again, Korsov mentally surveyed the faces of the pilots in the first flight. No. Not a one of them would have forgotten that single most vital concept.

Then who? It was almost as if—

A thought struck him like a bolt of lightning, and all at once everything made sense. The vague reports of a MiG firing on the antiair sites, the questions shouted out that one aircraft was at too low an altitude—it was a MiG, but it was not a Russian MiG!

Then who? A pilot from a former client state, drafted into the service of the Americans? Or an American himself?

Yes. An American. That explained the unexpected appearance of the MiG. It had launched from the aircraft carrier, closed the air battle, and proceeded on to Bermuda. Once finished there, it had noticed his aircraft departing, and chosen to give chase.

Outrage boiled over him. How dare they! Insult to injury— well, the pilot would pay for this. It was probably a Hornet pilot, the most comparable aircraft the Americans possessed. But, regardless of how experienced he was, he would never know the MiG as well as Korsov did. Training and experience would make the killing difference.

It was time for a sucker punch.

MiG 101
1554 local (GMT-4)

"I lost him," Greene announced. "He's in the sun somewhere, and I can't make him out in the glare."

"Let's just take a precautionary shot, then," Tombstone said. He toggled off another heat seeker toward the sun and followed up with a short burst of the gun. "Anything?"

"No. The radar's completely down."

A sudden thought occurred to Tombstone. "Do you remember how many rounds they carry in the nose gun?"

"Not exactly. I remember it was less than the Tomcat, that's all."

"Shit." Tombstone's instinct told him that he had expended approximately half of the rounds in his gun, but his instincts were based on the larger carrying capacity of the Tomcat. With a MiG, who knew how low he was? "Is there any way to check in the avionics?"

"No. It's down—everything down."

Suddenly, the aircraft came screaming in on them, coming out of the sun, apparently completely undamaged. Tombstone toggled off the short burst, falling away in a barrel roll as he did so in an attempt to evade the return fire. He took a visual on the sun to maintain situational awareness, then tried to duplicate the maneuver the other had attempted.

"He's coming at us, Tombstone—his radar's still working."

"I know—the heat seekers, though."

"You have to finish this, and finished it fast," Greene said quietly, his voice taking on an odd note. "Stoney, he knows his aircraft—we're just amateurs. If you try to fight him one-on-one, we're going to lose. So, at least get us down to a survivable altitude for ejection."

"No punching out, not unless we're hit bad," Tombstone said. He did, however, descend 2,000 feet, putting them at the very edge of the ejection envelope. "And if we're going down, we're taking him with us. You think he knows how to play chicken?"

MiG 102
1555 local (GMT-4)

Now content that he knew who the other pilot was, Korsov toyed with him. Yes, the man appeared to be a competent aviator, but he was not a veteran MiG pilot. He had a heavy hand on the controls and missed opportunities for maneuver that any one of his former students would have recognized.

Korsov turned again, trying to get the advantage of the sun again, but the other aircraft turned to intercept him. He turned as well, then began firing, positioning the nose gun carefully and directing its fire for maximum effect.

The first few rounds hit. The MiG pulled up nose high and the inexperienced pilot evidently overcorrected, sending her tail over nose, tumbling, somersaulting across the sky. Korsov watched the MiG depart controlled flight, faintly disappointed. ACM should end with fire and smoke, not with a quiet splash in the ocean three miles below.

Well, a kill was a kill. Korsov rolled his neck, working the tension out that always settled in during the combat. He turned back to the south. Critically low on fuel, he contacted the AGI and ordered the master to make best speed toward him. He proceeded at max conserve speed to the south. In another five minutes, he would commence his descent—his final descent. He would eject from the aircraft at 3,000 feet.

MiG 101
1555 local (GMT-4)

The aircraft shook violently, the engines screaming like banshees as the aircraft tumbled though the sky. Tombstone fought the disorientation as he tried to stabilize her motion into a flat spin. Anything was better than this wild uncontrolled motion— there was no way even to begin to recover from this, and there wasn't even a very good chance of ejecting. More than likely, they'd smash into the aircraft within microseconds of punching out.

Recovering from a flat spin in a Tomcat was almost impossible. But maybe, just maybe, if he stomped hard enough on the control surface and kicked in afterburners, he could manhandle the lighter MiG. The engines might be able to overpower, at least temporarily, through brute force, the aircraft's gyrating motion. Then maybe he could convert the flat spin into something he *could* deal with.

Sure enough, the MiG slowly went nose down, and after four more gyrations, quit swapping nose with ass. Now she was headed straight down, her speed increasing with every moment, every support structure howling in protest. Tombstone pulled back on her, watching all the controls redline, fighting against the blackness. Behind him, he heard Greene shouting, coaching him, insulting him, anything to keep him conscious.

Finally, when the strain on his arms was almost unbearable, the death dive flattened out slightly. The MiG's nose twitched upward ever so slightly. Tombstone cut back slightly on the power and increased the angle on the control surfaces. Ever so gradually, the MiG began to respond.

But would it be enough? The altimeter was already unwinding past 10,000 feet and he still had not regained control.

Can't rush it—too much too soon, and you'll stall. Not enough, and you'll never make it.

A Tomcat could withstand far more stress in her structural

members than the men in her, and Tombstone forced himself not to pull up too hard on her. But, dammit, she had to recover fast, or there'd be no chance at all.

Remember, your reflexes are based on a Tomcat. This aircraft is lighter—yes, she's tough, but not that tough. You don't know how much she will take.

Her wings were thrumming in the air, vibrating curiously as the air poured over them. She started to shake, more violently than she ever had before, and for a moment he was afraid they were not going to make it.

But, then, ever so slightly, her nose came up. Not much, but enough to send a surge of hope coursing through him. He eased back on the throttle.

Her airspeed indicator quivered and started dropping. He pulled back harder, willing with every ounce of his being into her sinews of hydraulic lines, making himself one with her. He felt her pain, the agony at her wing roots, the excruciating pain in her control surfaces. Yet valiantly she fought on, trying her best to respond to the insane demands he placed on her. And, gradually, she did it.

They could have been in the dive for hours. It seemed to him he had spent a lifetime inside the MiG's cockpit, straining to pull her up, fighting the forces of drag and gravity. How she had managed to hold together he would never know, but somehow she had.

He heard Greene gasp in relief in the back seat. Tombstone did not yet trust himself to speak.

Every second of level flight sent adrenaline coursing through him. He tried a few, cautious maneuvers, testing her aerodynamics—yes, she was fine, no sluggishness or unexpected jolts indicating damage control surfaces. Finally, when he was satisfied that she was not seriously damaged, he said, "So we're still here."

"Yeah," Greene managed.

There were a few seconds of silence, and Tombstone said, "Why didn't you eject? After all you've talked about it— well—I thought—"

Silence. "Because I thought you would pull us out," Greene said finally. "No, that's not fair. I knew you would. And I— *there he is!*"

Tombstone scanned the area outside of his canopy, looking

for what had caught Greene's attention. His eyes were burning fuzzy from the force of pulling down during the dive. "Two o'clock low—it's him!"

Now Tombstone had a visual on the other MiG. Yes, it was the MiG they'd been chasing, the one he simulated this death fall in order to trick into complacency. Because his plan had worked exactly as he hoped. Everyone knew—knew with absolute certainty—that a MiG could not recover from a flat spin.

Tombstone had known better. He had trusted his instincts with her, had put his life in her hands, and she had come through for him. Sometimes what you know wasn't as important as what you believed.

"The tail number—did you see the tail number!" Greene shouted. "It's the same MiG, Tombstone—the MiG in Chechnya!"

And so it was. Tombstone recognized the tail number, along with the odd streak of red along the vertical stabilizer. "How the hell—never mind! Any second now he's going to realize that—"

Too late. The MiG jinked violently out of the way as the pilot evidently looked up and saw his adversary still airborne.

Tombstone dove after him, holding his fire for a few seconds then slammed his finger down on the fire button.

MiG 102
1559 local (GMT-4)

It was like seeing a ghost. Korsov shuddered as he looked up and saw the MiG cruising above him. It could not be—no MiG could recover from that violent a spin.

An ancient dread crept into Korsov's soul, one born in the flat targas of Russian. This is no aircraft, not a MiG with an American pilot. It was a demon, a lost soul cruising these winds—and it was searching for him.

With a cry, Korsov cut away from it, thinking only of running. Panic threatened to overwhelm him and he caught himself, realizing that the surest way to die was to panic.

The AGI—she is so close! I have to find her. And if it's a demon, she can follow me to hell.

Korsov turned, his hand on the ejection handle, checked his altitude, and said a silent prayer to his ancestors that he'd survive the ejection at this altitude. He yanked down on the ejection bar.

MiG 101
1600 local (GMT-4)

"Oh, dear God," Tombstone breathed. His mouth dropped open as he stared in shock at what was happening.

Just as the first of his rounds splattered against the MiG, the canopy popped open, and a lone pilot smashed out into the air at a forty-five degree angle in his ejection seat. The helmeted figure turned toward them, as though taking a closer look at them. Just as he did so, the first of Tombstone's rounds passed just above him.

"I didn't mean to—I didn't know he was going to—oh, dear God."

Any aviator in the world would have understood Tombstone's anguish. Because as much as he wanted to down the MiG, as much as he had had every intention of blasting her out of the air, he would never, ever, strafe a pilot ejected from an aircraft. Never. Once the pilot was removed, he was no longer a factor. Pilot's didn't kill other pilots under chutes.

"He was clear when you fired, Tombstone. He was. The only thing you hit was his aircraft. What happens to him now is not your fault."

MiG 102
1602 local (GMT-4)

Even in the violent rush of ejection, Korsov knew vaguely what was happening. The sound of the rockets, the hard punch of the ejection seat, the fiery blast of the rocket that shot him clear of the airframe. As soon as he ejected, the force of the rocket spun him around until he was facing the other MiG. He saw the helm of the pilot in the front seat and he saw the tail number. One part of his mind registered astonishment. It was the same MiG he'd seen in Chechnya.

He saw the bright flash of the tracers, and cried out in fear, his voice lost in the tumbling air stream around him. Surely he wasn't strafing him! And then he realized that he'd ejected just as the pilot fired. No, he wasn't strafing Korsov. He was only shooting at the aircraft.

Why was he continuing to tumble through the air? By now the chute should have opened, should have started braking his mad disoriented fall through the air. Any second now—any second now—and then he saw it.

Overhead, the stark white collapsed fabric of his parachute. Although the shots had missed him, they had severed the lines connecting his parachute to his harness.

With a cry, he slapped the release button, and let the chute fall away from him, He deployed the secondary chute, jerked hard, and shouted at the violent deceleration, at the pain of the straps grinding into his crotch. Above him, the secondary chute was filling with air and slowing his descent.

The ocean was rushing up to the him. Fast, he was going too fast—but it was still survivable. Yes, he might break a leg, might sustain other injuries—but this was survivable. He would survive, just as Russia had survived. And would survive.

MiG 101
1603 local (GMT-4)

"His secondary deployed," Tombstone shouted. "He lost the primary, but the backup was okay."

"Wonderful, I supposed that means I have to call SAR to come get him," Greene said sarcastically. "That makes perfect sense, doesn't it? He tries to shoot us down and we pull him out of the water."

"It's going to be tough to call SAR with our radios out," Tombstone pointed out. "We'll have to wait until we're back on board the *Jefferson*. Maybe he's got a hand-held dialed to air distress."

"Another exciting experience, but no longer a first. We've

already landed a MiG on an aircraft carrier, haven't we?"

"I got half a mind to set down in Bermuda, swap seats, and let you try it," Tombstone shot back. "Show some respect for your elders."

Greene laughed and Tombstone knew that the pilot would be all right.

"So I suppose he's got a life raft?" Greene asked.

"At least a flotation device. There's probably a life raft in the ejection seat pan, just like ours."

"He better hope so. Pretty warm water out here . . ." Greene didn't have to finish the thought. Warm water meant an abundance of kelp and microscopic animals and plants that were at the bottom of the food chain. It also meant that you'd find the small fish that fed on them, and the larger fish that fed on *them*, and so on up the food chain to the ultimate predator in the ocean—the sharks. While warm water would not kill a man with hypothermia, it was home to sharks.

"He'll see the raft as he goes in," Tombstone said. "Swim over to it and wait it out." But, both of them knew that a life raft was no absolute protection against sharks. "That AGI he was heading for is still too far away to pick him up before we can get back to the ship and send the SAR out."

"It's going to be a bit tricky getting back to the *Jefferson* anyway, with no radios," Greene pointed out. "To them we'll be just another MiG that they missed somehow."

"The Hawkeye is keeping track of us," Tombstone said. "At least, I hope they are."

"Yeah. Let's hope so."

Tombstone put the MiG into a gentle bank and headed back toward the carrier.

South of Bermuda
1605 local (GMT-4)

Korsov hit the water feet first at thirty miles an hour. He hit so hard that at first he thought he'd broken his left leg, but that quickly became the least of his concerns. He punched down through the water, the dark closing over him as he descended until he floated alone in black water.

His training took over. He pulled his knife and cut the risers to his parachute. He kicked away from them and watched the bubbles for moment. They were rising, indicating the way up. He followed them, kicking harder, forcing protesting muscles to propel him upward. His lungs burned and some part of his brain was insisting he must breathe, must breathe, that he could breathe water if he really put his mind to it. He resisted, forcing himself up. Finally, when he thought he could stand it no longer, he broke the surface.

He gulped down great quantities of air, flushing his lungs of the carbon dioxide. A small wave splashed in his face. He choked, then started breathing again.

The life raft—he saw it off in the distance, and he figured he could probably make it. The AGI would probably pick him up before he could even reach it, but he had to try. He turned in the water, oriented on it, and started to swim.

Just then, something touched his shin. It molded itself to him and surged over him to wrap around his lower legs.

Blind panic descended. Visions of giant sea creatures and tentacled monsters out of his wild nightmares overcame him. He screamed, beating the water, trying to kick his legs and escape, but it continued enveloping, now up to his waist. He cut at it with his knife, but the nightmare wrapped around his hand. He jerked back, dropping the knife as he did. It disappeared into the blackness below almost immediately.

With one arm pinned against his side and both legs immobilized, Korsov sank lower in the water. Another wave washed over his head. He choked, and tried to cry out, gulping down more salt water. Panic overcame his reason and he screamed, twisting and fighting against the demon. It tightened around him and covered his face, plastering itself against his mouth and nose.

As his consciousness faded and he began sinking, he realized it was his parachute shroud.

TWENTY-TWO

Forsythe came to slowly, aware that something was wrong, feeling a growing sense of dread but unable to figure out exactly what it was. At first, he was aware only that he was cold and uncomfortable, and his arm was bent at an awkward angle under him.

We were running from the torpedo. Three torpedoes. There was a Yankee—am I hit? I was running, and there was—

He remembered the sound, *Seawolf*'s tumbling through water, and nothing else. It was dark, too dark, only red lights illuminating angles in the control room. He rolled over onto his back, and tried to push himself up into a sitting position. White hot pain shot through his right hip, forcing a groan through his lips.

Emergency lighting—what the hell?

"Welcome back, sir." The chief crouched down on the deck next him and placed a restraining hand on one shoulder. "Don't move too fast, sir. I think you broke something in your right leg, or maybe just dislocated something. I don't know for sure."

"Where are we?" Forsythe asked, barely able to force words on past the white hot pain engulfing his leg.

"Just where you left us, sir. The torpedoes hit the transport.

You surfaced just long enough to get a look at it, then you passed out." The chief paused, considering him carefully. "I figured it wouldn't hurt nothing to lie quiet for awhile, sir, so I took us down to the bottom and parked us. The men, they were worn out. Needed a couple of engineers, that's all that's awake right now. The rest of them are asleep on station."

"Help me up." Forsythe let his weight rest on the chief's shoulders, as the chief dead lifted him to his feet. He could put no weight on his right leg, and for a moment he considered asking for the doctor. But, when he looked back to the place where the doctor had been handcuffed to a water pipe, there was no one there.

The chief saw his look and shrugged. "He took a pretty hard hit, sir. He came to, but he was fried. He's under the chart table."

Next to the flag? The synchronicity struck Forsythe as odd. "I've had about enough of his medical care anyway," Forsythe said. "How is the ship?"

"As best I can tell, she's structurally sound. No leaks, and everything seems to work. We lost the sonar dome—came down a little rougher than I wanted—but we're not going to have any trouble getting out of here, sir.

"Who knows we're here?" Forsythe asked.

"Second Fleet, SouthCom. ELF has been ringing off the hook, but I figured it could wait. At least we know it's all quiet overhead."

"Anything happening?"

The chief shook his head. "Quiet as a tomb."

"How long was I out?"

"About three hours."

"Show me the ELF messages."

The chief handed him a sheaf of papers and stood by silently while the ensign read them. Forsythe thumbed through them quickly, then stopped and reread a second one. He looked up, his face wondering. "We can surface any time now. You read this. Why haven't you already taken her up?"

"Captain's prerogative," the chief said quietly. "I could have tried, but the crew wouldn't have stood for it. She's ready to surface, Captain. On your command."

Forsythe stood, still feeling shaky but better than he had before. His leg would bear some weight, if not all of it.

My last few moments as captain. He shot a glance of gratitude at the chief. His relief was standing by overhead, but he'd damn sure prefer to leave his own ship under his own power.

My last command—for a while. Maybe some day, maybe when I'm a full commander and have about a million years in the Navy, I'll command another submarine. But it'll never be like this. Never.

"Chief, surface the ship," Forsythe ordered.

TWENTY-THREE

Northern Maine
Omicron Testing Facility
1406 local (GMT-5)

Senior Chief Armstrong was unbuckling his flight harness before the helicopter even settled down on the concrete pad just to the west of the main facility. It was a small helo of the type normally used on the fishing boat. Not the best choice, not in this weather, but it had been immediately available and willing to help.

Armstrong ducked, although the rotors were still turning well over his head. It was an instinctive move, one that few could resist. He ran across the concrete apron and to the waiting delegation. Bill Carter grabbed him by the arm. "Does this mean what I think it means?"

Armstrong nodded. "If this works, I don't think you'll have any problem getting full operational funding for the prototype." He shouted to be heard over the noise of the helicopter. It was already lifting off and heading away, headed back to Brunswick.

"Will it work?" Carter's gaze searched his face, his eyes anxious. His face was drawn, intense, evidence that the realization of just how high the stakes were had finally hit him. This was more than an operational test or a first cut on next year's budget—this was the real thing.

"It better," Armstrong said. "God willing, we won't have to use it—but if we need it, it better work."

The two jogged the few hundred feet separating the landing area from the main operations building, and Armstrong shucked his heavy outer gear as he waited for the guard to admit them into the security area. Beside him, Carter was babbling on about something, about the test, the latest specs, but Armstrong wasn't listening. It was as ready as Omicron could make it, and now Lady Luck came into play.

And that was the real bitch of it, he thought, as the door opened and admitted them. No matter how much you trained, how well you engineered something, there was always an element of luck in everything. Even in warfare. Clauswitz had called it the fog of war, but Armstrong knew better. It was luck, either good or bad.

He knew every person inside the facility, with the exception of one radar console operator, and introductions were quickly made. Armstrong took the supervisor's seat, donned his headset, and leaned back to wait. Someone put a cup of coffee in his hand and his fingers closed around it reflexively, his gaze fixed on the screen.

In front of him, three large screen displays conveyed a variety of information. In the middle were real time detections from their own radar, the status bar across the bottom indicating the status of the laser targeting system. To the right, the system status and weapon status of each component was displayed, the numbers of the latest self-test results constantly shifting as a system continually self-tested. To the far left, the screen displayed the data link of the U.S. Navy. Right now, they were receiving via satellite the feed from the *Jefferson*'s data system.

Armstrong felt the sense of dislocation. The screen on the left showed just what he had been looking at not sixteen hours ago, with the exception of the ships moving around within their assigned boxes. And here he was, thousands of miles away, wearing jeans instead of his uniform, looking at the same picture.

The screen on the far right indicated that there had been no problems thus far, and that the information was streaming in a timely fashion. Now, it was a matter of waiting.

It happened without warning or fanfare. One moment a

screen was basically as he had last seen it, and the next moment a cluster of symbols popped up around the island of Bermuda. Simultaneously, the speaker tuned to the battle group, high frequency tactical channel relayed voice communications from the scene.

The E-2 Hawkeye's report came close on the heels of the first radar imagery. "Missile launch, we have missile launch. Number: ten. Classification: unknown. Initial trajectory indicates ballistic flight profile." Seconds later, the Air Force AWACs chimed in with its own assessment, adding, "Confirm classification as medium-range ballistic missiles. Cheyenne reports probable targets are D.C. and Norfolk."

Armstrong's blood ran cold. Washington and Norfolk—he had spent too much time in both places not to be able to imagine just how a missile detonation would affect each one of them.

Perhaps three seconds elapsed from the initial launch detection until the time the first shot was fired. In rapid succession, the Aegis cruiser rippled off wave after wave of her antiair missiles, the ship clearly operating in full auto. Even the fast frigate attached to the battle group added her missiles to the flurry, although she could not fire at the same rate or with the same accuracy and range as the others.

One by one, the missile symbols disappeared from the screen. The Aegis kept count, the TAO transmitting the current number of kills over tactical, his voice growing stronger as he numbered off each one.

But he stopped at eight, there was silence on the net, and then another missile went down.

"Nine?" the TAO said. "All stations, that is not a confirmed scale—it wasn't our missile. Perhaps an equipment malfunction or failure on the missile itself. But, for whatever reason, it has departed controlled flight and is now heading for the ocean."

"I don't care what the cause, I'll take it," Coyote said over the circuit. "Interrogative your intentions with the last one?"

"*Jefferson, Lake Champlain.* Sir, we've sent four more birds after it, but we're in a tail chase. It doesn't look good."

A long silence. Finally, Coyote spoke. "Recommendations?"

Still the silence continued. Coyote scowled. "All stations, all units, listen up. I'm authorized to disclose the following information to you." Armstrong's blood pumped faster. Here it came, the first indication to the rest of the fleet, other than Lab Rat, exactly what was about to happen. Or, he amended, what he hoped was about to happen.

"On the coast of the continental United States," Coyote said, clearly reading from a prepared statement, "there is a new facility that possesses some capabilities—and don't ask, as I can't tell you any more than that—that may be able to intercept the remaining missile. Time of flight to the United States is four minutes. We should know around then whether or not it worked. And, may I add a personal note to someone I know is listening: Senior Chief Armstrong, kick some ass. That is all."

A grim smile crossed Armstrong's face as Coyote's voice stopped. *Kick some ass, indeed.* "Well, Admiral," he said out loud, ignoring the startled looks from the civilians around him, "I'll do my best. You can damned well count on that—I'll do my best."

The four minutes ticked by impossibly slow. Armstrong drummed his fingers on the cold console, then noticed that that made everyone else nervous. He leaned back, and tried to project an air of calm, competent confidence. "Could I get some more coffee?" he asked Carter. "One sugar this time, please." He passed the plastic cup to Carter.

The tension in the control room abated slightly. Then Armstrong spoke. "Okay, folks. We trained for this, we know what to do. We're tuned up, tweaked out, and, like the admiral said, ready to kick some ass. So, let's do it!"

"Oooo-rah!" one of the technicians shouted, betraying his Marine Corps background. The others chimed in with various expressions of enthusiasm.

Finally, the radar sweep picked up the contact exactly where he expected it on the center screen. At first it was no more than a few pixels in size, and then the picture wavered and steadied into a hard contact. A speed leader stretched out before it, indicating a speed in excess of Mach 4.

"Commencing acquisition," the man at the acquisition console said. His voice cracked initially, then immediately steadied down into his normal calm tenor. "All sensors nominal, scanning—scanning—Central, I have a lock. Repeat, I have a lock."

"Very well," Armstrong said. "Recommendation for range gate?"

"At expected angle of descent, fifty to seventy miles off the coast," the target coordinator said. "That will give us time for a follow-up shot if necessary."

"Roger, concur." At that range, most of the debris would rain down on empty ocean. "Notify the Coast Guard to clear the area and stand by." The former was futile gesture—there would not be time to clear that part of the ocean, but at least they would be ready for any search and rescue missions.

"Ninety seconds," the target coordinator said. The room was silent.

The seconds ticked by. Someone coughed, another sneezed. It was a peculiar stillness, as though everyone was afraid even so much as to move for fear of disturbing the laser tracking the missile.

The monitor set high in one corner of the room gave them a good view, although there was really not much to see. The blue laser bit into darkness, sharp, so sharp that it almost hurt the eyes to look at. It moved in small jerks across the dark green screen, the stars almost indistinguishable behind it. The missile itself was invisible. Even though the picture was stunningly prosaic, everyone stared at it.

"Forty-five seconds." The target coordinator's voice was calm, as though he announced this every day of his life. And, indeed, Armstrong reflected, that was the advantage of constant training. You did it so often, pretending it was real, that, when the time finally came, the whole process was so familiar that it seems like just another drill.

Except it wasn't. Thousands, maybe millions of lives depended on the system now.

"Twenty seconds." His voice was slightly higher than it had been earlier.

Okay, so it wasn't exactly like a drill. Your body knew even better than your mind what was happening, knew with a deep and compelling realization what the consequences of failure would be.

Which warhead had slipped by the Aegis? Nuclear, chemical, or biological? There was no hard data on exactly what warheads the island missiles carried, which warhead was associated with a given location. All they knew was that all three were possibilities, maybe a combination thereof.

"Ten seconds."

"Commencing ignition warm up sequence."

And which would be the worst? The nuclear, most certainly. Thousands, maybe millions would die in the initial blast. Then those casualties that came later from radiation along the outskirts of ground zero, and poisoning of the land with radioactive dust. Depending on the warhead, it could be centuries before the radioactivity decayed. He tried to imagine Washington as a polluted nuclear wasteland and couldn't even begin to see it.

The biological warhead would be deadly, too, although many of the agents were notoriously unstable. Dispensing biological and chemical weapons from an airborne missile required generating a very precise density of aerosol mist to carry the spores or germs or bacteria or whatever the hell it was. If the drops were too large, they wouldn't flow through the air on the currents. Too small, and it couldn't serve as a transport mechanism.

Then again, a biological agent could be difficult to precisely classify and treat. It could spread quickly with casual contact, certain types could anyway, and it could be the most difficult of all to contain.

"Five seconds. All systems go. Stage two ignition sequence. Four, three—"

Chemical was his personal choice. Hard to treat, often fatal, but it suffered from the same problems of aerosol distribution. It couldn't be transmitted person-to-person, not without direct contact. So the kill zone was limited to the original dispersal pattern. Deadly, far more deadly than the biological probably, but in a more limited barrier.

"Two, ignition," the weapons coordinator said, his voice notably tense. There was a collective sigh of relief as of spot of fire appeared in the lower left-hand corner of the TV monitor. "We have booster ignition—we have a launch, we have a launch. Stand by for retargeting. Retargeting in five seconds. Four, three, two, ignition. Two missiles launched, no apparent casualties. On course, on track.

Now, there was a little bit more to look at on the monitor,

but nothing to indicate how deadly the situation was. Two brief arcs of white fire from the missile rockets dazzled the eyes, a stunning contrast to the laser that still pinned the missile into the sky. The missiles gained speed slowly at first, then shot out of sight, the rockets fading to mere pixels, then winking out in a matter of seconds.

And they waited. At this range, interception would take fourteen seconds.

The control room group began counting down together at ten. "Nine, eight, seven, six—"

Armstrong shut his eyes, just for instance, and tried to read his gut. Was it a good shot, or had something gone wrong? Normally, he had a second sense about these matters, and could tell immediately if things were going according to plan. Almost always, at least.

But, this time, the familiar sense of certainty was missing. Was it because it was a new system? He stared at the screen, trying to will the missiles to interception, convinced for no real reason that his direct and personal attention to what was happening on-screen would make a difference.

"Five, four, three—" He prayed. It wasn't something he was used to doing, but, in these moments, there were no atheists, not in this modern equivalent of a foxhole. If God could—*would*—make a difference, then Armstrong wasn't going to be caught wanting.

Nothing happened on the screen. Two more seconds, then three, before he concluded that the first missile had missed. The weapons coordinator was evidently of the same mind, because he waited a full five seconds before saying, "Negative intercept, first round. Stand by for second."

Five seconds separated the two at launch, but that might decrease slightly during flight time.

In the next instant, Armstrong's heart sung with joy. It was a small blip of light on-screen, searing, the pattern of the pixels lingering on the retina for seconds afterward. Small, but intensely brilliant.

"Interception!" The targeting coordinator's voice was jubilant. "Oh, dear God, we got it."

Armstrong slumped back in his chair as relief washed through him. They got it—it had taken two shots, something they would spend months and months poring over and ana-

lyzing, but they got it. Whatever the warhead, it was now
reduced to its components high in the atmosphere where they
would be disbursed by the jet stream. They would watch, of
course, but most biological and chemical weapons have notoriously short life spans. The nuclear, well, that might take a
while longer, but there would be more than enough nations
monitoring it.

"Senior Chief Armstrong, I don't know if you're listening.
But, if you are, my congratulations." Coyote was almost howling, he was so jubilant. "Damned fine job, gentlemen—
damned fine." Someone produced champagne. Armstrong took
a glass and bemusedly wondered what corporate planner had
thought to stock it and when. Surely it had not happened in
the last sixteen hours? No, and the fact chilled him, that someone had foreseen the possibility of this happening and had
made provisions for it. Did they also stock sackcloth and ashes,
in the case of failure? Or grief counselors, perhaps? Someone
who would insist that they share their feelings, bond, and do
all that other happy horseshit?

Bill Carter pounded him on the back, spilling some of the
champagne, but nobody cared. "You did it! You did it!"

"*We* did it," Armstrong corrected, and walked over to clink
his glass with the weapons coordinator. "We did it."

One final thought struck him. He had prayed that their system would work, that they would shoot the missile down. But
had there been someone on the other end praying that it would
work?

TWENTY-FOUR

Bermuda
Monday, November 13
1200 local (GMT-4)

Late fall had been unusually mild on the island. Tombstone walked down the sand near the edge of the water. Waves rushed over his toes, straining sand out from beneath his feet, then deposited it around his ankles. He felt like he was sinking into the earth and that if he stood there long enough he would eventually disappear beneath the beach.

He had been walking for two hours, conscious of being very alone, and trying to sort out what had happened over the last two weeks. Evidence of the conflict was everywhere on the island. In the distance ahead of him, he could see a black pile of twisted metal, the remains of a Russian MiG shot down in the second air battle. It was cordoned off with yellow police tape with an MP standing guard. The American casualty teams were dispersed throughout the island, counting and identifying casualties and preparing the mortal remains for transfer.

Instead of returning to *Jefferson*, Tombstone had reconsidered his options. Yes, he was certain he could get the MiG back down on deck. Certain of his own skill, at least. The airframe itself, after the death-defying pullout from the spin, he was not so certain about. Surely her metal had been stressed beyond anything her designers had intended. Was he willing to bet that she would hold together for another carrier landing?

No, he decided. She had done more than anyone could ask any airframe. So, he'd turned away from the carrier and headed back toward land. A military air traffic controller was in charge in the tower, but he was evidently getting guidance from the naval forces. Tombstone had done a flyby, waggling his wings to indicate loss of communications, and then turned in on a standard approach pattern. His IFF was set to the code indicating communications difficulties as well, and he hoped that the tower's gear was still operative.

It had not taken the American Marines long to completely retake the island. The air control tower at the airport had been the last holdout. When the American forces had finally broken in, they'd found that the Russians were already dead. The man who was apparently their commander had executed them, then himself.

And now what? Tombstone stopped walking and turned to look up at the sun. Was Tomboy alive? Would he ever see her again?

His uncle had not been so sure. He had become convinced that the photo of Tomboy was a fake, just another way to stir up doubt and contention within the United States.

But why? Over Bermuda? No, that didn't make sense. What possible motive could they have for trying to make America believe that Russia was holding American POWs?

The sun beat down on his face, forcing him to shut his eyes. He could still feel the heat on his eyelids and see the after-image of the sun on his retinas.

If she's alive, I'll find her. I have somewhere to start now—I will find her.

GLOSSARY

0–3 LEVEL The third deck above the main deck. Designations for decks above the main deck (also known as the damage control deck) begin with zero (e.g., 0–3). The zero is pronounced as "oh" in conversation. Decks below the main deck do not have the initial zero, and are numbered down from the main deck (e.g., deck 11 is below deck 3). Deck 0–7 is above deck 0–3.

1MC The general announcing system on a ship or submarine. Every ship has many different interior communications systems, most of them linking parts of the ship for a specific purpose. Most operate off sound-powered phones. The circuit designators consist of a number followed by two letters that indicate the specific purpose of the circuit (e.g., 2AS might be an antisubmarine warfare circuit that connects the sonar supervisor, the USW watch officer, and the sailor at the torpedo launched).

AIR BOSS A senior commander or captain assigned to the aircraft carrier, in charge of flight operations. The "Boss" is assisted by the Mini-Boss in Pri-Fly, located in the tower on board the carrier. The Air Boss is always in the tower during flight operations, overseeing the launch and recovery cycles, declaring a green deck, and monitoring the safe approach of aircraft to the carrier.

AIR WING Composed of the aircraft squadrons assigned

to the battle group. The individual squadron commanding officers report to the Air Wing commander, who reports to the admiral.

AIRDALE Slang for an officer or enlisted person in the aviation fields. Includes pilots, NFOs, aviation intelligence officers, and maintenance officers and the enlisted technicians who support aviation. The antithesis of an airdale is a "shoe."

AKULA Late model Russian-built attack nuclear submarine, an SSN is fast, deadly, and deep diving.

ALR-67 Detects, analyzes, and evaluates electromagnetic signals, and emits a warning signal if the parameters are compatible with an immediate threat to the aircraft (e.g., seeker head on an antiair missile). Can also detect an enemy radar in either a search or a targeting mode.

ALTITUDE Is safety. With enough air space under the wings, a pilot can solve any problem.

AMRAAM Advanced Medium Range Anti Air Missile.

ANGELS Thousands of feet over ground. Angels twenty is 20,000 feet. Cherubs indicates hundreds of feet (e.g., cherubs five is 500 feet.

ASW Antisubmarine Warfare, recently renamed Undersea Warfare.

AVIONICS Black boxes and systems that comprise an aircraft's combat systems.

AW Aviation antisubmarine warfare technician, the enlisted specialist flying in an S-3, P-3, or helo USW aircraft. As this book goes to press, there is discussion of renaming the specialty.

AWACS An aircraft entirely too good for the Air Force, the Advanced Warning Aviation Control System. Long-range command and control and electronic intercept bird with superb capabilities.

AWG-9 Pronounced "awg nine," the primary search and fire control radar on a Tomcat.

BACKSEATER Also known as the GIB, the guy in back. Nonpilot aviator available in several flavors: BN (bombardier/navigator), RIO (radar intercept operator), and TACCO (Tactical Control Officer) among others. Usually wear glasses and are smart.

BEAR Russian maritime patrol aircraft, the equivalent in rough terms of a U.S. P-3. Variants have primary missions in command and control, submarine hunting, and electronic intercepts. Big, slow, good targets.

BITCH BOX One interior communications system on a ship. So named because it's normally used to bitch at another watch station.

BLUE ON BLUE Fratricide. U.S. forces are normally indicated in blue on tactical displays, and this term refers to an attack on a friendly by another friendly.

BLUE WATER NAVY Outside the unrefueled range of the airwing. When a carrier enters blue water ops, aircraft must get on board (e.g., land, and cannot divert to land if the pilot gets the shakes).

BOOMER Slang for a ballistic missile submarine.

BOQ Bachelor Officer Quarters—a Motel Six for single officers or those traveling without family. The Air Force also has VOQ, Visiting Officer Quarters.

BUSTER As fast as you can (i.e., bust your ass getting here).

C-2 GREYHOUND Also known as the COD, Carrier Onboard Delivery. The COD carries cargo and passengers from shore to ship. It is capable of carrier landings. Sometimes assigned directly to the air wing, it also operates in coordination with CVBGs from a shore squadron.

CAG Carrier Air Group Commander, normally a senior Navy captain aviator. Technically, an obsolete term, since the air wing rather than an air group is now deployed on the carrier. However, everyone thought CAW sounded stupid, so CAG was retained as slang for the Carrier Air Wing Commander.

CAP Combat Air Patrol, a mission executed by fighters to protect the carrier and battle group from enemy air and missiles.

CARRIER BATTLE GROUP A combination of ships, airwing, and submarines assigned under the command of a one-star admiral.

CARRIER BATTLE GROUP 14 The battle group normally embarked on the *Jefferson*.

CBG *See* Carrier Battle Group.

CDC Combat Direction Center—modernly, replaced CIC, or Combat Information Center, as the heart of a ship. All sensor information is fed into CDC and the battle is co-ordinated by a Tactical Action Officer on watch.

CG Abbreviation for a cruiser.

CHIEF The backbone of the Navy. E-7, -8, and -9 enlisted paygrades, known as chief, senior chief, and master chief. The transition from petty officer ranks to the chief's mess is a major event in a sailor's career. On board ship, the chiefs have separate eating and berthing facilities. Chiefs wear khakis, as opposed to dungarees for the less senior enlisted ratings.

CHIEF OF STAFF Not to be confused with a chief, the COS in a battle group staff is normally a senior Navy captain who acts as the admiral's XO and deputy.

CIA Christians in Action. The civilian agency charged with intelligence operations outside the continental United States.

CIWS Close In Weapons System, pronounced "see-whiz." Gattling gun with built-in radar that tracks and fires on inbound missiles. If you have to use it, you're dead.

COD *See* C-2 Greyhound.

COLLAR COUNT Traditional method of determining the winner of a disagreement. A survey is taken of the opponents' collar devices. The senior person wins. Always.

COMMODORE Formerly the junior-most admiral rank, now used to designate a senior Navy captain in charge of a bunch of like units. A destroyer commodore commands several destroyers, a sea control commodore commands the S-3 squadrons on that coast. Contrast with CAG, who owns a number of dissimilar units (e.g., a couple of Tomcat squadrons, some Hornets, and some E-2s and helos).

COMPARTMENT Navy talk for a room on a ship.

CONDITION TWO One step down from General Quarters, which is Condition One. Condition Five is tied up at the pier in a friendly country.

CRYPTO Short for some variation of cryptological, the magic set of codes that makes a circuit impossible for anyone else to understand.

CV, CVN Abbreviation for an aircraft carrier, conventional and nuclear.

CVIC Carrier Intelligence Center. Located down the passageway (the hall) from the flag spaces.

DATA LINK, THE LINK The secure circuit that links all units in a battle group or in an area. Targets and contacts are transmitted over the LINK to all ships. The data is processed by the ship designated as Net Control, and common contacts are correlated. The system also transmits data from each ship and aircraft's weapons systems (e.g., a missile firing). All services use the LINK.

DDG Guided missile destroyer.

DESK JOCKEY Nonflyer, one who drives a computer instead of an aircraft.

DESRON Destroyer Commander.

DICASS An active sonobuoy.

DICK STEPPING Something to be avoided. While anatomically impossible in today's gender-integrated services, in an amazing display of good sense, the Navy has not required gender neutrality.

DOPPLER acoustic phenomena caused by relative motion between a sound source and a receiver that results in an apparent change in frequency of the sound. The classic example is a train going past and the decrease in pitch of its whistle. When a submarine changes its course or speed in relation to a sonobuoy, the event shows up as a change in the frequency of the sound source.

DOUBLE NUTS Zero zero on the tail of an aircraft.

E-2 HAWKEYE Command and control and surveillance aircraft. Turboprop rather than jet, and unarmed. Smaller version of an AWACS, in practical terms, but carrier-based.

ELF Extremely Low Frequency, a method of communicating with submarines at sea. Signals are transmitted via a miles-long antenna and are the only way of reaching a deeply submerged submarine.

ENVELOPE What you're supposed to fly inside of if you want to take all the fun out of naval aviation.

EWs Electronic warfare technicians, the enlisted sailors that man the gear that detects, analyzes, and displays electromagnetic signals. Highly classified stuff.

F/A-18 HORNETS The inadequate, fuel-hungry, intended replacement for the aging but still kick-your-ass potent Tomcat. Flown by the Marines and the Navy.

FAMILYGRAM Short messages from submarine sailors'

families to their deployed sailors. Often the only contact with the outside world that a submarine sailor on deployment has.

FF/FFG Abbreviation for a fast frigate (no, there aren't slow frigates) and a guided missile fast frigate.

FLAG OFFICER In the Navy and Coast Guard, an admiral. In the other services, a general.

FLAG PASSAGEWAY The portion of the aircraft carrier that houses the admiral's staff working spaces. Includes the flag mess and the admiral's cabin. Normally separated from the rest of the ship by heavy plastic curtains, and designated by blue tile on the deck instead of white.

FLIGHT QUARTERS A condition set on board a ship preparing to launch or recover aircraft. All unnecessary persons are required to stay inside the skin of the ship and remain clear of the flight deck area.

FLIGHT SUIT The highest form of navy couture. The perfect choice of apparel for any occasion—indeed, the only uniform an aviator ought to be required to own.

FOD Stands for Foreign Object Damage, but the term is used to indicate any loose gear that could cause damage to an aircraft. During flight operations, aircraft generate a tremendous amount of air flowing across the deck. Loose objects—including people and nuts and bolts—can be sucked into the intake and discharged through the outlet from the jet engine. FOD damages the jet's impellers and doesn't do much for the people sucked in, either. FOD walkdown is conducted at least once a day on board an aircraft carrier. Everyone not otherwise engaged stands shoulder-to-shoulder on the flight deck and slowly walks from one end of the flight deck to the other, searching for FOD.

FOX Tactical shorthand for a missile firing. Fox one indicates a heat-seeking missile, Fox two an infrared missile, and Fox three a radar guided missile.

GCI Ground Control Intercept, a procedure used in the Soviet air forces. Primary control for vectoring the aircraft in on enemy targets and other fighters is vested in a guy on the ground, rather than in the cockpit where it belongs.

GIB *See* Backseater.

GMT Greenwich Mean Time.

GREEN SHIRTS *See* Shirts.

HANDLER Officer located on the flight deck level responsible for ensuring that aircraft are correctly positioned, "spotted," on the flight deck. Coordinates the movements of aircraft with yellow gear (small tractors that tow aircraft and other related gear) from maintenance areas to catapults and from the flight deck to the hangar bar via the elevators. Speaks frequently with the Air Boss. *See also* Bitch box.

HARMS Anti-radiation missiles that home in on radar sites.

HOME PLATE Tactical call sign for the *Jefferson*.

HOT In reference to a sonobuoy, holding enemy contact.

HUFFER Yellow gear located on the flight deck that generates compressed air to start jet engines. Most Navy aircraft do not need a huffer to start engines, but it can be used in emergencies or for maintenance.

HUNTER Call sign for the S-3 squadron embarked on the *Jefferson*.

ICS Interior Communications System. The private link between a pilot and a RIO, or the telephone system internal to a ship.

INCHOPPED Navy talk for a ship entering a defined area of water (e.g., inchopped the Med).

IR Infrared, a method of missile homing.

ISOTHERMAL A layer of water that has a constant temperature with increasing depth. Located below the thermocline, where increase in depth correlates to decrease in temperature. In the isothermal layer, the primary factor affecting the speed of sound in water is the increase in pressure with depth.

JBD Jet Blast Deflector. Panels that pop up from the flight deck to block the exhaust emitted by aircraft.

JEFFERSON USS The star nuclear aircraft carrier in the U.S. Navy.

LEADING PETTY OFFICER The senior petty officer in a workcenter, division, or department, responsible to the leading chief petty officer for the performance of the rest of the group.

LINK, *See* Data link.

LOFARGRAM LOw Frequency Analysing and Recording display. Consists of lines arrayed by frequency on the horizontal axis and time on the vertical axis. Displays sound signals in the water in a graphic fashion for analysis by ASW technicians.

LONG GREEN TABLE A formal inquiry board. It's better to be judged by six than carried by six.

MACHINISTS MATE Enlisted technician that runs and repairs most engineering equipment on board a ship. Abbreviated as "MM" (e.g., MM1 Sailor is a Petty Officer First Class Machinists Mate).

MDI Mess Decks Intelligence. The heartbeat of the rumor mill on board a ship and the definitive source for all information.

MEZ Missile Engagement Zone. Any hostile contacts that make it into the MEZ are engaged only with missiles. Friendly aircraft must stay clear in order to avoid a blue on blue engagement (i.e., fratricide).

MIG A production line of aircraft manufactured by Mikoyan in Russia. MiG fighters are owned by many nations around the world.

MURPHY, LAW OF The factor most often not considered sufficiently in military planning. If something can go wrong, it will. Naval corollary: Shit happens.

NATIONAL ASSETS Surveillance and reconnaissance resources of the most sensitive nature (e.g., satellites).

NATOPS The bible for operating a particular aircraft. *See* Envelope.

NFO Naval Flight Officer.

NO-BRAINER Contrary to what copyeditors believe, this is one word. Used to signify an evolution or decision that should require absolutely no significant intellectual capabilities beyond that of a paramecium.

NOMEX Fire-resistant fabric used to make "shirts." *See* Shirts.

NSA National Security Agency. Primarily responsible for evaluating electronic intercepts and sensitive intelligence.

OOD Officer of the Day, in charge of the safe handling and maneuvering of the ship. Supervises the conning officer and other underway watchstanders. Ashore, the OOD may be responsible for a shore station after normal working hours.

OPERATIONS SPECIALIST Formerly radar operators, back

in the old days. Enlisted technicians who operate combat detection, tracking, and engagement systems, except for sonar. Abbreviated OS.

OTH Over the horizon, usually used to refer to shooting something you can't see.

P-3s Shore-based antisubmarine warfare and surface surveillance long-range aircraft. The closest you can get to being in the Air Force while still being in the Navy.

PHOENIX Long-range antiair missile carried by U.S. fighters.

PIPELINE Navy term used to describe a series of training commands, schools, or necessary education for a particular specialty. The fighter pipeline, for example, includes Basic Flight then fighter training at the RAG (Replacement Air Group), a training squadron.

PUNCHING OUT Ejecting from an aircraft

PURPLE SHIRTS *See* Shirts

PXO Prospective Executive Officer—the officer ordered into a command as the relief for the current XO. In most squadrons, the XO eventually "fleets up" to become the commanding officer of the squadron, an excellent system that maintains continuity within an operational command—and a system the surface Navy does not use.

RACK A bed. A rack-monster is a sailor who sports pillow burns and spends entirely too much time asleep while his or her shipmates are working.

RED SHIRTS *See* Shirts

RHIP Rank Hath Its Privileges. *See* Collar count.

RIO Radar Intercept Officer. *See* NFO.

RTB Return to base.

S-3 Command and control aircraft sold to the Navy as an antisubmarine aircraft. Good at that, too. Within the last several years, redesignated as "sea control" aircraft, with individual squadrons referred to as torpedo bombers. Ah, the search for a mission goes on. But, still a damned fine aircraft.

SAM Surface to Air Missile (e.g., the standard missile fired by most cruisers). Also indicates a land-based site.

SAR Sea-Air Rescue.

SCIF Specially Compartmented Information. On board a

carrier, used to designate the highly classified compartment immediately next to TFCC.

SEAWOLF Newest version of Navy fast attack submarine.

SERE Survival, Evasion, Rescue, Escape; required school in pipeline for aviators.

SHIRTS Color-coded Nomex pullovers used by flight deck and aviation personnel for rapid identification of a sailor's job. Green: maintenance technicians. Brown: plane captains. White: safety and medical. Red: ordnance. Purple: fuel. Yellow: flight deck supervisors and handlers.

SHOE A black shoe, slang for a surface sailor or officer. Modernly, surface sailors are also authorized to wear brown shoes. No one knows why. Wing envy is the best guess.

SIDEWINDER Antiair missile carried by U.S. fighters.

SIERRA A subsurface contact.

SONOBUOYS Acoustic listening devices dropped in the water by ASW or USW aircraft.

SPARROW Antiair missile carried by U.S. fighters.

SPETZNAZ The Russian version of SEALs, although the term encompasses a number of different specialties.

SPOOKS Slang for intelligence officers and enlisted sailors working in highly classified areas.

SUBLANT Administrative command of all Atlantic submarine forces. On the west coast, SUBPAC.

SWEET When used in reference to a sonobuoy, indicates that the buoy is functioning properly, although not necessarily holding any contacts.

TACCO Tactical Control Officer: the NFO in an S-3.

TACTICAL CIRCUIT A term used in these books that encompasses a wide range of actual circuits used on board a carrier. There are a variety of C&R circuits (coordination and reporting) and occasionally, for simplicity's sake and to avoid classified material, I just use the world tactical.

TANKED, TANKER Navy aircraft have the ability to refuel from a tanker, either Air Force or Navy, while airborne. One of the most terrifying routine evolutions a pilot performs.

TFCC Tactical Flag Command Center. A compartment in flag spaces from which the CVBG admiral controls the battle. Located immediately forward of the carrier's CDC.

TOMBSTONE Nickname given to Magruder.

TOP GUN Advanced fighter training command.

UNDERSEA WARFARE COMMANDER In a CVBG, normally the DESRON embarked on the carrier. Formerly called the ASW commander.

VDL Video Downlink. Transmission of targeting data from an aircraft to a submarine with OTH capabilities.

VF-95 Fighter squadron assigned to Airwing 14, normally embarked on the USS *Jefferson*. The first two letters of a squadron designation reflect the type of aircraft flown. VF: fighters. VFA: hornets. VS: S-3, etc.

VICTOR Aging Russian fast attack submarines, still a potent threat.

VS-29 S-3 squadron assigned to Airwing 14, embarked on the USS *Jefferson*.

VX-1 Test pilot squadron that develops envelopes after Pax River evaluates aerodynamic characteristics of new aircraft. *See* Envelopes.

WHITE SHIRT *See* Shirts.

WILCO Short for Will Comply. Used only by the aviator in command of the mission.

WINCHESTER In aviation, it means out of weapons. A Winchester aircraft must normally RTB.

XO Executive officer, the second in command.

YELLOW SHIRT *See* shirts.

SEAL TEAM SEVEN
Keith Douglass

__SEAL TEAM SEVEN   0-425-14340-6/$5.99

__SEAL TEAM SEVEN: SPECTER   0-425-14569-7/$5.99

__SEAL TEAM SEVEN: NUCFLASH

0-425-14881-5/$5.99

__SEAL TEAM SEVEN: DIRECT ACTION

0-425-15605-2/$5.99

__SEAL TEAM SEVEN: FIRESTORM

0-425-16139-0/$5.99

__SEAL TEAM SEVEN: BATTLEGROUND

0-425-16375-X/$5.99

__SEAL TEAM SEVEN: DEATHRACE

0-425-16741-0/$5.99

__SEAL TEAM SEVEN: PACIFIC SIEGE

0-425-16941-3/$5.99

__SEAL TEAM SEVEN: WAR CRY

0-425-17117-5/$5.99

__SEAL TEAM SEVEN: DEATHBLOW

0-425-18074-3/$5.99

Prices slightly higher in Canada

Payable by Visa, MC or AMEX only ($10.00 min.), No cash, checks or COD. Shipping & handling:
US/Can. $2.75 for one book, $1.00 for each add'l book; Int'l $5.00 for one book, $1.00 for each
add'l. Call (800) 788-6262 or (201) 933-9292, fax (201) 896-8569 or mail your orders to:

Penguin Putnam Inc. P.O. Box 12289, Dept. B Newark, NJ 07101-5289 Please allow 4-6 weeks for delivery. Foreign and Canadian delivery 6-8 weeks.	Bill my: ☐ Visa ☐ MasterCard ☐ Amex _____(expires) Card# _____ Signature _____

Bill to:

Name _____

Address _____City _____

State/ZIP _____Daytime Phone # _____

Ship to:

Name _____Book Total $ _____

Address _____Applicable Sales Tax $ _____

City _____Postage & Handling $ _____

State/ZIP _____Total Amount Due $ _____

This offer subject to change without notice.   Ad # 695 (3/00)

PENGUIN PUTNAM INC.
Online

Your Internet gateway to a virtual environment with
hundreds of entertaining and enlightening books
from Penguin Putnam Inc.

*While you're there, get the latest buzz on
the best authors and books around—*

Tom Clancy, Patricia Cornwell, W.E.B. Griffin,
Nora Roberts, William Gibson, Robin Cook,
Brian Jacques, Catherine Coulter, Stephen King,
Ken Follett, Terry McMillan, and many more!

**Visit our website at
www.penguinputnam.com**

PENGUIN PUTNAM NEWS

Every month you'll get an inside look at our upcom-
ing books and new features on our site. This is an
ongoing effort to provide you with the most
up-to-date information about
our books and authors.

Subscribe to Penguin Putnam News at
www.penguinputnam.com/newsletters

Think: *The Hunt for Red October*
Think: "The X-Files"
Think: The most original
techno-thrillers of the year.

Greg Donegan

__ATLANTIS   0-425-16936-7/$6.99

Three areas on Earth's surface defy explanation: the Bermuda Triangle, the
Devil's Sea of Japan, and a small region of Cambodia. Now, the destructive
force behind these mysteries has been revealed. They invaded before...when
they destroyed Atlantis. *And now they're back.*

__ATLANTIS: BERMUDA TRIANGLE

0-425-17429-8/$6.99

When a nuclear missile is launched from the waters of the Bermuda Triangle,
ex-Green Beret Eric Dane must lead a team into the depths to confront an
enemy which has but one objective: the total annihilation of all life on Earth.

__ATLANTIS: DEVIL'S SEA

0-425-17859-5/$6.99

In the jungles of Cambodia, mankind's ancient enemies waged their first
attack. From the depths of the Bermuda Triangle, they tried to launch a
global apocalypse. Now, from the bottom of the Devil's Sea, they rise again.

Prices slightly higher in Canada

Payable by Visa, MC or AMEX only ($10.00 min.), No cash, checks or COD. Shipping & handling:
US/Can. $2.75 for one book, $1.00 for each add'l book; Int'l $5.00 for one book, $1.00 for each
add'l. Call (800) 788-6262 or (201) 933-9292, fax (201) 896-8569 or mail your orders to:

Penguin Putnam Inc.
P.O. Box 12289, Dept. B
Newark, NJ 07101-5289
Please allow 4-6 weeks for delivery.
Foreign and Canadian delivery 6-8 weeks.

Bill my: ❑ Visa ❑ MasterCard ❑ Amex _____(expires)

Card# _____

Signature _____

Bill to:
Name _____
Address _____City _____
State/ZIP _____Daytime Phone # _____
Ship to:
Name _____Book Total $ _____
Address _____Applicable Sales Tax $ _____
City _____Postage & Handling $ _____
State/ZIP _____Total Amount Due $ _____

This offer subject to change without notice.   Ad # 891 (3/00)

"Fasten your seat belt! *Carrier* is a stimulating, fast-paced novel brimming with action and high drama." —Joe Weber

CARRIER

Keith Douglass

U.S. MARINES. PILOTS. NAVY SEALS.
THE ULTIMATE MILITARY POWER PLAY.

In the bestselling tradition of Tom Clancy, Larry Bond, and Charles D. Taylor, these electrifying novel's capture vivid reality of international combat. The Carrier Battle Group Fourteen—a force including a supercarrier, amphibious unit, guided missile cruiser, and destroyer—is brought to life with stunning authenticity and action in high-tech thrillers as explosive as today's headlines.

_CARRIER	0-515-10593-7/$6.50
_CARRIER 6: COUNTDOWN	0-515-11309-3/$5.99
_CARRIER 7: AFTERBURN	0-515-11914-8/$6.99
_CARRIER 8: ALPHA STRIKE	0-515-12018-9/$6.99
_CARRIER 9: ARCTIC FIRE	0-515-12084-7/$5.99

Prices slightly higher in Canada

Payable by Visa, MC or AMEX only ($10.00 min.), No cash, checks or COD. Shipping & handling: US/Can. $2.75 for one book, $1.00 for each add'l book; Int'l $5.00 for one book, $1.00 for each add'l. Call (800) 788-6262 or (201) 933-9292, fax (201) 896-8569 or mail your orders to:

Penguin Putnam Inc.
P.O. Box 12289, Dept. B
Newark, NJ 07101-5289
Please allow 4-6 weeks for delivery.
Foreign and Canadian delivery 6-8 weeks.

Bill my: ☐ Visa ☐ MasterCard ☐ Amex _____ (expires)
Card# _____
Signature _____

Bill to:
Name _____
Address _____ City _____
State/ZIP _____ Daytime Phone # _____

Ship to:
Name _____ Book Total $ _____
Address _____ Applicable Sales Tax $ _____
City _____ Postage & Handling $ _____
State/ZIP _____ Total Amount Due $ _____

This offer subject to change without notice.   Ad # 384 (3/00)